About the Author

Mark Hayden is the nom de guerre of Adrian Attwood. He lives in Westmorland with his wife, Anne.

He has had a varied career working for a brewery, teaching English and being the Town Clerk in Carnforth, Lancs. He is now a part-time writer and part-time assistant in Anne's craft projects.

He is also proud to be the Mad Unky to his Great Nieces & Great Nephews.

Third Eye

The Sound of Peace

Eleventh Book of the King's Watch

MARK HAYDEN

www.pawpress.co.uk

First Published Worldwide in 2023 by Paw Press
Paperback Edition Published
July 2023
First Edition
Updated with minor corrections 04 September 2023

Cover Design – Rachel Lawston
Design Copyright © 2022 Lawston Design
www.lawstondesign.com
Cover images © Shutterstock

Paw Press – Independent publishing in Westmorland, UK.
www.pawpress.co.uk

ISBN: 1-914145-04-6
ISBN-13: 978-1-914145-04-9

For Jade & Andy

Thanks for putting up with

My Niece & Nephew

Over many years.

THIRD EYE

A Note from Conrad

It's been a while, hasn't it?

As well as saving the world, I've been getting on with the important business of planning our wedding, and I must admit that some things have become a bit of a blur for me, so I can't imagine what you're feeling.

To help bring things into focus, Mr Hayden has put a list of new and recurring people from this story on his website, and you can also find a full list of everyone from the previous books, and a glossary of magickal terms on the Paw Press website. Go to the "Extras" page and download the Dramatis Personae for *Third Eye*:

www.pawpress.co.uk

And now on with the story.

Thanks,
Conrad.

Prologue — Winter in Yorkshire

Kathy Metcalfe hated her life. When she'd first come to the Abbey, the shrink at the time had said *the unexamined life is not worth living.* Kathy had then made a point of examining every aspect of her life, and she was pleased to report that she hated all of it.

She hated waking up every morning in an empty bed, and she hated the shock of knowing that she had to stay sober all day if she wanted to get back into the same empty bed tonight.

In between, she hated leaving the warmth of the Abbey kitchen in the mornings to stand in the shivering gallery with the red-eyed "guests" who couldn't sleep. She hated the way that the guests hung around her kitchen trying to make conversation when all they were doing was avoiding being alone with their sobriety while she prepared their breakfasts.

She hated dinner service from Monday to Thursday when the guests had to plan and cook the food for everyone at the abbey, and of the guests, she `didn't know which lot she hated most. Doctor Simon had told her off more than once for lumping people into one pot (he called it *stereotyping*), but when she'd told him what went on in the kitchen, he'd laughed and said, 'When it comes to the kitchen, Kathy, I am *not* going to argue with you.'

St Teresa's Alcohol and Narcotic Dependency Centre @ the Abbey – known universally as STAND – had three contracts, and when the guests rocked up fresh and *clean* from detox, they pretty much followed their script when it came to cooking.

One contract was with the West Riding Mental Health Trust, and a lucky few *guests* with no one to pay for their rehab got to live it up in Beckthorpe Abbey while they tried to put together an escape plan: escape from Doctor Simon back to their dealers, or escape from the shitty lives that had brought them here. As a rule, they all thought that *beef* came from creatures called *beeves*, and that somewhere on the moors were animals called *doners* which you could slaughter to make *doner kebabs*. Having said that, they were a bit like bread dough: give them a good pounding and you could soon knead them into shape.

As you'd expect, the West Riding NHS Trust paid peanuts for its patients' treatment, and to balance the books, STAND took private clients from down south: clients who wanted to recover well away from prying eyes. Usually, the wanker-bankers from London looked down their noses at Kathy while trying to impress her with their TV chef recipes which never worked. To manage *them*, she simply invited some of the NHS lot to watch while it went wrong. Kathy loved seeing a banker's ego deflate like one of his soufflés, and Dr Simon didn't mind the fallout, unlike Faye Langley, his fiancée.

Tonight, Kathy was watching one of the third group in action: the spooks. *And don't get me started on the spooks*, she thought. Of the Abbey's eighteen guests, no more than one or two would be spooks, and although they slipped in quietly, pretending to be from financial services, Kathy could spot them a mile off: it was the eyes that gave them away.

To a man (never a woman), the spooks' eyes would dart around, checking out the doorways, the hiding places and the escape routes. Then they would linger on each person in the room, weighing them up, and their stories were just so full of total *shit*. Kathy had pushed one of them, and then gone to see Dr Simon.

'What is he?' she'd demanded. 'He's not Julian from Aktiv Reinsurance, that's for certain. Are you taking *serious* criminals now? Like rapists and paedos?'

Dr Simon had nodded slowly. 'You deserve an answer, Kathy,' he'd replied in that measured way of his, and he'd paused for a second, looking out of the window. He'd turned back to face her and said, 'We will be having some guests from government agencies. Secret government agencies. Just let them have the same chance as everyone else.' He'd smiled then and added, 'The only thing they're allowed to lie about is their work, and given that everyone else lies about their jobs, who's to deny them that?'

It was a fair point, and to be fair to the spooks, they could be useful. Not only did they always take orders, most of them could actually cook proper food.

That didn't stop her from hating them, though. They'd appear in her kitchen on their first day and get the measure of her, and having measured her, they would put her in a box in their head marked *staff, domestic, be polite*. And from that moment, they would treat her with respect, ask her advice and let her get no nearer to them than she had been to Australia, and the nearest Kathy had been to Australia was Tenerife.

Because today was Friday, Kathy got to choose the menu and do some actual cooking instead of watching the guests ruin perfectly good food, and because a lot of staff were at home, and because a lot of the guests were away on supervised visits, she only had a dozen to feed tonight. The STAND calendar worked differently from most of the world, with the weekend being on Friday and Saturday; long experience had taught Dr Simon that guests found Sundays the hardest day, so they all had to be back at the Abbey for a communal dinner. It was also Kathy's day off, which made it even more special.

'Can you not chop those onions any finer, Michael?' she said to the spook.

He was an anonymous man in an anonymous grey hoodie, and he'd probably come from abroad, (judging by the deep tan at the end of winter). He was probably in his late thirties (like Kathy), and he was most definitely not called *Michael*. This was his first weekend at STAND.

'I'll try,' he responded, blinking back the tears.

Kathy took a moment to watch the spook try a finer chop with hands that still shook, and then winced when the inevitable red smear of blood appeared on the knife. 'Quick. Get away from the food and put your hand under the tap. I'll get the plasters.'

It was the spook's third accident in as many days, and it would have to go in the accident book. Kathy hated filling in the accident book.

She was checking the man's finger when the scullery door banged closed. She was winding herself up to tell the interloper to bugger off until she saw who it was, and had to bite her tongue as Faye Langley swept into the Abbey. *Fragrant Faye* she called her, but only in her head. Out loud, she didn't call her anything much. She hoped that Fragrant Faye would pass through, but there was no such luck today.

The Abbey's *Therapeutic Lead* took off her snow boots and shoved her feet into a pair of green sandals, then noticed Kathy and Michael at the sink.

'Is everything OK?' she asked.

'Nowt to bother with,' said Kathy curtly.

'It's just a cut, thanks,' said the spook. 'I'll be back at the onions in a moment, just as soon as Kathy's finished her tender ministrations.'

The Abbey kitchen was separated from the scullery and through passage by an archway, and that threshold marked the dividing line. Faye stepped forwards, then stopped, having thought twice about interfering. Instead, she shook out her hair from the hood of her down coat and smiled. 'What's on the menu tonight, Kathy?'

'Slow cooked beef casserole with winter veg.' It didn't do to upset Faye unless there was a good reason, so Kathy added, 'Reckon we could all do with a bit of warming up. It were brass monkeys last time I went outside.'

'Sounds delish.' Faye hesitated. 'You going out shortly? Once you've finished your tender ministrations?'

'Might be. What's up?'

'dJulie's on the prowl.'

Kathy grunted a response and reached for a blue plaster. Faye decided that she'd got as much as she could and clopped off into the Abbey proper.

'Is dJulie the one with the big hair?' asked Michael.

'That's her. Faye wants me to go and be bad cop. Now she's gone, I'll nip outside and see whether dJulie's started picking up rocks again.'

Michael raised an eyebrow and smiled. 'I'm not sure that I'm cut out for onions. They don't like my contact lenses. Is there any chance I could switch to potatoes?' He stepped back and admired his plaster. 'You know, that beef recipe would be perfect with a *dauphinoise*. If you've got any cream, I could have a crack at it.'

Kathy tilted her head. He was right, of course, a side of dauphinoise potatoes would turn a stew into something much more memorable. She pointed to his cut finger. 'You reckon that after this I'm gonna let you near the mandoline? You'll have no fingers left if I do.'

He grinned. 'Go and see to dJulie. I'll make a start while you're gone, and then if I've amputated myself, it won't be your fault.'

She stared at him. 'It don't work like that.' She went to her desk in the corner, fished the accident book out of the drawer and grabbed a pen. She plonked them on a clean stretch of worktop and said, 'You fill this in, but don't sign it. If you do a good job, I'll let you have a crack at the spuds.'

Kathy grabbed her coat from the back of her chair and headed outside. The back exit from the Abbey had a stupid pointed door that weighed a ton, and on its own had helped her cut down on smoking, especially when it started to stick, but Faye hadn't closed it properly, so Kathy had no bother getting out.

The old Abbey building housed the kitchens and the communal spaces, as well as therapy rooms, but only the resident staff lived there: all the guests lived in the House Block across the courtyard. Well, all bar one, but that would come later.

Between the Abbey and the House was a long, covered walkway with some benches in it, and it was the only place outside the gardens where anyone could smoke, and a *lot* of the guests smoked. Because the covering only amounted to the roof and one side, it was known as the *shivering gallery*, and that's where Kathy found dJulie, pacing up and down.

'What are you doin' here?' demanded Kathy. 'You have a visit booked with your kids today!'

dJulie gestured at the snow which had fallen overnight and lay on the courtyard. It was deep in most places, but where the wind had caught it, large drifts had built up. 'Useless effing social worker said it were too dangerous to come up the bank from Easingwold. She hates me.'

The thing that Kathy hated most about her life, above all others and even above the need to stay sober, was being separated from the only thing she truly loved: her children. The only thing that allowed her to get out of bed in the morning was knowing that she was one day closer to being reunited as a family.

Their breath was steaming around them, the temperature well below freezing. Kathy lit a cigarette and checked the time on her phone. 'It's only two o'clock, dJulie. If you *really* love your kids, you'll ask Faye to get on to the Social and tell her to pick you up from Easingwold. You can still be at the foster family's place in time to build a snowman and put them to bed after.'

dJulie bristled with antagonism, as she did every time that anyone pulled her up for *anything*. 'How am I supposed to get there, you stupid cow?'

'Walk. It's only three miles. Faye will lend you some gear: there's enough of it.'

'You're mad! Walk in this!'

'It's what I'd do. If the Social told me I could see my girls today, I'd walk all the way to flipping Headingly, never mind Easingwold. Every step of the way. And I'd give thanks when I got there.'

dJulie turned away, stung by Kathy's passion but unwilling to abandon her victim's mantle (which is what Faye called it). Kathy knew she'd need a stick and a carrot to get through, and she started with the carrot. 'The social worker won't want to bring you back, neither, will she? And didn't you tell me the foster family had a bed-settee?'

With her face still turned away, dJulie answered with a nod and a, 'Yeah.'

It was time for the stick. 'If you show willing, they'll let you stay over, and it's that or get your sorry arse into the kitchen and help Michael cook tea.'

dJulie turned back and shivered. 'Michael! God help me, no. I swear down I have not met anyone more depressing than him, ever. Have you seen Faye?'

'Yeah. Went inside, so she's probably in the office.'

There were no thanks as dJulie bustled off. Maybe thanks would come later. Much later, like when she left. Kathy put out her fag and returned to the kitchen to see whether she needed to call an ambulance or not.

Back inside the warmth of her domain, Kathy was pleasantly surprised. Yes, the mandoline was out, but no, Michael hadn't attempted to use it. The razor sharp cutter was sitting harmlessly on the counter next to the accident book and the spook was peeling potatoes with a confidence he hadn't been able to bring to the onions. Maybe he really did have problems with his contact lenses.

She glanced at the accident book. 'You've put your real surname, Michael. You might want to edit that.'

He dried his hands and looked at the book. He blinked twice and gave a hollow laugh. 'It's worse than that. I've put one of my cover names. Not the last one, thank God. I'll change it.'

Kathy took off her coat and slipped on a black kitchen jacket. 'I'll finish the onions and put the casserole together, then we'll see about slicing them spuds.' She got her favourite long knife and picked up where Michael had left off with the onions (once she'd removed the ones with blood on them). 'Bet it was hard getting used to winter,' she said casually. As well as the tan, Michael had put down a name that sounded Spanish or something and had funny accents on it. She liked to find out where the limits were with the spooks, because they could be here for months, and you had to talk about *something*, didn't you?

Michael returned to the sink. 'I'll never tell you where I was posted, but I can tell you that I spent Christmas Day having a barbecue on Copacabana beach in Rio. I made a life-changing discovery that day: my idiomat... my street Portuguese is not as good as I thought it was.'

Kathy slid the onions into the two casserole pots and took the beef out of the chiller. 'Oh yes? Why would you need to speak Portuguese?'

'Erm, it's what they speak in Brazil. Everywhere else in South America is Spanish-speaking. Or English.'

'Every day's a school day in STAND,' observed Kathy. 'Some lessons are easier than others. Go on then, what happened? It sounds magical, that: Christmas on the beach. Did you try and chat up someone's wife or something?'

He put the large colander on the worktop and shook his head. 'I'd already done that, quite successfully as it happens. No, my mistake was to confuse *Look out for Marco* and *Watch out for Marco*. As a result, I tried to score some speed off an undercover cop and then try to bribe him.'

'Way to go, Michael. That's an epic fail, that is.'

He looked at her. 'The cops delivered me to the consulate, and I was on the next plane home with a minder from Security.'

'Have you shared that in group?'

He shook his head.

'Then I wouldn't, if I were you. Not until you've found your feet.' She glanced at the huge clock. 'Right. Let's see you in action: I clock off as chef in ten minutes and clock on as carer.'

'Sorry?'

'Go on.' He placed a giant bowl next to the mandoline and took a potato. 'Why no cold water?' asked Kathy.

'Starch helps thicken the sauce.'

'Correct. Off you go.'

He was slow and careful, and utterly safe. Kathy really fancied something warm and creamy tonight, and he looked competent enough. 'Pause a second.'

He looked up and put his spud down.

'You can crack on, Michael. At weekends, I do a split shift as carer to our convent patient.' She paused to see if he'd correct her (the bankers always corrected her). When he only looked puzzled, she carried on, 'Or that's what I call him, 'cos it's easier than saying,' she paused and got the word lined up in her mouth. 'Our *covenanted resident*. There. When Doctor Simon bought the Abbey, it used to be a private asylum or something. He took over three patients, and it was in the covenant or something that they had to live out their days here. Two died before I turned up, within a few weeks of the takeover, I think. Not Don, though. Donald Bell soldiers on, bless him.'

Michael grinned. 'Does he live on the other side of the Group Therapy Room, through the fire door and next door to Simon's office? The one with the small private garden and the wheelchair ramp down from the french windows?'

Instead of grinning back, Kathy gave him a sympathetic look. 'Don't, Michael. Believe me, if you try to spend the rest of your life looking over your shoulder, you won't *have* a life. Or not one worth living. Let it go.' She paused. 'Have you signed up for yoga or Tai Chi?'

'Yoga. I don't fancy going outside in this weather.'

'You should try the Tai Chi. If you do, you'll see Don join in from his garden: Faye puts the class with their backs to him so he can watch her.'

'Oh. Right. So he's not completely…?'

'He's in his eighties, he suffers from crippling arthritis and at some point he had a stroke, so he's non-verbal. Apart from that, he's in peak form. Right. I'll see you later, and no nicking the biscuits until I get back. I'll be a couple of hours.'

What Kathy hadn't told Michael, and never would, is that Don wasn't *totally* non-verbal. The other staff, including Mingey Mora, thought that Kathy had a special gift with Don. Rubbish. She just listened to him, and the key was that silence didn't mean he couldn't understand, just as an inarticulate moan didn't mean he was in pain. And that he understood every word.

She breezed into Don's room, still buttoning her carer's tunic and glanced at the chair on the way to the sink. 'Hiya, Don. Bit nippy today, i'n't it? Brew? I'm parched.'

When he didn't say *no*, she put the kettle on and picked up the clipboard. The morning carer left at ten, and on Fridays, Don was fed with help from one of the therapists or cleaners. Today, wonder of wonders, it had been Faye herself, and there was nothing to note. She signed herself on to the sheet and poured water into the teapot.

While it brewed, she peeked and prodded around the room to make sure that nothing was out of place and that the useless cow who was supposed to clean had at least made *some* effort. Then again, the cleaner knew that Kathy would be coming, so she'd have to, wouldn't she? Satisfied that Don's home was habitable, Kathy poured herself a mug of tea and poured Don's into the two-handled china cup with the drinking spout.

That cup had been the breakthrough, just after Kathy had started as his weekend carer. She'd looked at the stained plastic beaker he was using and had said, 'Bet tea tastes terrible from that,' and Don had agreed with her. At least, that's what she thought he'd done.

From there, she had gone on to build a rapport that had, in her opinion, improved his quality of life no end. She went to place the cup on the table, and he moaned and shifted in his seat.

'Need to pee? Hang on.'

She put the mug to one side and braced herself to offer support. His hands were curled into claws, barely able to lift the cup, and his left hip had almost no movement, but he could stand, walk and sit down on the toilet perfectly happily. With help, of course. And if she steadied the toilet roll holder, he could clean himself up afterwards.

Business done, she helped him to the windows and opened the doors, just for a minute, so he could breathe the frigid air and see the trees off to the left. As always, he stared at the bare branches for a long time before he grunted something, and then it was back to the chair and story time.

She opened the tablet and it was already lined up with the latest audiobook. Still working his way through Terry Pratchett for the umpteenth time, she noted. Perhaps that had been her biggest breakthrough – realising that he enjoyed, or pretended to enjoy, books. Obviously she couldn't read to him, but he delighted in audiobooks – so long as someone sat and properly *listened* with him.

The weekend rate for carers wasn't much, but it added to her escape fund hugely, and it was a massive help in passing the time. *Money for old rope if you ask me*, she thought as she settled down.

Michael's dauphinoise was *exquisite*, according to Faye. Kathy didn't argue, but she would have been a lot less *fragrant* in her description. Everyone else agreed, and the absence of Mingey Mora helped lighten the mood no end. In company, Michael retreated into his shell a bit (and at communal meals, Kathy only ever listened), so their end of the refectory table was quiet. Good job, too, because Steve the ex copper was off on one again.

Steve was leaving the Abbey soon, and at Friday dinner he always had some mad new scheme for what he was going to do when he packed his bags. Today, it was riding a motorcycle from Beckthorpe in Yorkshire, England to Beckthorpe in New South Wales, Australia, via Beckthorpe in Tennessee, USA.

One night, he'd told Kathy that dreaming of a Big Adventure was all that had kept him going during detox and the short stretch in prison that had followed. 'I'll never go to the States with my record,' he'd said, 'but that won't stop me dreaming.'

'So what *are* you gonna do?' she'd asked.

'Doctor Simon's got me lined up to enrol on a counselling course in Liverpool and combine it with a job supporting squaddies with PTSD. That's if the Three Heads gang don't catch up with me.' He'd shrugged and changed the subject, and never spoken of it again.

When they were clearing up, Michael asked Kathy whether it was usual to have larger than life characters dominating like that.

'Doctor Simon says that there's always a natural entertainer in every group, and so long as they know what they're doing, it can be healthy. Mind you,' she added, 'Steve may be a laugh, but he's not a patch on Long Lenny.'

She regretted it as soon as the words were out of her mouth.

'Long Lenny?' said Michael with a smile on his face.

'Some other time,' she responded, looking away. 'I need to get cleaned up before my third job of the day.'

Steve organised the loading of the dishwashers, and Kathy went to have a bath before the second half of her shift with Don.

He might be in better shape than he looked, but he was still an old man, and she found him asleep in his chair. That was okay, because it meant he'd be more awake later, and Kathy rarely put him to bed at the time she was supposed to.

Doctor Simon had taught her a lot, including the Spanish phrase *quid pro quo*. When setting up Don's Audible account, her quid pro quo had been that he had to let her choose one TV programme to watch in the evenings, and with it being a Friday in winter, there was only one choice: Britain's favourite comfort-food show, *Death in Paradise*. She loved it.

Tomorrow, she would go through *TV Choice* and read out some of the programmes to him. He never watched daytime shows, but he did love a science documentary, especially if it was about genetics and stuff like that. Tonight, though, they were heading to Sainte Marie in the Caribbean to see which British guest star would be bumped off in the first scene.

She went to close the floor-length curtains, but a grunt stopped her. *Of course. It's the full moon tonight. No curtains on the full moon.* 'Sorry, Don. Do you want a fleece or summat for the draft?'

No, he didn't, and they settled down to watch DI Mooney name the killer with nothing but a peanut clutched in the dead man's hand to go on. Case closed, Kathy put the kettle on for hot chocolate. 'More Terry Pratchett, Don?'

Her mind did drift a little during the story, and she was staring out of the window when she saw a silver light coming towards them. At first she thought it was a drone or something, but it moved steadily across the fields at head height, through a hedge and towards the window. At that point, she sat up straight and jabbed the speakers to kill the story.

She glanced at Don, and he was staring at it too, and he was utterly transfixed, totally motionless. Kathy stood up and went to the window, sticking to the side. The silver light came straight on, and Don let out a huge moan. She still didn't know what it was, and then it was across the lawn, over the garden and plunged straight through the glass, bearing down on Don and exploding in a flash of light.

Kathy picked herself off the floor and rubbed her head. Don was *glowing*. And that wasn't all. His hands were clawing at his face, and in the light, she

17

could see something like cables or wire hanging from his wrists. She also saw something that made her rush to the bathroom: it looked like someone had *stitched his mouth closed with the same wire.*

When she'd heaved up her casserole and dauphinoise, she grabbed a towel and went to see if Don were okay. He was, and there was no sign of the wire through his lips. He was also staring at her, blinking and twitching. He shuddered all the way down to his slippers and fell back, his head lolling on the high backed chair.

She rushed to feel for a pulse. Strong. 'Don? What's happened? You all right?'

His eyes opened, and he pointed at the clipboard. No, not at the clipboard, *at the pen.* Kathy reached over and passed it to him with her mouth hanging open. He couldn't grasp it. No chance.

'Hang on,' she said. 'I'm gonna nip next door. There's a flipchart in the therapy room, and I'll get some paper and a marker. See how we do with that. Maybe you can tell me what the fuck just happened.'

Don didn't tell Kathy what had happened, and she never did find out. In fact, Don tried to convince her she'd fallen asleep and dreamt it, but Kathy knew what she'd seen.

Don himself didn't find out the details until much later, but he knew what it meant alright: part of his Binding had been released.

The exact trigger for the light appearing in Beckthorpe had taken place a short while earlier, and on the other side of the Pennines. It happened on the Fae Gallops above Longsleddale in the Lake District, when Princess Faithful scythed down the former Prince Galleny, killing the rebel and sundering all his magick.

Like all forces of nature, there is no action at a distance, and the skein of Ink riding the back of a Ley line took a while to unravel. When it did, Don knew that he had a short window before what was left of the binding killed him. He also managed to remember something he'd been struggling to get hold of for decades: his real name.

Part One — Peacemaker

Chapter 1 — Happy Holi-Day

Spring(ish) in Lakeland.

We are all familiar with the noises of war, aren't we, but what are the sounds of peace, I wonder? Given that my hearing is not what it was, and given that I was wearing a thick woollen hat over my ears, today's answer would be: *not a lot*.

The hat was necessary because it was half past six on a bitterly cold March morning, and the wind coming off the lake was pushing the temperature close to freezing with wind chill. It won't surprise you to learn that rain was forecast for later. Just another day in the paradise of the Lake District.

At least everyone was here on time, and when I say *everyone*, I mean that there were dozens of people shivering on the lawns and gravel paths of Waterhead Academy, close to the shores of Windermere.

The bulk of the boarders at the modern school beyond the screen of trees are weekly, and this being a Sunday they were no doubt fast asleep in the bosom of their families around the Lakeland Particular. Not so the Seniors.

The young Mages who live in the Gothic pile of School House can't go home at weekends: extra magick practice. However, as today is a feast day, some of their parents and siblings have joined them, and that accounted for part of the crowd. The students themselves were at the front, led by the Head Girl, and the staff were behind them. I was off to the left, and by my side was Mina. Of course.

The Keepers of the Peace, the assessors – *my* assessors – were huddling together for warmth behind me. Except for my Adjutant. Karina Kent does not *huddle* with humans. With Mannwolves, I'm told, but not with humans. Then again, there are reports that she's been *huddling* with a certain Witch of the Water. I glanced away to my right, where the white robes of the Sisters stood out from the sensible winter wear of everyone else. Alas, they had their hoods up, so I couldn't spot the flaming red locks of Becca Lewis. Maybe later.

I looked left again, and further behind the assessors were my guests for today, and in one of their hands was the leash of my trusty hound, Scout. He still has his winter coat, so he looked bored rather than bored and cold (which was the expression on many human faces).

And that left the VIPs, gathered to the students' right. I know all the movers and shakers of the Particular now, and most of their families, too. I was trying to tick them off my mental list as the pre-dawn light grew, and to work out whether my maths for the forthcoming vote was correct. At that point, Dr Judith Yearsley, Housemaster of School House spoke up.

'It's time, Willow.'

The Head Girl, Willow Torver, stooped down and picked up the elaborate wreath which has adorned the School Hall since Yuletide. She carried it reverently to a pile of logs by the lake, and placed it on top. She stood back and lowered the hood of her coat, revealing her Goddess Braid.

The Vernal Equinox is not a festival of the Great Goddess as such, but it is a special day: from now on, the power of light will outface the darkness. I just wish someone had sent that memo to the weather gods. Mina put her arm round my waist and snuggled in, turning me ever so slightly to make me a more effective windbreak. Good to know I have my uses.

'Do you think they'll go through with it?' she whispered.

'We'll find out in a second.'

Willow Torver, erect of back and very conscious of her audience, raised her arms. She spoke loudly and clearly, her words carrying over the water.

'As the sun returns, Goddess hear our prayers and fill our baskets that we may live to finish your work.'

March is a terrible month if you live off the land. You can't eat daffodils, and nothing else is growing yet, not even the grass. Last summer's harvest is a distant memory, and generations past have had to choose between going hungry and eating their seed corn. We are lucky not to face that choice. Most of the time.

Willow continued, 'Take our pride as our only offering.'

The wreath has no nutritional value, and its sacrifice is a sign of humility. Willow took the knee on our behalf and used magick to light the bonfire. 'So mote it be,' she concluded.

We echoed her prayer and watched the flames take hold for a second until there was a stirring among the group of young Mages. 'Look lively,' I whispered.

Two of the girls, Iolanthe and Jocasta, reached into their capacious pockets and dug out handfuls of coloured powder. Iolanthe stepped forwards and threw a great cloud of green dust over Willow and the baby bonfire. Willow gave a high-pitched squeak, and the powder flared in the flames with a burst of Lux that lit up the dawn with writhing tongues of green fire which turned into snakes, dragons and birds. Very impressive. And very distracting.

Jocasta and Io had already covered the other students with powder, and been covered back by their partners in crime. And now they were headed for the grown-ups, their figures blurring with Glamours as they criss-crossed paths and made it harder to identify exactly *who* was doing *what* when it came to the pigment hurling.

I turned to Mina and grinned. For a second. Until a ball of yellow burst on my chest. 'Traitor!' I roared, but I was talking to her back, because she'd already performed a hit and run on the assessors. Except one.

The Senior Assessor, Matt Eldridge, had taken his anointing with as much good humour as he could muster on a March morning, but not Karina. My Adjutant has the reflexes of a Ninja and a profound hatred of surprises. She used magick to blow the powder away, right into the face of Tanya, who was now complaining loudly.

Beyond the assessors, one of our guests lost their struggle with Scout. He bounded over, trailing his short lead, and came to see what the fuss was all about, barking loudly to announce his arrival. Poor lad couldn't work out whether this was an attack or a game, and if it was a game, why couldn't he join in?

The ordered groups on the lawn had dissolved into chaos as people instinctively dodged and ran from the marauding teenagers (and the overexcited Border Collie). It only stopped when they ran out of powder.

Mina sensed the ending, and scuttled towards the shore, where Judith Yearsley was about to read the riot act, and I was glad to see that the Housemaster hadn't escaped unscathed. Mina skidded to a halt on the gravel and bowed in Namaste. 'Happy Holi, Doctor Yearsley. I'm glad to see that your students are embracing the traditions of many diverse cultures.'

Judith pursed her lips and considered her options. All across her face, you could see her preferred response: *They'll be embracing the thick edge of my tongue in a minute.* She breathed out and gave a rictus grin. 'Such a shame you'll be leaving soon, Ms Desai.'

Mina bobbed her head. 'We'll be back often enough. You won't miss us for long.'

'I won't miss you at all,' muttered the Housemaster. It was rude, but it let her vent some of the steam, and the students probably wouldn't get in any trouble later.

Saul Brathay, President of the Grand Union and Chief of Clan Skelwith came running over to defuse the situation. He was also desperate to return Scout. It hadn't been difficult for him to capture the runaway mutt, because once Scout realised that no one was truly in danger, he'd followed the most interesting smell. That dog was once a Bonded Familiar, and the experience has left him warped. In a good way. Mostly. He can smell Lux, for one thing, and for another he has a clear sense of what non-humans smell like. The downside is that Gnomes are olfactory dog-nip to him, and he loves to lick them for some reason. It doesn't go down well.

'Here,' said Saul, thrusting the lead into my hand and turning to Judith and

Mina. 'Let's get inside out of the cold, shall we?' Judith turned and stalked off.

'Your doing?' he said to Mina, backing away from Scout and trying to keep a straight face.

'This is a festival, is it not?' she replied, the grin on her face belying the innocence in her voice. 'I distributed the Holi powder at the poker game last night.'

Saul's eyes lit up with alarm. 'You're joking, right, Mina?'

She wasn't, actually, but she smiled as if she were. 'I thought that the meeting of the Grand Union would be a lot more fun if everyone was tagged.' She looked Saul up and down, from his bull neck to his stout boots. 'It's hard to be pompous if you are covered in Barbie pink dye.'

'Right,' said Saul. He hesitated, following Mina's gaze. 'Pink, you say?'

'All over your back,' she replied. 'Don't worry, it is all water-soluble and bio-degradable.'

He shook his head and headed for School House at a fast pace that did nothing to enhance his diminished dignity. Mina and I linked hands and grinned at each other. 'It's good to leave your mark,' she observed. I snorted and said nothing because there was a confrontation looming ahead. At the moment, it didn't involve us, but it soon would. When Mina's eyesight caught up with mine, and when we were a lot closer, she said, 'Is that…?'

'Oh yes. And I'm not sure who's in the most trouble here.'

The Peace of Brothers Water has held for a month now, following the showdown and near battle at the lake of the same name – a month during which I'd criss-crossed the Particular with Karina, gritting my teeth in the face of much abuse and generally making sure that everyone got the message.

I did take a few days off for the Cheltenham racing festival, but that was it. Now that I reckoned they had fully absorbed the message of Peace, I had asked for this special meeting of the Grand Union. If we got through the doors alive.

The Peace had avoided all-out war, but it hadn't prevented casualties in the preliminary skirmishes. On that night in February, the Fae Queen of Derwent had tried to attack the Greening family of Grizedale, and the Queen had very nearly been wiped out in return.

The Greenings, with their human allies, had got the drop on the Queen, and they'd achieved that by hitching their wagon to a pair of misguided Spirits, who then introduced them to a bunch of Fae rebels. The Spirits had also suborned my magickal partner, Cordelia Kennedy, and their plan had very nearly worked: I'd had to put my own life on the line, and called on a lot of people to do the same. It was a close run thing.

All of the Fae rebels were captured and killed, the Spirits were destroyed, and I'd prevented an attempted poisoning of our tutelary Nymph and patron of the Watch, Nimue. In the aftermath of that, James Greening, political head of his family, had been wounded trying to kill me and had died in hospital. His niece, Alexandra, was one of the two people arguing outside School House, and her daughter was the other.

Jocasta – Jo – Greening had been the first casualty of the nearly-war. In a blaze of rage, the Red Queen of Derwent had given Jo a double compound fracture of the forearm; it was still strapped up, though the cast seems to have gone. Jo was liberally covered in Holi powder, as was her mother, and they were having the Mother and Daughter of all rows.

'Arff!'

Scout really doesn't like it when the Big People argue.

They stopped and turned to us. I raised my voice and said, 'Your arm seems a lot better, Jocasta. Glad to see it.'

Jo flashed a smile, then looked down at her trainers, unwilling to risk saying anything that would get her in deeper trouble.

Alex Greening reined herself in now that she had an audience, and confined herself to shifting the blame. 'Whose idea was it?' she said to Mina. 'Yours or Iolanthe Preston's?'

Alex, like any good mother, is convinced that any wrong-doing by their child is because they have fallen in with bad company. In the case of Io Preston, she's probably right. Not that Iolanthe is *really* bad. I hope.

Mina put on her innocent face, the one with a lot of eyelash-fluttering and head-bobbing. 'It's because I am an accountant, Lady Greening. Every so often I have to do something outrageous or people won't believe I'm human. The Holi powder was all my idea.'

In the face of such nonsense, Alex Greening's anger escaped like steam on the wind, and she shook her head to clear it. 'Don't call me *Lady* again, please. Some people will think I'm trying it on.' She took a breath. 'Go and make yourself useful, Jocasta. If you can.'

'I can't, really,' said her daughter. 'Most of the work needs two hands.'

I had an idea, and shoved Scout's lead at her. 'This only needs one.' She took the lead without thinking (well brought up, you know), then frowned at the responsibility. I took the roll of poo bags from my pocket and added to the burden. 'Don't try to hold the leash with your teeth. He's wise to that. Wrap it round a tree and fasten that clip to his harness.'

'Erm…'

Jocasta had no desire whatsoever to walk a lively Collie on a freezing morning, and her face said so very clearly.

'Off you go,' said her mother with a malicious grin. 'I need to talk to the Commissioner.'

'And I need to get warm,' said Mina, bowing to Alexandra and skipping through the doors.

Jocasta wandered off, trying to work out which way would lead to the most shelter, and I turned to face Alexandra. 'Have you made a decision?' I asked.

'Yes, but that's not the main reason I waited for you. Stella came to see me last night.'

'Oh?'

'If she'd told me what she was planning last year … if she'd told me about it before they started digging, I'd have told her to stop.'

Stella Ripley had spent her fortune on a manuscript. A manuscript that led her and her family to the tomb of an ancient human prince. A human prince who'd become the full consort of a Fae Queen. The Queen had loved him, lost him and buried him in a grave full of her gifts to him, a grave that had been forgotten when she too died. Until Stella bought that manuscript.

The Ripleys had dug him up, taken the Artefacts and sold them to the highest bidders, one of whom was Alexandra Greening. The excavation had cost the life of Matt Eldridge's brother when he tried to investigate, and of Sura Ripley, one of Stella's daughters when she was forced against her will to look after Mannwolves and made such a hash of it that they turned on her; they are now *my* Wolves.

When the Red Queen had discovered the full truth about the desecration of her ancestor's bequest, she'd broken Jocasta's arm and broken the fragile status quo of the Particular, nearly triggering an all-out war. As part of the Peace, I'd ordered that the Artefacts be returned to the Red Queen as the Queen of Grace's heir.

I'd wondered whether the Greenings were part of the excavation, or just eager clients. Alexandra was telling me that they were innocent of the greater crime. Or was she?

She'd paused after telling me about Stella, and she had something to add that was very difficult for her. I'd stayed silent, and carried on waiting while the wind whipped at the strands of hair that strayed from her braid. Someone closed one of the great doors with a bang, and that prompted her to speak. We'd both have to be inside very soon.

'Stella told me that James had been a party to the dig. He said nothing to me. I swear it.' That was big news. And there was more to come. 'Stella also told me that he was Sura's father.'

'Was he now?' I replied, to show that I'd heard and understood the implications of what she'd told me.

Alexandra Greening was the matriarch of the family, no question, but the political leader and public face had been her uncle, James Greening. James had done good in running the project to purge Nimue of mercury poisoning and he'd done bad when he tried to stab me. Oh, and he threatened Mina, too. He'd only avoided serious punishment by dying in hospital. To learn that he was Sura's unacknowledged father was news indeed, because Sura was Stella's older daughter, or had been. She'd also tried to kill me and been torn to shreds by her own Wolves. My Wolves.

25

'I am sorry for what he did to you, Commissioner,' she concluded.

'Not your fault. You were not your uncle's keeper.'

She nodded slightly. 'The only reason Stella told me about James was because she came to say goodbye.'

'Did she say whether James was Saïa's father, too? I'd hate to think that Stella had two children with a reason to dislike me, even if I did save Saïa from the Fae.'

'No, he wasn't. I only know that because it's clear that Stella's children had different fathers, and it's a moot point anyway. The Ripleys are broken.'

'Broken?'

'Their debts are so huge that they can't continue as they are. The holders of secured loans have called them in, and most of their estates will have to be liquidated to pay their creditors back. Yesterday afternoon they formally repudiated Stella and cast her out. They passed over Saïa and appointed Stella's nephew, Hunter, as head of the Family, even though he has less magick than your dog.'

Having heard that, I was even happier to be leaving. The fall of the Ripleys would help ensure the Peace, but seeing me around all the time wouldn't help them move on, that's for certain.

'Thank you for telling me,' I said. 'You didn't have to do that.'

'I did. You needed to know.' She gave a bitter smile. 'And it will help convince you that James acted alone at the Four Roads Cross and that he acted for personal reasons, not Family ones.'

I didn't point out the ambiguity she'd spoken, the ambiguity of Family versus *family*. James had most assuredly acted for *family* reasons: seeking revenge for your daughter's death is pretty *familiar*. As it were.

I shifted to more immediate concerns. 'Stella isn't here, is she? I didn't see her.'

'Gone overnight. The Ripleys no longer hold the Chair of the Eden Valley Union, either. The vice-Chair will vote for Saul's motion. As will I.' She breathed out, blowing her cheeks and letting her eyes unfocus for a second before setting her mouth and meeting my eyes. 'Shall we?'

'After you.'

Chapter 2 — Passing on the Baton

Half an hour after ushering Alex Greening inside School House and closing the main door behind me, my status in Lakeland changed irrevocably, and so did the Particular itself. Their near-absolute independence had begun to crumble two centuries ago when they accepted the authority of the Cloister Court, and it continued today when they made their Commissioner answerable to an outside authority: the Lord Guardian of the North. Me, in other words.

They then accepted my resignation as Commissioner and appointed Matt Eldridge to replace me. They'd created a long staff of Enchanted oak for the Commissioner, and I took great pleasure in handing it over to Matt. He accepted it with quiet dignity and said only two things, both of which were quietly satisfying to hear. First, he said that he'd do his best to be as dedicated and impartial as I had been, and second he said that he was confirming Karina as his Adjutant.

I led the applause and left him to take charge of his team: I'd said my goodbyes last night over Ukrainian food at the Oak Tree Hotel. With the meeting breaking up behind me, I made a dash for the canteen to beat the queue. I was bloody hungry.

The senior students (under supervision) had been up well before dawn to get the breakfast started, and by now it was all ready. Mina had missed the Union meeting to look after our guests (who weren't allowed into the meeting, not being registered members of the Union), and I found them exactly where you'd expect Mina to be: close to the warmest radiator.

Having said that, I had to double check, because at first glance there were *two* Minas, one at each end of the table. The real Mina looked up and smiled at me when I gave her the thumbs-up. The fake Mina isn't what they call in Turkey a *genuine fake*, but she does have Mina's hair. Literally, her hair is exactly the same as Mina's ('But Leesha is not going grey! What is happening to me!').

Why there exists a woman with Mina's hair is a long story, and not relevant to today. The owner of the hair, Alicia Lake, finished eating and put her cutlery down, knife and fork neatly together and at an angle. She stood, bowed to Mina, and scuttled out of the dining room to who-knows-where. Given that Alicia is a Fae Squire, she might go and wait in the freezing cold or she might go and burgle the strong-room. You can never tell with the Fae.

Three other women were clustered closer to Mina, chatting animatedly and finishing their breakfasts. I plonked my tray down and said, 'I'd better rescue Jocasta before she freezes to death.'

Mina shook her head and sighed. 'No need. The food is okay but won't survive if you disappear and let it go cold. I'll do it. You'll no doubt be talking magick anyway.'

She rose and squeezed around the chairs, stopping to give me a kiss. 'All good?' she asked.

'All good. I'll see you soon. Scout can be tied up for a bit if he's had a walk.' I slipped two of the extra sausages I'd picked up into a paper napkin and passed them over. 'These should help.'

I smiled at our guests and lifted my knife and fork. 'Is there anything left to discuss?' I asked hopefully.

'Lots,' said Princess Staveley. 'We haven't started on the contract yet.'

'So what *have* you been talking about?'

'The Wedding,' she replied. 'But I won't stand between my lord and his repast.'

She said it ironically but meant it literally: I am her lord and master. 'Good,' I replied, and speared the bacon with my fork.

The Peace of Brothers Water had seen a lot of losers, yes, but there had been winners, too. I'd looked at two of them in the School Hall when they debated the motion to change their constitution – Victoria Preston and Morgan Torver seemed quite pleased with themselves. With the collapse of the Ripleys and the setbacks to the Greenings and the Red Queen, the Preston and Torver Families were suddenly on the up. And yes, before you ask, it's not unusual to have the oldest daughters of three Families together at the Academy. Whether Willow Torver, Jocasta Greening and Iolanthe Preston will go on to be friends or mortal enemies is a question well beyond me, though I believe that Jo is nailed on to succeed Willow as Head Girl next year.

Another winner from the Peace was seated at my left. Princess Staveley, formerly Princess Faithful of the Borrowdale Fae, had bent the knee to me in exchange for my help and I had saved her life. For the next eleven months, she was mine to command, and I had commanded her to become Madreb to the Birkfell Pack. Reports of her performance are mixed, shall we say.

When her service is done, she will become a full Fae Queen, and what does a Queen need? She needs a Royal Sídhe, that's what she needs. Princess Staveley has the land and the cash, but what she doesn't have is time. Karina is Guardian to the Pack, and Faith answers to her as Madreb. Believe me, when it comes to the Wolves, Karina is a far stricter taskmaster than I am.

Seated on my right was a woman with both time on her hands and the necessary skills. All I had to do was bring them together. From the way they ignored me and carried on discussing Fae politics while I ate, it didn't seem like I'd have a lot to do. That's Mina for you.

It helped that Tamsin is a special friend of Mina's. You've heard me talk of her as *Tamsin Kelly*, but now that she's accepted that her marriage to Chris is over, she's switched back to her birth name and is Tamsin Pike again. She has also finished her stint as a student of Plane Shifting and there is nothing and no one to keep her in London any more. If you're wondering about her girls, they are fast asleep in our rented house under the care of Tamsin's Irish nanny.

Coming up here to work on Faith's sídhe would be a new start for Tamsin, and all I had to do was…

'How much are you offering?' she asked when I got to my last piece of toast.

'You might not be up to it, right?' said Faith, brushing back her hair, which was most definitely not in a Goddess Braid.

Tamsin nodded. 'No, but we'll find out soon enough.'

'Fine.' Faith named a generous amount and continued, 'I'll pay you half in monthly instalments and the rest on completion.'

Tamsin looked uncertain, and the third guest leaned over to put her hand round Tammy's shoulders. 'If the Queen of Richmond thinks you're ready, you're ready.'

Very, very few people are willing to be seen supporting the Bodysnatcher in public. One of the reasons Tamsin wanted to come to the Particular was the hope that the label wouldn't come with her. 'Deal,' she said.

'Good,' said Faith with a smile. 'If my lord will give me some time off, we'll start tomorrow.'

I took a swig of tea. 'Not my decision. That's the Pack Guardian's decision, though I'm sure she'll be flexible.' I paused. 'But bear in mind, she starts with a new boss tomorrow.'

Faith didn't freeze. She went *still*, suppressing her irritation and bringing the twin imperatives of royal biology and her bondage to me back into balance. She has begun to change from being a mostly human female into Fae royalty, a change as profound as that undergone in the hive by a bee pupa becoming a Queen, even if it's not visible to the mundane eye.

I'd see a difference if I were to open my Third Eye, though. Queens project magick in different ways to lesser Fae, and when I peeked at her on Friday, I could see a silver shimmer that wasn't there before. Not that my Third Eye is very reliable.

'Of course, my lord,' said Faith. 'I'm sure that Tammy would like a couple of days to explore child-care options first.' With that, she rose and went to intercept Karina, who was standing next to Matt in the queue for breakfast.

'Mmm,' said Tamsin. 'That reminds me. You were going to point out one of the Daughters, Conrad.'

'Look around,' I said drily. 'If you threw Holi powder over the canteen, you'd hit half a dozen of them. There are almost as many Daughters of the Earth up here as there are sheep.'

It's true. The Daughters of the Earth have pretty much sewn up the para-magickal economy in Lakeland. Need a magickal lawyer? It's a Daughter. Mage friendly hotel? It's a Daughter. Child care? You get the picture.

'Do you see that one? The one looking at you surreptitiously?' I said quietly.

'The one with the unreal blue eyes?'

'The same. That's Sapphire Gibson. Go and say hello. She's dying to meet you. She told me so at dinner on Friday.'

The same arm that had encouraged Tamsin to accept the job with Faith gave her a shove out of her chair and across the room. Tamsin walked nervously, slow steps at first, then Sapphire got up, snatched Tammy into a big hug and pulled her to their table. And then there was one.

'I can't see her,' said Francesca. 'Are they making her do the washing up? Like some Cinderella?'

'It's not like that, Francesca. Honestly. Every day since Persephone started at Waterhead, Willow has looked out for her. No one has bullied her or excluded her deliberately. It's just that …' I shrugged. 'She's always been on a different path. Especially since they discovered she's true to the Eden Line. If anything, they look up to her. Especially since she won the Waterhead Chase.'

'Childish games.'

I wouldn't call anything with that level of mortal danger *childish*. Before I could say something mollifying, Jocasta appeared from outside, her blue face adding to the rainbow dyes on her coat and jeans. 'Jo! Everything okay?' I asked.

She turned and saw me. 'Yeah. Mina's got him.' The cold got the better of her, and she added, 'Your dog is mad, sir. He kept trying to jump into the air over the flagstones.'

'Hopscout,' I replied. 'It's a game. Never mind. Could you tell Perci I need a word out here.'

She looked at the queue (gone), and nodded. 'Course I will.'

Francesca watched Jocasta's retreating back and whispered, 'When that one kicks back against her mother, she's going to be trouble. Mark my words.'

'Hopefully she'll be Matt's problem, not mine.'

As Jocasta approached the door to the kitchen, Judith Yearsley emerged with a bacon sandwich and a cup of tea. Presumably she'd been inside checking that the students weren't letting down the name of School House. They hadn't.

Jocasta dodged her teacher and disappeared into the kitchen while Judith surveyed the room, and was about to flick her eyes past me when she saw who I was with. Her brows shot up, and she came straight over.

'Doctor Somerton. What an honour. What brings the Keeper of the Esoteric Library to the Particular? Business or …' She looked at me and shook her head. 'I'm guessing it's not pleasure.'

'Judith. How lovely,' said Francesca, keeping an even, professional tone. 'There's not much business left for me. I don't know whether the new Warden has opened her internal mail from Friday afternoon, but when she does, she'll find my resignation letter. Three months and I'll be gone, and the first two months of that are accrued leave.' She peered at Judith over her glasses. 'You heard it here first.'

The Housemaster was taken aback for a second. 'Well, well, well. Change is all around. So this is a pleasure trip, then?'

Perci had emerged from the kitchen, seen the Housemaster, and was now keeping her distance while drying her hands vigorously on a tea towel.

Francesca took a deliberate look at me. 'I'm visiting friends, Judith. I may do some house-hunting as well,' she announced, speaking with a malicious grin which could have meant anything.

The Housemaster grinned back. 'Well good luck, Francesca, and have a good time. You know where I am if you want to drop in.'

'Thank you. I may well do that.'

With a nod, the Housemaster went to join another table, and Persephone sidled up to our corner. 'Hi, Conrad.'

'Morning, Perci. Have a seat. There's someone I'd like you to meet.'

Persephone fiddled with the teatowel, realised it wouldn't go into the pocket of her jeans, then dumped it on a free chair before sitting down as far from Francesca as she could. She didn't recognise the Keeper, but she guessed what was coming.

'Perci, this is Francesca Somerton. She's your grandfather's sister, so that makes her your great aunt.'

Perci flashed a nervous smile, then shrank back as Francesca got up, circumnavigated the table and stood waiting for a hug. The teenager got up and was enveloped by the relative she'd never met, and whose existence she'd only discovered a few weeks ago. The embrace was long, and for the first time indoors, I got a frisson of magick.

'You're Roly's granddaughter alright,' said Francesca. 'How lovely it is to meet you, dear. Are they feeding you properly? You're so… thin.'

'She's a jockey, Francesca,' I supplied. 'And it's all muscle and sinew. She can ride Unicorns.'

Francesca squeezed Persephone's bicep in the way that only matriarchs can do without getting a slap. 'Hmmph,' she observed.

The older woman started blinking away tears and made her way slowly back to her seat, finding a handkerchief and removing her glasses to dab at her eyes. When she'd sat down, she replaced her spectacles and stared. 'Just for a moment, dear. Let me look at you just for a moment.'

Perci lifted her head and tried to smile. Francesca stared, then lowered her head and spoke quietly. 'Conrad said you haven't taken a family name. Didn't the Torvers offer you theirs?'

Persephone's mother had more-or-less abandoned her and died shortly afterwards. She'd been assigned to the Torvers by the Union and brought up as Willow's younger sister. Fostered, but never adopted.

31

'Willow wanted them to offer, but I said no,' replied Perci. There was no anger in her voice, just a flat statement of fact.

'Then would you consider becoming a Quinn?' said Francesca. 'Roly didn't know he had a granddaughter until he became a Spirit.'

Perci looked uncomfortable, as well she might. I can't imagine what it must be like to be visited as a teenager by the Spirit of your grandfather, especially when your grandfather was the legendary Sir Roland Quinn, late Warden of Salomon's House and premier Mage of Albion.

'He mentioned it,' she said. 'I don't know. And before you say anything else, he told me about the will, too. That's just about all he said, though.'

'Good. So long as you know. We can do the boring stuff later. And the important stuff.'

'Sorry?'

'Conrad tells me that my brother's Spirit has been chained and imprisoned somewhere around this miserable place, and by *miserable place* I mean Lakeland before spring. I came to see you first, dear, but freeing Roly is the second reason I'm here.'

'And you want me to help?' said Perci sceptically.

I took over. 'I'm ninety-nine per cent sure that he's near Furness Abbey. It's the only place that Cordelia went on her own for an extended period. And she made Faith lie about what she was doing there. He's not going to be happy. He may even be … damaged, Perci. Having you there in the background should help him orient himself.'

'Don't worry, dear,' added Francesca. 'I'll make sure you're well protected.'

'But I can't just take time off.'

'I'll square it with Judith, and with your … Fae sponsors. You can drive, I take it?'

Perci was stunned, not quite sure what was coming next. 'Yeah. Got an express test so I could tow the horse boxes.'

Francesca sniffed at the mention of horses. If she was going to spend much time with Perci, that would have to change. 'Good. You can drive my hire-car when we've telephoned their unhelpful desk to put you on the insurance. Or maybe there's an App thingy. You can sort it while I drive us to Lunar Hall, then you can drive back. You'll need to change first, of course.'

Perci's horse was now adrift in an unmapped wilderness. 'Where and what is Lunar Hall?' she asked, bewildered.

'Where your maternal grandmother lives, of course!' Francesca looked at me suspiciously. 'Didn't Conrad tell you?'

I hadn't told her because Persephone would have bolted like a scared colt. 'Sorry,' I said innocently. 'Been a bit busy trying to keep the peace and all that.'

Persephone didn't win the Waterhead Chase by being a total doormat. It was her turn to stare at me. 'You had enough time to come to the stables last week to ride your horse! You could have told me then.'

I waved my hand airily, slightly camp, I know, but Fae Queens seem to be able to dismiss all sorts of problems with a wave. 'You were busy. Just let Francesca be your human shield, and don't worry about Sister Theresa.'

'Sister who?'

Francesca was now looking daggers at me. 'He talks rubbish, dear. He's a man.'

Mina reappeared at that point. I breathed a huge sigh of relief, and as they'd accused me of talking rubbish, I thought it was time to live down to their expectations. I took a packet out of my pocket and slid it to Perci. 'When you get to Lunar Hall, ask to speak to Anna and meet Kracik. If you give him these, you'll have a friend for life.'

Perci looked at the packet. 'Curried mealworms! Euew! Who in the Goddess's Name is Kracik?'

'A huge, magickally enhanced mole.'

A lightbulb came on over Francesca's head.

'Why would I want to be friends with a mole?' asked Perci.

'Because you wouldn't want him as an enemy,' I replied.

Francesca noticed that Mina hadn't unzipped her coat and said to Perci, 'Go and get changed into something warm but smart, dear. We'll be outside a fair bit, I suspect. I'll look after this snack for you.' She pocketed the mealworms and stood up, leaving Perci no choice but follow. 'I'll see you outside. It's getting a bit stuffy in here.'

'Right,' said Persephone. Now that the shock had worn off, she was getting excited. Nervous, yes, but excited, too. She stepped back, turned and almost skipped out of the canteen.

I took the empty trays to the returns trolley, and we all gathered our things. I didn't say any goodbyes as we followed Persephone out of the dining room and towards the entrance hall, but I did nod and smile to my friends and allies. When the swing doors closed behind us, a thought struck me. 'Francesca, why was Judith the only one to say hello – to you, I mean? Almost all the Mages here have done at least a term at Salomon's House.'

'They have,' she replied. 'And to all of them but Judith, I was the scary Librarian who made sure they didn't try to get away with anything. Judith was the only one who I got to know properly. She earned that doctorate.'

There was something in her voice that made me raise my eyebrow. 'But...?'

'But nothing. It's just that I told her she was mad to take a teaching position up here instead of staying at the Invisible College. I told her she was wasted, and it didn't go down well. She's spent the last thirty years proving me wrong: the Waterhead Academy graduates all have a much better grounding in the Art than any of our own Aspirants. Are you two off now?'

'Yes,' replied Mina. 'We have to finish packing, and it's a long drive to

Chester.'

'Then I wish you well. Thank you for bringing me here. And don't worry, Mina, I shall keep my eye on Tamsin until I go back.'

'And I'll be here on Tuesday, if I'm not in hospital after tonight.'

She was serious. 'I shall take a good look at Persephone today. I want her there when we go hunting for Roly, but not if there's a risk. You know, in some lights she has a real glow of the Fae about her.'

'Of course. One of the many reasons for having Faith with us.'

Francesca glanced back at the dining room. 'I wasn't happy about that, but you really have subordinated her, haven't you? Let's go.'

There were proper goodbye hugs as we left Francesca to wait for her great niece and the difficult encounter which lay ahead of them. I'd have loved to go with them, because I really do have a lot of unanswered questions about Perci's great-great grandmother, Madeleine, but they could wait: our appointment in Cheshire couldn't. Not if I wanted to see Midsummer alive.

We walked off, and I was about to say something when Mina's phone rang. Mendelssohn's *Wedding March* blasted out towards the lake, and she reached for her pocket. 'What on earth does the vicar want at this time on a Sunday morning? Does she not know that this is a day of rest ... Hello, Libby. You're up early.'

She put the phone on speaker, just as the vicar let out an exclamation. 'Oh. Erm, I didn't expect you to answer. I was going to leave a voicemail.'

Mina looked at me and frowned. My love is a master of the strategic voicemail for bad news. 'No, no. It is Holi and now we are going to Middlebarrow. What's up?'

'Desmond – the organist – came to see me last night. He's not going to be available for your wedding. Sorry.'

Mina frowned at me again, as if I were responsible for all the residents of Clerkswell. 'What's the problem, Libby? You said that he would love to play in the morning and have the afternoon off.'

'Ah. Here's the thing.' The vicar paused, bracing herself. 'That was before he found out who was getting married.'

Mina's eyes hardened, and it was her turn to pause. I think she was trying not to take it out on Libby. 'Well, he can't use the excuse that I'm a divorcée, so what *has* he come up with?'

'Officially, he's just not available. He doesn't have to be. Unofficially, I'm afraid that he's heard about the shrine to Ganesh at Elvenham Grange. I'm really, really sorry, Mina.'

There was no pain in her eyes when she looked at me. Instead, I saw a mixture of anger and uncertainty. She turned her eyes back to the phone and nodded to herself. 'Has anyone else said anything?'

'No. No one. Then again, you haven't tried to book the choir, so...'

'And you, Libby? What do you think now that it's in the open?'

There was no hesitation in the vicar's reply. 'I think that there's a good reason why he's the organist and I'm the vicar. I also think that I've changed my mind about the party later. Even if I'm dead on my feet after a shift in the ICU, I'm going to turn up and be seen.'

'Thank you. That means a lot.' She sighed. 'Now we shall have to find a replacement.'

'I'm seeing the assistant organist at Family Communion later. I'll have a word with her if you like. She's completely different to Desmond.'

I touched Mina's arm urgently and made a *kill it* gesture with my hand.

'One second,' she said, putting the phone on mute.

'I've heard her play,' I hissed. 'She *is* completely different to Desmond: he has musical talent.'

Mina unmuted the call. 'Perhaps not just yet, Libby. I'll get back to you on that one.'

'Fine. I really am sorry, Mina.'

'It's not your fault. Have a good day.'

When she'd disconnected, I said, '*Have a good day*? Where did that come from?'

'My mother. It's what she said when she couldn't get what she wanted from someone.' She looked up. 'I shall try not to channel her again. Is this organist woman really useless?'

'A year ago, I heard her massacring *Away in a Manger*. If she couldn't cope with that…'

'This is Ganesh's work,' she declared, entirely without irony. 'He has closed the door to Desmond that it might be opened to something else. Come to think of it I don't even *like* the sound of a church organ.' She shoved her hand deeply into her glove. 'I am too cold and it is too early to think of this. In fact, it should be your job. You are the one who knows about formal music, and you are doing nothing towards this wedding.'

'I'll call a medic I used to know. She's an RAF bandsman now. If the Central Band aren't busy…'

A look of pure horror came to her face. 'A *brass band*? That is even worse than your idea of Scout carrying the rings up the aisle.' She jabbed a finger in my chest. 'You're doing it deliberately, aren't you? Coming up with *stupid* ideas so that you can get out of things.'

'Would I do that?.'

'Aaagh! Ayaieee! Ganesh give me patience. Go and get the dog and let's get out of here.'

'Will do. And I won't tell Scout that you don't want him to carry the rings.'

When I didn't get a rise out of that, I woke our sleepy hound and slipped him off the leash. He shook himself awake, sniffed the air and bounded off towards the lake. We followed him slowly, arm in arm again, and I gave Mina a blow-by-blow account of the Grand Union meeting. When we got to the dock, the little fire which Willow had consecrated was still burning. Someone must have added more logs after we came in. We fell quiet for a second, enjoying the view and taking a moment to separate the past from the future.

It had been an intense couple of months. Violent at times. Sobering. But also filled with promise: with more beginnings than endings, and with more friends made than enemies spawned. Spots of rain started to land, blown in off the lake and already dissolving the Holi powder. As the vibrant reds, oranges and yellows merged together, a realisation came to me.

'I know what it is,' I said out loud.

'Mmm?' said Mina, trying to tug me towards the path home.

'The Sound of Peace. It's children screaming with pleasure, grown-ups grumbling, lovers talking about their wedding and everyone looking to the future. *That's* the sound of Peace.'

'I'm sure it is. Now can we go before my hair gets ruined?'

From now on, it was no longer my job to keep the Peace here, and I silently wished Matt and his team all the very best of luck. Prayer over, I whistled for Scout and we headed off into the future.

Chapter 3 — Guardians

'Where've you been?' grumbled Evie Mason when we arrived at Middlebarrow Haven, Locus Lucis of the Lord Guardian of the North and, once again, office of the Deputy Constable. Evie looked at me. 'Typical man. Avoiding all the hard work.'

I was about to say something about Mina avoiding it as well, when Evie's mother bumped her daughter out of the way to get to the Aga.

'Just because you've had to do some work yourself for a change,' said Saskia. 'Conrad is the first Deputy in living memory to load the dishwasher and make breakfast, so count your lucky stars. It's not his job to make up guest beds, it's yours.'

'For which I am paid rubbish wages,' responded Evie. 'And they're only staying one night, so it'll all have to be washed tomorrow.'

What is it about the Vernal Equinox? Do mothers and daughters everywhere have a go at each other? Is it fathers and sons in Australia?

The white-blonde cloud of hair which signals the arrival of Saffron Hawkins emerged from the scullery carrying prepared root vegetables. She flicked her eyes from Saskia to Evie and decided on the solidarity of youth. 'We should have told them to get here in the afternoon, then *all* the men could have joined in. It's ludicrous that the whole feast has been prepared by women.'

'Says the woman who lives here rent free,' observed Saskia. 'And who was caught trying to break into the Deputy's wine cellar.'

'I was not! I was testing the Wards,' protested Saffron.

'A likely story,' I said, risking an input. 'We shall have words about that later, Hawkins.'

'Whatever.'

Mina had slipped away as soon as we'd got through the door, and now she returned with an expression somewhere between a smile and a frown. 'Whoever did it, the dining room looks a-ma-zing. Totally. I haven't seen anything so grand in my life! But why are there only seven places?'

Normally we eat in the Country Life Kitchen, where it's warm and comfy and near the cooker. The formal dining room is a long way away from here, and hostess trolleys may be involved. Woman's Weekly optional.

It was Saskia's turn to frown. 'Didn't Conrad tell you? Murray Pollard sent his apologies.'

Mina instinctively knew that I hadn't told her because I hadn't a fucking clue what was going on. She went still as a statue.

'He did what?' I said.

When she heard the tone in my voice, Saffron vanished like a ghost at sunrise. Only Evie seemed oblivious, taking the vegetables to the worktop and muttering.

'He called me out of courtesy,' said Saskia. 'He said he'd emailed you. Or would email.'

Mina stayed rooted to the spot while I got out my phone and opened the email App. It was the first time I'd looked since leaving the house to go to Waterhead at six o'clock this morning. Anything urgent would have come in as a phone call. I'm insistent about that.

About an hour ago, Murray Pollard, Watch Captain of Cleveland, had sent me a short email. Here it is:

Hi Conrad,

Sorry but I won't be coming to Middlebarrow tonight. Let me know when you want to meet up. Happy to travel down to you or whatever.

Hope it all goes well,

Murray.

I carried on staring at my phone while deciding on the best approach. Having decided, I clicked the lock button and put it back in my pocket. 'Scout's been in the car a long time,' I announced. 'I'm going to take him for a walk before it gets dark, and call Captain Pollard on the way.'

'You…' began Evie.

'Leave it,' snapped her mother. 'Get those chopped.'

Mina gave my arm a squeeze as I passed her, and she said, 'What can I do, Saskia? Please. The smells are getting to me already.'

I left them to it and dropped into the Deputy's Study to grab a souvenir of my trip to Ireland before I went back outside. I collected Scout from his luxury lean-to at the side of the house and headed for the public footpath. It was only when water got into my eyes that I realised it had started raining again. I looked down. 'Sorry, lad. Have I dragged you out of bed for this?'

'Arff.'

'We'll take the golf-course route.' I bent down to ruffle his neck. 'Don't tell Auntie Saskia, but I'll let you off the leash in the field with rabbits in it.'

'Arff!'

Fifteen minutes later, I released the hound and he shot off over the hillocky meadow. One day he's going to catch a rabbit unawares, and I'll have a lot of explaining to do. I got out my Undercover Ireland phone and held it next to my iPhone. I brought up Pollard's number on my iPhone and manually dialled it on the unlisted one. I didn't somehow think he'd take the call if he saw it was from me.

'Hello?'

'Pollard, it's Wing Commander Clarke. What's all this about?'

'I… Sorry. I thought you were someone else.'

I said nothing.

'Hello?'

'The email, Captain Pollard. Explain yourself.'

'There's no need to take that tone. I was going to explain it when we met up, but now you're on the line. It's just that I don't want anything more to do with Nimue. I don't think it's right.'

'I didn't invite you here, I ordered you here and dressed it up as an invitation. *All Watch Captains are to report to Middlebarrow Haven Command at sunset* is pretty unambiguous. You've got about two hours to get your arse down to Cheshire, Captain, or you'll be posted AWOL.'

'Sorry?'

'You'll be listed as Absent Without Leave. The Military Police from Catterick will no doubt pay you a call tomorrow. They quite enjoy arresting officers. Makes a change from squaddies.'

'Is that a threat?'

'Of course it's not a threat, you abject moron. It's an order.'

'I think I'd better call the Constable.'

'You do that, Captain.'

I disconnected and got out my fags. Scout was still trying to dig out bunnies when Monti's *Czardas* rang out over the field. 'Ma'am?' I said.

'You could have handled it more sensitively,' she said without preliminary.

'How?'

'You didn't need to call him an *abject* moron. A simple *moron* would have sufficed.' She sighed. 'I always knew it would come to this. When you started to do the job properly, I mean. Murray was never going to accept you as anything but a *senior colleague*. He was never going to buy into the idea of having a *commanding officer*. A year ago, I'd have bitten my lip and ordered you to back off. Not any more. He's on his way to find open water and surrender his Badge of Office. I've accepted his resignation from the service with effect from the end of the month, to allow for a handover. '

'A shame. I mean that,' I told her.

'I know you do, and it *is* a shame. What do you want to do about the vacancy?'

'The only one who I think is both willing to relocate and ready for the responsibility is Saffron. I'd suggest Vicky, but you're not going to give her up, are you?'

'I know you two have a bond, Conrad, but Victoria has been doing a lot of growing-up since you last worked together. It's been a while. I think if I tried to push her out of London, she'd leave the Watch. Unless it were an emergency, of course.'

I reflected for a moment. 'I think I knew that, Boss. I just didn't want to admit it.'

'Saffron for Cleveland it is. That leaves a vacancy in the Marches. I should make you cover it as penance for losing Murray Pollard.'

'And I'd deserve it, but we both know that Andy's ready to strike out on his own. I can supervise him to take some pressure off Rick.'

She *humphed*. 'I was going to send him to Wessex to actually *help* the poor man, but you're right. Andy to the Marches as well.' Her tone lightened. 'How's Karina getting on? Is she still keen to rejoin the Watch?'

'Karina is doing very well, but she's even more settled than Vicky in some ways. And she still needs to work under a closer supervisor than she'd get in the Watch.'

'Well, the good news is that we're back in fashion. I have half a dozen applications from the current crop at Salomon's House, but they won't start until the summer. Late summer. I even had a couple of calls from Circle Witches last week.'

'Now that *is* good news. I'd better get back and have a difficult conversation with Mina and Saffron.'

'I was going to call you anyway, Conrad. I know why you've gathered the troops tonight, and I'll never forget what a close call it was last time. If I could be with you myself, I would.'

'I know, Hannah. Thanks.'

We said goodbye, and at my feet, a very happy, very wet and very tired dog was asking if he could go home now. I told him he could.

There was a man in the kitchen when I got back, a man with a bright future ahead of him. I know this because he was doing the washing up and listening to Evie witter on about her plans to turn *The Ballad of the Fair Queen and the Hound of Gloucester* into a rip-roaring Paranormal Romance.

'Evening, Warren,' I said. 'Have you actually heard that pile of drivel? *Riding came the Hound of Gloucester, Riding, riding o'er the sea...* A horse that can ride on water would be nice, though.'

'It doesn't translate well,' said Evie with a huff. 'And it would be a tragedy, told from the Fair Queen's POV.'

'Tragic romance doesn't sell,' I informed her. I have no idea whether that's true or not. 'Good trip, Warren?'

Tonight was my first meeting with the three – now two – Watch Captains who make up my command, along with Saffron. We've video-called and spoken a few times, and emailed a lot, but this was the first face-to-face meeting.

Warren Knott, Watch Captain of Northumberland, put the last pot on the draining board and shook suds off his hands before offering one to me. 'Aye, thanks. Traffic's not so bad on a Sunday.'

His Geordie accent isn't as raw as Vicky's, and it almost has a Scottish burr at times. Warren grew up in the rural Tyne Valley and is on the young side at twenty-seven. He'd left Salomon's House just as Vicky arrived, though they know each other quite well now.

'About the Shield Wall...' he began.

'Later, Warren. I think that's Jordan.'

Saskia escorted another man into the kitchen. Jordan Fleming is older than Warren: broad and flat-faced, and mostly laid back. He's also happily married, which makes him in the minority for the Watch. The married part, not the *happily* part. His patch is the Danelaw, and if you're wondering where all these places are, there's a handy map somewhere.

Jordan nodded to me, but he was lingering behind Saskia while he checked his phone.

'Are you going to the Grove soon?' asked Saskia.

'Now Jordan's here, I want to get it over with,' I replied.

Jordan was frowning at his phone, and looked up. 'Just got a message from Murray. *That fascist bastard has forced me out of the Watch. Watch your back.* What's going on?'

'Captain Pollard is leaving to pursue interests beyond the service,' I said.

Warren's jaw dropped. 'Eh?'

Saskia and Evie looked away. Saffron took a deep breath and said, 'I'll tell you later. Murray's wrong though. We don't have to watch our backs. That's the Chief's job. Our job is to watch his.'

'Chief?' said Warren.

Saff pointed at me. 'That would be him.'

Jordan looked at me, shoved his phone in his back pocket and came over with his hand extended. 'Nice to finally meet you, Chief. Mind if I nip to the loo before we head out?'

41

Chapter 4 — Feasting

I didn't take my coat when I led the three Watch Captains out of the house and up the drive. What I did take was an umbrella, which I put over my shoulder. My other hand held Mina's, partly because it can be painful for her to cross the Wards on her own but mostly because I needed it.

We processed up the path, over the rise and down to Middlebarrow Grove, also known as Nimue's Spring. When we got to the gate, I kissed Mina and handed her the umbrella.

'Are you sure I can't come?' she asked for the one hundred and ninety-ninth time.

'Only those who have drunk from Nimue's hand,' I repeated automatically.

'Then I shall be waiting.'

Her gloved hand came up to stroke my face, and I turned to walk down path to the spring.

I didn't realise that they weren't with me until a loud curse echoed through the trees. I stopped and turned round: Warren Knott was some way behind and caught in a bramble.

'Sir! I've been calling you,' said Saffron plaintively.

'Sorry. You'll have to shout a bit louder.'

'Ouch! Ow!' said Warren as Jordan put his foot on the bramble and the younger man pulled free. He looked towards me with a hurt expression on his face. Saffron put her hand on his arm.

'The Chief's gone a bit … hard of hearing recently,' she told him in a speaking-to-your-elderly-relative voice. 'He's also got night vision, which is why he forgot to issue Lightsticks.' She glanced at me. 'I'll speak up next time.'

Phones were taken out, and torch functions switched on. I waited until they'd caught up and moved more slowly until we reached the clearing. At its heart, water bubbled out of the mossy grass and flowed down the slope to join the many tributaries of the River Dee. Before stepping forwards, I opened my Third Eye.

Most Mages, but especially Sorcerers, have their Third Eye open all the time. It isn't a real eye, though it's true that the more Lux sensitive parts of the brain are just behind that little depression in the middle of your forehead.

Since my Enhancement by the Allfather, I've been able to *detect* Lux using that sense, but only recently have I been able to *see* it. The *Third Eye* is so called because it maps the detection of Lux on to your visual cortex, and for me (at the moment) it takes a conscious effort.

The spring came alive with light, a deep reddish hue that wafted above the water like steam above a thermal spa. Keeping my Third Eye open, I walked towards my appointment with Albion's tutelary Nymph.

She rose to greet me, and the cloud of Lux took shape into a creature of water. Every previous meeting has seen her as just that – water. With my Third Eye, she was still water, but now she shimmered and glowed. She was also more solid, which meant I got to see her nakedness as more than a half-perceived state. I looked up, into her eyes.

'Welcome, Lord Guardian. Twice since the turn of the year we have met, though under a happier star today.'

I bowed low. 'My lady.'

'Spring approaches,' she announced. 'Time of growth and renewal. I see that all is as it should be and that your acolytes are waiting.'

Amongst my many titles is *Priest of the Dyfrdwy Altar*. It was why I was here: to lead us in making an offering. A blood sacrifice.

The first time had led to a near fatal exsanguination as I bonded with her and with the magick underneath Middlebarrow Haven. The second time was less traumatic, but today is the day of obligation: I have to sacrifice blood to continue my status as Lord Guardian. Down in London, Hannah is about to do the same thing, as is Dan McCabe up at a grove near Scone Palace in Scotland. The only saving grace is that my "acolytes" get to share the burden with me, as others will share it with Dan. Hannah will be doing it alone, for reasons that will become clear shortly.

Nimue's face stiffened for a second, and the outlines softened like melting ice. 'One has left me. Murray has renounced me and gone.'

How the Elderkind – the gods and their peers – manage to have one consciousness in many places is a mystery for the metaphysicians. I just deal with the Nymph before me. 'We blow in the wind, my lady,' I observed, 'and our names are writ in water.' It's what we mortals say at times like this.

She went even more liquid and shrank down a little. If I had to guess, I'd say that Hannah was doing her bit at this exact moment. When Nimue rose up again, she was as clear as before. 'You have an offering for me?'

I knelt down on the sodden grass and presented my left arm. She lost her lower legs and sank to my level. As her face approached my arm, she recoiled. 'You have changed! You have the flesh of the People in you!'

'Forgive me, my lady. One moment.'

Interesting. After a deep sword cut into my forearm, a piece of Fae Princess had been grafted in as part of the repair. Either it hasn't been absorbed, or I'm going to be permanently part Fae. I rolled up my right sleeve and offered my other arm.

Her mouth sprouted fangs of ice, and she bit down. Blood flowed into her, nourishing and fortifying and renewing our bond. And it kept flowing. My vision dimmed, and I heard muffled noises around me. Not again. Please not again.

Everything went black, and then I was no longer kneeling in a Cheshire wood. Or I was, but not in the same way. The scrappy trees and scrub of the modern wood had been replaced by giant specimens that rose into the darkness. I was on a path, and the only light down here came from a glowing Nimue, bright silver and almost impossible to look at without hurting my eyes. Illumination also came from me: my lower left leg glowed, too. As I stood up, I caught glimpses of little white flowers around – wood anemones, just coming into bloom. No foreign daffodils in *this* wood.

'Oy! Eyes front!' said a voice from behind me. I jerked my head round, then jerked it right back again.

We'd been joined in this place by Warren, Jordan and Saffron, and it had been Saffron who spoke, because we were all naked, and she was not amused. Now you know why Hannah would rather die than have witnesses to the ceremony.

I drew a quick breath, and I got the scent of Nimue properly: earthy and pent-up, like Spring about to awaken. Her silver hand touched my arm and stroked it. 'Aren't you going to reconsider, Conrad? Mina need never know.'

I gently lifted her hand away. It was like touching liquid metal, not flesh. It wasn't unpleasant, but it was definitely weird. 'I trust the Watch Captains with my life. And I trust their silence, but I don't trust their faces not to give everything away the second we leave the wood and they see Mina. If I leave the wood.'

She laughed. 'You will leave. I take what I need, and today's need leaves plenty for you. And them.' She hesitated. 'Though it has been a long time since I tasted blood with the tang of sand iris. Your roots go deep, Conrad. Let us go.'

She led us down the path a short distance to a lake that once lay here, millennia in the past. As we walked, she observed, 'The realm has been more quiet of late. One of my priests once shared the wisdom of the east: *It is a curse to live in interesting times.* Do you feel cursed, Conrad?'

'Peace is a blessing, my lady. I hope it continues for many moons.'

The first time I met her, Nimue wasn't the full Nymph by any means. She's been getting better since then, and she even asked about the newest Watch Captain, Andy. I answered, and then we were at the lake.

'Bring forth the sword, Lord Guardian,' she told me. Right. If being naked wasn't enough of an embarrassment, I now had to make a magick sword out of water. My only hope was that the punishment for failure would be dismissal rather than anything more … drastic. Here goes.

There is a real steel sword, bound in leather and embellished with gold. It lives in the well under Merlyn's Tower and had just been wielded by Hannah, down in London. That sword, Caledfwlch, is only a symbol, though. If you have drunk the blood of the First Daughter, you can summon your own version from any water that lies on the earth. I squatted down at the edge of the lake and plunged my hand in.

I've done it once before, with Nimue's help. Now I had to do it for myself. Hannah had coached me a little. *You need to add Lux and withdraw heat*, she'd said. Given that I manipulate Lux *as* heat, it was a bit of a tall order. At least the Third Eye would help, and I gathered Lux in my hand. What I did next is hard to put into words from the inside.

If you watch elite sports, you may have seen the officials make a square in the air with their hands, signalling that the video assistant is involved. You could do the same without thinking about it. Now imagine trying to explain what you were doing to a dolphin without using the words *arm* or *TV* or *rectangle*. Not easy.

What I did is this: I made the shape of a sword under water, using a combination of willpower, visualisation and muscle memory. I felt a resistance grow in my fingers as the water became sticky.

See what I mean? *Sticky water* is something you have to feel to understand. That was the pattern, the template of magick, and to make Caledfwlch, all I had to do was freeze the water. As Hannah said, *Lux in, heat out.*

I drew on the reservoir of Lux in my leg, and the sticky water started to become chunky. Not enough. I was using my left hand to balance, and it got cold on the muddy shore. I shifted it forward and wobbled precariously as I laid it on the water. Water and Earth together. I used my connection to Mother Earth to draw Lux from the lake bed, and the water in front of me turned reddish. It's almost impossible to direct Lux through water (like electricity), so I had to draw more. And more. And more again until it surrounded my right hand and I could complete the Making. There.

I rocked back on my heels and drew my hand from the water. Then I fell on my arse and had to hold Caledfwlch up in the air to stop it hitting me. Did I hear a snort of feminine laughter? Perish the thought. I struggled upright and took a good look at my handiwork. Not bad.

The Artefact in my hand was made of ice, but you wouldn't know it. As part of the schema to Caledfwlch, the Glamour of the steel sword had replaced the ice one. You'd have to be one of the Elderkind to tell the difference.

'Present the blade,' said Nimue.

I turned round and lifted the sword for my comrades, keeping my eyes firmly on the tree line.

'The bond is renewed,' said the Nymph. 'Caledfwlch protects me once again. Go well, Guardians.'

Blackness again. Blackness and cold. Into the blackness came Jordan's voice. 'Let me help you up. Are you okay, Chief?'

I let him put his hand under my shoulder and add his strength to my rather uncertain attempts at standing up. Warren and Saffron were close at hand, ready to steady me. I blinked and took a deep breath. A little light-headed, but

Nimue had been as good as her word: there was plenty of blood left.

'Saffron…'

'On it,' she replied, and turned to leg it up the path to tell Mina that I was okay.

'We'd better get you inside,' said Jordan. 'You're wet through. Can you walk?'

'I think so.'

He kept his hand on my elbow as I took a few steps. Ow, that hurt. I put my weight on him and shook out my bad leg. 'I think I'll be all right now. I think.'

He took a step back, his arm still raised in readiness. 'Don't overdo it.'

Mina flew into the grove on light feet and rushed towards me. Jordan put out a hand to discourage her. 'Careful. He's none too steady.'

She slowed down and put her arms round me to hug me, anchoring me and giving me an extra squeeze to let me know how glad she was. It lasted about two seconds.

'Urghh. You are soaked, Conrad. Did she immerse you again?'

'I don't know.'

Warren coughed. 'I don't think so, Mina. I think he just fell into the spring when we translated to her realm.'

I turned to take one last look at the Dyfrdwy Altar. 'My lady,' I said with a bow. 'Thank you.'

Mina started to lead me away, trying to avoid getting mud on her coat. 'I don't know what you are thanking her for. You are going to have a hot bath and drink sweet tea before you even *think* of alcohol or tobacco.'

I was already *thinking* of them, but she was right. I needed to let my system recover gently. The others had gone ahead, the light from phone torches dancing in front of them. They were talking at a volume where I couldn't make out what they said, until Saffron raised her voice deliberately.

'Look, guys, when I said we had to watch the Chief's back, I had no idea it would mean watching his hairy arse as well.'

'It's hard to un-see, isn't it?' said Warren.

Something made me look ahead of them – an instinct or something in my peripheral vision. A small shape came running down the path, following my scent and almost gambolling with joy.

I stopped to bend down and embrace him, allowing Scout to lick my face for once. 'Now did you get out on your own, or did someone bring you?' I asked.

'Arff,' was his answer.

I felt round his fur and found the doggy harness. He wasn't wearing that when we left, so Evie must have brought him through the Wards. And there she was, swinging his lead.

'He was going mad,' she said. 'I found him running round the garden like a demon. I thought he might burst if I didn't bring him out.' She smiled, and I knew that Scout was an excuse. She'd been worried, too. 'Hurry up,' she added. 'I've run that bath for you.'

I stood up again, more easily this time, and the four of us headed back to the Haven.

Half an hour later, I was still soaking in the bath and starting my second cup of sweet tea, delivered by Mina. While the hot water was doing its thing to restore me, she'd got changed, and now she was perched on the bathroom stool by the open door to avoid exposing her shiny hair to the steam.

'You've had a message,' she said. 'Two, actually. From Francesca and Persephone. From what I could see on the screen, Perci thinks that her grandmother is lovely and Francesca wants to know who's kidnapped Sister Theresa and replaced her with an android.'

I wasn't surprised that Theresa had dropped the curmudgeon act: whatever had driven her daughter to the life choices which meant an early grave would no doubt weigh heavily on the old Witch.

'Oh, and Perci thinks that Kracik is terrifying. I must meet him one day.' She sighed. 'I'm going to miss you. Again. I've got used to being together, even if it was in a rented house. I love it here, Conrad, but I can't wait for the weekend. To go home.'

Saskia is taking Mina to Crewe tomorrow so that Mina can catch the London train for round three (or is it four?) of the Flint Hoard hearings in the Cloister Court. We will meet up again on Thursday night in Clerkswell. Maundy Thursday, as it happens. It's a very early Easter this year.

Over the holiday weekend, we are having several Wedding Summits. Mum and Dad are coming over from Spain; we've got video calls booked to Gujarat in India and to Boston in Massachusetts, and we're even expecting a visit from Faith and Alicia. Or Mina is. I don't have a lot of need for a hairdresser. Sadly.

'I can't wait to go home, either, love. The Elvenham Dragon will think I'm on a tour of duty again.'

'You are. Middlebarrow Haven may be safer than Camp Bastion, but this is still work.'

As you may have noticed, Mina is not a fan of the Lakeland Particular, for all sorts of reasons. Uncomfortable. Cold. Wet. Full of people who want to kill me. I try to believe that the last one is the most important.

'Talking of the Haven, Evie and Saskia are asking why they have to host a Fae Princess while we're not here.'

'What did you tell them?'

'Not the truth, that's for certain. I did not tell them that Lucy Berardi has to sneak away from Tom to meet Faith and Alicia. He's your friend…'

I interrupted decisively. 'Tom Morton is *not* my friend! He may be going on the stag-do, but that's more because he wants to make sure I don't cause another international incident.'

'If he's not your friend, then what is he?'

'My associate. Like Eseld. So there.'

Mina ignored the comparison with a sniff and said, 'Are you done?'

'Ready. And very, very hungry. Could you ask Saffron to come up in five minutes?'

'Of course.' She came over, kissed me carefully, and swept out.

Saff knocked on the door, right on time. 'Are you decent, Conrad?'

'I'm dressed, if that's what you're worried about. Come in.'

She peeked gingerly around the door, then entered with a grin. 'Seeing my boss naked twice in one night would be grounds for a week's sick leave. Are you feeling better?'

'Much, thanks. And hungry, so I won't beat about the bush. Do you fancy taking over from Murray Pollard in Cleveland?'

'Oh. Right. Are you sure?'

'I'm sure I'm sure. You've done a great job in the Marches, and here in the Palatinate. I think you're ready for a proper, meaty, Mage-ridden posting with lots of local attitude to overcome.'

'You make it sound so attractive that I can't say no, can I?'

'You can. We can't order you to relocate – a Watch posting is for life, in theory. I know you want to go to London, but making a good job of Cleveland would be a huge step on the way. And things might change down south.'

She tilted her head. 'What do you know that I don't?'

I put on a grave face for her. 'I know many things, my child, including the best place to buy fish and chips in Whitby. It will be a crucial part of your induction.'

'Has Murray gone completely?'

I shook my head. 'Hannah let him resign with an unblemished record in return for showing you the ropes. Does that mean you're interested?'

She reflected for a moment and said, 'Mum's trying to marry me off to one of the Geldarts, but that shouldn't be a problem. If I have to investigate them, I'll be straight on the phone to you anyway.'

I opened the door and turned off the lights. 'Good. If you hadn't learnt that no one is above investigation, I wouldn't have put your name to the Boss. After you, Captain of the Cleveland Watch.'

As a special treat, we let Scout lie by the fire in the dining room while we enjoyed the fruits of the earth. By tradition, it has to be from the store cupboard, and Saskia had laid down some very fine German sausage at Christmas to go into a monumental casserole.

There were toasts to Nimue, to Saffron and to the Boss. Jordan led one to me, and Evie led one to Mina on her impending wedding – it's only six weeks tomorrow. Gulp.

After the toast to Hannah, I'd made a short statement. 'You may remember that I took this job for a year. Then I lost it, and now I've got it back. The Boss and I have agreed to reset the clock, so at the next Spring Feast, I'll be handing over to a new Deputy Constable.'

'Did we know that?' asked Jordan with a frown.

'We did,' said Warren with a dark look at me. 'According to the Boss, he only agreed to do it for a year, and only on condition that he got long weekends to play cricket.' He forced himself to be generous. 'Then again, he does get beaten up a lot.'

When talk turned to the immediate future, I told them of my plans for the week (well, not the part about releasing the Warden. That's a personal mission) 'And after Easter,' I concluded, 'we're *both* off to London. The new Warden would like to make our acquaintance.'

'Oh her,' said Jordan.

'Yes, her. Do you know her?'

He shook his head. 'She was quite close to Murray, or so I've heard. He even campaigned for her a bit.'

'Well, getting rid of her favourite Watch Captain should get the meeting off to a good start,' said Evie brightly. 'I'll open another bottle, shall I?'

Chapter 5 — *The Things We Do*

When that weird silver light had burst over Donald Bell in February, there had been a rush of discovery: he couldn't speak, but he could now nod, shake his head and point at things in ways he hadn't been able to before. And how come Kathy had never noticed before that he couldn't nod like normal people?

She'd fetched the flipchart paper, and although Don couldn't hold the marker pen, she'd quickly discovered that writing the letters of the alphabet in a circle meant they could spell out words by pointing, and she could guess them like that autocorrect thingy on her phone.

There had been two problems, and the first was that Kathy was no better with words when taken one letter at a time than she was with words in a string. That took some getting used to. The second problem was that Don's first message had been this: *Don't tell anyone about this. You and your family will be in terrible danger if you do. Not even Simon.*

And he'd made her promise not to tell, then he'd fallen fast asleep and she'd had to wake him up to get him into bed.

In the weeks after that, he wouldn't let her take on more shifts as his carer (*Too suspicious*), and all he wanted to do was get her to collect things and wait for spring so that she could plant weird things in his little garden. The closest she'd come to falling out with him was when she'd found out about the gold.

It was hard to tell what was Don's stuff in his room and what had always been there. One day, though, he pointed to an ancient statue's head thingy with weird writing on a back shelf. Kathy had carefully moved it many times to check that cleaner was doing her job (not often), and Kathy had noticed that it looked wrong because the bottom was so big and also quite light. She took it to him, grunting with the effort, and laid it on his lap. He stroked the base with his twisted hands. She couldn't see how, but something like a plug came out, and along with it came *two dozen* gold sovereigns.

'Chuffing hell, Don! Where did they come from! There must be a fortune there!'

He pointed to the chart and started to spell out … *Yours … Buy my things and keep the rest.*

'No. I can't and I won't. What am I even gonna do with them? How am I gonna turn them into money without getting arrested? The likes of me don't walk into Ramsdens with gold sovereigns.'

She had taken them, though, because Don couldn't put them back in the statue's head and she wasn't going to leave them for the cleaner to walk off with, was she? And now it was nearly Easter, and she was having four days off next weekend.

She'd volunteered to work the Sunday before Easter, and on Friday and Saturday, Don had insisted she look up a foreign word: *equinox*. Apparently, Sunday was the official start of spring, and there was all sorts of weird hippy rubbish as well. All that mattered to Don was that on Sunday evening, she wheeled him into the garden and put out food for the birds (something that Faye normally did for him).

Dr Simon had caught her on the way to the kitchen and said, 'You're not going to take it easy and let us cook communally, are you?'

Sunday was normally her day off, and because it was a working therapy day at the clinic, Doctor Simon and Faye usually watched the guests organise themselves to cook the full Sunday lunch (and the vegetarian option).

'Not a chance,' she told him. 'That's my kitchen, so help me God, and I will not stand idly by and watch food go to waste. It's bad enough Monday while Thursday when I'm "supervising" them.'

The corner of his mouth twitched. 'Perhaps it would help you improve your teamwork skills, Kathy.'

She turned and carried on towards the kitchen, answering the good doctor over her shoulder. 'And perhaps I might knife dJulie. Your choice.'

She marched on, and Simon chuckled to himself. 'I'll leave you to it, then. See you later.'

Kathy reached her domain and stood at the threshold. Michael's spook sixth sense made him look up from his station, and he frowned in puzzlement. 'Chef? What are you doing here?'

Since the dauphinoise days, Michael had shown that he *must* have had training at some point. He had even ordered himself a kitchen jacket, and Kathy had permitted him to assist her at breakfast, an honour that she rarely bestowed on guests of less than six months, and he was going to be in charge over Easter (not that there would be many to feed). As you'd expect, Dr Simon had said that Michael was using the kitchen to hide from his problems, and after Easter he'd be barred for a week. Bloody typical. And talking of bloody…

'Michael! Why isn't the beef out of the chiller? It needs a good couple of hours to come to room temperature.'

'Yes chef! On it!'

The sun was going down over the wood as Kathy pushed Don's wheelchair out of the doors and into what was rapidly becoming a herb garden with his new suggestions. Kathy had pretended to Fragrant Faye that it was all her idea, that Don wouldn't know what was growing anyway, and he might like the smells, and wouldn't Faye like the fresh tastes, especially for the veggie stuff?

With Michael to help breakfast service, Kathy had taken to joining Don for Tai Chi, and she was amazed how graceful he could be when he got in the zone. She glanced at her phone and checked the pattern for tonight which he'd actually drawn for her (only took seven attempts), and which she'd photographed.

She walked through the pattern in a dummy run, and he nodded approval. She opened the bag and repeated her walk, scattering the bird food as she went. Don stared intently at the ground, then nodded and pointed back to the windows (it was not a warm evening). Back inside, he got her to spell out this message: *You must sell some gold soon. Please. I beg you.*

She put down the pointer and took a seat. 'I've not bothered you with this, Don, 'cos you've got enough to worry about. I'm seeing my girls next weekend. It's Easter, but I'm sure you know that, what with you being so hot on the calendar.'

She took a deep breath and plunged on. 'The social worker says it's time to re-establish contact, on neutral ground, so I'm going to Leeds. One hour with them on Friday in the community centre, then one hour on Saturday in the park. It would be so much easier if I could afford a decent hotel to stay in. And taxis.'

He nodded and did something unusual: he held her hand. Just for a second. Then he let go.

'I know a place in Chapel Allerton,' she continued with a wink. 'They'll give me a good price for the gold, no questions asked. I'll do it. Though after that, where I'm gonna find a thermometer with mercury in it, I have no idea.

He pointed to the paper, and she grabbed the pointer A - N - T - I

'Anti-theft?' she suggested. He shook his head.

A-N-T-I-Q-U-E

'Anti-queue? What's that?'

He shook his head and started again. A-N-T-E-A-K.

'Antique shops! Of course! Why didn't I think of that? Probably because I've never been inside one in me life except to try and nick stuff.'

Chapter 6 – Isolation Unit

One of the things I learnt very early after taking up residence at Middlebarrow Haven is that you should minimise your exposure to Pacer Trains. These relics of the 1980s are noisy, slow, and very uncomfortable. You have been warned.

Thankfully, the rather more twenty-first century West Coast Main Line to London or to the Particular can be accessed fairly easily, and Mina had volunteered to suffer the horrors of the Pacer service from Helsby to Warrington Bank Quay, a mere twenty minutes. She had also negotiated a lunchtime journey in case things had not gone well with Nimue last night, so it was me who drove Mina to her appointment with joint pain.

We had a Watch meeting in the morning while Mina worked in the Deputy's Study, and when they dispersed, I stuck my head inside to find her hunched over her laptop. 'You can take equality too far,' she said, before dragging her eyes away from the screen to smile at me. 'Have they gone?'

'They have. What's the problem?'

'There are issues with advertising yourselves as an *All Female* string quartet. Apparently. Everyone says a string quartet is the best value for money, especially in a church with good acoustics. I've found one, though. I shall call them in a moment, then I'd better get myself ready. Oh, and I've had another achingly polite message from Libby the Vicar about our vows. She's still not happy. See you in a minute.'

We were chatting amiably on the short drive to Helsby station when she checked her phone and swore.

'What's up, love?'

'This string quartet is what's up! They jumped at the chance of a booking until they got the email with the confirmation and the playlist. They flat out refuse to play Pachelbel's *Canon* when I walk up the aisle. What is this? Does it have a secret meaning that no one has told me about?'

'Not as such. It's just that jobbing musicians can get … passionate about what they play.'

'They are not jobbing musicians! They are recent graduates from the Worcester Conservatory, whatever that is, and they should be grateful for the work.'

'Did they offer an alternative suggestion?'

There was a scrolling of the screen. 'They even have the cheek to suggest that to make it really good, we should hire a Baroque trumpeter. Does that mean he dresses up or something?'

'No, it's just that his trumpet doesn't have valves … Never mind. Why a trumpeter?'

'For handling the re-juice-ance, whatever that is.'

My brain fought to make sense of what she'd said, and then it clicked. 'Actually, it sounds like they know what they're talking about. Tell them you'll take the trumpeter, so long as they throw in a free percussionist, and get them to email the final choices to me. Then it's ticked off your list.'

'Good. If the music is rubbish, we can always overdub the videos, and it will be something I can use against you for the rest of our married lives. In fact, you can deal with them as they won't be going to the house.' There was a pause and a *whoosh* from her phone. 'Done. Will you have time to sort this?'

'Of course. A small price to pay for knowing that you won't have to worry about it on the train to London.'

'Hah! That means I shall have to worry about something else, like working out where so many people are going to stay. Anything to stop me thinking about what you're doing tomorrow.' She paused, drew breath and finished with, 'I shall miss you every second that you are away. It gets harder to say goodbye the closer we get to the wedding. I love you.'

I paused in the drop off zone to Google the Worcester Conservatory String Quartet. They were good. I don't know how they'd handle Beethoven's Great Fugue, but they could certainly handle Handel. Mina made it safely on to the train, and I headed back to the Particular to plan for tomorrow and to get an early night. I may not have been exsanguinated yesterday, but it was still exhausting.

'I don't see why you've dragged me into this,' grumbled Faith.

'Or me,' added Persephone.

Scout was sniffing around the gate with interest, and I was tempted to point to him and say *Why have a dog and bark yourself?* And then I remembered that Faith is not just Mina's handmaiden and my Madreb, she will soon be Queen of Westmorland.

'Francesca is here because Roly was – is – her brother, and I'm here because my partner imprisoned him. You're here because we don't want to damage the Red Queen's property, do we?'

Faith looked from the field beyond the gate to Perci and shrugged. Both the land and the girl were the property of the Queen of Derwent. Not literally, of course, but close enough. In law, Persephone is a bonded servant. As for the land, when a Fae Queen dies, her sídhe is sealed: completely sealed and totally inaccessible for a period of time equal to her lifespan, and I may be the only mortal to know the truth about that closure. Everyone else thinks it's a side-effect of the collapse of the magick, but I know different. When a Queen dies, her death is swiftly followed by a visit from the Morrigan, and it is the Dread Goddess who puts the seal on her resting place.

We should be safe from divine intervention today, because the Radiant Queen died during the Early Mediæval period, also known as the Dark Ages, and her sídhe was held under the royal (human royal) warrant. There were no takers until the Grand Union of the Particular was founded, and the Crown sold the land on which the sídhe was located to them – a quick profit for the then Constable. The Union planted a magickal junction there, and it has leased, but not sold, the ruins to the Red Queen. And we are about to find out what she uses it for.

The Furness Peninsula (home to the town of Barrow) sticks out into Morecambe Bay, and until the railways arrived, the quickest way to get to Furness was to pay the King's Guide to escort your carriage over the treacherous and ever-shifting sands and waterways, and that's why Furness Abbey became such an important monastic institution in economic terms. In magickal terms, the consensus seems to be that being located next to a Royal Sídhe had something to do with it. At a cost.

If you've a long memory, you might recall that the Codex Defanatus, that compilation of dodgy magick, had included quite a chunk from Furness Abbey, and Francesca has looked deeply into this. According to the Esoteric Library, the monks down the road did not have a very savoury reputation. Nor does the abandoned Radiant Sídhe.

Faith swears that she doesn't know, that she's never been inside, and that the higher levels are very hard to access. I believe her. I could just *ask* her Queen, but I'd rather we didn't tip her off. The only thing that Faith can say for certain is that the Red Queen never talked about it beyond saying that it was, 'My predecessor's place, really.' In other words, a lot of money to pay for somewhere you don't go.

Someone who *had* been there was my former partner, Cordelia. Along with two Spirits, she had somehow Confined the late Warden in here, and we had come to get him out. Before you say anything else, yes, I am trying to put off going through that gate.

Faith had never been to the sídhe itself, but she had been to the fields around it, and she knew the Wards on the gate. I gestured for her to open it, and when we were inside, I studied the lie of the land. Large, grassy hillocks were all I could see of the Radiant Queen's home. That and a glowing red patch off to the side. Even without opening my Third Eye, I could sense the magick, and when I did, a large iron cross with a Celtic top revealed itself. That was the terminus of the South Road, one of the great Ley lines running across the Particular. Not relevant today.

'Arff!' said Scout. He too had surveyed the land, and he'd seen something much more interesting: sheep. They're here to keep the grass down (and be meat for the royal table in time), and in Scout's opinion, they needed a good herding.

'Later, boy. If we've got time.' I relaxed my grip and allowed him to take us towards the centre. There were a few trees around the hillocks, and I secured his lead before we began the ascent. At least Faith could work out how to get in without any help.

There were five hawthorn trees scattered amongst the beech and ash, and we moved between them, tracing the points of a star, each time going to a slightly higher plane. By the time we got to the last tree, everyone was loosening their clothes. It did not feel like late March up here.

'What had she become, Conrad? What had Cordelia become that she could stomach *this*?'

Francesca had been the first to speak after the transition and after the sheer shock of what we'd found. It was not like March in England up here, it was like Hell: roasting hot, full of demons and rotten with the stench of sulphur.

We coughed, we spluttered and we tried to make sense of the nightmare. Faith had gone rigid, her back to us, and Perci looked ready to bolt. If I'd known it was like this, I wouldn't have brought her. Francesca took in the scene and spoke my thoughts for me. How had Cordelia come to a place in her life where this was all in a day's plotting? She'd done her dirty work here and then lied to me through her teeth.

Without moving a muscle of her spine, Faith pirouetted on her heel and looked at me, then she dropped to one knee. 'Forgive me, my lord. On my life, I knew not that this place was as it is.'

'What in Nimue's name is it, then?'

'Her Grace is skilled in breeding, my lord, and at ... another place, she has the royal pens. This is the same thing, but not of her doing. This must have belonged to the Radiant Queen and somehow survived the collapse of her sídhe. I say again, I knew nothing of it.'

'Get up, Faith. I believe you. The question now is what the fuck are we going to do? Can you see what's under these ... lids? Trapdoors? Whatever they are?'

I don't know exactly what the others saw, but with my Third Eye, I could see a green space. I won't call it grass, but it was green and alive and it was broken up by pulsing lines of Royal Violet magick that formed smaller squares, and under each square was something trying to get out.

'Cork Hatches, we call them. As in the Irish county, not the stuff that keeps your wine in,' said Faith, showing more fear today than when she'd faced death at the hands of Galleny and submitted to me. She was almost babbling, whether that was from nerves about the task in front of us or from naked terror at the thought of the future now that we'd seen this place, I'm not sure. Could have been both, because now that I knew about it, I'd have to pursue it, and Faith had broken a direct order from the Red Queen to bring us here.

'Does anyone have a clue where the Warden might be?' I asked, keen to regain some focus.

'Look for the rainbow,' said Francesca. 'When he came to say goodbye, he was coruscating colours like his robes. How about that one?'

'I can see at least two with rainbow aspects,' said Faith. 'That one and that one in the corner.'

'And that one three up and two across,' I added. 'But if we can all see the one that Francesca pointed out, shall we start there? How do we get in, Faith?'

She turned to me and wiped her face. It was a gesture I hadn't seen for weeks, not since the gaping wound on her mouth had healed. She used to do it all the time because she had no lip to stop the saliva running out of her mouth. 'Are you okay?'

'Of course, my lord. Now we are here, it is right to find and release Sir Roland.'

'But we shouldn't be here. I get it. We'll cross that bridge later, okay?'

'Yes, my lord.' She shook herself and tried to focus. 'The pens are physically underneath but spatially on a higher plane. The energy is trying to push the beasts up and out, and the Cork Hatch is keeping them in. You just lift a corner and…'

Francesca lashed out verbally. 'My brother is not a *beast*, you foul creature! Go and release whatever *prisoner* is held over there, and if it eats you, I won't be sorry.'

'But I will,' I said, stepping between them. 'If nothing else, we need Faith to open those Hatches, but Fran's right: we should start there.'

'My lord.'

'Perci, you stay here, by the hawthorn. If we come under attack, execute a tactical retreat.'

'In other words, run like fuck,' added Faith. 'He means it.'

'And so do I, minus the profanity,' added Francesca.

Faith turned and set off, leading us across the strips of green between the Hatches until we came to one over on the right. Faith held up her hand to stop us at a distance, then walked slowly forwards. Rainbow sparkles flickered above the surface like diffraction around the froth on a waterfall. Faith didn't hesitate: she bent down, pulled at the corner of the Hatch and then jumped back as only a Fae can, using the Lux flooding the plain to make her look like a Superhero. Bloody good job, too.

'By the Goddess…' began Francesca. Perci screamed, and I tried not to lose my breakfast. Having landed upright at first, Faith dropped to her knees and covered her eyes. There are some things you just know you will never un-see.

The proud race of centaurs once roamed the forests and plains of Greece. Allegedly. If this … *creature* … had ever roamed anywhere, I'd be surprised. Some power in magick, human, Fae, divine or demonic, had put a human head at the end of a horse's neck. I won't say any more than that. Whatever you've just imagined, it was worse. Much worse. If you want to know why they did it, the answer was still there on its back: a racing saddle. Sport indeed.

As the creature tried to charge us, then bucked and reared, we stared in shock, and we were lucky that the thing wasn't completely free. A short, silver chain was attached to its hind leg and kept it close to the pen.

I coughed and spat, and tried to get my voice to work. 'What do we do, Faith?'

She turned, and I have never seen a Fae noble go white before today. 'Sorry, my lord?'

'What do we do? Release it? Put it out of its misery?'

She coughed, too; Fae lungs are no happier with sulphur than human ones. 'I think it would be very ill-advised to release it, and it's protected by the binding. I … I believe there's an umbilical element to the Work, keeping it alive and making it hard to self-harm. I suspect it's mostly asleep, too. We should put it back in the pen.'

Francesca took a step forwards. 'You said *Work*. That binding is no part of the Great Work. It's Quicksilver magick if ever I saw it.'

Faith licked her lips. 'Please forgive me, Keeper. I don't believe this binding was Inked, nor is it a Charm of the Woods. I said Work for want of a better word.'

'Let me see,' snapped Francesca. She took another step, and Faith moved aside. I shook myself into action and got ready to draw my sword. Francesca saw me and grabbed my arm, using it to balance as she bent down and peer at the chain. She grunted and said, 'Fair point. I'll call it *origin unknown* for now, but that doesn't mean it wasn't the Red Queen's handiwork.'

One of the many things I've learnt about the Fae is that they're lazy. If the Red Queen had a Quicksilver spell for this, she'd have used it. That didn't mean she wouldn't have to answer for its presence here, though. 'Enough,' I said. 'Faith, can you send it back.'

'Yes, my lord, but I need to grab that corner. Can you distract it?'

'Let me,' said Francesca. 'Knowing Conrad, he'll take out his sword. You go right, Faith.'

I forced myself to look at its eyes, and I saw that the light of thought had flickered out long ago. There was pain and rage, but no capacity to work out that the flickering Fae to its left was the real threat and that the illusion of the tiger to its right was only a construct of magick. When it had been folded back underground, we all turned away and returned to a shivering Persephone, our shoulders slumped and our hearts sore. Mine and Fran's were sore, anyway; I simply don't know the Fae well enough to say whether it's a thing for them.

'What did he do?' said Perci. 'The man who was joined to the horse? What did he *do*?'

'Let's not dwell on the details,' I said rather abruptly. 'I think we can all see what happened.'

'No, I meant *what had he done wrong?* To get punished like that, it must have been…' she trailed away, lost for words.

'I think we *should* dwell on one detail,' said Faith, an entirely human expression of anger on her face. 'You and the Keeper think that's a human, don't you my lord?'

'Not any more, I don't. Maybe once?'

Faith shook her head. 'It was a Fae Prince before the merging. Perhaps that's what confused the Keeper about the binding.'

'Are you sure?' asked Francesca.

'I would not lie to my lord about that. And before you ask, there are no stories of missing Princes amongst the Borrowdale People.'

'There is going to be a reckoning for this,' I said. I touched the mark of Caledfwlch on my sword and added, 'In Nimue's name, I will not let this rest. You say that the prisoners are mostly asleep, Faith?'

She gestured to the green sward. It was moving gently, especially over the Hatches. The whole field must have sensed something. 'They dream, my lord. Mostly they dream, I think. That much I saw, and yes, the Dreaming is an Inking of the People. It can be copied, though.'

'Then we can leave them in peace for a while longer. Except Roly, of course. I won't leave him here longer than I have to, Fran.'

'I can help,' said Perci. 'Let me approach the rainbows. I'll know him, and I don't want to see another of those things come out. The next one might not have such a short chain.'

She said the last part like someone much older, and she was right. 'With me,' I said.

I led, with Persephone to my left, and I suggested the rainbow that only I could see. It turned out I was right – don't forget, Roly left a piece of himself in me when he died. When Perci pronounced that we'd found his cell, she made it clear she wasn't going to stand by the trees again. Faith didn't wait for me to ask, and went up to the corner of the Hatch.

The Spirit of Sir Roland Quinn, late Warden of Salomon's House reared up before us. I focused on his eyes to see whether Roly was at home or whether his incarceration had driven him mad. Big mistake.

Faith barrelled into me and knocked me flying as the jets of rainbow flame shot out of Roly's hands. They caught her right in the leg.

'Grandfather!' screamed Perci. 'Peace!'

'Child? Is it you?' boomed the Spirit.

'Yes! It's me, Perci, and Auntie Fran.'

Roly lowered his hands. 'How?'

'Faith? Are you alright?' I asked. Her leg clearly wasn't alright. I know how she feels.

'Yeah, thanks Conrad. I'll live, but it's not what I wanted to be spending my energy on. Can you take me to the Stables? Maybe the Hlæfdigan can speed things up a bit.'

'Is there anything I can do now?'

'In a bit. This is gonna need … Owww. Shit. This is gonna need a splint.' She went still for a second, then looked up. 'There. No pain now. What's up with Perci?'

I jerked my head up. The young Mage was crying into Francesca's shoulder. Great, racking sobs. From the look on Fran's face, comforting her great-niece was all that was stopping her from collapsing herself. I gave Faith's shoulder a squeeze and stood up.

'Warden,' I said. 'I'm sorry to meet again like this. Thank you for saving my life at Newton's House.'

'I wish I could say the same to you, but thank you for releasing me. And bringing my family.'

'What's wrong?'

'The chain. It was not designed for human Spirits. My thread has been cut, Mr Clarke. When the binding is released, I will blow away.'

Oh. No wonder Perci was distraught. I had no words for him, and he smiled at me.

'A shame is what it is,' he said. 'I was so looking forward to chasing down those three and taking my revenge. What has happened? If Perci is here alive and well, then Lucas's plan must have failed.'

'It did, Warden. Lucas and Helena are gone, as is Madeleine. Cordelia fled. You knew what Lucas was up to?'

'I did. I was being hunted by Spirits even more powerful than him, and I couldn't intervene directly.' His ethereal shoulders slumped. 'It was hard to watch him reel in your partner and not be able to stop him. He picked his moments carefully.'

'What did he do?'

'Convinced her that Raven was alive and trapped by the Red Queen. Once Cordelia had joined him in binding me here, I imagine there was no way back for her. Will you do me one last service, Conrad?'

'No!' said Francesca. 'Let me go back to the Library, Roly. I can help.'

'You can't, Fran. Take Perci away. This is no place for a child. Please.'

Persephone is made of strong stuff, but Roly was right. Underneath, she's still a child, a child who's lost too many people already. Francesca took one last look at her brother. 'Goodbye, Roly.' She had tears streaming down her face as she led her great niece away, and then there were three.

'What *is* this place?' I asked him. Call me callous, but you have to get your intelligence where you can.

'What it seems. A cross between a zoo and a prison. Or Frankenstein's reject pile if you prefer. I was trapped here for a short while before they bound me, and that's all I could sense. Once the Hatch closed, I faded. Tell me one thing, Conrad. Why did Cora pull out of the election? She's been ready to succeed me for a while.'

I smiled as best I could. 'She had her reasons, Warden.'

'Then don't tell me that Heidi has taken my place. Anything but that.'

'Lois Reynolds. By a nose.'

'Well well. Cordelia has fled, you say?'

'Completely. Left everything behind and disappeared. We're fairly certain she left the country.'

'The death of the Fair Queen and the sealing of the Codex did not end things, of that I'm certain. There is something rotten in the realm of Albion, Conrad, and I wish you well in your hunt for it. Now, give me the key.'

'Are you sure?'

'He's sure,' said Faith. 'Sorry, my lord, but I might have to amputate myself if we don't get out of here soon. It's not a healthy environment.'

'Should I unlock it, Warden?' I asked. 'I think I can manage this one.'

'Just tell me the sequence. I won't do it now. I'm not quite ready. If you're up at dawn, look for the rainbow. The Gallops at Sprint Stables would be an excellent viewing point.'

Which was a rather macabre thought, but I could understand him wanting a witness. I spelled out the dashes and dots that would release the binding, and Roly made marks on his arm, like a tattoo.

'Farewell, Conrad.'

I bowed. 'Warden. Thank you again.'

I put my arm under Faith's shoulder and we made our way to the down escalator.

Chapter 7 — Relative Values

The wind whipped across the meadow, chilling the sweat down my back and on my head. Even so, I gulped in great lungfuls of the fresh air. So did Faith. We'd been so keen to get out of that Hell-hole that I'd risked putting my back out by taking all her weight on my shoulder. Good job she can hop like an Olympian.

A furious barking told me that we'd been missed, and Scout had a most aggrieved look on his face. 'In a minute, lad,' I shouted. Getting Faith back to the car without a splint wasn't an option, so I set to on an ash tree and broke off a couple of branches. When I walked over to my distressed hound, he thought it was Christmas – not only did he get treats, I had to let him off the lead so that I could use it to bind the splints. 'Fetch the sheep, Scout. Go on.' And off he shot. It's a dog's life in the Watch.

Francesca and Perci were still comforting each other, oblivious to what was happening around them, so I went back to Faith and started work. Believe me, when treating someone who can opt not to feel pain, first aid is a lot easier. 'Thank you for saving my life up there. I should have been better prepared.'

'You risked more for me at the Gallops. And I need you alive. For later.'

It was the first time she'd referred to the secret clause in the Peace of Brothers Water, the clause which commits me to providing the First Seed when she becomes Queen. I try not to think about it. 'I'll do my best. Should I try to straighten this or just support it.'

She examined the leg. 'Give me something to bite on and I'll open it up again. If we can set it here, so much the better, but I'll have to feel it. You'd better do a Silence, too.'

I passed her my handkerchief and made the Work. It stopped the rest of the county from hearing her scream, but I was manipulating a double fracture, so the magick had no effect on me. Good job my hearing's not what it was.

Job done, I collapsed on to the wet grass next to her. 'I don't know why you're out of breath,' she said. 'What have you done today?'

'Ha bloody ha.'

'Meeeh! Baa!'

'Arff!'

'Give me strength! Your dog is a maniac, Conrad.'

'But very good at his job. He gets it from me.'

We sat there, surrounded by irate sheep and being circled by an excited Border Collie until we both burst out laughing. We were still in hysterics when Francesca walked over, hand in hand with Persephone.

'Take us back to Windermere Haven,' she said. 'Please. Perci is going to stay with me for a couple of days.'

I looked at Faith, not because she needed to give permission, but because I don't know Perci's treatment schedule. The doses of Quicksilver have to be regular. Faith nodded, and I hauled myself upright before offering her a hand. The drive back to Ambleside was a quiet one.

When I'd dropped the Quinn family off at Windermere Haven, I didn't start the engine again straight away. Instead, I poured two mugs of coffee from the flask and stood outside the car to smoke a cigarette. Faith accepted the coffee and said, 'Can we not do this now? I don't think I've got the capacity, Conrad.' She sipped and grimaced. 'Please, my lord. Take me to the Hlæfdigan and wait. By this afternoon, I should be stable enough.'

I had one question. 'Will she know?'

'I doubt it. She didn't know when Lucas imprisoned Sir Roland, did she? And other mortals have got in before. We usually find the bodies later. Or what's left of them.'

'I'll pretend I didn't hear that. I'll wait. Of course I'll wait. We're in this together, Faith.' I peered in through the window at the ash and dog-lead splints. 'You're supposed to be driving to Clerkswell on Thursday.'

'Shouldn't be a problem. I'll just do what you do, my lord.'

I stood up straight. 'And what might that be, my loyal bondswoman?'

'Drive an automatic and limp a lot.'

There have been a lot of changes since my first visit to Sprint Stables – the top Fae here should be the Count of Force Ghyll, only I've killed the last two. The current leader is only a Knight, Saerdam Felix, and he's on probation. Poor bloke must get nervous every time I come to ride my horse. One thing doesn't change, though: I saw the impassive figure of Aidan Manning in the distance. Counts may come and Counts may die, but the Trainer goes on forever.

The Fae took their Princess underground, and another Sprint fixture came nervously over to ask what had happened. Flora is now senior amongst the Assistant Grooms, and she was joined by Sophie, the very first person I met in the Lakeland Particular. Like Flora, Sophie is not a Mage – she's just a young girl who's mad about horses.

'Is Perci okay?' asked Flora. 'You took her away yesterday…'

'And dropped her with Francesca. Her great aunt. As far as I know, they're having some bonding time in Ambleside. Faith has had a bit of an accident, that's all.'

'Faith will be fine, though, right?' asked Sophie uneasily. She's going to be Faith's senior groom when the Staveley sídhe has been equipped with stables, but Sophie's employers have a habit of dying or passing her round like an orphan in Dickens. No wonder she was worried.

'You'll get used to it, Sophie. Working for the Fae means accepting that their bodily wardrobe is as extensive as their fashion one. Isn't that right, Flora?'

Flora put her hand on Sophie's back. 'Yeah. Course. Are you gonna be here long, Conrad?'

'This afternoon and overnight. Would one of you mind getting up extra early and prepping Evenstar for a ride before dawn.'

'I'll do it,' said Sophie eagerly. Then she bit her lip. 'Do you want to be on your own, or would you mind if I came with you?'

'I'd love your company. Now, if you'll excuse me, I have to make a few calls. Scout! Here boy!'

The sheep herding had been enough exercise for my hound to collapse on to the floor of the stable office and go straight to sleep. After I'd kicked out Saerdam Felix, that is, not that he was sorry to leave the computer and get back outside. When he asked me if I understood spreadsheets, I was tempted to give him Mina's number. Or Tom Morton's. Perhaps I will.

I began by sending Mina this message: *For once it's not me in hospital, it's Faith. She should be OK for Thursday, though. Not so good news for Roly. Will call later with full details. Got to ring Hannah first. There might be a bit of a situation with the Red Queen.*

Mina didn't reply straight away, which told me she was probably in Chambers with Judge Bracewell. The Boss, however, was available, and for once she didn't interrupt while I gave her a quick report.

'You must have an enhanced magickal sense of smell,' was her dry conclusion, 'because you have a knack for uncovering enchanted cesspits.' The video blurred a little as she shuffled in her seat. 'Is it really bad?'

'Yes, ma'am. I'd rather not go into details if you don't mind.'

She shuddered by way of an answer. 'Quite. Hmm. Do what you think best, Conrad. This is can of worms and no mistake. Feel free to pass the buck if you're not happy with what the Red Queen says.'

'Thank you.' I sat back and breathed out. 'Are you looking forward to the Hen Party?'

'No, because I hate being on show, and Vicky tells me there's no getting around it. I asked Tennille if that's grounds for dismissal and she laughed at me. And who's this Alicia person?'

'Not so much a person, more of an enthusiastic Fae Squire who's going to help Faith discharge her duties as handmaiden. Try not to freak out when you see Alicia's hair for the first time.'

She pointed her finger at the camera. 'If I get embarrassed, I will blame you, not Mina. Understood?'

'Perfectly.'

'Good. Take care, and good luck.'

'Thanks.'

Talking of Alicia, I had to ring her and tell her what had happened to

Faith. She went very quiet at that point. I also had to ask her if she and the rest of Faith's household could cope overnight. Her voice brightened. 'Of course we can! We will not let our lady down.'

Could they cope? Of course they could, from the Pack side. So long as there wasn't an invasion, they'd be fine.

I made some more calls, sent some emails and tore a sheet of paper off Felix's notepad. I wrote Mina's number on top and added, *Spreadsheets a speciality. Reasonable rates. Discretion assured. Conrad.* I wonder if he'll take the bait?

Faith emerged from the sídhe mid-afternoon, sporting a crutch and with her left leg bandaged from the knee down. She didn't need a cast because the bone had already knitted.

'You okay?' I asked.

'Unfortunately, yes. Unfortunately because you're going to ask awkward questions and we're going to have a difficult conversation with Her Grace.' She took out her phone and waved the screen at me, showing a slew of unopened WhatsApps. 'Why do I get the impression that she already knows?'

'Because she does. I video-called the Constable from the office in the house, so I imagine she had someone listening in.'

She narrowed her eyes. 'Why on earth did you do that? Am I missing something here?'

'It was a way of letting her know without letting her know. I don't want a confrontation about this, Faith, I want an explanation and a solution. If I wanted a confrontation, I'd call Alex Greening and tell her what the Red Queen has been up to.'

'Don't. It's not funny.' She looked at the hills, over towards Grizedale. 'Word has got out about Lucas, you know. That you killed him. There are some mortals who say that Lucas had the right idea: let's bring back the Pale Horsemen.'

I opened my mouth to ask why this was the first I'd heard of it, then remembered that it wasn't my business any more. Not directly. 'Does Matt know?'

'He does. Where are we going to do this?'

'The next conversation has to be without an audience. We're going into Kendal for a bit, because I know someone who can lend me a totally secure room. And don't worry, I'm leaving Scout here, so you can have the back of the car to yourself.'

We needn't have bothered going all the way down Longsleddale to Kentdale and the market town of Kendal, because when I dialled the Red Queen, I got her right-hand woman instead.

'Good afternoon, Countess,' I said. 'Is her grace on her way?'

Countess Bassenthwaite made a face, as if she were trying to tell me that this wasn't her fault. Or mine. 'The Queen says that this is an issue best discussed in person.'

'I can't argue with that,' I responded. 'So long as it's sooner rather than later.'

'I'm sure you are all very busy with the wedding, my lord. We would hate for this to become a distraction.'

I smiled at the Countess. 'Her grace is thoughtful. She has also submitted to me until the first of June, four weeks after the wedding. I want this sorted by then.'

'Aah. That may be difficult, my lord.'

'I will be at the Radiant Sídhe on the seventeenth of May, as will her grace.' I glanced at my watch. 'By now, Matt Eldridge and Karina will have finished putting a trigger ward around the fields. I am charging the Red Queen to protect it, is that clear?'

It was one of the calls I'd made earlier. Matt is good at Wards, and he had Karina to help him, so if her grace was thinking of removing evidence, she'd have to think twice. Especially as I'd now told her to guard the damn thing. It's not often the Fae are held fully to account for what they do. This was going to be an exception.

The Countess glanced to her left, a sure sign that the Queen was in the room watching. Bassenthwaite looked completely boxed in and she wasn't going to have any help getting out. In the end, she had no choice but to bow her head. 'It is as my lord wishes.'

'Good. Another reason for sorting this out promptly is that word will leak. Sooner or later. Neither of us want that, do we?'

'No, my lord. I shall convey your wishes to the Queen.'

'No you won't, you'll convey my orders: guard the sídhe, turn up when I tell you and bring the wherewithal to sort this mess out. Thank you for your time, Countess.'

'Of course, my lord.'

The screen went dark, and I reached for the mouse. 'Do you think I went too far?' I asked Faith.

'It's not for me to say. It depends on how much Her Grace can shift the blame.'

I grunted and closed the laptop.

When Mina finally escaped the clutches of Judge Bracewell, she definitely thought I'd gone too far.

'Is it ever wise to box the Fae into a corner?' she asked. The way she asked it, you'd think she'd been taking lessons from the judge on how to skewer witnesses, not that Mina needs much help when it comes to that.

'You're right, my love, which is why I told the Boss and Matt. Insurance. She can't eliminate the problem by eliminating me, as it were.' I pulled my lip.

'My biggest worry is Persephone. She's still a kid at school most of the time, and one of her classmates is Jocasta Greening. I won't be able to stop a war twice.'

'Let's pray that it does not come to that. Is Faith really going to be able to come on Thursday?'

And with that, we moved on to the wedding, to the coming Easter weekend, and finally to the thorny issue of our vows. Progress on that issue is, shall we say, slow. My fault, of course, because whatever I say, it's going to be binding…

When we'd got as far as we could, Mina said, 'Is this message from "Saerdam Felix" genuine? Is he really so scared of the Red Queen that he would allow me to see her accounts?'

I was stunned. 'Bloody hell. He must be. Up to you, love.'

'I shall take him on. Of course, if I do, it will be confidential.'

'You should call him and tell him that. And if he sounds extraordinarily pleased, then triple your fee, because there's something he wants to hide from me.'

I could hear her smile over the line. 'I have taught you well.'

And then we forgot about spreadsheets and Fae and vows and focused on why we're getting married. You know, the closer we get to tying the knot, the further away it seems.

One of the reasons I opted to stay at the stables is that I fancied trying the Royal Bedchamber for size. The Red Queen often arrives at Sprint late and stays over for an early start, so naturally there's a room reserved for her use. It was very comfortable, thank you, if a little disconcerting. I'm not used to silk sheets. Especially not red ones.

After a night of undisturbed sleep (not all Fae beds are Enchanted, you know), I was woken by the Elder Hlæfdigan, Morag, who brought me tea and toast in bed, and when I got downstairs, I found that she'd even fed Scout. I must come here more often.

Sophie was waiting in the yard, both mounts saddled and ready, and both of them familiar – my own mount, Evenstar, and an old four-legged friend called Agrippa. 'You're not risking Hipponax?' I asked.

She made a face and started to blush. 'I'm getting better with him, but there's a problem, 'cos Evenstar might be coming into heat according to Mister Manning. He uses magick, so I wouldn't know. Unicorns are hard enough to control at the best of times…'

'You do right, Sophie. I would not want to be on Evenstar's back if Hipponax got frisky.'

She turned her face away and took Evenstar to the mounting block for me. When we were both up and ready, I signalled for her to take the lead. 'I've only transitioned a couple of times, and I've got to try and make sure Scout is nearby or he'll get left behind. I'll see you up there. We'll meet at the top of the straight.'

We set off, and I was glad I'd let her lead, because I had to circle the meadow twice before I got the hang of engaging the magick. Sophie has no magick at all, and all the hard work is done by the saddle. And the horse. She can manage this transition to the Gallops, but a proper multi-plane race would be beyond her, which is why she'll never become a trainer in the world of magick. Only Mages can do that, and I wondered if it was what she wanted to talk to me about, because she wasn't coming along for the pleasure of my company. She's grown out of that.

It was barely pre-dawn when we got to the higher level, and I trotted carefully through the course and the woods to the viewing point, where I pulled up and turned to face south-west. Sophie was waiting patiently for me. 'I need to watch for something,' I told her. 'If you don't mind waiting.'

'No. Course not.'

We sat and waited, and in a couple of minutes our bodies grew shadows when the first rays of the sun hit. Two more minutes and the sun hit the Radiant Sídhe over in the Furness Peninsula. Right on cue, my left leg throbbed, the distant sky lit up with a burst of rainbow light as Roly Quinn unfastened his binding and his Essence dispersed with only a whisper of sound.

'The cunning old bugger,' I said.

The Rainbow of Lux, as seen through my Third Eye, runs from Mother Earth's Red to Royal Fae Violet, via the regular seven mundane colours. The two magickal shades *didn't* disperse. Instead, they twined and re-formed and made a shape.

The image burned itself into my magickal Sight, and I can still see its mixture of Earth red and Royal violet whenever I think about it, as if I were remembering it differently to other things.

I've tried to sketch it, but every time I try to realise it in two dimensions that are visible to mundane sight, it doesn't come out right. Anyway, for future reference, this is the best I can do:

As the image formed, thirty miles away as the raven flies, I wondered whether others would see it. There would be Sisters of the Water making early devotions. Fae out hunting. Insomniacs and early risers. With all those possibilities, I somehow got the feeling that they'd miss it, that there was something in the Work of magick that would turn their eyes away, that would in fact turn away all eyes and ears but mine: the Fraternal Magick that Roly had once used to save lives had bonded him to me, and down that bond had come the image and the message.

Neither image nor message made sense, yet, but I could hear him whispering the words just as clearly as I could see that twisted sigil: *Beware of Homer.*

No sooner had it burned itself into me than the image grew thin and it, too, blew away on the wind, and now he was truly gone. Sir Rowland Quinn was no more, and sharing that weird shape was the last thing that he had done. I pulled my lip and wondered not about the fact that he had shared it with *me* but about the fact that he had set up this long-distance dawn encounter to avoid sharing it with someone else yesterday. Who? His sister? His granddaughter Persephone? The Fae Princess?

Or was it someone they knew. Someone they would talk to. I shrugged: that was for another day, and it would go into my Larder of Unfinished Business under the heading "Infinite Circle".

The Lord Mayor of Moles (like his mundane cousins) had a larder where he stored live worms. He used to bite the heads off to stop them escaping, but they still wriggled around. I have much the same storage for unfinished business, and it's full of things I need to look into. One day.

Chapter 8 — Affairs of the Heart

'Did something just happen?' asked Sophie. 'I'm getting better, you know. Most of the time I can spot when someone uses magick, and you've just seen something, haven't you?'

She hadn't seen a thing, not even the main light show. 'Something did happen, Sophie. An old dog wanted to show me that it's never too late to learn new tricks. Shall we put them through their paces then have a break?'

'Yeah. Race you to the Margin and then back here.'

I swung my rucksack off my back and dropped it to the ground, and Sophie, being a teenager, was already half way to the course. 'Come on, girl,' I told my horse, 'we're not going to let her get away with that, are we?'

Okay, so I cheated in the end. What's the point of having a highly trained Border Collie and not using him to distract the opposition? I think I might have won anyway, because Agrippa is a superb horse, but he's at that stage in life when he doesn't put himself out unless he has to, and Sophie doesn't quite have the experience to get the better of him.

'What kept you?' I said mildly. 'I take it the flask with milky coffee is for you.'

'Bloody dog! Where did you get him, sir?'

'Long story. Handy tree, this. I've sat here quite a lot recently.'

'Have you? Thanks.'

We got our breath back for a moment while the horses (and Scout) took a drink. When I'd finished my fag, I turned to Sophie. 'What's up? Having second thoughts about an Entangled career?'

'Yes and no. I wanna work with Faith for a bit. At least a year. I won't get that sort of experience anywhere else.' She smiled. 'Not that it's gonna appear on my CV or in a reference, is it?'

'There is that.'

'This is really hard, but you're the only one I can talk to, and, no offence, Conrad, but ... well, you're old enough to be my dad. And you're a bloke.' She sighed. 'Am I allowed to mention Miss Kennedy?'

My hand hovered over my mug. Just for half a second. 'Of course you are, Sophie. Matt Eldridge asked me if I should question you about your time together during riding lessons, but I said no. I didn't think that she'd have confided in you.'

Sophie shook her head. 'She didn't. But I did to her.'

When she looked up, she could have looked at the trees or the grass or the weirdly distant fells, but she didn't: she looked at Evenstar (who was being ignored by Agrippa, because Agrippa is a gelding). I decided to take a risk.

'Sophie, is this about your love life?'

'Oh my god! Are you a mind-reader?'

'No. Thankfully. I noticed that you've made an impression with Flora.'

She put her fingers in her ears. 'Nah nah nah nah. Not listening.'

I held up my hands in a surrender gesture. She unplugged her ears and pointed her finger at me. 'Just don't, alright?'

I lowered my hands. 'Not only am I old enough to be your dad, I was there when Force Ghyll shot Verona in the back and I saw Flora mourning her. I've always known about Flora's preferences. There is someone you *can* talk to, though. Erin Slater.'

'I've never met her. Heard about her, though. She's like old, too, though.'

'She is. She's ancient. Almost *thirty*! But she's a great friend, Sophie. And she works just down the bottom of the dale, at Sprint House. Even more importantly, I know that she can keep a secret. I'll give her your number and tell her to swing by.'

'Thank you, Conrad. I mean that.'

I shifted on my perch and looked at her properly, giving her Dad signals. 'If this is about the Fae, and I think it is, then she's exactly the person to talk to.'

'Message received.' She threw away the dregs of her coffee and poured fresh from the flask. 'Talking of you being old enough to be my dad…'

'I'd rather you didn't, but go on.'

'Saerdam Felix was helping me with the paperwork on Evenstar's horse passport, and I saw that the ownership is partly traceable to George Baxter. Who's he?'

'Can you keep a secret?'

'Course. He's not your secret gay lover, is he?'

'No. That's someone else. George Baxter is my go-to alias, that's all. I wanted to keep Evenstar legal but off the grid a little.'

'Oh. So George Baxter doesn't exist?'

'Erm, no. Only on paper. Why?'

'I've just discovered that I'm related to a George Baxter. Or his sister Jaylene to be exact.'

I grunted in pain, twisted sharply on the branch and grabbed my leg. It's a great cover story when I've just been shocked out of my skin. After I'd hopped around, I topped up my own coffee and pretended to make polite conversation. 'Jaylene Baxter? Weird name. How are you related, and why has this come up suddenly?'

'Mum was in care before she was adopted, and her file went "missing" when she asked the local authority about her birth family. Dad bought her a voucher for her fortieth birthday last month. Not a real present, like, it was a hint. It was a voucher for one of those genealogy websites. Mum went weird at first. She even asked me if I was happy.'

'My mother asked me if I was happy when I was your age. It freaked me out as well. I'm sorry, Sophie, I can't imagine what it's like growing up without knowing your family. Then again, I did discover a half-sister last year.' Before she could ask about her near namesake, I changed the subject back. 'So what did your mum do?'

'She thought about it for a bit, then she uploaded a DNA sample, and a couple of weeks later, it said she had a match to the Baxter family, 'specially Jaylene. Mum was thrilled at first, but there's no information in their public profile, and they haven't responded to any messages.'

There's a very, very good reason why the Baxters haven't responded to messages – George mislaid the access code to the website and hasn't been bothered to look for it, but I'll come back to that. For Sophie, I put on my Uncle Conrad face.

'I can find things out, you know. I won't break the law, but I can bend it a little. There are people who owe me favours who could help your mum. What's her name?'

'She's Sky Guest now. Couldn't wait to take dad's name, but she was born Skylark Wilson. Can you really help? I don't want men in suits knocking on their door or nothing.'

I patted my pockets, lit a cigarette, then went back until I found a suitable business card. 'It has to be her decision. Tell her that if she wants me to look into it, she should take a good picture of her birth certificate and WhatsApp it to this number. Completely confidential. How about that?'

'Thanks, Conrad.' She stared at the card for a few seconds, then shoved it in her jeans. 'Better get back. Some of us have work to do.'

'You're forgetting something, Sophie.'

She looked around. 'What?'

'You work for Faith, and she works for me.'

She grinned. 'Is that why you swan around all the time? 'Cos you've got so many people to do your work for you?'

The first time I came to the stables, they tried to hide the mini-unicorns and the nest of Sprites from me. They don't bother any more. Half way to the Margin, the mini-beasts raced up from the lower plane and shot towards us in a wave of screams, shouts and whistles. We pulled in and let them pass.

'Still can't get used to them,' said Sophie. 'Just a bit *too* creepy. It's like my brain won't accept that Robbie was one of *them* a couple of months ago.'

That explained a lot. Robbie is one of Faith's new Squires, like Alicia, and Robbie is a handsome devil: young and muscular and already an accomplished swordsman. 'Do you want me to warn him off?'

'God, no! I can handle him. He's like a puppy, not a man. Even if he could slice you up in seconds.'

'Fair enough. Did you see where Scout went?'

When we returned to the stables, Faith was up and about, and she was already walking without the crutch. I grabbed a quick breakfast, woke up Scout and loaded the car. Faith joined me up front and we headed off. 'Quick stop at Sprint House on the way,' I told her. 'I'd do this by phone, but sometimes you need to get Erin in front of you to get the message through. Could you text her and ask her to come to the gates. I don't want to meet the Sextons unless I have to.'

'No problem.' Two minutes later, she added, 'Erin says "Fine, but you tell him you're not his secretary."' She grinned. 'I may have neglected to tell her that you were driving.'

The entrance to Sprint House is grand but not opulent. I parked in the driveway and spotted Erin coming down the path. I got out and moved away from the car.

'What's up?' she shouted.

When she was close enough for us to talk, I said, 'Need a favour. You know Sophie, from the stables?'

She thought for a second. 'The kid who fancies you? What's the problem?'

'My ego may never recover, but she's over me, Erin. She needs some advice, and I thought of you. I'm sure you'll be the perfect Agony Aunt.'

'Less of the Aunt, thanks very much! What's up?'

'I'll let her explain, but could you nip up to the stables later?'

'Yeah. We're winding down for the Easter weekend today, so that's no bother. You've got me intrigued.'

'Thanks. I'd better go.'

It is a long way from Sprint House to Birk Fell, unless you've got a helicopter. Faith and I discussed her trip to Clerkswell tomorrow rather than the mess waiting for us at the Radiant Sídhe. Priorities and all that. I dropped her at the marina on the western side of Ullswater and waved at the Pack King, Alex, who'd brought the launch over to collect Faith and save me an hour's drive. Even so, it was going to be late by the time I got to Middlebarrow Haven. Plenty of time to think about what Sophie had told me about her mother's origins.

Raven. Simple name, very complex person. In every way.

The giant Witch who'd once been a leading light in the Daughters of Glastonbury was casting a very long shadow. Cordelia had loved her, and that love had been twisted by Lucas to corrupt a good woman. That was bad enough, but Raven's size and Gift were more than a freak of nature, she was through-and-through an unnatural creation who'd been delivered to Glastonbury by a raven (hence the name).

That bird had been the creature of either the Morrigan or the Allfather, both of whom were there. According to Odin, someone tried to create a Valkyrie, using a young Witch as host. It had not gone well for the mother, and the Elderkind have no knowledge of who was responsible or how it was done. I also think they tried to cover things up.

Raven grew up being told that if she ever left the Daughters, she would die, like the Lady of Shallot. I was there when she broke the ties to Glastonbury, defying the prophecy and making a stand. Less than four hours later, she picked up my gun and tried to save my life, and she did, but it cost her dearly. The Work of magick in my ammunition blew back and erased every ounce of Lux in her body, totally destroying all that she'd ever been. Accident or divine intervention? The jury is still out on that one.

When we committed Raven's remains to the fire, I took a sneaky swab of her DNA. I didn't dare put it through the National DNA Database, so I created a fake family tree for the Baxters, then uploaded Raven's DNA. If you're wondering why I chose *Jaylene* as a name, don't forget that jays and ravens are both members of the crow family, and talking of family members, there had been no matches to Raven at the time, but now…

I'm sure that this is not a bluff by the Elderkind. The Allfather wants to know who was behind Raven's creation, and so do I. Unfortunately, I was now obliged to have a difficult conversation with Hannah, because she has no idea of my little investigation. I stopped at our rental in Windermere and threw stuff in the car, then came to a decision: it could wait until after Easter. Coward? Moi?

Guilty as charged.

Part Two — Interested Parties

Chapter 9 — Easter Greetings

I can't say that I'd been ready for what greeted me when I'd got home on Maundy Thursday. There was me, tired and exhausted after discovering the Radiant Sídhe, lonely and ready to be received by my true love and what had greeted me on the doorstep?

My mother, that's what, standing ramrod straight and with her arms folded. Oh. The last time she'd looked like this was twenty years ago. I bowed to the dragon and unleashed Scout, hoping he'd provide a tactical diversion. No such luck: he took one look at Mother and ran off to mark his territory.

'Hi Mum. Good flight? Raitch pick you up okay? Where's Mina?'

Her arms had stayed resolutely folded. 'Your father is in high dudgeon with me and everyone else is with those creatures in the stables pretending it's a beauty parlour.'

Oh. Erm. Well, riddle me this: how *do* you tell your mother (who lives in Spain, don't forget) that you've arranged for two Fae to do the girls' hair? Damn the bloody M56 for making me late. I was coming back via Crewe next time. There was nothing for it. I had to change the subject.

'What's wrong with Dad?'

The arms unfolded and took up position on her hips. Oh. Bad choice of tactic. 'Your father should *not* be exposed to magick unnecessarily, Conrad! It's bad for him. And I know all about their reputation.'

Scout returned from the bushes and looked at the two humans. He'd been in the car for hours and wanted to play. From his point of view, neither of us looked like good prospects, so he lifted his nose, took a good sniff and headed for the gardens.

There was no alternative: I'd have to get physical. I limped over the gravel and up to the steps. I put my arms round her unyielding body and gave her a hug, ignoring the flinch. 'I'm so glad you came, Mum.' Instead of letting go like she expected me to, I clung on. 'They'll be gone soon and it'll just be us.'

She softened. Maybe she's mellowing in retirement. Or maybe she's just running out of energy. She lifted her hands to my ribs and gently pushed me away. 'Yes, I know, dear, and I can't wait to catch up with everything. But that creature! The *hair!* How? Why?'

'Mum, I give you my word that I have no idea *how*. In fact, I don't *want* to know how. As for the *why*, it's just what they do. When you can have a perfect replica of your client's hair to practise on, why wouldn't you? And don't worry, it will be gone by the actual wedding.'

That mixture of suspicion, concern and worry that I knew so well came into her eyes. 'Really?'

'Yes. What did you think was going on?'

'Promise not to tell anyone?'

I nodded.

'I thought it was a plot. To get you to marry one of their kind instead of Mina. You know, like a Changeling bride.'

That was the most alarming thing I'd come across since the Radiant Sídhe. Possibly *more* alarming. And the most alarming thing of all is that it used to happen a lot. Probably still does.

'No, Mum. I'm safe from that particular nightmare. Wouldn't work in our case for all sorts of reasons.'

She managed a smile. 'Good. Now go and tell your father that he can go to the pub tonight to calm down if he wants.'

'Tell him yourself, Mum. I'm off to see what's going on and give Scout a walk. We'll all be safer if he's tired.'

Faith's 4x4 was parked up to the garden wall, somewhat drunkenly. I'm guessing a close encounter with Eseld's Wards would have had a profound effect on the two Fae passengers. I opened the garden gate, and Scout ran through, eager to see if his nose was telling him the truth: that there were lots of people and almost-people to check out.

I followed him up the garden path (pun intended), and found him sniffing happily around the old stables where Erin used to have her Scriptorium and was, for one day only, the headquarters of the Bridal beauty team. They even had a board outside proclaiming it to be the premises of *Shear Magic*.

Sitting in the opening on a padded chair was the happy, round figure of the very pregnant Myfanwy, and she still has a couple of months to go. Behind her on another chair was Rachael, and hovering between them were Faith and her Squire, Alicia, who is possessed of an exact (but longer and glossier) copy of Mina's hair. Yes, it does look utterly bizarre on her, and I'm not surprised Mum freaked out.

Scout had been sniffing at something outside the pop-up salon, and was now happily saying hello to Mina, who had come out to greet him. I looked at them all, and you know what? I'm *sure* they're up to something. You could argue that a group of five women together are, by definition, up to *something*, and before you ask, I am nowhere near brave enough to ask them about it.

Instead, I smiled and said, 'Evening Ladies. Are you going to be much longer?'

'Not me,' said Myfanwy. 'That casserole will be nearly done.'

'And I'd better go and make my peace with Mary,' added Mina.

'In that case, I'll wait a bit,' said Rachael. 'I don't fancy being collateral damage. Did I see you with a stash of Sofía's finest, Faith? That would put me in the mood for Easter quite nicely.'

That was quick work. Rachael had never met them before, and now she's sharing a joint with a Fae Princess. *Obviously* Rachael was up to something. She always is, but her I can leave alone. 'Come on, boy,' I said to Scout. 'We know when we're not wanted. Let's go herd some sheep.'

And after that, it was a very harmonious, very busy and very happy holiday. Great for me, but I suspect boring for you, so I'll cut to the chase.

On Sunday afternoon, I got a WhatsApp attachment from Sophie the groom (not to be confused with Sofía the sister, who was back in Spain – another reason Mother relaxed a lot).

As well as her mother's contact details, Sophie sent me a photograph of her mother's birth certificate and this message: *Hi Conrad, Mum says to go for it. She also thinks I'm too nice and that you're hiding something, so I said course he is. Please keep her up to date, yeah? SopheeeeeXXX.*

I zoomed quickly over the full birth certificate, and I can honestly say that the only two parts I believed were Sex: "girl" and Name: "Skylark". Everything else I took with a pinch of salt: date, place of birth, mother's name, name of notifying physician, signature of registrar, the lot. There were two significant omissions which also told me something, though. First, this was definitely not a hospital birth, and second there was no father recorded.

On reflection, I was inclined to believe the County of Birth as being Westmorland. If you wanted to hide something in the world of magick, you'd choose one of two places: Mercia or the Lakeland Particular. Mercia has a Watch Captain, yes, but it was something of a magickal jungle up there back then, with millions of people and very few Mages, and that makes it easier to work under the radar.

You don't need me to tell you why it's easy to get away with things in the Particular. Or it was forty years ago; I hope it isn't so much any more.

I sat back and looked out of the library window. Spring would soon be here, and so would our wedding. I had a slowly growing pile of coincidences in my folder now, and the biggest was Sky Guest's genetic match to Raven. Unfortunately that's all I really had: coincidence. Reluctantly, I closed the folder for now and put it back into my Larder of Unfinished Business.

Chapter 10 — Where the Heart Is

Kathy climbed out of the taxi and retrieved her case carefully from the boot. The driver had offered to do it, but she'd been adamant. She didn't want him dropping it on the flagstones: that thermometer thingy was made of glass, weighed a ton and was very close to something infinitely more precious.

After the long drive from Thirsk Station, she really wanted a fag, but the thought of facing the shivering gallery without her big coat was too much, and besides, the sooner she got rid of the stuff to Don, the sooner she could unpack properly. She turned left instead of right and went through the main doors to the Abbey, then she skirted the therapy rooms and followed the dim lighting through the fire door.

On the other side, sensors triggered the LEDs and dispelled the darkness of the corridor. With it being Easter Sunday, Faye would no doubt be standing in for Don's carer (no way would they fork out the overtime, and weren't the Poles big on Easter or something?). Kathy knocked on Don's door, waited a second, then went in.

Seeing Nika instead of Faye was the first surprise; seeing Michael sitting next to her on the little sofa was the second.

Nika blinked but didn't move, while Michael jumped up with concern. 'Hello, Kathy. What are you doing back tonight? Everything okay?'

She ignored his question, because she wasn't going to discuss it in company, so she said, 'Since when have you been on Don's visitors' list?'

Michael looked a little hurt to be treated with suspicion, and he looked down at Nika (who still wasn't giving anything away except mild amusement).

'Since Simon twisted his back doing triangle pose on Friday and I offered to fill in, that's when. I joined in the Tai Chi as well, but Faye thought there should be a professional here in the evenings, so…' He shrugged and looked down at Don. 'I didn't realise how much he understands.' He gave a sad smile. 'Shame you can't tell your story, isn't it, Don?'

Kathy stepped into the room, leaving her case by the door. She stood in front of Michael and bent down to Don's chair. 'How are you, Don?'

With her body in the way, hiding him from Michael, the old man gave her a knowing look and the tiniest shake of his head: *Michael doesn't suspect* was the message. Probably. Kathy stood back and smiled.

'I will take my break now,' announced Nika, standing up and straightening her tunic. 'If you are good, Kathy?'

'Yeah. No problem.'

When the carer had left, Michael jumped to the kettle. 'Can I get you anything? Tea? Have you had supper?'

'I've eaten, thanks.' His concern was genuine, and she relented. 'Make us a brew, will you Michael? I'll be back in five. You've got me number.'

'I think I can cope for five minutes.'

She pushed her case into the corner and jogged up the emergency stairs to grab her down coat and have a wee. After a quick visit to the shivering gallery (where she ignored everyone), she dodged back to find Michael adding a splash of milk to her tea.

Nika's break was twenty minutes, and Michael wasn't going anywhere. Telling both of them and telling them tonight would save her the hassle of doing it twice tomorrow.

She took another chair rather than sit next to Michael, and blew steam off her mug. 'I've come back early because I had an amazing time with the girls. Simple as that.'

'So it went okay?'

'Better than okay. I was panicking that they wouldn't recognise me, but they did. The little one cried when I left yesterday, and I cried all night.' She shrugged and drank some tea. 'Funny thing, but it was the best feeling I've had for months. Years.'

Both men were looking at her, and the look on Don's face said that he understood what she meant, and he knew why she was back; Michael's face showed nothing but confusion, and it confirmed that he didn't have any kids. She explained it for him.

'I cried myself to sleep last night, then I woke up at seven this morning. It was so early that I had to go for a walk in Roundhay Park until the hotel dining room opened for service. Then after that, all I wanted to do was see the girls, and if I couldn't see the girls to go to the pub.'

A lightbulb lit up behind Michael's eyes. 'You were tempted.'

'I was. There weren't even any shops open today. Bloody Easter Sunday. So, instead of getting drunk, I spent the whole day fighting with the effing rail replacement bus service, because there's no sodding trains as well as no sodding shops. And here I am, back where I can do some good. I…'

The last remark, about *doing some good*, had slipped out without thinking, and it wouldn't do for people to think she was getting above her station, so she covered it by saying, 'And no way was I buying overpriced biscuits from the station shop. Is there any in the tin?'

Michael stood to check the biscuit tin, and Kathy looked at Don. She pointed to her suitcase and gave him a double thumbs-up. He grinned back, then dropped his face again when Michael turned round.

'You're in luck,' said Michael. 'An unopened pack of chocolate Hobnobs.'

'Can this day get any better?' she asked, taking the packet.

'Make the most of it. Are you going to get up and do breakfast tomorrow when you're on holiday?'

She bit into a hobnob and considered the options. Her contract was quite clear: she couldn't dine with the guests on a scheduled holiday. Sod it. 'I'll do breakfast and tell the Fragrant Faye that I've cut my holiday short. She can like it or lump it.'

'The *Fragrant Faye*. That's so wrong, but so right, Kathy. And now I will have to find a way *not* to say it out loud.'

They grinned at each other. Kathy took another biscuit, and said, 'So, you won't have to do breakfast solo in the morning.'

'But you will on Tuesday.'

'You what? You can't be leaving already.'

He spluttered into his tea. 'As if. No, but the Fragrant Faye took me aside for a chat on Friday. She said I was getting too dependent on cooking – and my relationship with you.'

Kathy couldn't help herself. She flushed bright red and said, 'We don't have a relationship! You're one of the first men who hasn't hit on me as soon as their libido's recovered after detox.'

'I'm not gay, if that's what you're thinking.'

She gave him a withering look. 'And why would I think that? Leaving your magic power of resisting my charms aside, why is Faye banning you from the kitchen?'

'Like I said. She thinks I'm too dependent on a routine where I'm comfortable. I've to do a week in the gardens, starting Tuesday.'

Kathy hooted. 'And I'm going on Masterchef. Load of bollocks. They're doing all the spring graft outside, is all, and they need as many hard workers as they can get. Would you set dJulie to digging over the flowerbeds?'

'Erm. Probably not. Definitely not with those nails.'

So Michael checked out women's nails. Hmm. She looked at the time: Nika would be back in a few minutes. Kathy leaned forwards. 'So, have you resisted my charms because you prefer someone younger?' She leaned her head towards the door to emphasise the point.

Michael looked down. 'No. I lost someone because of what I did, and I want them back. It's as simple as that.'

Don grunted at that point, and Michael volunteered to take him to the toilet, under Kathy's supervision, and Nika returned while Kathy was trying to persuade Michael to fill in the log.

'I'll do it,' said Nika. 'You look tired, Kathy, but good, yes?'

'Yep, thanks. All good. I'll leave you to it, Nika. See you tomorrow,

Michael.'

She couldn't leave her case here, so she slowly lifted it one step at a time, then round the landings until she was back at her room, almost directly above Don's (though not with the same spectacular view). She carefully unpacked her things and the weird stuff she'd bought for Don, leaving the two fragile objects until last.

The combination barometer/thermometer filled with mercury stayed in its blanket (which she'd nicked from the hotel), and she transferred the bundle straight to the top shelf of her cupboard. Contraband safely stowed, she gently unwrapped her true treasure.

The community centre had been brilliant, putting on all sorts of activities, including Easter egg decorating, and with Don's gift she'd been able to afford the luxury option, with the free ornamental giant egg cup. She placed the cup on her desk-cum-dressing table, away from the radiator and from the sunshine, then she placed the cellophane-wrapped chocolate egg on top of it.

The word *Mummy* in pink edible ink was front and centre. She stared at it for ages before getting up to go and hunt for a sandwich (she'd lied about having supper), and the egg was the last thing she looked at before she went to sleep.

Chapter 11 — A Night Out

There's a lot about London that takes getting used to when you've grown up in a village and when your Great Metropolis is Gloucester. One of the many, many novelties is that the location of a property isn't just a *thing*, it's the *main thing*. I got out of the taxi and considered what the Kensington Roost might be worth on the open, mundane market. My head couldn't cope with that, so I gave up and rang the bell.

Tonight was going to be a strange one for all sorts of reasons, and for one it was my first visit to the London base of the Hawkins family: I was very much looking forward to poking my nose into their mansion. According to Saffron, the place is a total money-pit and her mother would sell it off if she could. The only problem is that Lady Celeste Hawkins, the family matriarch, doesn't own the place outright.

Lady H does own the Cherwell Roost down in Oxfordshire, but apparently all Hawkins Mages have some sort of voting rights in the Kensington property but no equity, so there's no incentive for them to sell. I was expecting some sort of servant to answer the door, but no, it was Stewart McBride, Saffron's uncle by marriage. He came out and stood on the step.

'Hello Conrad,' he said drily. He also looked me up and down quite obviously. I raised an eyebrow. 'Don't worry, I'm just checking that you've still got four limbs – I want to make sure my sponsor is still in one piece.'

Stewart has a camp dial that goes up and down like the volume knob on a taxi driver's sound system, and he knows it doesn't bother me in the least. 'Hello, Stewart. I know I've said thank you by message, but it's good to say it in person: sorting out the conference means more to Mina than you'd believe.'

He smiled the sort of smile that said he shared some of her pain. I don't know anything about his family background, and I'm guessing that not everyone he knew was equally supportive when he came out. Attitudes have changed so quickly in my lifetime that someone like Stewart, who's a bit older, would have emerged into a very different climate than the one today.

Thanks to my intervention and Stewart's support, Mina's older brother is coming over to the UK to co-present a conference on the relationship between the individual and the state in the age of Big Data, with Arun focusing on technology and Stewart on the politics. It was the excuse that

Arun needed to overcome his pride and his anger and to present himself at St Michael's to walk his sister down the aisle.

'You should consider a change of career to events planner,' said Stewart. 'It's going to be a sell out crowd. Your sponsorship won't cost much at all.'

'I'll bear that in mind,' I replied, looking anxiously over his shoulder at the glimpse of majestic Georgian hallway behind him. He still hadn't opened the door wide enough to let me in.

He sensed my thought and raised an eyebrow. 'They're in the dungeon, I'm afraid. Tradesman's entrance.' He tilted his head. 'According to young Victoria, you quite like calling yourself a tradesman.' He left his observation hanging. 'Round the side, down the alley and look for the glowing portal into another realm.'

I stepped back. 'Thanks.'

'Have a nice evening, and don't worry, you'll get a proper invitation one day.'

'I'll look forward to it.'

He waited until I'd limped along the road a few yards before calling out, 'There's a dripping tap in the servants' quarters that needs fixing.'

The rear (tradesman's) entrance to the Kensington Roost was as you'd expect: Warded, reinforced and creepy. Stewart does like his games, and he must have messaged or used the old servants' speaking tube to inform them that I was on my way, because Saffron was waiting to let me in. I followed her down the steps and into the Hawkins magickal workshops.

I'm told that Heidi Marston is banned from working here on account of her profession as an Artificer being noisy, smelly and dangerous. Either that or they just don't like her and ganged up on her.

Since I joined the Watch, Mages have been a lot less reluctant to share things with me, but that's relative. When it comes to the Art or Craft of magick, they're still a secretive bunch, and all the Hawkins Mages (Saffron, Emerald, Bertie, Julius, GG and Lady Celeste herself) each have their own space down here in a basement that was built as part of the house and not dug out as an extension. Saffron showed me through a door with a small wooden plaque on it, hand painted at some craft stall many years ago. It said *Georgina's Room Keep Out* and it was written in purple glitter ink on a pink background. It also thrummed with magick. I gave it a wide berth.

Inside GG's den, seven people were gathered and divided into two groups: those who were staying sober for now, and those who were starting early; Mina was drinking tea. After a general Hello, I gave Mina a kiss and glanced at the group gathered round the Prosecco bottles.

This was the first time I've seen Chris and Eseld in the flesh since Georgina announced to the world that they were having an affair. They were standing close to each other, with Ez leaning in slightly to Chris, and they'd been talking to Rachael, Vicky and Alain. They looked relaxed and happy, and tonight was partly about us all going out and having a meal together ahead of my twin ordeals tomorrow.

Having nodded to the drinkers, I embraced Mina and asked how she was feeling.

'Alright so far. This sitting room has very little magick in it, so I haven't fainted yet.'

This was the other reason for gathering tonight, and the reason we were meeting at Kensington Roost. We needed somewhere private and somewhere magickal to test a new Artefact. A very special Artefact, custom made for Mina. Tomorrow was my – our – appointment with the new Warden in Salomon's House, and Mina needed help. Help to get in without fainting.

Mundane people often visit Salomon's House, and once a Mage has helped you over the threshold and signed you in, there's no problem. If you have a little latent Gift, you will be creeped out beyond measure, but that says nothing. I'm a Mage and I'm creeped out by the place. The problem is Mina's arm.

When her Ancile was tattooed on to her chest, her struggles against the restraints made the priest miss his first stroke, and he ended up scoring a line across her bicep. It was only later she discovered that this tiny, unfinished Work of Alchemy actually functioned. What it does is itch furiously whenever it detects other Works being used, which is useful in dangerous situations, but problematic when you go to the most intensely magickal place in Britain.

The tattoo may be passive, but it draws Lux from Mina to work, and with her Ancile doing the same, it can drain her Imprint quickly. Hypo-Lux they call it, and it works a bit like hypoglycaemia in diabetics: you faint. Helping Mina get round the problem has been a bit of a challenge.

There are magickal isolation outfits. Of sorts. They take an atmospheric diving suit, as used for extreme water depths, and stick runes on it. Or you can have two Mages walk round holding your hands. Neither appealed to Mina for some reason.

I had realised that we were one short, and said, 'Where's Julius?'

Julius Hawkins is Saffron's cousin and, more recently, Vicky's boyfriend. He works as jobbing Enscriber and as assistant to Georgina, down here in the basement and in Oxford.

'Train was late,' said George. 'He should be here … now!'

I turned and saw what the others had heard – Jay wheeling a small suitcase.

'Sorry I'm late everyone.'

He parked the suitcase and was going to greet Vicky when George stuck a hand out. 'You can kiss her later, Julius. Some of us are dying of thirst here. Come on, get it out.'

He opened the case and took out a long, black quilted coat. Georgina looked at it, then looked at Mina. 'Oh dear. I keep forgetting that you're not as tall as me.'

Jay rolled his eyes. 'I bloody told you, George. Ten times I told you that this would swamp her.'

Mina stared uncomprehendingly, then the penny dropped. 'You want me to wear *that*! To meet the Warden!'

GG took the coat and felt inside it, running her hands into the sleeves. 'Tilly spent hours stitching the copper into the sleeves and across the back. That's why it's only just been finished and Jay had to bring it up on the train. We can't change it now.' She smiled brightly. 'I'm working on a version that goes in a medical sling. Might have it finished for the summer. Try it on.'

I did sympathise. I really did, but there was nothing useful I could do about it, and empty words were no use here.

Mina frowned. She pouted, then she lifted her nose and aimed the point at Georgina's chest. 'You could at least have got a red one, as befits a princess.' When the laughter had died down, she held out her hand. 'Do we do it here or next door?'

'Put it on here, then I'll whip you into the workshop and see if you collapse. Hopefully not. There you go.'

It looked as daft as you'd think, and it was going to be a complete sweatbox, too, because the zip had to stay fastened to complete the circuit of Lux. It worked, though, as Mina confirmed when she and GG had nipped through an impressive security door and into the darkness beyond. You'll note that none of the other Mages were invited to go with her.

'Nothing,' Mina said to me. 'No itches or burning on my mark. Thank you very much for all your trouble, Georgina.' She slipped off the coat and passed it back. From the look on her face, she was mentally redesigning her outfit for tomorrow.

'Time for dinner,' said Georgina. 'Shall we?'

There are restaurants near the Kensington Roost. If you can afford them and know the owner to get a table big enough. Thankfully, it's only a short walk to the more cosmopolitan zone of Notting Hill, which is well served for all manner of eateries, and one of which had a reservation for ten.

We left the basement and fell into line, mostly by couples, and I ended up with Saffron, because Mina was talking in hushed tones to Eseld. GG and Chris walked at the front, leading us like the teachers at a school outing.

'How's the Cleveland Watch?' I asked Saffron.

'Fine. Nice to have a weekend in London, though. Thanks, Chief.'

'Don't thank me, thank Jordan for agreeing to cover for you.'

'I already have. Three weeks in the summer while he goes to Florida.'

I left it a second, then changed the subject. 'How was Murray Pollard?'

'Professional. Thorough. I've never been so well briefed on a new Watch.' She said the last with a sideways glance. I rose above the implied accusation. 'He also got lots of digs in. About our *reliance on the divine*.'

'Hmmph. Did he give any indication of his plans?'

'He's up to something, I know that. We did the first part of the handover at his house. Nice place. He went outside twice to take long, meaningful phone calls. I tried to sneak a look at his phone. No luck.'

We had arrived at the restaurant, and I grabbed a bottle of beer and headed back outside for a smoke; I was soon joined by Eseld. 'What were you on to Mina about?' I asked, wondering if it might be about Tamsin's decision not to object to Eseld's presence at the wedding.

Mina and Eseld will never be friends as such. Mina wants us to treat Ez as if she were my sister, but I already have two sisters, and neither of them has made sexual advances to me even once, let alone twice. Nor have they saved my life or exchanged partial Imprints. At the wedding, Eseld will be standing with the ushers, not the bridesmaids. Or so I thought.

'I've been doing Saffron a favour,' she replied.

'I've always said you were selfless and noble, Ez. Shame no one believed me.'

'Ha bloody ha. And I always thought it wasn't fair that Saff had to be escort and bodyguard.'

I agreed with her, as it happens. Saffron's ticket to bridesmaid status had been dependent on escorting Mina to the church for the legal ceremony and spending most of the service hanging around outside. 'Did you offer to swap?'

'I did more than that. I offered to provide a carriage and drive the bride and her brother from Elvenham to Saint Michael's, with Maggie to act as footman.'

I was stunned. It actually *was* selfless and noble. 'Does this have anything to do with your impending visit to the Bloxhams?'

She frowned. 'How d'you know about that? Did that Faith creature blab to you or something?'

'Don't call Faith a *creature*, Ez, even though she is one. I'm treating her with all the respect due to her station, because before you know it, she'll be a Queen, and Queens have eternity to get their own back for all the insults they suffered, right back to when they were Squires.' I put my hand on my heart. 'If not for your sake, then for the sake of yours and Chris's children.'

She sputtered in outrage. 'Do not go there again. Ever. Not without written permission, okay?'

'Noted. And you're changing the subject.'

'Did Faith tell you?'

'No. Nor Mina. I have other sources.'

'Right. Well, you have Clarke secrets, and we have Mowbray secrets. I trust you that if they ever crossed over, you'd tell me.'

'I would.'

'And so would I.'

'Could you answer me just one question, though. Does it have anything to do with Ethandun?'

It's a long story, but Eseld has inherited a ruined palace from her father. I'll fill you in about it if she answers yes…

'That money pit! You're joking. It's as magickal in its way as Pellacombe, so no, the Bloxhams have nothing to do with it.'

'Fair enough, Ez. My mind is boggling about what on earth you'll talk about with the Spotless Bloxhams, but there you go. How did Mina react when you offered your services as carriage driver and bodyguard?'

'She was grateful. And suspicious.'

I could tell from the sparkle in Eseld's eyes that Mina had good reason to be suspicious. 'What are you planning, Ez?'

'Me? Nothing. You know me, Conrad. I wouldn't do anything to spoil your wedding day.' She sucked on her tatty roll up. 'And besides, I need all the friends I can get. I wouldn't upset Chris, either.'

They are an unlikely couple, it's true. Vicky thinks that Chris Kelly is the most boring man in Salomon's House, an opinion which seems widely shared by staff and students alike. I don't think that. I think of him as a good friend, but then again, I don't have to consider his qualities as a potential soulmate.

'How's it going between you? That's you and Chris, not you and Mina. I know all about that.'

She was serious for a moment, the barriers down. 'Good, thanks. I think we're good for each other. I'm very happy, most of the time, and that hasn't happened for ages.'

'Then I'm pleased. For both of you. Will I see you tomorrow?'

'Oh yes. You need all the friends you can get, too.'

'Tell me about it. Come on, Ez. We're getting filthy looks from inside.'

Chapter 12 — Into the Warden's Den

'I suppose it's too much to hope that there won't be pictures,' said Mina. 'Not a chance, love. Not a chance. Just grin and bear it.'

She lifted her chin. 'I will do no such thing. I will *own it*, Conrad. Shall we go?'

'Give me your hand.'

We linked fingers, and I opened my Third Eye to get the full effect of the Baroque front door to Salomon's House. Because we were joined, Mina could see it, too. Not the magickal dimension of course, but to her, the previously blank wall was now an entrance to rival the one at Seville's cathedral.

'Goodness me. I didn't pay much attention last time, and it was dark. Those carvings wouldn't be out of place on an Indian temple.'

'As far as I know, there are no carvings of a sexual nature here.'

'Not *all* temples have X-rated carvings, Conrad. There's Vicky. And that coat.'

Vic slipped out of the massive doors and held up the padded jacket. To my bemusement, Chris followed her. I had an encounter with Chris booked for later, so what was he doing here now?

Mina passed me her bag and slipped on the coat. Vicky zipped it up and activated the Work, then stood back. Chris stepped forwards and offered Mina a scrunched up wadge of nylon fabric. 'This should do the trick,' he said. 'Works in fog, this does.'

'Thank you, Chris. Let's see, shall we?'

Mina untangled the fabric, and it turned into a runner's waterproof, bright red and sized to be short on Chris. On Mina, it reached her knees. Chris rolled up the sleeves for her and surprised me by also doing zip duty.

'Wow!' I said. 'You're not kidding, Chris. I could land the Smurf with that as a beacon.'

'Good,' said Mina. She glowed. Properly glowed, like a street lamp.

Vicky looked aghast. 'Where the hell is the Lux for *that* coming from? Not from her, surely?'

'Panic not,' said Chris. 'Right now, it's coming from the coat underneath, but it'll pick up the ambient inside. Better hurry, though.'

He put his hand on the door to bridge the threshold and ushered Mina inside. When I brought up the rear, the red light was so bright that you could see the carvings move on the panelling. There wouldn't just be pictures of today – I saw at least three Aspirants recording videos as we walked up the Junction staircase. Good job it was the Easter vacation.

Vicky and Chris had left us downstairs: they weren't invited to our first appointment, and we walked slowly up the staircases pinned to the sides of the hollow core of Salomon's House. I pointed out the few places I'd visited before – the King's Watch suite, the Esoteric Library and the corridor to Cora's office. I pointed to the top (Mina was starting to hug the wall as we got higher) and said, 'Warden's Parlour and the roof where they hold Inner Council meetings. We're going to the Warden's den itself. It's down half a level and through there.'

'Why is it like this?' she asked, her shoulder not leaving the plaster. 'Why have such a waste of space?'

'No one's saying,' I replied. 'If you ask me, it's a huge safety feature. There is so much Lux and so many Works in the basement that if there were an explosion, the energy would vent up here. Bad luck if a Council meeting were in progress, though.'

'Explosion! How is that possible?'

'Francesca told me that some idiot tried to precipitate nuclear fusion using magick in the early 1960s. Mind you, she'd had a few, so she might have been making it up. Roly Quinn put a stop to that sort of thing. Here we are.'

We turned through an arch into a well-lit, thickly carpeted corridor. It was well lit from above, and Mina got her first good look at the Skyways which make up for lack of windows in here. This one was a simple feed from the roof: a bright, spring day in London. 'Impressive,' she observed. I know that tone: she was making a mental note to see if she could use one herself. I didn't say that they cost millions to set up.

'Even more impressive,' she added when we came to a foyer with views over … the Yorkshire Dales? Ah yes, the new Warden hails from near Hebden Bridge. It was even brighter up there, apparently. Looked nippy, though, judging by the way that the grass rippled in the wind.

I was going to suggest we took a seat when a masculine voice said, 'Whoa! That's what I call an entrance.'

Proof that the mundane can frequent Salomon's House was here. Instead of a receptionist or the Warden's PA, we were greeted by her son.

'I think it's time this came off,' said Mina, lifting the running waterproof away from her neck. I could see sweat beginning to form at her hairline already. I hastened to help her out, unpeeling the Work of magick in the zip carefully.

Freed from the beacon, Mina made Namaste, then shook the lad's hand. 'Richard Reynolds,' he said. 'Glad to meet you properly, wing commander,' he added when it was my turn.

Our previous encounters had been at the Manchester hustings, and then the Election for Warden. He'd acted as his mother's campaign manager, and he'd been a tense, driven figure in the background. He was all smiles now.

'The Warden's PA had this week booked for holiday,' he said, looking behind him at the open door. A door that wasn't there when we came in. 'And the receptionist retired when Sir Roland died. The interviews for her replacement are soon, so I'm filling in for a few days. As best I can.' He cracked something close to a genuine smile. 'It's not easy when you can't open any of the doors from the outside except the Gents toilet. I can boil the kettle though. The Warden's ready. This way.'

The new Warden of Salomon's House, Dr Lois Reynolds, must have had her only child fairly young for a Mage. He was in his late twenties, and she was early fifties at most. We followed him through a deserted office and were shown a small door. He continued his theme. 'Which is why you're going through the tradesman's entrance, not the Grand Portal. My fault.'

'As is fitting,' I said. 'For me at any rate. I'm proud to be a tradesman, Richard.'

I left him with a puzzled expression and said, 'After you, love.'

'And I am not a *tradesman*,' said Mina in a stage whisper as she preceded me into the Warden's study. It was everything you'd expect from Albion's Premier Mage: wooden panelling higher than me, a vaulted roof and books.

Lots and lots of books on the opposite wall, books in piles on a long bench, mixed in with Alchemical paraphernalia. Cupboards so old they must pre-date the building seemed to lurk with intent in the shadows. I'd been hoping for a crocodile suspended from the ceiling, but the most outlandish item was a tailor's dummy in the corner, half draped with pinned together patches of white fabric covered in marker pen squiggles. Whatever.

The main doors were to our left and barely stood out from the panelling; the other side of that Portal must be hidden by the Yorkshire Skyway. A portrait of the Duke of Albion (looking rather accusing) hung opposite the doors, and in front of the picture was a Warden-sized desk. The Warden herself was already half way round to greet us.

Lois Reynolds had gone for the unrobed barrister look, with a fitted white blouse and black trousers. 'Welcome to the most masculine room I've ever seen,' she said after greetings were exchanged. 'I don't know whether Roly did it for effect or if he actually liked it. Talk about *inhabiting* your role.'

'I hope you're planning a makeover, Warden,' said Mina.

'Please call me Lois in here. And no, I'm not *planning* a makeover, I'm *dreaming* of one. I can't change a thing until Halloween.'

'Whyever not?' said Mina. 'Making you work in here is harassment at the very least.'

'Don't I know it.' She gestured towards the half-covered mannequin. 'Everyone calls me Warden, and I have the Warden's authority, but I'm not *actually* the Warden until Her Royal Highness pins the badge on my robe of office. Until then, I'm legally Chair of the Inner Council. That's all.'

'Is that a template for new robes?'

'It is. Well spotted, Mina. Every Mage bar Francesca thinks that the Warden's official robes are rainbow ones because that's what Roly wore. His robes are in storage, waiting to go on display, and I need to come up with something of my own. Please, sit down.'

A couch and easy chairs were clustered around a coffee table in front of an unlit fireplace in the corner. When we'd sat, the Warden said to Mina, 'What do you think of Salomon's House'

She smiled. 'Worth getting dressed up for.'

'I wasn't going to mention the coat.'

'Unless forced at gunpoint, I shall wait for the improved version before I come back.'

The Warden managed a brittle smile. She doesn't have a dour face, by any means, it's just that her default expression is *serious*. 'Noted, Mina. Aah, thank you Richard.'

Tea was poured, and I took the chance to speak. 'I really am very grateful for getting my job back. Thank you, Warden.'

When I'd been sacked as Deputy Constable, my reinstatement had only been possible because the new Warden took the risk of demanding it. In one stroke, her first political action in supporting me (and the Boss) had made her several enemies. Whether she's made any friends remains to be seen.

'It was the right thing to do, Conrad,' she responded. 'Thank you for coming to see me today. Both of you. I had a word with Hannah and Justice Bracewell before I invited you, of course.' Another smile flitted and vanished. 'Do you know what Hannah said? She said, "No skin off my nose. He'll listen, smile, say nothing then come and tell me everything."'

I nodded. 'Sounds like the Boss.'

'And Marcia?' said Mina with a grin.

The smile was both scared and more genuine this time. 'The Judge pointed her finger at me and said, "Don't even *think* of poaching her, Lois." Shame.'

'So why *are* we here?' said Mina, sipping her tea delicately. Credit Richard, it was a good cuppa.

'Because I want to put my cards on the table in private. Give you a chance to ask questions. I'd also planned to have Murray Pollard here to help explain things.'

We both stiffened. I raised my eyebrows to show that I wasn't going to respond to that. She got the message. Instead of expanding on her remark, she went back to her desk, stepping lightly in lace-up shoes. With her back to us, her long, naturally coloured hair swung gracefully in its Goddess braid and she looked twenty years younger. She waved some folders at us, and I recognised them straight away: Merlyn's Tower Special Issue. Most of them were stamped *Class I Restricted*. 'Mine?' I said.

'Who else's?' She replaced them and came to sit back down.

It is right and proper that the Warden should know what's in those files. It directly affects her role, and ignorance would not be bliss. I also know that there are other, unmarked files. They are kept in Hannah's safe and will only ever be read by the *next* Peculiar Constable. There was nothing in the

Warden's files that I wouldn't defend in the Court.

She put her hands on her knees and looked up. 'Murray Pollard and I agree on one important issue, and disagree on another. The disagreement is on the military nature of the King's Watch. As you've discovered, it doesn't sit well with him.' When I still didn't respond, she continued. 'Long term, I think he's right, but right now, I would not have anyone other than you as Deputy Constable. That's why I wanted you back in post. The King's Peace is safer with you around.'

Mina crossed her legs. 'Don't flatter him too much. It goes to his head.'

The Warden flicked her eyes to Mina, trying to work her out. *Good luck with that, Lois*, I nearly said out loud. What Mina actually meant was something closer to *Cut the crap*.

Lois pointed to the files. 'I've done my reading, and I'm sure you've done yours. I saw copies of my manifesto lying around the polling station, so you'll know about my views on jurisdiction.'

'We do,' I replied.

If you go to the Invisible College and train as a Chymist (old name for Alchemist), then you have to be registered there as long as you continue to practise magick. Even I do, although the fee is waived for serving Watch officers. If you're registered there, then your activities are subject to regulation by the Provost of Salomon's House, which is great in theory. In practice, Mr Parrish does not go round chasing down homicidal Chymists. Oh no, he leaves that to me.

If you're not a Chymist, then you're most likely a Witch or Warlock and trained in the Circles. This makes you directly subject to scrutiny by the King's Watch, and it explains why they call us Witchfinders.

Even though I'd just said that we understood her, she told us anyway. In the short version. 'Separation of powers is always good. Governance should be separate from education, and religion should be no barrier to membership of the Community of Mages.'

You could hear the capital *C* in *Community of Mages*. It doesn't exist yet, and the reason she mentioned religion is the old entry requirement for the Invisible College: you had to be a communicant member of the Church of England. That's no longer a barrier, but the Loyal Oath to the Queen is still required. Very few who have trained in the Circles are willing to take it. The Unions of the Lakeland Particular are, as usual, somewhere in the middle.

'Which brings us to your authority, Conrad.' She sat back a little and became even more of a politician. 'From where does it derive? From the Queen and the government? Or does it derive from a Nymph? And if it derives from a Nymph, is that any way to regulate magick in the twenty-first century?'

Without waiting for an answer (which I wasn't going to give, anyway), she leaned forwards again. 'You gave your blood on the Equinox, Conrad, and were no doubt offered the chance to give your seed as well. For what? For the power of arrest? For the power of Judgement over those who submit, and sometimes over those who do not? You carried out a death sentence on that rebel Princess, and you did it in Nimue's name. The Peace of Brothers Water is sealed in her name, too.'

They were all very good questions. And they were all well above my pay grade. I think she was expecting me to say that, and she was certainly surprised when Mina chipped in.

'Aah, now I see why you wanted Conrad to resume his authorised post as Deputy Constable, Lois. You didn't want him to continue as a rogue Lord Guardian, did you?' Mina smiled and pushed a bit further. 'You didn't want the issue forced while you're still getting fitted for your Warden's robes. You are playing the long game, are you not?'

The tight smile was back on the Warden's face. 'It's a shame I can't offer you a job, Mina. You are quite right, though. I hope to be Warden for many, many years. It was once considered outrageous that there might be a female Warden, but here I am. All three candidates were women this time. One day it will seem outrageous that we relied for justice on a Nymph who demands blood sacrifices.'

There was a discreet cough, and Richard said that we were due in the Examination Room. Lois grabbed her jacket and a briefcase and offered to escort us down.

'Thank you, Warden,' I said. 'And thank you for sharing your vision. I mean that. I would hate there to be a Warden who didn't value the Watch for what we do today, even if your vision for tomorrow is rather radical.'

On an impulse, we shook hands. I'm guessing that something similar had happened when she spoke to Hannah. I hadn't finished, though. 'You may well meet my father one day, Lois.'

'Oh yes? I'm sure it will be a pleasure.'

'I hope it will, so long as you don't get him on the subject of Her Majesty's Revenue and Customs. He once stood in our village pub and declared, "What are taxes if not a blood sacrifice that we have no choice but make?" If he didn't live in Spain and wasn't blind to magick, Hannah might hire him to run the campaign against you. Lead the way, please.'

Chapter 13 — A Chymical Examination

There was a lot to think about in the Warden's words, and no time to think about them because I had another appointment. On the way down the staircase, I decided that seeing the Warden first had been a good thing, because it had stopped me thinking about what was coming next.

'You know what,' I said to Mina when our little bubble of Silence had excluded Lois. 'For the first time since we met, your fingers are hotter than mine. Usually it's the rest of you that's hot. Very hot in my opinion.'

'Conrad! Shush! I'm sure there are CCTV cameras and lip-readers in here. This place is a living nightmare, and this coat is making me pine for Gujarat in the summer. If I bolt, it's not personal.'

I looked at her forehead. She looked very uncomfortable, but nowhere near heatstroke yet. I gave her fingers a gentle squeeze. 'Shouldn't be long. I hope.'

We passed the ground level door to the Receiving Room and continued down. The shadows became denser, the doorways darker and the sense of things lurking beyond your vision became even more acute. I was deeper than I'd ever been before.

We weren't quite at the bottom when the Warden led us through an arch and into a wide entry space with four doors off it. Waiting outside one of them was the Dean.

My ears had registered the end of the general Silence, and the Dean confirmed it by saying, 'Morning, Lois. I need a quick word with Conrad before he goes in.' She arched her eyebrows a little, and the Warden got the message.

'I'll take Mina inside and find her a seat,' she replied.

The Warden opened the door, which was marked *Senior Examination Room*, and led Mina inside. When it closed, the Dean embraced me, and when she did so, she made a new Silence all of our own. With her arms still around me, I said, 'How's it going, Cora?'

'Still tough. I have some big decisions to make soon, but unlike your friend Chris, I'm still married. For now.'

'You'll work it out, Cora.'

Cora once did something that she doesn't regret, but is rather ashamed of. If you see what I mean. If it became public, it would end her career at Salomon's House in a stroke: it has already made her pull out of the Warden election, and telling her husband (which she did last summer) might yet lead to the end of her marriage. I can't go into details, I'm afraid, because I gave her my word that I would tell no one but Mina.

With my arms still around her (because hers were still around me), she said, 'Mike wants something I don't think I can give him, and he thinks I'm denying him to save my career. I'm not.'

'How about if I came up with a radical solution?'

'Then you really would be superman.'

With a squeeze, we parted, and she became the Dean of the Invisible College again, and not a troubled woman with a terrible secret.

'I wanted to tell you about the supervising committee,' she said. 'Just to give you a heads up.'

'Thank you, but I'm sure it will be fine. It's not like you've chosen Heidi Marston, is it?'

'Aah. About that...'

'What! Et tu, Cora?'

She was holding her hands up to deflect my horror. 'Listen, Conrad, in your heart of hearts, do you truly want to be a Doctor of Chymic?'

She said it with a smile, and I couldn't help but smile back. 'I think you know the answer to that. I want to do right by Chris, and I don't want him embarrassed.'

'Neither do I. If Heidi *wasn't* on the panel, she'd snipe from the sidelines and cause trouble. If she *is* on the panel, then she has to operate knowing that if she does something wrong, you can appeal to me. Worst case scenario, she sets you an impossible thesis and you never complete it.'

Cora had a point. 'Fair enough. Let's get it over with.'

She led me through the door and into the Senior Examination Room. Not for nothing do the students call it *The Bear Pit*, and I was about to be the bear.

The large room was divided into four zones, and my zone was in the centre. One of the reasons for being in the basement was that we could have a stone floor, and into the flags, a dormant Circle of the Art had been Enscribed: practical demonstrations are often a feature in here.

In the centre of the circle was an antique stool, polished by the bottoms of many candidates. If you're into academic trivia, I can report that it had four legs, not three. Also inside the Circle of Art was a stiff-backed chair for my Sponsor, Chris Kelly. Both of us would be under the spotlight today.

The zone outside the Circle was divided in three, and my eyes immediately looked behind Chris to find my Supporters, and I got a pleasant surprise. In the front row was Mina, and she was coatless. However, she couldn't wave at me because Vicky and Georgina Gilpin were holding a hand each to suppress the Work in her scar. Had they planned this? I ask that because Mina was only wearing a vest top and her other tattoo, the swastika, was on display for everyone to see. Another second and I twigged: of course she'd planned it. *Whatever happens to you, I have exposed myself to scrutiny as well.* My heart surged, and we locked eyes. Cora was right. Nothing bad could really happen here.

Behind Mina sat the rest of my crew for today: Eseld, her brother Kenver, Francesca Somerton, Saffron, and Vicky's friend Desirée Haynes. They were all sending me enthusiastic good luck signals except Eseld. She was grinning like a Cheshire cat and going to enjoy herself immensely.

To their left were the Spectators, though *Observers* would be a better word for their role. The Warden and the Dean sat front and centre, and most of the Inner Council were arranged behind them. If it hadn't been Easter week, I think they'd all have been here for the baiting. I nodded to them and turned around. It was time to face the Panel.

The Mages in charge of my fate had a table to sit behind, a table adorned with a cloth showing the golden sunbursts and blue background of Salomon's House. Very official, unlike the Custodian of the Great Work. I think Heidi must have wandered up from her workshop (which is in the deepest recesses of the basement), because she was still wearing a singed, stained brown smock. At the moment I turned to face them, she was trying to pick bits out of it. The way they glinted, I'd swear she'd splashed molten gold on herself. After a successful peel, she dropped them in her empty water glass.

To her left and right were the other members of the Panel, and the one on Heidi's right winked at me. Oighrig Ahearn is the Oracle, chief of Sorcery and the most junior member of the Inner Council. For now. Her great mane of red hair was tamed with a blue scarf and her Glamour was firmly in place: no sign of her whole-body coating of freckles today. The third member was an even bigger surprise – I know so little about the Steward of the Great Work that I couldn't remember his name at first. Andrew Ormerod. That's it.

Chris coughed and said, 'Custodian, may I present the Candidate, Mister Conrad Clarke, admitted as a Master of the Art.' No rank, titles or honours today. Until I left the Bear Pit, I was a Chymist, with the lowest level of qualification.

Master of the Art may sound grand, but it's the magickal equivalent of a badge for twenty-five metres of breast stroke. And now it was time to swim the Channel. Wish me luck.

Heidi Marston looked up and looked at me. She didn't look happy. 'Welcome Mister Clarke. Normally, you'd have to stand, but given your bad leg, I'm sure you no one will mind if you sit. Please.'

I sat. 'Thank you.'

'On another day, I'd also tear you off a strip for making us twiddle our thumbs, but you've got a good excuse.' She looked over my shoulder. 'Perhaps someone could tell the Warden that we work on London time here, not Yorkshire time.'

Andrew Ormerod looked down. Oighrig looked at me with raised eyebrows. Clearly Heidi Marston had not forgiven Lois for snatching the election away from her. Not that Heidi would have won anyway. She picked up a sheaf of papers and waved them in Chris's direction.

'Shall we begin with this farrago of nonsense? Are you seriously suggesting that this qualifies the Candidate for Part I?'

There are two sorts of ChD in the Invisible College. One sort is all thesis, the other is part thesis and part certification. I'm going for the second kind, and Heidi was holding the signed, completed forms which certified my abilities as a Geomancer. Or so Chris said – I just did what he told me and wrote it up. In fact, I was the first ChD candidate in Geomancy since Chris himself, and he'd had to write them specially for me. You can see why I didn't want to disappoint him.

Chris is a quiet man. Most of the time. He blinked at Heidi and said, 'Are you questioning my certification, Custodian?'

Heidi slapped the papers on the table and fanned them out. 'I am questioning whether …' She stabbed her finger on one of the pages. 'Whether *Accessing Ground Lux on a Higher Plane* meets the Doctoral standard.'

Chris turned to the Steward. 'Andrew, have you got the Academic Board minutes where this was discussed?'

'I have.'

'Do you remember what I asked you to put in the minutes?'

'I do. I also remember refusing your request.'

Heidi turned to Ormerod. 'What is Kelly wittering on about now?'

Ormerod pointed to Chris, and Chris said, 'I asked him to minute that the Custodian had *snored loudly* during discussion of my proposed criteria. For some reason he refused.'

A low rumble started in Heidi's chest, somewhere between an angry bull and a hungry lion. It gathered steam, then burst out of her mouth in a gale of laughter. Ormerod blinked once, and Oighrig chewed her knuckle.

'Is *that* what I slept through?' said Heidi. 'No wonder I fell asleep. And it had been a heavy night.' She sat back, and Oighrig flinched. I think Heidi's chair must have groaned alarmingly. I am going to get my hearing checked, you know. I promise. After the wedding.

'In that case, we're bang to rights, aren't we?' She looked from side to side. 'I take it we *don't* question the Certification.' A twin shake of the head. 'Then let it be recorded that the Candidate has achieved Part I of the degree. Now on to the fun bit. What are you proposing for the thesis, Earthmaster?'

Ormerod had already lifted a piece of paper, and Oighrig followed him with one of her own. Chris pointed at them and said, 'In the bundle, Custodian.'

Heidi peered over Oighrig's shoulder and read the proposal. When she'd got to the end, she stabbed her meaty finger at it, forcing Oighrig to lean right over to avoid a close encounter. 'Load of tosh,' said Heidi. 'Not only do we not care about Dwarven/Gnomish Ley line interfacing, I also believe you've written a paper on the subject, Earthmaster.'

It was Chris's turn to be *bang to rights*. 'Errr…'

'Thought so.' Heidi leaned back again. 'I'm late for my next appointment. I propose this: That the candidate finds out who's stealing Lux from the Nether

Orchards. Not only is it useful, it's also been beyond my skills, so that puts it over the Doctoral threshold. What do we think?'

Ormerod frowned. 'I can't speak for the Oracle, but I think that the Nether Orchards are your private property, Custodian, and that the Invisible College should not be asking Candidates to do your dirty work.'

'So? He'll be rewarded with a Doctorate if he's successful. I'm open to alternative suggestions.' She turned right. 'What do you think?'

Oighrig was trying not to corpse. 'I think we should ask the poor sap what *he* thinks of it.'

Heidi turned to me. 'Fair enough. What do you reckon, Conrad? Sorry. *Mister Clarke?*'

'Where and what are the Nether Orchards, Custodian?'

'They're an old Fae wood above Brompton Cemetery.'

I forced myself not to look at Chris. If this was an impossible task, I didn't want to know. I didn't care. What I did care about was being set up. 'I have one observation, ma'am. If there really is theft, and criminal theft, then I reserve the right to call for help and for the task to be voided. You can set me another.'

Heidi clearly hadn't thought of that, and raised her eyebrows, checking with the others. They nodded in agreement. 'That's fair enough. I thought you were going to ask for a percentage, Conrad. Done. Just to tick the box for Andrew here, I must advise you that the dissertation must be submitted no more than three years from now.' She gave me an evil grin. 'It may be submitted posthumously, so long as your Spirit is available for a viva afterwards.'

Andrew Ormerod didn't look up from what he was writing and spoke in a matter of fact way. 'Let's hope he's still alive, shall we? I for one do *not* want to conduct a viva examination in Valhalla.'

Heidi went ever so slightly pale at that point and gave a tiny shudder. She pointed to her daughter and said, 'I'm sure GG will be happy to show you round the Nether Orchards if you want to get started. She used to play there as a little girl. In the cemetery, mostly.'

I distinctly heard a hiss from behind me, and equally distinctly I heard Eseld say, 'Don't. She's not worth it, George, and you can *not* let go of Mina now.'

Heidi stood up and pushed the whole mound of documents to Ormerod. 'You sort out the paperwork, Andrew, and send it to me for signature.' She looked up. 'And good luck, Conrad.'

She picked up her water glass with gold flecks and left the Bear Pit with her mind already focusing on something more important. Lunch, probably. I stood up and turned round to see what the rest of the room thought of all this.

I had to wait a second and shake out my leg before I could go over to Mina, which meant that there was a quite a crowd by the time I got there. With Mina being hand-in-hand with her magickal carers, everyone made a big ring, and it wouldn't have been out of place with today's events for everyone to join hands and start a dance.

The Warden was near Francesca, and I heard her say, 'How did Roly cope with her? Heidi, I mean.'

Francesca snorted. 'The same way we all did: let her get on with it.'

Chris clapped me on the shoulder. 'Sorry about that, mate. I had no idea she'd come up with summat like that. Don't worry, though. I have every confidence that you'll find out what's going on.'

'If there is anything going on,' I said. 'It could just be a windup.'

'Oh no, Conrad, there's something there alright, and I'll tell you this. If you can't find it, I'll go up there and look meself, and if I can't find it, I'll come back here and hold her arse so close to the fire, you'll be able to carve chunks off it.'

'Thank you for sharing that image, Chris,' said the Warden. 'I shall pray that it doesn't follow me into my dreams. I also take it that you consider the test a fair one.'

'Harder than the one I set, but fair it is.'

'Then good luck, Conrad. If you'll excuse me.'

She left us, and I went to kiss Mina.

'It's not half brave of you to show your mark like this,' said Oighrig from behind me. 'I wouldn't have the balls to do that in here.'

'Hmph,' said Mina.

'About that,' said Georgina. 'Sorry, Conrad, but there was a failure in the Work. The coat malfunctioned when Mina crossed the Circle. I should have thought of it.'

'Yes, you should,' said Selena Bannister. 'It's a good job Heidi didn't know you were responsible for the failure, or you really would have copped it from her. In public.' From her tone, you'd think that Selena was Georgina's aunt or something.

Selena looked at the three of them holding hands and shook her head. 'When we leave, I shall weave a Glamour for you, Mina. So long as I'm with you, no one will see through it.'

Chris was not to be deflected from his purpose. 'When are you thinking of going to the Orchards, Conrad?'

Mina answered for me. 'There is another sitting of the Court in June. We can both be in London together. If the Constable gives him study leave.'

'I've told you, it's in the contract,' said Vicky. 'Hannah won't mind.'

'Then let's see, shall we? We don't want to be late twice in one day, so if you could sort me out, Selena…?'

As soon as we arrived at Merlyn's Tower, Hannah ordered me up to the roof with her, leaving Mina to make polite conversation with Tennille while they unwrapped the lunch. I went out of the hatch first and held out my hand to give the Boss a pull. When she was through, she didn't let go. Instead, her grip got stronger. 'Take me round the chimney,' she snapped.

She stared at her feet until she was able to sit on the roof with her back to the chimney stack. No wonder I'd never heard of her coming up here before. I was about to take a look at the view when she almost shouted. 'No you don't! You sit there. Right there.'

'Yes, ma'am.'

When I was sitting down, and when her brain had convinced itself that we weren't on a high tower with a long drop to the river, she breathed out heavily. 'Call me superstitious, but we can't talk about Nimue inside. I can't help thinking she can hear it when her name's mentioned.'

'I'd call it a wise precaution, not superstition.'

'I don't want to be here for one second longer than I have to. What do you think of Doctor Loose's mad scheme, then?'

'I don't actually think it's a bad idea in itself. Her basic point about humans running their own affairs is a good one. We've both seen how badly Nimue was affected by the Quicksilver poisoning. Who's to say it won't happen again?'

'As it happens, I agree. Our Nymph hasn't done too badly, though, has she? And she refused to wash her hands of you after your little trip to Ireland. Unlike the Oversight committee. That's what worries me, Conrad. The King's Watch is supposed to be above politics.'

I've been thinking more and more about our heritage here. Now that I'm part of the management, a little reflection can be a good thing. 'Nimue didn't stop the early Watch Captains from persecuting Witches and mundane women, did she?' I observed.

Hannah frowned. 'I know that, too. I've heard it said that she put the brakes on, though. Without her, it might have been worse.' She sighed. 'Only the Lord is perfect, and he's not offering to sponsor the King's Watch.'

I held out my hand to help her up. 'At least the Warden doesn't want to pull down the old temple before the new one's ready. I like that about her.'

Hannah brushed muck off the back of her skirt. 'There is that, there is that. Right. There's a lot else to discuss, once you've told me how you got on in the Bear Pit.'

'Do I have to?'

'Oh yes. I've already heard about the coat debacle. One of the reasons I left Mina downstairs was so that Tennille could share the videos with her. She's much better at that sort of thing.'

'Ouch.'

'At least that won't be a problem tomorrow.'

I handed her through the hatch before I replied. 'I thought Newton's House had as much magick as the Invisible College.'

'It doesn't, but that's not the issue. I tried, but they won't give her a Stranger's ticket. You'll have to make do with me.'

Chapter 14 — Fool's Council

Only a truly hardened bureaucrat would schedule a meeting of the essentially bizarre Occult Council for the morning of April Fool's Day. Guess what? They have hardened bureaucrats to spare.

My previous encounter with the Looking Glass world of the Occult Council had been via video link from Barrow in Furness, and today I got to meet them in person. Sort of. I'll come back to that.

The Invisible College doesn't just offer degrees in Alchemy (like the one I'm supposed to be working towards), they also offer doctorates in the Philosophy of Magickal Governance, because the laws and politics of magick are more complex than the Art itself. One of the few people I know who has one is Cador Mowbray, and he has a brain the size of a planet.

Also, the word *Council* implies a sort of democracy, and I suppose it is, in an eighteenth century kind of way. If I had *my* way, it would be renamed the Occult Commission, because that's what it is: it supervises the wider world of magick and does its best to keep it in check.

I know some of the members now, and three of them were waiting for us when the Boss escorted me into a small room in the bowels of the Invisible College's other building – Newton's House in Whitehall, just north of the Houses of Parliament. Hannah went to talk to the Warden, and the other two were keen to talk to me. The first to stride over with a smile was the great Henry Octavius of the Gnomish Clan Octavius.

He shook my hand, and we caught up on some Gnomish gossip. When he saw that Síona was hovering, he shook hands again and said, 'You've come a long way since we first met, Lord Dragonslayer. You're the first human brother in blood to a Clan Chief that I can remember.' He smiled. 'Even if it is only Clan Condiment.'

It's actually the Salt Clan – *Clan Salz* – but Gnomes do like their little jokes. Little being the operative word. 'I've always found the world tastes better with seasoning,' I replied.

He chuckled and left me with Síona, 1st of Hawthorn in the Daughters of the Goddess. The triple Coven of the Daughters is located in Glastonbury, of course, but they have daughter covens all over Albion, and the most senior Witch outside the Homewood is Síona. 'Is it true about Cordelia?' she said as soon as Henry was out of earshot.

'That she betrayed me? That she abandoned me in a Fae realm with a host of rebel Fae, then yes it is, I'm afraid.'

That wasn't what she meant, and I knew it. She inclined her head. 'Of course. I can't believe it. I can't believe that she'd abandon her children, either. She's really gone without trace?'

'I think the *abandoning* part had already happened, Síona. I don't know what she was up to. Not really. She *has* gone, though. Rick James has been in touch regularly with updates. Or lack of them. No signs or activity from her whatsoever. Not that I expect any for a long time.'

She sighed. 'Such a shame. Such a waste. And I shall make sure the Daughters know all the facts.'

'Thank you. I believe that Kiwa is set to become the Eldest Daughter?'

'She is. She became 1st of Oak at Imbolc and will take over as Eldest at Beltane. The day before your wedding, I believe?'

'So it is. I wish her well.'

'And you, too, Conrad. And Mina. May the Goddess bless your union. You two are well suited, I think.'

'Thank you.' I was about to ask what she thought of the new Warden (who had disappeared), when Hannah waved at us and said, 'I think we're wanted, Síona. Well, you are.'

I didn't add that the Great Goddess would have to join the queue when it came to blessing my wedding. An invitation to the Allfather has already gone out, Enscribed with special charcoal by Erin Slater. I watched her write it, and I watched it burst into flames. As we were in a room full of flammable materials, Erin had gone into a panic and hadn't noticed that every molecule of the paper had burnt. Not a cinder remained.

I said I'd come back to the *in person* part of the Council. Well, this was the public reception room, complete with a Salomon's House carpet, and there is a private reception room on the other side of the Council Chamber. Henry and Síona had made a choice to come and see me, which is reassuring. The other members of the Council had chosen not to. Or not today, at least.

Everyone but me disappeared through a door round the side, and I heard it click shut. Must have been a very loud click. As briefed by Hannah, I turned to look at the floor to ceiling mirror that was fixed to the dividing wall between here and the Council Chamber. I also poured myself another cup of coffee. This could take a while.

The members of the Council are not anonymous as such, but they are all listed by title not name. I recognised the voice of the President as he brought the Council to order and began the meeting. You can listen, but you can't look.

He moved through the first couple of items (of no interest) at a fair pace and then introduced *A Report from the Deputy Constable*. That would be me. I straightened my uniform, moved to a respectful distance from the mirror and stood at ease.

The mirror swirled and the Council Chamber came into view. Most of Newton's House is classically Palladian in style, but the Chamber was done out by the Victorians: confident and powerful. And empty, apart from one person sitting at the far end of a large table. At least it *looked* empty: the rest of the seats were filled, but Council rules say that the other members remain invisible. The only one I could see was a grey suited man, and I have no idea of his name, but he didn't buy that suit on a Civil Service salary.

'Welcome, Wing Commander,' he began. 'Thank you for attending in person.'

'Sir.'

He looked at the magickally empty chairs. 'We've all had the Deputy's report. Does anyone have any questions before we accept it?'

They did. A lot of questions. Before they started, I heard the Boss speak up. 'Can my Deputy sit down before we begin? We don't want him keeling over when his bad leg plays up, do we?'

They did not want that. I took a chair and began fielding questions. If you've read the accounts of my adventures, there's nothing you don't know, so I'll skip over them. As well as the people I've mentioned, I recognised several other voices. Cora, Heidi and Michael Oldcastle from Salomon's House. Lady Hawkins, Saffron's mother. One voice I remembered from last time also spoke: it was pure, musical and intimate. I heard someone call her *your grace*, and I knew it to be a Fae Queen. Probably Highgate. She's the most powerful in London.

Cross-examination complete, they accepted my report and moved on to an item I'd actually asked for. I stood up for that one.

'The Deputy Constable would like us to vary the orders regarding Seclusion,' said the President. 'Would you care to explain?'

'Thank you, sir. As the Council knows, when a Mage is sentenced to Seclusion by the Cloister Court, they may not leave for any reason until their sentence is complete. I'm sure the Council also knows that I am hosting such a Mage in my own home.'

'We do know that.'

'The Council may not know that she is six and a half months pregnant with twins. I have arranged for a midwife to attend her, and everything is going well. She plans to have the birth at Elvenham Grange. But what if there is an emergency, sir? At the moment, there would be severe magickal consequences for her. That cannot be right. It has not been an issue for generations, but I cannot believe that the Council is happy with this.'

'Well, I'm not,' said the Warden, making sure her voice was heard before the President could say anything.

'Quite,' he said, and I'll give him full credit for what he said next. 'Is *anyone* happy with this?'

It was a good move: force people to speak up if they wanted to stand in the way of change. No one supported the status quo, and plenty made it clear that they were against.

'Good,' he concluded. 'We'll need to draft something that satisfies the lawyers, of course, but I move that we resolve to change the law with effect from today. The actual change can then be backdated.'

'And I second it.'

The resolution was passed unanimously, and they moved on. I felt a prickle on my neck. It wasn't magick as such, and I didn't look round. What I did have was the distant echo of laughter, as if Fate was laughing at me. They'd all played nicely with the first two items because the third one was a total minefield. For me.

'We now come to the Commission on Dual Natured residents,' announced the President.

You may recall that *Dual Natured* is the official name given to creatures who have two bodies and shift between them. I've had a very close encounter with Pramiti, the snake woman from India, but today is effectively about Mannwolves, because they are the most common species in Britain, and they are all watched over by Protectors. As far as I know, *all* the Protectors are Fae except me. The other Dual Natured creatures who are rumoured to exist are pretty solitary and keep a low profile.

The Occult Council has spent three hundred years ignoring this problem, and by taking a Pack under my protection, I'd forced their hand. As far as the Council were concerned, there needed to be some sort of regulation. Hopefully. There were still voices around who want every single Mannwolf sterilised.

In short, the Council are not happy, and they want me to get my arse in gear and actually start holding the meetings – it's been on my to-do list for a long time. Hannah pointed out to them that I've been rather busy, and it was Heidi who responded.

'Things are supposed to get quieter now, aren't they?'

I groaned. Out loud.

'What?' said the President. 'Did you say something, Wing Commander?'

In for a penny…

'Sorry, sir, it's just that no one in the front-line services likes to hear the *Q* word. My fiancée would say that it's *bad karma*.'

'Noted. Can you just make this commission a higher priority? The longer this issue goes unresolved, and the longer it looks like we're not doing anything, the more difficult it will be to keep the initiative.'

'Yes sir.' I left a slight pause, then asked mildly, 'Is all the litigation complete? I believe that there was an issue with Scotland. There often is.'

The President gave me a hard stare through the glass. 'You're not going to use that as an excuse to delay things *again* are you?'

'I'm sure the Council wouldn't want me to start something that had to be changed midway through. I know the Constable wouldn't want that.'

I didn't know that for certain, but I know the Boss. She would be most unhappy if I wasted *any* time on this.

The President bent to listen to the empty chair on his left, presumably some sort of Clerk or Secretary, then he announced, 'I believe the Scottish Grand Committee have it on their agenda for next month. Time for a break, I think.'

I knew it was time for a break because I'd been thoroughly distracted a few minutes ago when two women came in to change over the refreshments. The break would also be my cue to leave, once I'd sampled the coffee.

Only Hannah and the Warden came to the public room this time, and Hannah headed straight for the toilets. Lois let me pour her a coffee and asked how I felt about the Commission.

'So long as it allows my Pack – and other packs – to enjoy the same right to Peace as everyone else, then I don't mind if they get inspected and I have to pay taxes on them.'

She stirred her coffee absently. 'You make strong chains, don't you Conrad?'

What under the earth was she on about? 'Sorry, Lois? I'm not with you.'

'You forge unbreakable links, and I don't just mean you and Mina. There's you and the Constable. You and Lloyd Flint. You and your Pack. You and a Fae Princess, if rumours are true. And that's not all of them by any means.'

'Cordelia's link broke,' I responded. 'Fairly spectacularly.'

'So it did. But not the others.' She smiled. 'And the strongest is Mina, of course. How are the wedding plans coming along? I didn't want to ask when you came to visit yesterday because she looked so uncomfortable in that coat, and I didn't want to make things worse.'

'It won't be long,' I said. 'We're going to a Naming Ceremony tomorrow, then the Hen party starts next Thursday.'

'It's going to be epic, is it?'

'I have no idea. I'm sure it will be, though. Vicky Robson is in charge, so...'

'They do like to party in Newcastle. I should know. And your stag do?'

'Dos, plural. I have to be ready for a surprise. My best man told me to pack my passport and my dinner suit. Mind you, I did get that message this morning, so knowing Ben it could be an April Fool.'

She looked almost human when she laughed. Oh, hang on. She *is* human. I keep forgetting.

'And the groomsmen have insisted on another outing the afternoon before the wedding itself,' I added.

She raised her eyebrows. 'Risky.'

'Tell me about it,' I said with feeling. 'And there's the fact that the whole weekend is also Beltane / Walpurgisnacht. It could get *very* interesting.'

'It could! Do you have plans to be in London before the big day?'

'Not at the moment.'

'Then I wish you all the very best, Conrad. Both of you.'

'Thank you, Lois.'

I shook out my leg, went over and wished a Good Shabbos Eve to the Boss then headed out into a day that bore more than a passing relationship to Spring. I'd go further and say that it positively put a spring in my step. Half of my steps, anyway. The other half tried their best.

Chapter 15 — A Change of Plan

Michael did his time in the gardens, and more.

On the Tuesday of the second week, Kathy overheard Doctor Simon and Faye having an argument. Faye said that the morning counsellors and therapists were complaining that breakfast was taking too long, and could Michael go back in the kitchen, please love?

Doctor Simon said that it was doing Michael good, and it would give some of the newer guests something to do if they helped in the kitchen for a change.

Kathy decided to interrupt them and coughed loudly. 'No,' she said, 'Not having that shower in my kitchen while Michael's still here', and she walked outside for a fag. Michael was back with her on Wednesday morning.

On Thursday, he stayed behind to help do a deep clean ahead of the Abbey's Weekend (which of course started on Friday). Kathy checked that he wasn't missing Group Therapy or something, then after tossing the cloths into the washing machine, they sat down for a brew. She looked at his skin: the deep tan had returned quickly after the outside work, even with the weak sunshine of April. In fact, it hadn't faded much since his arrival. Maybe he did have Spanish blood or something.

'Are you due any visitors soon,' she asked. He'd been here long enough for that to be a legitimate question.

He shook his head. 'It's too far for the people I'd really like to come. I love Beckthorpe, but it is a long way from civilisation.'

'Careful. There's a few Yorkshire folk here who'd lynch you for saying that. I wouldn't join in, but I wouldn't get in their way, neither.'

'Point taken.' He grinned at her over his mug. 'Have I been here long enough for you to tell me about Long Lenny yet? You've hinted enough times.'

Kathy crossed her legs, put down her tea and stretched her arms. There was nothing else to do, was there? 'You know I don't like talking about past guests. They're entitled to their privacy, same as you? You wouldn't want me tattling about Michael who can't chop onions, would you?'

'I'm an open book, Kathy.'

He was telling the truth. Sort of. Michael had never boasted about stuff;

the spooks rarely did, but they did let you see what was left of their lives now that they were no longer secret squirrels: kids, hobbies, plans. With Michael, all she'd got, despite spending hours together, was a picture of a boring flat in London and the fact that Michael used to go to watch Fulham Football Club with his dad. That was it. Everything else was related to cooking or to Kathy; it had been a long time since a guest asked her questions and actually listened without having an ulterior (usually sexual) motive. Quite flattering, really.

Lately, Michael had taken to asking about previous residents whenever Kathy mentioned them. He'd show an interest, and occasionally asked more than Kathy was willing to share. He always backed off then and respected her, which was another thing she liked about him, but Long Lenny was different. Long Lenny was a legend.

'I can't really do him justice,' she began. 'He was Scottish, for one thing, and some of the things he said just don't come out right in Yorkshire.'

'I'll do my best to imagine.'

'Well, he were addicted to speed, not coke, for another, which is unusual. And he were an actor. Not that I ever saw him on telly. Claimed he was on stage a lot, but I've never been to the theatre since Mum took me to the panto.'

'He was a good laugh?'

'He used to come into dinner and stand over the table. He'd take a big sniff and say things like, "Are we about to dine on the food of the gods or has my nose been destroyed completely?" Then he'd pick on someone and say, "David, I am in love with you and want to spend the next hour gazing into your eyes. Either that or move your sorry arse out of the way."'

'Sounds like a bit of a drama queen.'

'You have no idea. He was never boring, though, not like some of them. He'd never say the same thing twice, and he really did know drama. I were in Group with him once.'

'Group therapy?'

'Aye. It were a new kid in charge. Young girl from York. Well, she had a degree and stuff, so not so young, but you know what I mean.'

'Not old has-beens like you and me.'

'Speak for yourself. Anyway, she wants to do some drama therapy. Have you had any?'

He shook his head, 'Not yet. Go on.'

Kathy paused for a second, because she was sure that Michael had been in Group with Faye last week, and Faye does a mean role-play of *my worst boss*. Whatever. 'Right. Long Lenny, we called him that because he was so tall, well Long Lenny volunteers to play the fixed point. Erm,'

'Where the same character interacts with everyone. Got it.'

Which Michael would only know if he'd done Faye's role play. Maybe it hadn't gone well.

'The fixed point in this was *My Dealer* where everyone had to describe who they got their stuff from and he'd play the part. He was amazing, 'cos they're not all men in hoodies, are they? Or undercover cops pretending to be men in hoodies.'

'No they're not,' said Michael with a flinch and a smile.

'So, this bloke says, "My dealer was my doctor," and Lenny says, "Where from?" "Mangalore, India," and Lenny does this amazing impression of an Indian doctor. "Graham, are you still in pain?" he asks, while at the same time writing out a prescription. "Next!" and that was it. He gave Faye the perfect chance to put Graham on the spot about dependency.'

'And what about you?' said Michael, the empathy in his voice inviting her to open up a little.

'He just sat at the table and pretended to scan me shopping. Didn't even make eye contact. How that man *knew* that's what happened when I bought booze at the supermarket, I have no idea.'

'And was it easy for Faye to get him to be himself with all this role play?'

'She didn't get the chance. Lenny left after four weeks, and don't ask me why because I have no idea. Place was like a funeral after that, like all the life had gone out of the Abbey. Until the weekend, then someone new came in. There's none but me left now who actually remember him.'

'Sounds like an awesome guy. Anyway, have social services been in touch about another visit to your children? You said it wasn't your girls who you went to see last weekend.'

Ouch. She should have expected that. She'd asked him about visitors, so it was only natural he'd ask her back. She breathed out. 'Yeah. I was gonna tell you: I'm going on Saturday. Trains are running this time.'

'Brilliant. I'm thrilled for you.' He ran his finger round the top of his mug. 'You'll tell me to sod off if it's none of my business, Kathy, but what is the endgame for you?'

'What game?'

'What do you want at the end?'

'To get me kids back, of course. They're only on a temporary order, but if I can show I've cleaned me act up, they've promised I'll get them back.'

They hadn't promised, but she'd been to see her solicitor last weekend, and the solicitor had said that a full court hearing would definitely give Kathy custody, if Kathy could afford a barrister…

Kathy had taken out her credit card and waved it under the solicitor's nose. Deal done, she went back to Chapel Allerton and cashed in another sovereign. Mind you, she couldn't go there again: they'd remembered her this time, and three times would mark her card.

Michael nodded, weighing up her determination. 'So you're absolutely dependent on a good reference from Simon, Faye and Mora?'

'Yeah.'

He sighed. 'Then you need to be more careful about Don.'

The mug stopped half way to her mouth. 'What are you on about?'

'Last week, you brought your big bag in, and you were in such a rush that you just plonked it on the side. Five minutes later, it fell off and all the stuff came out. I went to pick it up, because you'd gone outside. I couldn't help notice the flipchart paper. It had unfolded itself.'

'So?'

'So, I thought why is she taking an alphabet wheel to look after a non-verbal man? Later on, after dark, I went and spied from the gardens. Those binoculars they have in the hobby room are as good for spying as they are for bird watching.' He shrugged. 'Sorry. I saw you spelling things out with him, and he's quite sharp, isn't he?'

She was bang to rights. For the first time since the corner shop had caught her stealing, she was bang to rights and couldn't deny it. Naturally, she'd denied it to the shop owner, because back then she couldn't admit to *anything*, but she was different now.

'What are you going to do, Michael?'

'I don't want to – what's the phrase? I don't want to *dob you in it* with the Fragrant Faye, but I do have two questions. First, who else knows, and second, how long has he been like this?'

This time, she was prepared to lie. She'd even worked out a cover story, because she wasn't going to be talking about weird silver lights and silver wire holding Don's mouth shut.

'No one knows. I think it's happened slowly. You know, people do recover from strokes. Maybe it's been Faye's Tai Chi. He's surprisingly good at it. I think it's down to the turnover in carers, and them simply not looking, or not realising. You know, so long as you can understand when he needs the loo, why bother going any further? Maybe Mingey Mora changed his medication, you know what she's like: you don't get stuff unless you're dying.'

He nodded, accepting what she said. 'And the alphabet chart?'

'I left my pen next to him one day, and he picked it up. Don't forget, my shifts are an extra. It's not my job, so I don't have blinkers on. I just messed around with him for a bit, then I got the flipchart paper.' She shrugged. 'It doesn't make much difference. And he said he's happy enough.'

'But there's more to it, isn't there?' He didn't wait for an answer. 'My second question is this: what in God's name are you doing with that thermometer thingy? I saw you showing him, and I saw you taking it away again. You must have bought it for him, and he must have had a reason. That's why you're not telling anyone: he's got access to money.'

She blushed again. 'It's not like that! I haven't stolen anything! I'm just looking after it, and it was him who gave it to *me*. I've even got receipts for most of it.'

'I believe you. I really do. I know you wouldn't steal from him. But all that

112

means is that you're up to something *together*. What is it?'

'And if you believe this, you won't tell Faye?'

'Depends on what you're up to.' He said it with a smile, but she knew she had to answer. So far, Michael hadn't given a single indication of not being trustworthy. It was tell him or risk him going up to Don asking the question himself, now that he knew Don could give him an answer.

'Alright then, it's like this. Don has family. He's been here thirty-five years, you know, and one of his family put him here out of the way. Beckthorpe is a very civilised place, thank you very much, but you're right, it is a bit far from anywhere.'

Michael looked mystified. Not unbelieving, just mystified. 'Why?'

'Dunno, and he won't say. What he has said is that he wants to get in touch with some of the other family members. The ones who didn't put him in here. He used to be an electrical engineer and inventor. He says that he can build a special bio-communicator. I've seen him do stuff, Michael, and I believe him, but it won't happen because there's no way I'll be able to get hold of some of it.'

She didn't specify *what* stuff. No way. Not to Michael. Nor had she got round to telling Don that the spinal cord of pigs has been routinely removed at the slaughterhouse for decades. Mad Cow Disease and all that.

'And what about the thermometer?' asked Michael.

'He wants the mercury from it. Acts as an adjustable trans-thingy for his whatsit.'

Michael was already shaking his head. 'No, Kathy. I won't let you. Do you realise just how *toxic* that stuff is?'

'I'll be careful!'

'No! It's beyond dangerous, it's *deadly*. And disabling. Do you want your girls to lose their mother twice?'

She jerked back. 'Leave them out of it.'

'Fine. I'll do it for you, then.'

'What?'

'If you don't hand that thing over to me, I'll tell Faye and Simon.'

She could see he meant it, and she would be Googling mercury poisoning as soon as he left her in peace.

'What about Don? It'll break his heart.'

'I'll tell him. He needs to know that I know anyway.' He stood up. 'We'll write his family a letter instead of trying to make some crackpot ham radio.'

It was a good job Michael was looking away, because Kathy flinched visibly at the words *ham radio*. Lucky guess? Did it mean something else? He went to get the teapot, and she Googled *Ham Radio* with lightning speed. Good job she could spell both words. *Amateur radio, also known as ham radio...* She breathed a sigh of relief. Coincidence, then.

When he came back with the teapot, she said, 'Don't you think I've tried that, Mister Clever Clogs? It was the first thing I said. He said no. Said it were too dangerous. Said that the ones who put him away might still be alive, and if they intercept the letter, I'd be in deep shit. Only he didn't say *deep shit*.'

'We'll find a way. Technology has evolved exponentially since Don was messing with radios, not that I doubt his skills. If you let me use your phone…?'

Guests were strictly barred from having mobile phones. After a couple of incidents, they were routinely scanned after visits, and any parcels had to be opened in front of a member of staff. They were allowed to use one special computer, and that only gave them access to a special email address – @standabbey.co.uk, and Dr Simon had access to all your emails, if he wanted to. And he often did.

Early in her time as a *resident* rather than a *guest*, Kathy had been forced to choose. She hated the idea of telling on people, but Dr Simon was right: *all* staff had to buy in to the Abbey's process. Kathy had no hesitation in reporting people if she thought they were trying to smuggle drugs or alcohol, but phones…

She compromised by leaving anonymous notes on Faye's desk when she knew someone had smuggled in a phone. Faye knew who the notes were from, but Kathy could live with herself if her name wasn't at the bottom. She shook her head and smiled at Michael. 'Sorry. If I can't give Don his thermometer, you can't have my phone.'

'I understand.' He sat back and drank some tea. 'What's Don's story, anyway?'

'He won't say, and no one knows a thing about him.'

'It's a mystery, though. Why does he have an ancient bust of Homer, for example?'

She was past caring now. Michael must have picked it up and found the secret compartment when he was ignoring the come-on signs from Nika. 'How did you know?' she said wearily.

'It has his name on it. Well, it says *Homeros* in Greek, but that's the man.' He peered at her, and he guessed that she was hiding something. 'What's up?'

'That's where he hid his stash. A pile of gold sovereigns in the bottom. Said he'd been waiting for someone he trusted.'

For the first time since his arrival, Michael reached out to take her hand. 'And he can trust me, too. I give you my word, so long as the mercury stays safe and Don is not at risk, I'll do nothing to give you or him away.'

She squeezed back. 'Thanks, Michael. You can tell him tomorrow night, and don't fret: the thermometer's going nowhere.' To change the subject, she asked, 'Who's this Homer when he's, you know, at home?'

'Ancient Greek poet. He's the Greek answer to Shakespeare, only much older.' He frowned. 'And that's the weird thing. I'm no expert, but that bust is solid carved marble. It's definitely *old*, but whether it's ancient, I don't know.

Part Three — Stags and Hens

Chapter 16 — The Stags Take Flight

The condemned man ate a hearty breakfast. As he should. After all, he'd cooked it. 'Are you sure you don't mind giving me a lift to the airport?' I asked Evie when I'd finished loading the dishwasher. 'Given that the Hen Hordes are going to descend on Middlebarrow tonight.'

'Course I don't mind. It's not as though I've got to feed them is it? All I have to do is put buckets next to the beds.'

'You have a very low opinion of the Sisterhood, Evie.'

'They're gonna be eating a big meal, drinking a spring load of wine and getting in a helicopter. What do you think the most likely outcome is? Wanna put a bet on it?'

'You haven't met the pilot. Leah won't let them on if she thinks the leather seats are in danger.'

'Even Mina?'

'There is only one thing Leah loves more than the Smurf, and that's her infant child. Her husband knows he comes third, so Mina is well down the pecking order.'

Evie tilted her head on one side for a second. 'Yeah. I can see that. After all, Mum loves Middlebarrow Haven way more than she loves me. Are you all packed?'

Evie Mason and her mother fell out spectacularly two nights ago. We've become immune to it, and I decided not to intervene on Saskia Mason's behalf. 'I am all packed, and I shall go and get my case. See you outside in five?'

'Sure.'

I got my case from upstairs and found Scout waiting by the car wondering if we were going on an adventure. I gave him an extra long scratch behind the ears. Naturally, he gave me a suspicious look.

'I won't be long, lad. I hope. I'll see you soon, and you be good for Evie, eh?'

Today is the day that Mina and I commence our Stag and Hen events, and when (if!) we get back safely after the weekend, we only have a few days more at work before we both clock off and adjourn to Clerkswell for our nuptial preparations. You won't believe how much I was looking forward to that. We'd be back in Middlebarrow before long, though: it's the venue for what I am refusing to call our *second wedding.*

I shoved my case in Evie's car and got ready to fight the front seat to get leg room.

I turned round as we drove out, and watched Scout follow the car until we crossed the Wards. You might think that the loyal dog was chasing after his master: I know better. The damned hound was checking to make sure that we had really left so that he could continue his project of digging under the fence by the Ley line. I sometimes think that dog is part mole.

'Shouldn't be too long,' said Evie. 'No traffic problems for once.'

We chatted amiably for ten minutes (by avoiding mention of her mother), then I turned the conversation to her writing, and I'm pleased to report that she has ditched her project to turn my Irish adventure into a paranormal love story.

'Can I visit the Pack at Birk Fell?' she asked. 'Think of all the stories there. The passion! The struggles! The adventures!'

That was not going to happen. Not if I had anything to do with it. Naturally I had a cunning plan to stop it. 'You should speak to Karina about that. And Faith, of course.'

Evie went quiet. She knew Karina before her fall from grace and redemption at the First Mine, both of which involved extreme violence. And she's also met Faith.

'Why don't you write something set in Middlebarrow?' I suggested. 'I'm sure there are plenty of stories about goings-on there.'

'Mmmm. Maybe.'

She turned off the motorway in south-west Manchester to begin the final leg of our journey. Everyone knows about the two-runway giant of Manchester International Airport. What they don't know about is Manchester Barton airport, tucked in next to the rugby stadium and in the shadow of the Barton Motorway Bridge. For a light aircraft hub, it seems to be thriving.

'I had no idea this place existed,' said Evie as we drew closer. 'In my time, visitors have usually come via Chester airfield. Like you. Mum says she did a bit of ferrying around back in the day. She gave Heidi Marston a lift, once. Heidi put her hand on Mum's knee while she was driving. Allegedly.'

'Now there's a story for you!'

'Just no, Conrad. Just *no.*'

Evie dropped me off and wished me the best with an evil grin. 'I'll get the truth about the Stag Event from Lloyd, you know.'

'And I shall get the truth about the Hen Party. Bye, Evie. Take good care of Scout.'

I hefted my case and headed for the restaurant. My crew were already laughing in a corner and completely failed to notice my arrival. Or didn't care. As I limped over, I counted them off. Tom Morton, Chris Kelly, Lloyd Flint, Barney Rubble…

'Where the devil is Ben? And Alain, come to that?' I said in a loud voice. They finally looked up and grinned at me.

'Stuck in traffic,' said Tom Morton. 'For some reason Lloyd thought that you might bail out if you knew there was a delay, so we didn't message you.' He sat back and looked more like a rugby player than a detective for once. Being next to Barney Smith helped. 'I told Lloyd he was wrong: you're no lightweight.'

'Have a beer, Conrad, I brought a case to get us started.' That was Lloyd, as you might have guessed. He was already on his second.

'That depends on whether we're really flying or not,' I replied. 'Old habits, but I don't drink even when I'm a passenger.'

'Are we not flying?' said Barney. 'What else would we be doing at an airport? We haven't come for the food, that's for certain.'

I pointed out of the window, past the planes, past the stadium, past the flyover, and towards the weirdly shaped building that houses a huge ski-slope with real snow. 'Ben's a cricketer, and we devotees of the hard ball game are known for our cunning. It wouldn't surprise me if we were due at the Chill Factory for indoor skiing, and that this is a ruse. Excuse me while I get a coffee.'

I was being served at the bar when Lloyd announced, 'Here he is!'

My oldest friend and best man, Ben Thewlis, strode across the lounge with a wheely case and a big grin. With him was Alain Dupont, founder member of the Merlyn's Tower Irregulars when they were still known as #TeamConrad. Alain looked a little worried, but that's pretty much his default expression. Being French, he hasn't had the years of training in drunken excess which are part of the Englishman's birthright. And women, too, of course.

'Sorry, lads,' said Ben. 'I see you've got the party started, Lloyd. Pass one over.'

Lloyd wrenched off two bottle tops with his fingers and passed them to Ben and Alain.

I took a seat next to Lloyd and Barney, and said, 'Did Erin and Anna get away alright?'

They both nodded. Barney had driven down from the Particular this morning with Erin and they'd performed a shuffle so that Erin could take Lloyd's (very pregnant) wife, Anna, down to Clerkswell.

I had no idea what was going to happen to me tonight (and for the coming weekend), but we all knew how the Hen Event was starting: a dinner in Mina's honour thrown by the Clerkswell Coven Ladies Cricket Team. With a couple of extras, including Anna (who has no interest in cricket).

Why is this, you may ask? Myfanwy is the answer. Myvvy wanted to be part of the action in *some* way, despite being unable to leave the village, and as Vice-Captain of the Coven, she'd subtly hinted that a dinner might be a good idea. As for Anna, she was going to have a break from her existing children and spend a few days at Elvenham.

Once the Hens climbed on to the helicopter tonight, I knew that they were flying to Middlebarrow, but after that I have no idea what's going on. Ben knows, and he and Vicky have been co-ordinating mischief of some kind. I dread to think.

'Oh, there's our pilot, I think,' said Ben. 'Over here!'

A man in a blazer with pin-on wings came over and smiled. He shook hands with Ben and said, 'Good morning, gentlemen. We should be good to take off very soon. I do need to complete the manifest beforehand, though. Sorry to be a pain, but because of where we're landing, I need to see your passports. If I fly you over there without checking them, I'll be in serious trouble.'

I slipped my passport out of my pocket and glanced at the visa stamps. 'Where *are* we going?' I asked. 'Just which country. There may be issues…'

Tom piped up at that point. 'Please say we're going to Ireland. Please, please, pretty please, Mister Pilot.'

The pilot looked worried. 'Erm, do I want to know why?'

Barney lifted his beer bottle. 'Because the groom will be arrested on arrival and Tom's boss will dance a jig for joy. Win-win all round!'

The pilot was now looking seriously alarmed. I wasn't worried, yet, but…

He looked at Ben. 'Your call, Mister Thewlis. You swore me to secrecy, so it's up to you.'

'France,' said Ben.

'Good,' I said. 'I'm not banned from there.'

As the genuine Frenchman, Alain decided to make his point while we were still sober. He waved his passport at us and said, 'And you will all be'ave with the utmost respect for *La France.*'

'We'll give France all the respect it deserves,' said Ben.

I extended my hand to the pilot, then offered my passport. 'Here you go.'

'Is that a special passport?' said Lloyd with some seriousness.

The pilot had now edged away from *worried* towards *concerned.* He glanced at the burgundy document and asked, 'Why would Mister Clarke need a special passport?'

''Cos he's in the RAF.'

'Are you, sir?'

'He is! A wing commander, no less, and he'm staying sober in case he needs to fly the plane. You never know if there might be Dragons out there.'

The pilot looked at the takeout coffee cup in my hand and went past *concerned* and on to *bewildered.* I find I often have that effect on people. I never used to. Honest.

Chris stepped forwards and clapped his arm around the pilot's shoulders. 'Ignore Lloyd. He's from Earlsbury. You focus on flying and leave the Dragons to us.'

With all six foot six of Chris Kelly embracing him, the pilot visibly wilted. 'Thanks. Excuse me. If you make your way to the plane in five minutes, the cabin crew will tell you where to stow your luggage.'

Chris gave him an extra squeeze and let go; the poor man started backing away, but Ben was frowning.

'Cabin crew?' said Alain, also with a frown. 'Do we 'ave to pay extra for them?'

'Free of charge!' said the pilot, trying not to run towards the exit.

Lloyd plonked his empty bottle on the table and turned to his right. 'Hey, Barney, what'm you writing?'

Barney looked up from his police issue notebook and smiled. 'Just making notes. I reckon the Sheriff will be next down the aisle.'

Tom "Sheriff" Morton looked most alarmed at that thought: whether it was the idea of impending matrimony or the thought of any of us having a hand in it, he didn't say.

'Let's sort ourselves out,' said Ben. 'There may or may not be cabin crew, but there are definitely no toilets on this plane, and if anyone gets caught short on the way, you'll have to pay the diversion fee yourselves.'

After much hefting and sorting (and visits to the Gents), the seven intrepid explorers weaved their way towards the plane, an eight seat turbo-prop of some vintage but with a good reputation for reliability.

The only other completely sober person was Alain (he never drank his beer), and as I limped after the others, he pointed to the aircraft. 'You were very generous with the budget, Conrad. I know how much these things cost to hire.'

I had been generous, as it happens, because the good people of Lakeland had paid us £100K in compensation for nearly killing us. As Alexandra Greening observed, it was *A contribution to the wedding fund*. What Alain didn't know was that I'd only paid for the non-Mages. Chris and Lloyd could buy and sell the charter plane several times over.

We arrived at the apron with Ben firmly in the lead now, and I was quietly glad that I'd chosen him to be Best Man. There were positive and negative reasons for my choice, because in some ways I'm closer to Lloyd and Chris than I am to Ben, but he and I go right back. Ben knows the dorky kid who got packed off to boarding school at eleven and who was more famous for having an eccentric mother than for being himself.

As for the negative reasons, if I'd asked Lloyd or Chris, I'd have been letting myself in for all sorts of potential madness. Despite a reputation for being a boring old fart, Chris is a huge overgrown kid when let off the leash, and Lloyd is a Gnome. Say no more.

'What the fuck!'

My polite reverie on friendship was brutally ended by a cry from Chris, and I looked up at the open door to the plane. He was right: *What the fuck?*

'Welcome aboard your pleasure flight, gentlemen,' said Cindy Crawford, resplendent in a flight attendant's uniform from the 1990s that matched her apparent age.

My blood ran cold. The last time I'd seen a projection of my teenage crush, it was on Helen of Troy. Don't tell me…

The Glamour dissolved under magickal assault from Lloyd, and the reality was even more disturbing than Helen of Troy. Leaning against the door (and still in uniform) was Eseld Mowbray, sporting an evil grin.

'Whaaaa….?' said Chris plaintively.

'You should see your face, mate,' said Lloyd.

'Is that Chris's girlfriend?' said Barney in a stage whisper.

'Shh!' said Tom. 'Don't let her hear you call her that.'

'Why not?' Barney looked worried. 'They haven't split up or nothing have they?'

'No! Eseld does *not* like being defined as anyone's *girlfriend*. If you value your balls, be nice to her.'

Eseld finished striking her pose and walked carefully down the steps. 'Cases in the hold over there. Chris, you take Conrad's. The Groom gets to take it easy on this flight.'

She turned her back on the man whom no one was describing as *Eseld's boyfriend* and ignored his open mouth to come over to me. 'I don't suppose I can have a crafty fag out here, can I?' she asked.

'Sorry. Nearest naked flame zone is on the other side of the building.'

'Damn.' She grinned. 'I suppose you're dying to ask what I'm doing here?'

'Not as much as you're dying to tell me. Not that it isn't always a pleasure, Ez.'

'Yeah, well, not so much of the pleasure. Blame Myfanwy.'

'Myfanwy! How on earth…?'

'Ben says to her, "What if I end up with three paralytic Mages and we get attacked. Or three Mages who get pissed and decide to climb up the chateau walls?" and Myvvy says, "Good point."'

'It's something I had wondered about,' I replied, and I wasn't lying. Ben can keep a whole cricket team in order, no matter how much they've had to drink, but this was a different challenge entirely. 'And Myfanwy suggested you?'

'Who else? All the usual suspects are in the Hen Party.'

It made sense: Eseld is a powerful Mage and completely trustworthy. When sober. 'Are you a late addition to the Stags, or are you our tour guide, Ez?'

She gestured to the uniform. 'It's symbolic. I am under strict orders to remain sober at all times, to put your safety first and not to spoil your fun. I even have a separate room, and you won't believe this, but I've brought some essays to mark while you … well, I don't want to spoil the surprise.' She gave me the evil grin again. 'I don't know who's in for the bigger rollercoaster – you or Mina. Come on, I've put the silly hat and cape on the seats with the most leg room. Got to look after the men in my life.'

And she was as good as her word. She flew up front with the pilot and left us to party all the way to the tiny airstrip of St Georges, right in the heart of the St Emillion wine region, and I had a pretty good idea who was responsible for this part of the Stag Tour.

'Hey, Alain, you're from round here, aren't you?' said Chris when we disembarked and when he'd worked out where we were.

Alain waited until we were all on the ground before waving to a minibus in the distance. 'Yes I am.' He raised his voice. 'Okay everyone, listen up. For the next 'alf an hour you will all be English gentlemen.'

Lloyd burped. 'First time for everything, I suppose.'

The reason for the lecture was apparent when the minibus driver turned out to be a woman in her late forties with a big smile who came straight over to embrace Alain. He couldn't help himself and grinned, 'Maman!'

There was some quick fire French (not a clue), and Mme Dupont turned to Chris. 'Monsieur, it is a pleasure to meet you, and thank you so much for introducing Alain to your sister.'

'Erm…' said Chris, somewhat bewildered. When it comes to social situations, he isn't the quickest out of the blocks.

'*Non, Maman…*' began Alain, pointing at me.

Mme Dupont's eyebrows arched. 'You are Monsieur Clarke? Alain said you were the tallest person he knew, so…'

I shook her hand. 'Pleasure to meet you, Madame.'

'Lisette, please.'

'And I'm Conrad. I like to have friends who are taller, stronger, richer, cleverer, better looking and have more hair than me. Helps keep me grounded.'

She looked around the group, trying to work out who was *stronger, richer…* 'And I think we will stop there before one of us says something we regret,' she concluded. 'Alain, help me with the cases.'

They disappeared towards the back of the plane, and Eseld said, 'Well I'm richer, cleverer, better looking and have more hair, so that doesn't leave much for the rest of you.'

'Excuse me, Ms Mowbray,' said Tom Morton. 'You neglected to mention your modesty.'

Ez stood tall in her heels and looked down her nose at him. 'It's *Doctor* Mowbray.' Then she winked. 'Conrad forgot to mention *sexier*. I tick that box, too.'

This had gone over Lloyd's head. Gnomes are nothing if not secure in their skin. He was looking disgusted, and said, 'Is that Alain's Mom? Some Stag Do it's gonna be with Chris's woman and Alan's mother here. OWWW!'

'I am no one's *woman*,' said Eseld. How she grabbed his ear without being stabbed, Odin only knows. She let go and stepped back.

Lloyd rubbed his ear and put on a pained expression. Ben broke his self-imposed silence and patted Lloyd on the shoulder. 'Don't worry, mate: Lisette is only the driver. Tonight's entertainment is being provided by Alain's second uncle thrice removed. Or something.'

'Oh yeah?'

'Yes indeed. He owns a chateau. A proper one. And a very extensive wine cellar.'

Lloyd rubbed his hands together. 'Now you're talking.'

Chapter 17 — Late Night Encounters

She heard me coming, of course. Anyone but me would have heard me coming. If you see what I mean. Limping up the spiral stone staircase after more glasses of wine than I care to remember meant that I had no chance of surprise. However, given that Ez can be a bit twitchy, *surprise* might have been dangerous.

'Beautiful, innit, Conrad?' she said without turning around from her spot on the battlements. The flight attendant uniform was gone, and she looked relaxed and comfortable in a huge jumper which must have been Chris's, and a pair of Mowbray blue leggings. I limped over the turret roof and joined her. It was indeed beautiful.

The Chateau Dupont de St Georges is nothing like the scale of the Loire chateaux, but it does have a proper tower and a view over the shallow valley to the village. There was a waning moon to light up the carpet of vines and friendly lights to mark the houses in the village. Very restful. I lit two cigarettes and passed one to Ez.

'How'd you know where I was?' she asked.

'I paid attention when Uncle Christophe told us where our rooms are. When you didn't answer my knock, I worked out that the shortest distance from there to a cigarette was up the stairs. And here you are.'

She looked at me properly, and looked a little alarmed. 'Conrad! Don't go so close to the edge!' She looked even closer. 'How much have you had to drink? 'Cos you stink of wine and summat else.'

'Alain and the noble Christophe organised a tournament!' I declared. 'Mages and Lloyd versus the mundane. The challenge was identification and the field of battle was cheese and wine.'

She snorted smoke and coughed loudly into the night. 'By the gods, you're smashed.'

I grinned. 'Just a bit. Not too much.'

'And was there really a competition?'

'Yep. A dozen wines and a dozen cheeses. Prize to the team which gave the most accurate and poetic analysis of each offering.'

She did the maths. 'You've drunk two bottles of wine?'

'Mmm… maybe.'

'And the winner…?'

'The competition was abandoned when Lloyd challenged Barney to a duel over the *Epoisses de Bourgogne* from down the road in Burgundy.'

'Wine?'

'Cheese. Fifth smelliest in France, and banned on public transport.'

'No wonder you came up here for a break.'

'I came up here for more than that, Ez.'

She actually stepped back. Oops. I may have overdone it here. I held up my hands. 'Peace! I had something to say, that's all.'

She still looked suspicious. 'What?'

'How's it going with Mowbray College? Any ideas?'

'You what?'

'Mowbray College. Your father's legacy…'

'I'd rather you made a pass at me than discuss that out here!'

'I know. Which is why I needed a few glasses of wine to say this, and you can pretend it never happened in the morning if you want.'

'So it's a bit like most of my one night stands, then: a few glasses of wine and the walk of shame in the morning.' She put her hands on her hips. 'Give me another fag and either talk sense or go back downstairs to the boys.'

I passed her a cigarette and paused. 'What's the biggest problem with Mowbray College, Ez? Seriously.'

She threw her arms in the air. 'Where do I start? None of our Entangled contractors will work outside Kernow, and I'm not going to the Gnomes for this, for all that Lloyd's your mate.'

'Blood brother. Lloyd is my blood brother, which means more *and* less than a friend.'

'Whatever. I can't find an Entangled builder to turn the ruin into a campus, and for all that Chris keeps telling me I can run it myself, I know I can't. I'm *showing promise* as a Tutor in Wards, but if I tried to become the first Dean of Mowbray College, you can bet all the cheese and wine in France that I'd be the last. I'm not up to it.'

'Not yet, but you will be. Look, if I make a genuine suggestion, will you promise not to tell anyone else? And especially not Chris.'

It was her turn to pause. 'Really? Why?'

'Because of who it involves. I want to make their life better, not worse.'

'Go on then.'

'Pick a moment very soon. Invite Cora Hardisty to Mowbray House in London for a drink when Chris is away and tell her you've got a job for her. And for her husband.'

She turned and looked over the countryside. Lights were winking out in St Georges as its citizens turned in for the night, and she spoke to the darkness. 'You had this idea when you were sober, didn't you? So you must be serious.' She turned back. 'Why? Just why?'

'You may never know why, Ez. That's up to her. I can't say *why*, but I can say that it's serious. She wants out of Salomon's House, and her husband wants to break into the world of magickal property. And it might save her marriage.'

'Fuck me, Conrad. That's *beyond* serious.' She stubbed out her cigarette in the helpfully provided ashtray. 'Is this to do with her pulling out of the Warden election?'

I nodded, scared to say more.

'How come you know about it?' She frowned. 'It wasn't *your* fault, was it? Don't tell me you and her had an affair.'

It was on the tip of my tongue: *Don't judge me by your standards.* I was sobering up fast, and it stayed unsaid.

I think she guessed from my face, though. 'Sorry. I didn't mean that. It's just too much to take in, that's all.'

I took a deep breath. 'You were in mourning for your father at the time. You probably didn't realise how far I stuck my neck out when I agreed to stand on her election ticket as Security Attaché. When she pulled out, she felt she owed me an explanation.'

The sleeves of the jumper were at least six inches too long for her, so definitely Chris's. She pushed them up for the umpteenth time and shook her head. 'That's … that's mad, that is.'

'I know. And I'm going back down to face the no-doubt ribald remarks. I'll see you in the morning.'

'Yeah. And it never happened, eh?'

I was halfway back to the staircase. 'It never did.'

There was no *walk of shame* on Friday morning. More of a *hobble of hangover*, and I was by no means the worst. Even Lloyd's constitution was struggling to process the quantity of wine he'd downed last night.

He stared at the breakfast selection and groaned. 'Only to be expected, I suppose.'

'What's that?' said Tom. 'And could you groan a little more quietly, please?'

'We're on the continent, so we've got a continental breakfast. I could murder a full English right now.'

I was inclined to agree about the breakfast, but I wasn't going to complain. The Duponts have been incredibly hospitable, and they had cancelled all the other bookings last night so we could have the chateau to ourselves. If I allowed myself to use TripAdvisor, the *Hotel Chateau Dupont St Georges* would get every star going.

'Good Morning France!' announced Eseld from the doorway, with all the virtuous energy of a woman who has slept sober and alone in a king size bed; I had shared a twin room with Chris, and believe me, that was not happening again in a hurry.

'You can go off people,' muttered Lloyd, grabbing a plate and half a baguette. He added ham and observed, 'I think I'll pass on the cheese. Turns out you can have too much of it.'

'I know,' said Barney, his feud with Lloyd now gone with the morning mist. 'Did anyone else have weird dreams last night?'

'Plate?' I said to Eseld, before Barney could start to elaborate. I do not like hearing about other people's dreams. After all, if they slept through it, why should I find it of any interest?

'No thanks,' said Ez. 'I had breakfast ages ago. Some of us had to get up and remove the Wards so that the bakery van could get through the gate.'

'I really hope we're not flying again,' said Lloyd.

'We are not,' announced Ben. 'Today we are being driven into Libourne. It's not far. Lunch on the train, then we will take the TGV to Paris and finally Rouen. Just so you know.' He put on an evil grin. Or his best impression of one. Evil does not come naturally to Ben. Mischief, yes, but evil not so much. 'However, our final destination is a mystery, and will remain so.'

He looked around. 'Does anyone speak French?'

'Alain,' said Chris. 'He speaks it really well.'

'Ha bloody ha. Anyone else? Tom?'

'Spanish, I'm afraid,' said Tom. 'Oh, and I'm learning Italian, as you'd expect.'

'Eseld? You're looking disgustingly wide awake. French?'

'Why would I? I had enough trouble learning Cornish. And why not Alain?'

'I wanted to get something for Lisette. Google says there's a florist in St Georges, but when I called to order some flowers to be delivered, there was a bit of a communication breakdown.'

'That's a lovely thought,' said Eseld. 'I'll handle it, not that I speak French. What was the name of the shop?'

Ben picked up his phone and frowned. 'Who the hell is Sapphire Gibson?' he asked the room. 'And why is she suddenly taking pictures of the Hen Party and posting them on Instagram?'

Eseld ran over to the table and grabbed a secure metal box. She flipped the lid and started passing out phones. We'd sworn a solemn pledge on the plane that we'd hand them in before any event where alcohol was involved, with only Ez and Ben allowed to keep theirs. So why had Ben heard first?

The thing is, the only one in the Hen Party who is actually Eseld's friend is my sister Rachael, and another of the Hens is Eseld's sworn enemy, which is why she knew nothing until Myfanwy started messaging Ben. Rachael would have told her straight away, but Raitch isn't due at Middlebarrow until a little later.

I took my iPhone and powered it on. WhatsApp messages flooded the screen and the boys swapped notes. Ez peered over my shoulder and whistled in awe. She'd rightly figured out that I'd be the only one with the inside information on Sapphire's presence in Cheshire. 'It's a long story,' I told the group. 'One to be told over a drink.'

I looked at the pictures. Sapphire may be intense and slightly scary, but she is a bloody good photographer. The Hens were all getting ready for their first big event – Ladies Day at the Aintree Grand National meeting.

For those who don't know (and can't remember me telling you), the Grand National is British horse racing's biggest, longest and hardest steeplechase, full of high hedges, deep ditches and nasty water hazards, and it's happening tomorrow. Today is the day for the well-heeled, the wedge-heeled and the spike-heeled to strut their stuff around the special course obstacles: the Prosecco bar, the gin bar and the oyster bar. I am not a lady. I make no judgement.

This was the one part of the Hen Event that was telegraphed in advance, and was partly due to logistics but mostly due to advance notice. If Vicky had announced their destination on the day, there would have been a riot and a strike on the basis that they had nothing to wear.

Mina had shown me the invitation, which helpfully included dress codes for the weekend as follows:

Friday Day: Ladies Day at Aintree.

Friday Eve: Dress to Impress

Saturday Day: Casual wear and gym gear

Saturday Eve: To Be Supplied (text me your shoe size if I don't already know it)

Sunday: Casual/Comfortable.

'Why are there no pictures of the actual outfits? Much as I love to see hairdressing and attitude shots, they don't say much.' I said to Ez (who was still looking over my shoulder).

'This is GRWM,' she replied.

'You what?'

'Get Ready With Me. There will be Reveal pictures later.'

I zoomed in to a picture of Faith, who was doing something to Mina's hair. 'Does she look okay to you?'

'Who? Mina? She looks like she's having the time of her life. Is that one of the Fae doing the hair?'

'Yes. It's Princess Faith. She looked fine the other day – full of life and as healthy as the fells. She looks positively ill here.'

'I…'

Eseld's response was cut off by a strangled, 'What!!!' from Ben.

We all looked at him, and he looked wildly round the room, finally fixing his eyes on me. 'Who the fuck is Elodie Guerin and why is she meeting us off the train at Gare Montparnasse in Paris.'

'Guerin, did you say?' asked Tom, who clearly knew he'd heard the name. Luckily, the hangover was stopping his normally excellent memory working properly when it came to French Mages.

I put my hand up. 'That would be my fault. Nothing to worry about.'

Lloyd laughed out loud. 'Last time *I* said there was nothing to worry about, I ended up chopping off me own arm. Best of luck, mate.'

I tried to give a disarming smile and said, 'Wasn't somebody supposed to be ordering flowers or something?'

I managed to avoid the subject of *Elodie Guerin* and what she meant until we were well on the way to Paris. At first, I had Alain's relatives to distract my friends, and then the first Definitive Hen Picture arrived, only it didn't come on Instagram. We were just looking at the SNCF food app and deciding what to order from the buffet car when Sapphire messaged me directly: *Check out the Celebrity Enquirer Website! Fame at last!* I dread to think.

It was Chris looking over my shoulder this time, and he promptly announced the message to the group.

Alain won the race to Fastest Finger First, and his eyebrows shot up, along with a totally Gallic *Mon Dieu!*

I arrived at the website and rapidly discovered something: you had to register first. 'Alain, why have you got an account with Celebrity Enquirer?' I asked.

He ignored me and grinned at Tom Morton instead. What on earth?

'Congratulations, Tom. I did not know you were engaged even.'

'I'm not engaged,' said Tom. 'Show me that phone or I'll get Lloyd to wrestle it off you.'

Alain passed over his phone with a smirk, and Tom stared at the picture. 'What am I looking at?'

'The caption.'

Tom groaned. 'Oh no. Listen to this: *Best Feet Forward! Strictly winning celebrity Tara Doyle joins her friend and business partner Lucia Berardi's Hen Party, along with bridesmaid Mina Desai, while the rest of the Hens form a guard of honour and show off their footwear. Picture credit: Jewel Images.*'

'Whaaaat!' said Lloyd. 'You are in for some stick, Tom. Look! Barney's already messaging Cairndale nick.'

'If I don't, someone else will,' said the unrepentant detective constable. Tom must be an extremely nice boss for Barney to be doing that. Then again, most of my lot would be even worse.

'It's not the *wedding* part I object to,' said Tom through gritted teeth. 'It's the *business partner* bit. I shall be having words after we get back.'

I held out my hand to borrow Alain's phone just as Eseld completed her registration and got to see the picture. 'What's going on, Conrad? First Sapphire bliddy Gibson turns up, and now *Oighrig Ahearn*. How come she gets to sit at the top table, eh?'

I stared at the picture. Tara Doyle is stunningly beautiful, and her purple silk jumpsuit looked more expensive than my car. Tara Doyle is a former model, winner of Strictly Come Dancing and wife to a famous footballer. She has a model's height and comfortably rested her arms on the shoulders of Mina and Lucy, both of whom are very firmly *petite*. Mina was wearing lilac, and Lucy yellow, if you're interested (and Mina has much nicer ankles).

I smiled at my soon-to-be-wife's picture, then scanned the seven Hens standing a clear metre away from the trio in the middle. On Mina's left, at the back and trying to hide herself was the mischievous grin, green eyes and shocking red hair of Oighrig Ahearn. I smiled to myself and passed Alain's phone back to him. 'Can you Airdrop that to me, Alain?'

Oighrig Ahearn is Irish, a step-cousin of Eseld and The Oracle of Salomon's House. She is also covered in tiny freckles, and I don't know that Mina's exchanged more than ten words with her, so no, she should not be there (though she is coming to the wedding).

'That's not Oighrig,' I told Ez.

'Eh? Who else could it be? I work with her, so I should know!'

We'd allowed Chris and Eseld to sit next to each other on the train, and after peering over my shoulder, Chris had plonked himself back down to look at her phone. 'Look who's *not* there who *should* be there,' he suggested.

'What do you … No. Please do not tell that's Hannah with a Glamour on. I will be in *soooo* much trouble.'

'Of course it's Hannah,' said Chris. 'And why would you be in trouble? This is nothing to do with you.'

She rounded on him. 'You know that, and I know that, but no one else does at Salomon's House, do they? And no one's gonna get arsey with the Peculier Constable, so I'll get it in the neck instead.'

Ben had finally got on to the website, and said, 'You're not the only one. Looks like Lucy's in trouble, too.' He read from the Comments under the picture. '*Lucy Berardi, you are dead to me. How can you get engaged without telling your best friend?*' He looked up. 'Who do we think *Angel of Mersey* might be?'

'Bridget Gorrigan,' said Tom. 'She's Lucy's Operations Manager. She's not Entangled, though, so this will be a complete mystery to her.'

'Hold your horses,' said Ben. 'Celebrity Enquirer have issued a correction in the Comments, but not changed the main caption for some reason.'

Eseld shifted in her seat and looked around for something, like a young mother who's left her baby somewhere and can't remember where. She stood up. 'Budge up, Chris. I need to get out.'

'What's up?'

'You lot. That's what. I may be on a Stag do, but that doesn't make me a bloke. I'm going to go down to the end of the carriage and talk about the important things.'

'Like what?' said Ben, bemused.

'Like the fact that Tom here is banging on about his alleged fiancée's *business partner* and hasn't said a word about her new hair extensions. And who got Saffron's hair under that hat, and why is Erin wearing a mini skirt, eh, Mister Rubble?'

She swayed off down the aisle to get some privacy, and we all looked at each other, no one quite daring to laugh out loud, and that was Tom's cue to change the subject.

'Tell me, Conrad, why is a Prefect from the French version of the King's Watch meeting us in Paris?' he asked in that infuriating voice he uses when he has a suspect cornered.

'Eh?' said Lloyd.

'Lunch?' I suggested hopefully.

Chapter 18 — Fun and Games

The one and only time I've met Elodie Guerin was at a rendezvous over a dead body. I've been on worse dates, but not by much.

Elodie is the *Préfet de sorcellerie étrangère*, from the *Sûreté de magie* (the French answer to the King's Watch), and she keeps an eye on the many non-French Mages who have made their home in the Republic.

If you haven't read our French Leave adventure, you might need reminding that the dead body was from my second case, the Welshfire affair, and that the deceased was Adaryn ap Owain. That business is history now, but the fallout from my *first* case, the search for the 13th Witch, is still alive and kicking. And living in France. What could this be about? Has Keira Faulkner been getting into trouble?

When we'd returned from Brittany after our French Leave, Mina had asked Alain to describe Elodie. She would have asked Vicky, but Vicky was gone before Elodie turned up, and Mina hadn't trusted me to be objective. 'You will miss out the important things,' she'd said to me. I'm used to it.

I'm afraid that Alain's judgement on Mme Guerin is not printable here, and it involved several serious slurs on the good citizens of Paris. I know a lot of people who say the same things about Londoners.

Whatever you think of Elodie's relaxed attitude to marital vows (her own and other people's), she is not someone you want to get on the wrong side of. Instead of following meekly behind Ben and Ez when we left the TGV, I had to put myself front and centre. And when we walked through the ticket barriers, there she was.

I turned and said to Ez, 'I hope you're taking notes.'

'About what?'

'Elodie. Mina will want all the details.'

The Prefect was wearing a closely tailored black trouser suit, white shirt, killer heels and sunglasses. I'm sure Ez will give you the specifics if you message her. Elodie lifted the shades and put on an amused expression when I approached. Instead of going in for a kiss, I stood back and offered my hand. The boys kept well back. I think. Given the level of background noise and my hearing, they could have run off.

'*Bienvenue à Paris,* Conrad,' said Elodie. 'You are having a good time?'

'So far. How did you know we were coming here?'

She gave me an enigmatic smile. 'When your name came up on the Immigration system yesterday, I called the Constable and told her that I was surprised that you had not notified us. When she told me that it was a surprise to you, I believed her. What I do not believe is that she is going on one of these … *fêtes debauchées.*' She shuddered. The reputation of British Hen Parties abroad is even worse than Stags.

'I don't think Hannah will be there for the debauchery,' I replied. 'Further than that, I can't comment.'

She looked over my shoulder and nodded a greeting. So the others were still behind me. Reassuring.

'I had a free moment, so I thought I'd better come and see for myself,' she stated. 'And it is true: you are as described, and last night you locked yourselves in a wine cellar, according to the Bordeaux Prefect.'

I smiled and tried to look relaxed. 'Is Keira behaving herself? I haven't heard from her mother in a while, so I'm hoping that no news is good news.'

'Keira has done what you call *keeping her nose clean*.' She grimaced. 'She has learnt French and even a little Breton. She works hard for Madame Ménard. She has friends. She dated a mundane boy for a while. Bad news, I'm afraid.'

'You mean you'll have to give her a clean bill of health?'

Elodie nodded and drained the coffee she'd brought with her. '*Oui*. If she keeps this up for another year and a half, she will be asking to be let back into England.'

I sighed: another worm wriggling in my Larder of Unfinished Business. 'Thank you for that. I think.'

She checked her phone. 'Now that I know you really are here for what you call pleasure, I have only to wish you well and good luck for the wedding. *Au revoir*, Conrad.' We shook hands again, and she smiled at the others before clicking her way towards the Metro entrance.

'Well?' said Ben. 'Are we clear to party?'

'We are, and you are back in charge.'

'Good,' he said emphatically. 'Alain? Can you find us the taxi rank and get us to Gare St Lazare?'

'But of course. Follow me.'

Should you ever find yourself in North Normandy, and looking for somewhere different to stay, I can thoroughly recommend Les Manoirs de Tourgéville (if someone else is paying). This recommendation is partly because it's very nice and partly because it is totally bonkers.

Imagine you've become an incredibly successful and very rich film director and you want to set your next movie in a luxury hotel. What do you do?

If you're British, you find a hotel that's closed in January, then make your actors freeze to death filming the exterior scenes in summer clothes (and you hope it doesn't actually snow). Then you build the interiors at Pinewood and crack on.

If you're French, you buy a chunk of the Normandy countryside and *build* a hotel to film in. That way, you have total control over everything and you get to keep the hotel afterwards.

It would never happen in Britain, of course. Why? Because you'd never get planning permission, that's why. It didn't go to plan in France, either, because it took so long to build that the director had lost interest. He got to keep the hotel, though.

Oh, and another thing you'd do is that you'd dig out a huge basement and put a cinema in it. Of course you would.

The original Tourgéville complex is half-timbered and faux-mediaeval in the extreme; they even pre-aged the wood to make it look ancient for his film, and if you squint, you really could be in some sort of monastery. Four rectangular accommodation blocks make a square round a lawn worthy of an Oxford college and there's a luxurious looking restaurant, too.

I say luxurious *looking* because after I was given my room key, I was about to check the menu when Ben announced, 'We're eating somewhere else tonight. If you earn it. Everyone back here at five.'

'Look at 'er,' whispered Lloyd, pointing to Eseld. And when I say *whispered*, I mean that he could be heard half way across Reception. 'Like the cat with the cream,' he concluded.

'That's right, Lloyd,' she responded. 'Because I get to be referee tonight!'

'Tell me again: 'oo brought 'er?'

We rested, explored our accommodation (a rather nice triplex in my case, complete with outdoor seating area), and then gathered in reception at the appointed hour. We had to wait for Alain to give directions to the hired driver: no friends and family up here, and when the bus showed up, Ez stood at the door with the metal box. 'No alcohol just yet, but time for the phones to be locked away.'

It took about half an hour to get to our destination, and the driver must have been under strict instructions to take roads with no signposts to confuse us, because I know for a fact that he took us in a circle at one point. Either that or he was completely clueless. I'll let you decide.

The Normandy countryside looks a lot like southern England with lots of pastures for the cows to do their bit in Camembert production, and then we drove into a huge commercial orchard that looked spectacular in the spring sunshine. I smiled and put my hand on the window. Who doesn't get cheered up looking at apple blossom. It had been a hard and violent winter in many ways, and now I felt … at peace, I suppose.

We bounced down a track that only ever saw tractors, and I looked at Ben. 'Why are we going in the back way?' I asked.

'Don't want to spoil the surprise, do we, Conrad?'

The bus reached the farm complex, and on this side it was all modern grey sheds and the industrial face of farming. The path into the yard was unfenced, and I noticed that the proper gate leading out was robust and covered in signs we couldn't see. So, these Norman farmers were expecting a lot of people on the other side of the gate who needed to be kept out. But not us.

'Follow me,' said Eseld with way too much enthusiasm. On the way out of the bus, she grabbed a carrier bag with something in it, and I noticed that Ben, who knew exactly what was coming, was way too happy.

I stretched out my leg, inhaled a lungful of sweet apple smell, then hopped behind the group towards one of the smaller structures. The door had the French equivalent of *Fire Door: Do Not Obstruct* written on it, and the front of the building was on the public-facing side. Eseld stopped in front of the door and turned round. From the look on her face, that feeling of peace wasn't going to last long.

'Right, you lot. We thought long and hard about your next challenge.'

We??? If Ez had a hand in planning this part of the tour, may Freya preserve us.

She looked at me and Lloyd, then continued. 'Laser Quest didn't seem appropriate, somehow.'

'Shame,' said Lloyd. Ez ignored him.

'So we hit on the idea of a themed Escape Room, or, as they call them in French, *Escape Games*. You are about to enter the universe of *Sous le Cosmos*.

'What?' said Alain. 'As in the worst show on French TV?'

'A hotly contested category, I'm guessing.' Lloyd again.

'The most popular French Language Sci Fi show ever,' insisted Eseld. This was going to be a tough sell. She glared at Lloyd. 'And remember, we are guests here.' She checked her watch, then hammered on the door.

On the other side of the fire door, another world awaited us, and we were ushered into it by the *Commandant de Navigation, Cuirassé Jacques Cartier*. At least that's what it said on her impressive ID badge. It also said that she was Manon Roussel, and she was certainly dressed for the part, if outer-space pilots wear tailored white boiler suits with silver inset panels. And huge glasses.

'*Voilà, le geek de jour! Ow!*

That was Lloyd being rude and getting his foot trodden on by Tom Morton of all people. I didn't know he had it in him. Tom, that is. I'm afraid I'm all too familiar with Lloyd's shortcomings.

'*Bienvenue à l'expérience,*' announced Mlle Roussel. 'I am Manon, and I am the pilot of the Battleship Jacques Cartier, but today I will be your guide to the Puzzle of the Dying Light. You must be Mademoiselle Mowbray?'

Ez shook hands. 'Eseld. Yes. We're not late, are we?'

'Not at all. You are the last ones booked in, and we have as long as it takes. Please, come in.' She had an open, enthusiastic face and an infectious smile, and she was clearly proud of what she was doing. Goes a long way, does that.

We shuffled forwards, and I took the chance to have a quick word with Lloyd under Silence. I'll tell you why if necessary. Beyond the door, we found ourselves in the future of locker rooms (which is very similar to the current state of locker rooms but with a lot of silver paint). She shook hands with us as we came in, and you could see that she'd memorised the guest list, because I got special treatment.

'Congratulations on your wedding, monsieur. I wish you all happiness.'

'You can tell she hasn't been married, then. Ow! Barney, that hurt, that did.'

Manon looked a little nervous. As well she might. 'You are our first visitors from England,' she told me. 'It is a shame that *Sous Cosmos* has not been shown there.'

'I'm sure you're right,' I told her. 'You've gone to a lot of trouble in here. That stencilling is very neat, and did you get your uniform specially made?'

'Oh no! I made it myself. I'm afraid that yours are not so detailed. We have not been open long. Perhaps one day I can get you all one.'

The last person to shake hands was Alain, and naturally he switched to French. Not a clue what he said, but Manon liked the sound of it. She said something back, he asked a question, and she realised we were all looking at her, so she answered in English. 'Yes, I run the fan group on Facebook and the Youtube Channel. Perhaps you can look at us later. Now, please to get ready. I have already put your names on the lockers, and Eseld says she has taken your phones.'

My locker was helpfully marked *futur marié*, and I took out the XXL boiler suit in powder blue, complete with embroidered *Cuirassé Jacques Cartier* badge. Very NASA. I turned to see whether Chris had the 4XL or whether they'd given up and got him separates, because Manon was nothing if not prepared for us, and yes, the kid had cut his suit in half and added an extra panel so it didn't strangle his manhood. Been there, know how he feels.

He grinned in surprise and looked around. 'How come there's some in blue and some in white?' he asked.

'Because there are two teams,' declared Ez. 'And I might as well tell you the prize.' She smiled politely at our Norman hostess and continued, 'This is Manon's project, but the family business is apples, cider and calvados.'

Alain looked at Manon. *'Calvados Roussel est ici?'*

'What's he on about?' said Lloyd.

'This place is to apple brandy what the Isle of Islay is to malt whisky.'

'Oh. Right,' he said, suddenly looking more interested.

'Yes, Lloyd,' said Eseld. 'And not just that, Manon's aunt has a five-star rated family restaurant on the other side of that door. And we have the main room to ourselves tonight. If you get out of the escape room in time, that is.'

There were appreciative murmurings, and Ez continued, 'The only problem is that they can't wait on a big group all at once, so the losing team has to wait on the winners. And me. And do the washing up.'

Lloyd knows Ez. He looked at Chris and figured that Ez would absolutely make her boyfriend wait on her and wash up afterwards. And he was on Chris's team. 'Will the losers get to eat and drink?' he asked plaintively.

'But of course,' said Manon. 'Tante Léa is preparing the special *Menu Normand* for you.'

'One more thing,' said Ez. 'Lloyd? Come here.'

He approached nervously, and Ez brandished the carrier bag, from which she pulled a boxing glove.

'I know about what you've been doing with your prosthesis, so either you wear the glove or you take it off.'

I wouldn't have said that, because you don't push Gnomes into a corner: they respond in *exactly* the opposite way to the one you really want.

Lloyd slipped off the left arm of his overall, unfastened his shirt cuff and pulled off his left arm. 'Take good care of it, Ez,' and Eseld had no option but to gracefully accept the offering.

Manon had gone slightly green, and quickly got on with the game. 'Now we have the briefing, and I am very proud of this part normally. I am so excited when I show it because Captain Champlain himself gives you your mission, but … *quelle dommage* … it is in French only. Alain, will you translate?'

Alain wasn't wearing a boiler suit, so presumably he'd be neutral. And presumably the game would be in English or both teams might end up serving breakfast, not dinner. The big screen came alive and there was a handsome Frenchman, wearing a uniform identical to Manon's. He was also sitting in the control room of a starship. Manon must be a *very* dedicated fan to have got the producers to allow filming on set. The video was on pause, and Manon passed a remote to Alain with some advice in French.

He pressed *Play* and Captain Champlain began a stirring speech that continued for quite a while. When he froze in mid-exhortation, Alain turned to us, and his face was struggling not to laugh. 'The crew of Battleship Jacques Cartier and the people of Dying Light Rock are relying on you to save them from a deadly threat. Agents of our great enemy have planted two bombs, one in the reactor room and one in the … air plant? Where they make oxygen. You must remove all the booby traps and find out who has sabotaged the system.'

He played a bit more, and the actor started getting technical, pointing and gesturing and lifting a couple of objects for our inspection. Alain continued by saying, 'All of the codes can be found in the clues, and you can use your communicator if you need help. However, as the starship is outside the rock, it will take at least three minutes for us to answer your questions.'

He was about to go on when Manon interrupted him and asked something in French.

'Yes. Of course.'

The remainder of the briefing was more exhortation to do our best, and then Alain reached into his locker and pulled out a white boiler suit. That did not bode well for Team Groom, who as you may have noticed consisted of the Mages. And if all the challenges were electronic, we couldn't use our ability to pick locks to cheat. We were digesting this, when Eseld had another announcement to make.

'Team Groom have an *extra* challenge at the beginning, and they can win an *extra prize*.'

'How come they get the extra prize?' asked Tom, looking slightly aggrieved.

'Because your team don't have much use for a French Dictionary, do you?'

'Merde,' said Lloyd. 'Ever get the feeling we've been stitched up?'

That feeling got a lot stronger about an hour later, when Lloyd, Chris and I came to the conclusion that Alain had been a trifle economical with the truth. 'Or should that be *economical with the actualité* as we're in France,' I observed.

'The slimy git,' said Lloyd.

'Precisely.'

We had quickly retrieved the French dictionary (it was only chained up with a padlock), and we were making good progress. It helped that a lot of the flim-flam was designed to appeal to fans of the TV show who wanted a totally immersive experience. There was even a scene filmed on set with Manon wearing her uniform and sitting in the pilot's chair. In the background was the gunnery officer, and I quite liked the look of her, too. If the actress's career doesn't go into orbit, she has a great future as a dominatrix. Not that I voiced my opinion out loud: I did *not* want a clip of me saying that turning up at the wedding: I was fairly sure that room was being video recorded.

Within the game, we were doing quite well at dismantling the booby traps around the rather ominous looking bomb next to the reactor control panel. Except for one thing: we were going round in circles without the radiation readings.

'We need a Geiger Counter,' concluded Lloyd. 'Are there any boxes we haven't been able to open?'

'Only the ones that you need a radiation reading for, so they can't have the Geiger Counter in them.'

We looked at the selection of old mobile phones, Chinese tat from Amazon and discarded props from the actual production. As the unofficial team leader, I made the call. 'We need to ask for help.'

'I'll do it,' said Chris, picking up a mobile phone that had been hacked so that it did nothing but run an App simulating communication to the mother ship. He typed the message, and we got ready to drum our fingers.

'No way are you gonna win that bet,' said Lloyd.

'What bet?' asked Chris.

'I can't say, Chris, because we're being observed.'

'And laughed at. We look a right set of idiots.'

Time for a change of topic. 'What's your room like at the Manoir?'

Five minutes later, the answer came back: *You have the Geiger Counter. It is on the Samsung Multi-Function Device. You need to use the Curie Code as it was told in the briefing.*

And that was the moment we realised that Alain had deliberately failed to translate part of Captain Champlain's introduction, and Manon's English hadn't quite been up to spotting the omission. Lloyd was right: Alain is indeed a *slimy git*.

Once we'd unlocked the Geiger Counter, we were back in business, but we'd lost a lot of time. 'Can we catch them up, do you think?' asked Chris.

'Let's see,' said Lloyd. 'There's two Mages and a Gnome in here versus two detectives, a cereal agronomist and a sneaky French investment manager over there. We're doomed.'

We did lose: but not by much. It turned out that the name of the challenge – Dying Light Rock – was part of the game. Once either team got to a certain point, the lights were lowered, then extinguished. As two of our team have night vision, we did a lot of catching up at that point. I think Ez must have missed that bit in the referee's notes, or there's no way she'd have let it happen, because she had a lot of explaining to do when Manon started asking how come our team could see in the dark.

We emerged, blinking, into the locker room to find a very harassed Eseld and a very embarrassed Ben. He started first.

'I'm sorry about Alain's little joke. We'll toss a coin for who waits at table, and don't take it out on him, okay?'

Another reason I love Ben: his sense of fair play is impregnable. And so is Lloyd's, in a rather twisted way.

'No chance, mate,' said my Blood Brother. 'All's fair in love and Stag Parties. We'll wait at table and wash up, and Alain can spend the next forty-eight hours looking over his shoulder waiting for our revenge.'

Tom and Barney joined us, and I pointed to the now open door to the front of the property. 'You owe me fifty Euros, Lloyd.'

'Shit! How does he do it?'

'What's going on?' said Tom.

'When we were outside, I bet Lloyd that Alain would have Manon's contact details before dinner. She's handing them over now, and Lloyd's going to hand over my winnings when he's taken off his rather fetching uniform and put his arm back on.'

Lloyd looked at us mutinously. We'd all noticed that he was wearing a Small overall, but none of us had said anything.

He took off the suit, and Eseld held out his prosthetic arm. 'I am gonna kill you, Lloyd. One day. Not only did I have to explain your night vision, your bloody arm started moving on the desk. I had to suppress it, and now I've got a huge headache and Manon thinks we're spies. I had to spin her the MI7 line.'

Lloyd grinned and accepted his arm back. 'I don't know about you lot, but I could murder a drink.'

Dinner *Chez Tante Léa* was as good as promised, and we got a lot of envious glances from the regular patrons who'd been squeezed into the back room. At one point, Alain joined Eseld and I outside for a smoke (the slow-baked pork belly deserved digestion before we moved on to cheese).

I started having a go at Alain about his subterfuge in the game, and he could see it coming, so he pretended I was going on about his interest in Manon. 'She is incredible! All of this is her design, you know? She programmed all the computers, she created the visuals and she did most of the set dressing.'

'He's not wrong,' added Ez. 'She's got a mind like a humming bird, flitting about and going too fast for me to see. She ran both rooms like she'd been doing it for decades.'

Alain was nodding. 'And what you do not know is that the show has been cancelled after two seasons. Poof. No more. And Manon, she is refusing to accept this, and she is going to start a campaign to save it. She has no chance, and then she will be so sad. A new project will help take her mind off it.'

Ez shook her head. 'You're worse than an open book, Alain. You just want to get her into bed.'

He actually looked hurt. 'Non! We were talking, and she has spent two years on this project, and her father has been a very patient man, because he paid for it. He wants her to get a proper job, and I am going to suggest that she comes to the UK, because there are so many more opportunities there. I am living proof of that, and I am going to suggest to Rachael that we invest in her.'

That stopped Ez in her tracks: Rachael and Alain's company looks after Eseld's investments. And her family's. 'You serious?'

'I am. If I show her how much money she could make from … say, a Doctor Who franchise, she will see that *Sous Cosmos* is as limited as the sets it was filmed on.'

'You're gonna take on the BBC?'

'I will pretend to. They have already franchised Doctor Who, but what about that show *Zero Hour* on Netflix? I am telling you, it will be as big as Star Wars.'

Ez and I looked at each other. 'Never heard of it,' I said.

'Me neither.'

Alain stubbed out his cigarette. 'That is because you are old. Conrad, I think it is time you fetched the cheeseboard.'

We weren't the only ones who'd had a break. Manon had helped her Aunt Léa finish the cooking, and now she reappeared, dressed as the gunnery officer. Either she is supremely confident in herself or she has never come across a room full of inebriated Englishmen before.

Alain leapt up and applauded and heaped compliments on her. 'She won an award for this costume at a convention last year,' he announced.

Those amongst us with other halves (i.e. everyone but Alain) exchanged glances and uneasily picked up our phones. None of us wanted to be the first to take the picture of the young woman in black leather, nor did we want to look rude and pretend that she didn't look spectacular.

Eseld cracked first. Not only is she female, she has done her fair share of cosplaying over the years. She stood up and went to take a picture, then stopped when something pinged into her phone. 'Bloody hell! Have you seen this, guys?'

Cue everyone reaching for their phones.

'Seen what? I said.

The only message for me was from my mother, hoping I was having a nice time.

'Mina and the stripper,' said Lloyd. 'Has anyone got video?'

I stood up as gracefully as I could, and said, 'Manon you look totally like the character. Do you mind if I take a picture of you and Alain with his phone? He may kill me if I don't.'

I tried to ignore the others and focus on Manon and Alain, but that wasn't going to happen. I finally cracked when Barney said, 'Do you think Mina's enjoying it or do you think she's embarrassed?'

'Have a look at this,' said Eseld. 'She is totally enjoying it.' Then she looked up and looked at me. 'Of course, if we'd arranged a stripper for Conrad, that would just have been *so* wrong. Sometimes it's good to be a woman.'

Chapter 19 — Must Try Harder

There were no more surprises from the Hen Party, and we finished our evening quite happily. And yes, there is a picture of me kneeling at Manon Roussel's feet. No point denying it. I'm not entirely sure how it happened, I must admit; her family's Calvados is *very* good.

Ben and Ez let us sleep it off in the morning, and a beautiful early spring day greeted me when room service delivered a flask of coffee to my room. I was just soaking up the sun when Ez appeared. 'There's a cup in the room,' I said. 'But no conversation yet.'

She reappeared with a mug and a sour expression. 'That room smells, Conrad. Yeah, I'll shut up.'

She did, and we enjoyed the moment as much as I was enjoying the croissant. When I'd dusted crumbs off my hands, she grinned. 'You're looking better than Chris.'

'But then again, I always do.'

'You wish.' She grabbed another cigarette. 'The trouble with being sober is that I've got nothing else to do but think. Do you really reckon that Cora would walk out on the Invisible College now, just as the new Warden is all set to open a campus in Manchester?'

'Or Leeds. Or Newcastle.'

'Whatever.'

'Politics, Ez. The anti-Lois Mages will look to Cora to be their leader, to oppose the setting up of this Community of Mages. I don't think Cora has it in her to do that,' I added diplomatically. The truth is that Cora wouldn't be *allowed* to lead the opposition, because someone put pressure on her, and will continue to put pressure on her. If only Cora would let me try and find out who's behind this … But no. She wants to do the right thing.

'In that case, I've got nothing to lose, have I? Should I ask her before the wedding or after? With all of the Mowbrays in Clerkswell, and her and her family, too, it would be a good time to have a few discussions. If Mina doesn't mind, of course.'

'Mind! Mina would love it – having the future of magick in England thrashed out at her wedding would be an honour. You don't get it yet, I don't think. This wedding is so big precisely because there's more ways of being the centre of attention than walking down the aisle in a white dress, not that she's doing that anyway.'

'Eh?'

'Never mind.'

She nodded and sat back. 'Do you remember Alain's last proper girlfriend? I never met her, but I saw the pictures. Do you reckon that Manon looks a lot like her? I'm only asking because I don't want him running off to France every five minutes like he did last time.'

'There speaks the caring employer.'

'Says the man who was ready to court martial his Watch Captain.'

I lifted my coffee cup in salute. Who'd grassed on me about Murray Pollard, I wondered? 'Aah, but I'm not their employer, am I? I'm their CO.'

'And in case you'd forgotten, I'm not his employer, either, but your sister is. As her friend, it's my job to give her an accurate report. Morane versus Manon. Spill.'

'I only met Morane a couple of times before they split up, and I've only met Manon once! Yes, the girls are of an age, and they both wear big glasses, they can both be a bit intense, and they're both attractive.'

'And they're both French.'

'Don't let Morane hear you say that. She's Breton first and last. She's also a Druid, for goodness sake. And a singer, not a techie..'

'Hmph. We'll see. Alain has already told Ben that he *has* to see her again before we leave or his heart will break, and I told Ben no way.'

'Talking of the others, it's time we showed our face at the no doubt elegant buffet.'

We sauntered over and found Tom checking his phone and ignoring the (yes, very elegant) buffet.

'There's something Lucy's not telling me,' he said.

'Yeah, I get the same feeling about Raitch,' added Eseld. She looked over at the Stags who'd already grabbed their plates. 'Hang on a sec. Barney is looking very guilty.' She strode over and pinned him to his seat with a glare. 'Spill it, Rubble. What's Erin told you?'

'Erin? Nothing. Still comatose, no doubt.'

Tom had joined us. 'But someone has told you something, haven't they?'

Lloyd put his prosthetic arm on Barney's shoulder. 'Give it up, mate. She'll drag it out of you sooner or later.' I saw the fingers flex, digging into Barney's flesh. 'That's like a love-tap compared to what Ms Mowbray will inflict on you.'

Barney didn't wince, even though his eyes started to water. 'It was Liz. She was checking a report flagged via South Lancs.'

'Oh?' said Tom, suddenly serious. South Lancs is the police force which covers Manchester, scene of last night's Hen-related shenanigans.

'Erm, yeah. Something about a car ending up in the Manchester Ship Canal, and did we know the owner, Lucia Berardi? Or the respondent, Sapphire Gibson?'

'What!' exploded Tom. 'Excuse me.'

We stared at his back, and then at each other. I shrugged as Gallically as I could. 'It'll all come out in the wash. Get me some breakfast, will you Ez?'

It didn't come out in the wash at all. Despite much prodding and pressure, no one in the Hen Party would say, and a lot of them were pretending not to know. The one person who *might* have told me the truth regardless is Hannah, only she is at a cousin of her in-laws for Shabbos, and she was nowhere near the Manchester Ship Canal. Ah well, maybe one day we'll learn.

The basic facts were true, though, and Lucy will be looking for a new car when she's recovered from the Hen Party. As for today, the girls are off to an as yet undisclosed destination, and so are we.

After breakfast, Ben stood outside the hotel and cast nervous glances between his phone and the sky.

'I take we're outdoors today, Ben?'

'Either or. It's flexible.' He turned round and saw some of the others. 'Okay, listen up everyone and pass the word on to the others: dress code is something you don't mind getting dirty, and pack a few layers.'

Chris looked around. 'If this involves an assault course, I may kill someone accidentally.'

'Believe me,' said Ben enigmatically, 'there are plenty of obstacles before Ez hands out the next prize.'

'Next prize!' said Lloyd indignantly. 'We haven't even had one prize yet, just a penalty for last night's losers. And I am not taking my arm off again. It gives me bad dreams after putting it back on.'

We grumbled, dispersed, and returned; the minibus was already waiting.

'We're not going far,' announced Ben, 'and for once you can keep your phones, because you might need them, and because we won't be drinking much today.' He paused and did his best to keep his face straight. 'Tonight's another matter.'

Less than fifteen minutes later, we turned off a minor road and on to a rough track, then stopped short of a gorgeous old farmhouse made of limestone, with a slate roof and cottage garden.

Ben stood up and faced his troops. 'We're a bit early.' He glanced behind him at the clock over the windscreen. 'Fifteen minutes early, in fact. I just wanted to run through today's activity and why we're doing it. And who gave me the idea.' He rested his arm on a seat back. 'I said to Myfanwy, "What can we do that won't give an unfair advantage to Mages and doesn't involve strenuous activity?" and she said, "I know! Painting! There must be someone who does painting classes. Organise a nice lunch, pray for good weather, and off you go!" And that's what we're doing.'

'Painting?' said Lloyd, as ever first off the mark. 'As in decorating or as in arty stuff?'

'You know, that does sound good,' added Tom. He got a couple of quiet nods, and we looked expectantly at Ben (except Lloyd, who looked disgusted).

'Yep,' said our leader. 'This is the home and art school of Madame Clémence Laurent, and we will be taking a watercolour class in her barn and, hopefully, by the river. Prize to be awarded after a blind judging by a guest judge.'

'Who?'

'Wait and see. Myfanwy had more to say, too. "I don't want to give no one an unfair advantage, so why don't I find out if they're any good at art? I know you and Conrad are rubbish, so why don't I do a little digging?" And so she did. You may remember she was laid up a couple of weeks ago, well she used the time to get in touch with your mothers.'

'You what!'

'Eh?'

'How?'

Ben held up his hand. 'Would you believe that every single mother barring Chris's has hung on to our school reports? And Oma Bridget didn't need to hang on to his because she remembers them word for word.'

There was a stunned silence. 'Tell me you'm joking,' said Lloyd. 'How in the name of Mother Earth did Myfanwy find *my* mom?'

'Simple. She asked Anna, and Anna shared her number, then Myfanwy and your mum Facetimed, and I have a message for you, Lloyd: just because you've moved to Cheshire, doesn't mean you can skip Sunday dinner more than once a month, so get your arse in gear. Her words not mine.'

'Fuck me.'

Not the most appropriate remark, given who we were talking about, but I forgive him (even if his mother won't). As it happens, he did once tell me about her. All Gnomes have (at least) seven older sisters in theory, even though fewer in practice. In Lloyd's case four of them grew up to become feisty women, and Lloyd's mother lives in an annexe to his oldest sister's house near Worcester.

We'd been so busy looking at each other that we hadn't noticed Ben produce a sheaf of printouts. 'It so happens that I have them here. These are all from Year 9, the last year that art was compulsory for all of us, and we'll start with mine. *Benjamin showed some promise in still life work, but sadly chose to concentrate on doodling rather than drawing. I wish him the best.*'

'Ow.'

'Harsh.'

'Wait till you hear Conrad's. Mary was most keen to dob him in it. *Conrad lost interest in my subject when the trainee teacher left us. After that, he preferred trying to watch the cricket out of the window until he was excused art to concentrate on modern pentathlon.*'

'Was she good looking, and does Mina know this?' asked Barney.

I tried to look wistful. 'The trainee was *very* good looking, and I was at an impressionable age.'

'No change there,' Barney responded, then turned to Ben. 'How did you track my mother down? *Did* you track her down?'

'She was a tough nut to crack until we discovered that she'd re-married. Yours is pretty straightforward, mate. *If Barnabas put the same energy into art as he did into rugby, he might not have failed all of the tests.*' He shuffled the papers. 'I didn't get this one until the night before last, and Lisette helpfully translated it for me.'

'Non!' said Alain, outraged. '*Pas possible!*'

'I'm afraid it is. *Alain lost interest in this subject when he realised that life drawing is only available to older students.* I think we could have guessed that one. Now, Lady Morton was a tough nut to crack. Very guarded, your mother, Tom.'

'How come she's a *Lady*?' asked Lloyd.

'Because she's married to Sir Thomas Morton,' said Barney, quite happy to dish the dirt on his boss. 'He's told us that if we try to call him *Tom Junior* we'll all be transferred to London, so that's why we call him *Sheriff*.'

Alain has looked at sea a few times since we flew off from Barton airfield, and the thought of London being a punishment worse than death was clearly something he couldn't adjust to, so he shrugged and said nothing. Or nothing out loud.

Ben turned to the next page. '*Tom is the most polite and well adjusted failure at art who I have ever had the pleasure of teaching.*'

Eseld was grinning and enjoying every second. I should also point out that she doesn't know Myvvy as well as she thinks she does. Ez shook her head and observed, 'This Madame Laurent doesn't know what she's let herself in for, does she? Mind you, I'm surprised she took a booking from a British stag party at all.'

'I lied,' said Ben. 'Well, Myfanwy lied. Only three more.'

Eseld clearly can't count, either, because she was still grinning. I debated moving seats, because this could get … interesting. Nah. I was enjoying myself too much.

'We'll do Lloyd's first, shall we?' Ben held up a piece of paper that was obviously blank. 'Your mum said to ask you why there is no art report.'

'That's 'cos I dropped it early to do more metalwork.'

'She said you'd say that. Go on, Lloyd, I'm dying to know.'

Lloyd looked shifty. 'It's true!'

Ben put the papers down and picked up his phone. 'I've got her number. Shall I?'

'No! Alright, alright, keep your hair on.' He went a sort of slate green colour and swallowed hard. 'It wasn't my fault. How was I to know that sable hair brushes cost that much?' He shut his lips and folded his arms.

'Go on,' said Ben.

Lloyd unfolded his arms and gesticulated randomly. 'I got kicked out of art class when I borrowed some of the teacher's brushes to do acid etching on metal.'

'No!' said Eseld. 'That's gross.'

'Mom made me do housework for two weeks to earn the money to pay him back. *Two weeks.*' He looked disgusted. And about twelve years old all over again. Mothers, eh? They never stop having that effect on their sons.

'I'm not sure which is my favourite,' said Ben. 'Chris has a strong contender though.' My friend already had his head in his hands. '*Christopher has a meticulous line, superb control of his pencils and grasp of scale that would make him a natural, if only he had any imagination to go with his talent.*'

'Ooh.'

'Ouch.'

'Did you get him back for that?' asked Lloyd.

Chris looked up. 'Yep. I did. On the last day, I scrubbed every single paint palate until it was spotless. Then I rearranged all the coloured pencils into alphabetical order.'

'Wow,' said Tom. 'That takes … dedication, Chris.'

'And now we come to Eseld.'

I felt it, Lloyd felt it and the others must have noticed *something*. Chris may or may not lack imagination, but has superb reflexes. He grabbed Eseld's hand before she could lash out. He couldn't put on a Silence, though.

'What the fuck have you done!' she hissed at Ben. 'How dare you! How did you find her? You bastard. If you read that out, I'll make sure those twins Myvvy's carrying are the last children you ever have, Ben.'

Without a word, Ben handed the report to Chris, not Eseld, and turned to the driver. 'Take us to the barn, now, please?'

Luckily it was only a hundred metres, and Alain made a point of saying loudly how beautiful it looked, and he was right: if that director who built Tourgéville had seen the barn and the view over the river valley, he'd have snapped it up in a second. A more suitable location for a country romance with lovelorn swains and capricious maidens could not be imagined.

Then again, if it had been a French film, they would no doubt have died of the plague in the last act. The bus stopped and we got off sharpish.

Madame Clémence Laurent was waiting for us, and I think there may have been a hint of nerves around her eyes when such a mixed bunch of men formed a line in front of her (Chris left Ez on the bus). Madame L forced a smile and shook hands with Ben. '*Bienvenue, messieurs.* I hope that you are all well?'

We were shown into the barn and she pointed to some flasks of coffee. 'We will start with a short demonstration in five minutes. There are facilities through there.'

I grabbed a coffee and manoeuvred Chris into a corner. 'How is she?'

He had the report stuffed into his pocket. He unfolded it and showed me. *Eseld's imagination knows no bounds, and if she allowed her technique to catch up, she could achieve great things. I hope she takes up art in the future and I wish her well.*

He took it back and looked hurt. 'What's wrong with that?' he asked.

I shifted my leg a little. 'How much has she told you about her time with the Daughters and about her mother?'

'Nothing, and Isolde is the only topic off limits. Always has been, even before we went public.'

Eseld's mother is Isolde (see? It's not just the Mortons who have this problem with names), and Isolde is currently a Guardian with the Daughters of Glastonbury. Eseld lived with her mother until she was a teenager, then they fell out. They fell out so badly that Ez refused to speak to her for nearly twenty years until I tricked her. 'You know about the family therapy?' I said to Chris.

The trick I'd played had been to make Ez attend at least three sessions with an Entangled therapist, and that at least two of them had to be in the same room as her mother.

'I know that two of them have happened,' said Chris. 'That's it. Could you try to talk her down, Conrad? I know it's your day, but Clémence seems really nice, and I don't want it all spoiled.'

I poured another coffee, put it in his hand and steered his elbow towards the door. 'Of course I'll talk to her, but only if she talks to you, too. Just hold your nose, Chris.'

Chris hates smoking. Ez has a smoking room at Mowbray House in Mayfair, and he made her move it to the top floor. I think it's the only time he's put his foot down. So far.

Ez being stubborn, took it as a challenge and spent a fortune getting an interior designer in. Her smoking boudoir is now the chicest room in the house.

We found her round the back of the bus, rolling a second cigarette. She looked daggers at the two of us, but she didn't tell us to go away. I took that as a good sign. Chris waited until she'd lit the roll-up, then passed her the coffee.

'What did it really say?' I asked.

'Eh?' said Chris. 'Ben can't have put a Glamour on, and Ez didn't, so what are you on about?'

'Your mother doctored it, didn't she?' I said. 'She didn't want to embarrass you in public, because she loves you. Tell Chris what it really said.'

'Why should I?'

'Because he needs to know. Not all of it, and not now, but Chris loves you, too.'

She turned her head to blow smoke away from Chris. 'Bit late for that. Couldn't have been more embarrassing if she'd tried.'

'No, love,' said Chris. He pressed his lips together and tried some tough love. 'You created the embarrassment yourself by reacting so ... instinctively. Contrary to my school report, I *do* have an imagination, and I'd rather not have to use it. If you tell me, I can stop thinking the worst. If you'd rather do it back home, then fine, we can just get on and enjoy the day.'

She drew smoke in and held it, then sighed. 'Okay. The original report said something like *I have had to ask Eseld to refrain from using such violent imagery in front of other students. It is not appropriate for a lower school setting. I have also suggested that if these scenes really are from her dreams, that she should seek counselling.* There. Satisfied?'

Chris went to give her a hug, and she let him. I left them to it and went to find my own spot for a smoke. What are the odds, eh? Does it say more about my friends that none of us were any good at art, or does is say more about the way that art is taught in schools? Not for the first – or last time, no doubt – I'll let you decide.

Chapter 20 — Eye of the Beholder

Clémence turned out to be a brilliant teacher. Her demonstration consisted of two things: how to mix paint ('No etching acid, Lloyd,'), and secondly that it really, really does make sense to start with lighter colours and then go to darker ones.

'And I shall say no more than that. We will have half an hour in here, and I want you to get used to the paint and brushes. No one is allowed to leave their easel until they have thrown at least three pieces of paper into the recycling.'

Shortly later, the sun had made an appearance and we were headed outside, with the instruction to space ourselves well apart and find a view that spoke to us. Some headed towards the river (which looked like it had once been dammed, and was quite broad here).

I moved upstream a little and found a diagonal view that included lots of meadows, some rolling hills and a little wood. Perfect. The fields also included some hefty French cows who were just starting to lie down after a busy morning munching on the grass.

I was tempted to include them, until I realised that handling animals might be something for an advanced class. On the other hand, their relaxed attitude to life reminded me this adventure was another dimension to peace: inner space to explore something in a way you never have before. I smiled a silly smile and wondered how Mina would react if I suggested we go on watercolour trip together. No, don't worry, I have no such intention. I want my marriage to be a long and happy one.

Peace. I like it. There's a lot to be said for it. I picked up my brush and set to.

After some moderately successful attempts to move from sky to ground, I rinsed my brush and decided I needed more water. I headed for the barn, and was joined by Lloyd. 'We still haven't got our revenge on Alain for stitching us up in the Escape Game yesterday. We can't let him get away with it.'

I changed the water and looked over to the corner of the yard where Alain was exploring the play of light on the texture of the farmhouse walls. 'You're right, Lloyd.' I lit a fag and gave it some thought. 'Can you make a Glamour that will be triggered by an approaching small Artefact? Some token?'

'I could. What do you want to do?'

I did a quick Google. 'Make a Glamour that will turn Alain's canvas into *this* when Clémence comes to give him help. I'm before him on the circuit, and when she comes to me, I'll slip it in her pocket.'

'That's evil, that is. I like it. Here.' He rubbed a two Euro coin in his false hand and passed it to me. 'That'll last an hour or so. Get Alain away from his easel, and I'll put the suppressed Glamour on it.'

'No problem.' I raised my voice. 'Alain! Come here a sec. I was just wondering which picture of Manon to send to Rachael. I think the one in the Gunnery Officer uniform.'

Alain scuttled over with alarm on his face, and Lloyd slipped away.

'You can't send *that* one,' said Alain.

It was the one with her standing with one foot raised on to the chair. He got out his phone and messaged me a much less raunchy image.

'Thanks.' I double checked my phone: another message from mother, and several laughing emojis from Sofía when she saw the one of me on my knees, but none of the Hen Party girls had been in touch all day, a point I made to Alain.

'No. It is true. Strange. Check with me if you have any more silly ideas.'

'Will do.'

And I would do. The only problem was that Ez had already sent Rachael *all* the pictures. Never mind.

About half an hour later, Clémence came to me and said, 'I like your grass, Conrad. There is a lot going on there.' She smiled and leaned in to point at the wood I'd inserted in the corner; the coin went easily into the pockets of her baggy trousers. 'You are having trouble here, I think.'

'I don't think. I know.'

'My best ever student taught me an English phrase. *When you can't see the wood for the trees.* She had your problem. Don't try to paint the trees, Conrad, paint the wood. You should have another go.'

'I will.'

She sauntered towards the house, and I messaged Chris. He came hot-foot from the river, and Lloyd joined us under a Silence, which we kept up until Clémence got three metres from Alain's easel. I lifted my phone and pressed *Record*.

She stopped dead and gawped. Alain shot up from his stool with a *merde*.

Clémence swallowed hard. '*C'est magnifique, Alain, mais pourquoi vous avez peint un portrait du Duc de Wellington????*'

'Conrad! Where … Oh. There you are. And Chris and Lloyd. Very funny, guys.'

'What do we think, gentlemen?' I asked. 'Are we even for yesterday?'

'Not even close,' said Chris.

'No chance,' said Lloyd.

Clémence had turned to face us as well, and while her back was to the canvas, Lloyd dispelled the Glamour. We returned to our easels and left Alain to explain as best he could.

A late lunch was delivered by minibus, and it included just enough wine to go with the superb picnic. By common consent, we ate it in the barn because the weather was a little less warm than the sun suggested, and Clémence had put on a fan heater to warm our fingers. When I went for a smoke, I even took gloves.

Eseld had cheered up a lot, and was laughing with Chris and Alain, and I think that the Iron Duke may feature in a future costume party. I was expecting to have time with my thoughts until Lloyd emerged from the barn, saw that I was alone and strode towards me with a purpose.

'Alright, Conrad?' he began. 'Mind if I get serious for a minute? May not get another chance to talk before we fly home, and then you're all gonna be busy with your new job as Deputy Constable, and then with wedding stuff.'

'Everything okay, Lloyd?'

'I'm fine. I had a chat with Albie this morning. He's been to see Niði to keep the relationship going.'

Lloyd doesn't have a son, and until he does, his heir is a young Gnome called Albrecht, universally known as Albie, the only other (living) member of Lloyd's old Clan in the new Clan Salz. Given Gnomish humour, Albie is of course known as *Lloyd's left hand*. I make no judgement.

So, Albie has been to see the Dwarf, Niði. Both Lloyd and I have a close bond with Niði; the difference is that Lloyd also has a commercial relationship with the bearded terror, and I prefer to keep the silicon monster at arm's length. No, that was not a joke.

Lloyd was unusually uncertain, and took a long pause before he spat it out. 'Niði asked Albie if he knew what you thought of the new Warden.'

'Me? Why does Niði care what I think of the Warden?'

'You're a bright bloke, Conrad. You went to see her last week, and I'm sure you've thought about her plans, and I'm equally sure that you've noticed the name of her pet project.'

'The Community of Mages? What about it?'

Lloyd gave me a look that said, *Stop pretending to be dense.* Actually, I wasn't pretending: I really had no idea, and tried to convey it in a shrug. I don't think shrugs translate well to Old High Proto-Germanic.

He rolled his eyes, and said, 'Community of *Mages*, not Community of *Magick*. I'm many things, Conrad, but I ain't a Mage. Nor are your pet Wolves, and nor is your bloody cockroach.'

Gnomes and Dwarves often refer to the Fae as *cockroaches*. I let it ride this time, because he had a point. 'Politics is the art of the possible, Lloyd. I think that Lois is just trying to convince people to join in.'

'I wish I shared your sunny disposition, mate. I really do. Look at it from my perspective, will you: the thought of *all* human Mages banding together and locking us out is pretty disturbing. It didn't go well for the Creatures of Light when the Catholic Church had a monopoly, did it? We've only started to properly prosper since the Reformation.'

Third Eye

I didn't know what to say. In his shoes, I'd think exactly the same thing. What I didn't say was that the Catholic Church never had a total monopoly and spent more time hunting Witches than it did exterminating Gnomes. No comfort in that thought.

'Why me, Lloyd? You know I'd never let that sort of thing happen.'

'I know that, but you're human. You won't be around for ever, and more than that, you're special.' He sighed. 'I even asked Princess Poncy about the confluence.'

'Hang on, you do actually mean Faith, don't you?'

'Yeah. Who else?'

'Never mind, and never mind how you came to be talking to her, just tell me what in the Mother's name you mean by *confluence*?'

'Just that!' he said, shaking his head. 'You! You're the confluence.' He started ticking things off on his fingers. 'You wear the Allfather's ring. You've swapped blood with the First Daughter of Mother Earth. You've swapped blood with me, come to that. You have a seat reserved at Niði's table. You are Nimue's anointed priest and Guardian. What is it you say? You *hold the Queen's Commission*. You have friends at the high table in Salomon's House yet you also have a sapling of the Glastonbury Oak growing in your garden, and now blow me if you don't have a cutting of the Morrigan's Tree growing next to it. According to Myfanwy, anyway. You are blood brothers with me…'

'Already done that one.'

'Yeah, but I was gonna say that you're my brother *and* you have the Noble Queen of Galway's favour *and* a Princess as your handmaiden. You have a pack of Wolves. Oh, and the cherry on top of the biscuit is that Ganesh is going to join the flippin' queue to bless your wedding.'

'Gnomes never were known for pastry. I wouldn't put cherry on a biscuit.'

He actually turned purple, a colour normally reserved for angry Dwarves. 'Shut the fuck up, brother!'

Magick radiated off him, and not in a good way. I shut up.

He jabbed a finger at me. An artificial finger which extended and turned pale blue. 'I spoke to Princess Faithful to ask if her People had any – what do they call them? *Stories*. Any *stories* of a human having so many connections. I'd already asked Francesca, and the Children of Mother Earth certainly don't. No, was the answer from Faith, too. You're a confluence of interests, Conrad, and you should use them to stop the Warden from trying to build something that excludes the Creatures of Light. There. I've said it, so help me, Mother.'

He's got it wrong, of course. He thinks I'm building a power base, and he couldn't be more wrong. I'm like … I don't know. Prussia, perhaps? A small but perfectly formed territory surrounded by bigger players and desperately in need of allies. I want things to stay like that. I have no intention of establishing my own empire. On the other hand, alliances work two ways: not only do I have a lot of obligations to my allies, most of them are people I

153

actually like. I would not see them marginalised or threatened through inaction on my part.

'Not me, Lloyd. I have too many enemies of my own. What you need is someone at a loose end with a grudge against the Warden.'

'Who? Selena Bannister? Not Heidi Marston, surely?'

'Closer to home. You should see the Chief of Clan Blackrod and get him to raise it at the Manchester Alchemical Society. You should find plenty of hounds who'll run after that hare.'

The metaphorical lightbulb came on over his head. 'Seth Holgate! Of course. He's done more to integrate the Creatures of Light into human magick than anyone. He'd love to make it a cause after Lois Reynolds beat him to the nomination.'

'And I'm a member of Malchs, as well as being Lord Guardian of the North. I'd be willing to commit to it in public, so long as Seth took the lead.'

He clapped me on the back. 'You are such a devious sod, Conrad. No wonder I love you so much. I think Clémence is getting worried about us.'

He was right. The whole party was standing in the barn doorway wondering what we were up to. 'You did create a Silence?' I asked him.

'She can't understand me accent.'

But there were plenty who could, and none of them looked comfortable with what they'd heard. Except Barney. He just looked confused.

Chris, Lloyd and I refrained from further revenge on Alain after lunch, and following a final spurt in the afternoon, the whole group all produced something we felt inordinately pleased with. Until the judge arrived.

Around four o'clock, a filthy, battered Renault bounced into the yard and a woman in paint splashed dungarees over a bright orange top got out. Clémence's face lit up, and she winked at me. 'My best ever student,' she said. 'A much better artist than I could be. The only shame is that she gave up watercolour. *Excusez-moi.*'

She quick-stepped to the new arrival and gave her a kiss. A very affectionate kiss which her wife/girlfriend didn't return at first, and then did so with interest. Clémence half turned and said something in French to Alain, then followed her partner inside.

'Allo!' shouted Alain. 'We are to put our canvases in the barn and be ready for judging in twenty minutes. Remember, no signatures yet!'

We drifted in, cleaned up and arranged our canvases. Ben took a little posable wooden mannequin (you know the sort) out of his bag and put it on Clémence's table. 'Eyes on the prize, guys. This is the trophy. No expense spared, as you can see.'

We stood in a huddle and awaited our fate. Right on cue, Clémence returned and introduced her star student/wife as Jenner. Our judge turned out to be Scottish, and she'd also changed into clean dungarees and a more subdued top. We huddled by the sinks and awaited our fate.

'A whole English stag party, eh? Never thought I'd see one of those here. Clémence almost called me back when she realised who you really were.'

Alain had raised his fingers as if he was going to object to being referred to as *English*, then thought better of it. No such restraint for Eseld.

'I'm Cornish,' she announced with all the attitude you'd expect from someone with pent up energy looking for a lightning conductor.

Jenner was not happy. 'Are you the token woman to show how enlightened they are?'

Ooh. Wrong day to pick a fight with Ez. I dread to think what she'd have said if Ben hadn't stepped forwards. 'We were just saying what a peaceful, amazing day it's been. Clémence is an amazing teacher, and so patient! Eseld is actually from the Royal Protection Squad. She's our bodyguard, and I may have been a little economical with the truth about names on the application form.'

Jenner was totally wrongfooted, and looked along the line, trying to match what she saw against her mental register of the British royal family. She was about to come up empty when Lloyd looked at me and rattled off something in the Mother's Tongue. I think it was something to do with the weather in Wurtemburg, but it sounded impressive. He finished by bowing to me and saying, '*Prinz Conrad.*' That shut up the judge, and she got on with what she was here for.

I can't swear to it, but I'm sure she was trying to work out which was Eseld's canvas, and if she'd known, would she have awarded the prize to the only woman out of sisterly solidarity, or denied it because Eseld is clearly a traitor to her sex? We'll never know.

When she came to my effort, she studied it carefully (as she had all of the others, to be fair). 'Nice. I'd definitely picnic in that meadow, but you wouldn't catch me going in *those* woods after dark.'

And the prize? It went to Chris Kelly. 'This is by far the best executed picture, and Clemmy swears you are all complete beginners. If so, then hats off to the only one who felt up to tackling livestock. That cow practically moos at you.'

As we got back on the bus, Ben had an announcement for us. 'Vicky says to tell you that the girls are all fine, if totally exhausted' He shrugged. 'No idea why they should be exhausted, but there you go. Vicky's taken their phones off them today after last night's debacle with … with Mina and the stripper. She says that Sapphire Gibson is official photographer and will be uploading a full selection to the cloud tomorrow for them to delete ones they don't like. After that, we'll get to see what they've been doing. If we're lucky.'

My leg ached after so much standing, and I was looking forward to a bath and some stretching. Ben had other ideas.

'Afternoon tea will be ready when we get back. I'd tuck in if I were you, lads, because tonight's meal won't be served until after the main activity, and that could be late. Dinner suits on and ready for the bus at seven-thirty. Ez is coming on the bus but not inside where we're going.'

'I have no idea why not,' said Ez loudly. 'He won't tell me, and I brought an evening gown specially.'

'You can still wear it,' said Ben.

'No thanks. I'm going to the gym to try and work off some of last night's desserts. I am not gonna be Billy No Mates at wherever we're going.' She looked at Chris. 'For one thing, I don't want to have to keep fending off men if I'm not on the pull.'

Lloyd snorted. 'Hey, Conrad, will you get to be nursemaid on her Hen do to repay the favour?'

'Let's not go there,' said Tom diplomatically. 'That's a whole kettle of worms we don't want to open.'

Chapter 21 — Level Playing Field

'Yep. You lot really do scrub up nicely. Squeeze in a bit.' Eseld took the picture of us in our dinner jackets, and we filed on the bus after dropping our phones in the secure box. Except Chris. She held him back to get a solo shot, posing moodily in the hotel entrance.

'How did you and Chris get your penguin suits to fit?' asked Barney. 'I look like a bouncer in mine.'

'Don't ask,' said Tom. 'The answer involves multiples of your salary. On you get.'

Another short trip around the Normandy countryside, and Ben got up again. 'I can't take credit for tonight's agenda, I'm afraid.'

'What the hell did he do, then?' asked Lloyd.

'He's got it pretty much right up to now,' I supplied. 'Myfanwy again? She's been busy.'

'No, not Myfanwy. So far, I've done my best to avoid anything magickal, and that's about to change. When we pull up at the abandoned farmhouse ahead, some of you may be able to see something that I can't. On the right.'

We did pull up, and there were four sharp intakes of breath and two expletives. The ruined farmhouse (cottage really) positively *glowed* in the evening sunshine, and on a battered *immobilier* board were glittering letters in a script favoured by the Fae: *La Tentation*. Bloody hell.

'Have a good time, lads,' said Lloyd, ''cos I ain't going in there. Not *won't*, *can't*, as in they *won't* let me over the threshold. No Children of the Mother allowed.'

Notwithstanding Lloyd's confusion with his modal verbs, he was right. And I was with him – I wasn't going in there, either.

'Don't panic,' said Ben. 'None of us are going in there, despite Tara Doyle telling me that it was the best restaurant and private club in the whole of France.'

'You mean the most exclusive brothel in the whole of France,' added Eseld.

'Seriously?' said Barney, with a little too much excitement mixed in with his puzzlement.

'Yeaaah,' drawled Ben. 'When I double-checked Tara's suggestion with Faith, she fell about laughing. Because this place is so exclusive, we'd need a sponsor to even get a booking. I'm not sure that Tara would have gone through with sponsoring us, but she wanted it on the itinerary. Said we'd have a mind-blowing experience.'

Chris shuddered. 'I'll count that as a lucky escape, thanks.'

Tom looked rather annoyed, as if he'd been left out of something and didn't fancy the alternative. 'So where *are* we going? And what does magick have to do with it?'

'*Allez a Deauville, s'il vous plaît*,' said Ben to the driver, then sat down and refused to answer any questions except to say that our actual destination was Faith's idea.

When we got to the posh seaside town, Ben handed a slip of paper to the driver. Our driver in Normandy had been carefully chosen to speak no English whatsoever, and he chuckled when he read the paper, then he said something to Alain, put the coach in gear and drove off.

Alain looked alarmed and swallowed nervously. 'Go on,' said Ben. 'We're dying to know.'

'In English, he said that he hopes our tuxedos have deep pockets.'

Eseld swung herself athletically out of her seat and went up to Ben. 'Give us a sec, Alain. Yeah?'

When Alain had scuttled away, Ez put her hand on Ben's arm and whispered something under a Silence. Ben turned his face away to answer, and Eseld looked slightly put out with his words. She dropped the Silence and put on a smile. 'Right. Alain, tell the driver to stop on a side road near where we're going. I'm gonna go in and check it out. If I'm happy, then off you go and have a good time.'

We pulled up with a view of the sea ahead but no other clue as to where we might be. Ez grabbed her gym bag and hopped off. As she got close to the end of the road, she swirled her fingers and her short jacket morphed into a Mowbray Blue gown. With a wave, she went round the corner. Yet again, Alain had to intervene with the driver.

It only took five minutes for Ez to reappear, during which time a competition to guess the event was nearing its climax. I think the most likely (and most bonkers) was definitely Chris: 'I know, I know! We're going to a Live Action Role Play where we are all James Bond!'

Who said Chris has no imagination, eh?

From the end of the road, Ez gave a thumbs-up and looked at her phone, then she set off in search of some gym or other. The coach moved up to the junction, turned right and then swung into a drop off zone under a very impressive portico. We were going to the casino. Alain went white and used two swear words I've not heard before.

'Follow me, gents,' said Ben. He waited until we were all off, then he put his arm round Alain's shoulders and led him to the front door. Ben said something about a *Salle Privée*, then we were being escorted through the public rooms by a most attentive security guard. He left us half-way down a red corridor, and told us to turn left at the end, and that our hostess would meet us.

Ben still had his arm close to Alain, which was a good thing, because around the corner we beheld Manon Roussel in all her leather glory. Poor lad would have bolted if Ben wasn't there to hold him in place.

I spotted it first, because casinos smell of many things but not usually damp earth. Our hostess was a Fae, and I'm betting that Eseld was responsible for this.

Lloyd chuckled. 'I think we're even now.' He raised his voice. 'Alright, love, you can knock it off now or poor Alain will faint.'

Rather than disrobe her Glamour in public, the Fae slipped through an open door, and we found her standing by a card table and dressed in the uniform of a casino croupier. Ben stood aside and let me go first.

I bowed. 'Well met…?'

She returned the bow. 'I am Seigneur Ambre. Well met in peace, my lord. Her Grace La Reine de Normandie bids you welcome to her lands. And now, I think, a drink.'

A waitress emerged from the shadows to hand round glasses of Champagne, and we admired the little den. I have no idea (and don't want to know) whether the Fae have a stake in the Casino Barrière du Deauville, or whether they'd just rented the room for tonight. Either way, it had been dressed and draped in Rococo fabrics and suitably adorned with soft-porn pictures. I couldn't resist it. 'Nice choice of decor, Ben. Are you planning to redecorate your cottage like this for when Myfanwy moves in?'

'Ha ha, Conrad.' He turned to our hostess. 'Excuse me, erm, Ambre? Does the room always look like this?'

The Seigneur looked like butter wouldn't melt. 'No, monsieur. The booking specifically requested it for the groom. Said it would make him feel at home.'

Ben looked at me, and I looked at him. 'Faith,' we said in unison.

Ambre's staff uniform had one addition I hadn't seen in the public rooms. 'Are you expecting trouble?' I asked, pointing to the dagger at her waist.

She frowned at me. Quite seriously. 'My lord has good Sight and a strong Third Eye. It marks my status as a *Seigneur*. More than a Knight in your country, but less than a *Comte* in mine. To bare it in mortal company would be a serious matter.'

'Your grace has honoured us with you,' I replied. I was going to ask where the Royal Sídhe might be, but Ben had an announcement.

I'd seen him talking to Alain, presumably reassuring the lad that he wouldn't lose his shirt. That was kind, but he should have remembered that Barney and Tom may have relatively rich girlfriends, but they are both on police salaries.

'Tonight's game is Texas Hold'em, lads. Has anyone *not* played before?' Tom and Chris put their hands up. 'Don't panic. Ambre is going to give you a quick lesson in a minute, and I just wanted to say that apart from tipping our hostess, you can keep your wallets safely in your pockets.'

That was good news, though I couldn't see us having much fun with dummy chips. Ben had thought of that, too.

'Conrad gave me a generous budget for this weekend, and we were going to fly up from Bordeaux until Faith suggested we come here. I booked TGV tickets instead, and the difference will be tonight's pot. You'll all get four hundred Euros in chips, and the winner takes all.'

Chris spoke up, too. 'In case you're wondering, Lloyd, Señor Amber is an expert on suppressing magick at the card table. It's a level playing field.'

'It is *Seigneur Ambre*,' said Alain. 'She is not a Spanish gentleman.'

'That's what I said!' protested Chris. 'Where do we sit?'

Ben left the newbies to their lesson, and we adjourned to the bar for a short while, then wandered past the roulette table. 'Can you really fix the wheel, Lloyd?' asked Barney.

My blood brother held out his left hand. 'With this, I could make the ball stop on any number you like.'

I coughed. 'Lloyd. You're attracting the attention of that gentleman with the frown and the earpiece. I think he may be a Mage.'

Lloyd gave the pit boss a cheeky grin and stepped back from the table. 'Their lesson should be over by now.' He rubbed his hands together. 'I reckon Anna's getting a new necklace tonight.'

We returned to the boudoir (can't think of it as anything else), and Seigneur Ambre put a Seal on the door. What happened behind that door is going to stay private, if you don't mind. Nothing of any great import was said, and nothing unexpected happened. I can tell you this, though: Anna Flint did not get a new necklace. Not even close.

'Looks like you had a good time,' observed Eseld when we returned to the bus. 'By the gods, you stink. The lot of you. How much booze did you put away?'

'I think we ought to lay Tom out on the back seat,' said Chris. 'He's a bit unsteady on his legs.'

'Grmblre,' said Tom. 'Grmm.'

'Lloyd, you sit on the floor in front of him,' said Ben. 'In case he rolls off.'

'Why me?'

'Because it was your side bet with him about whether Conrad was bluffing which tipped him over the edge.'

Without another word, the driver passed everyone a sick bag before we set off. And he drove very slowly. Don't blame him.

The last act of my Stag Weekend took place over a glass of calvados outside my triplex. Seeing the Roussel label had driven Alain wild, and we'd forcibly removed his phone to stop him calling Manon and waking her up. When he realised we were serious, he called us *a whole family of badgers* and went to bed. And then there were three: Eseld, me and (suitably upwind), Chris.

'Was it what you wanted?' asked Ez. 'Do you feel you've put your bachelor days behind you?'

I nodded slowly. 'It's going to be at least three years away, but I'll be hard-pressed to better this when Ben gets married. He did a brilliant job.'

Okay, I'd had a few, and it was very late. That's my excuse. When I talked about Ben's wedding to Myfanwy, I completely forgot that Chris and Eseld might get married, too.

Eseld slapped my knee. 'Don't worry, Conrad, I won't ask you to ride shotgun on my hen party. If I ever have one. There's a lot to be said for living in sin, as my Gran used to call it. C'mon, lover boy, lets get you up the staircase.'

And then there was just me, the stars and a last glass of calvados. I settled back and enjoyed the peace, until my phone pinged. I grabbed it and saw a message from Sapphire Gibson. *For your eyes only* said the text, with several wink emojis. I opened the image, and there was Mina, dressed as some sort of Bollywood warrior princess, complete with twin daggers.

There was still a silly grin on my face when Sapphire's follow-up message landed. *I'm barred from sending the other pictures, but they all had a great time and none of them were actually arrested. See you soon.*

I made Mina's image my new screensaver and went to bed the happiest man in France. Four weeks tomorrow, I'm getting married. Plenty of time to get nervous yet. Amongst my father's many pearls of wisdom, one of my favourites has always been, *Clarkes never go looking for trouble, son, because trouble will always come looking for us. It's what you do when she finds you that makes the difference.*

I always wondered why Dad personified *trouble* as female. If Mina and I are blessed with children, I shall spend their junior years considering that question carefully.

Technology doesn't solve *all* problems. Kathy knew it, Don knew it, and eventually Michael admitted it too. He wasn't happy.

Michael had spent three weeks suggesting apps for Kathy to download and print from, even though the office printer was locked up tighter than the Confidential cupboards. Michael said he could crack *that*, but it didn't matter because he couldn't come up with any ideas for how Kathy could find an app with which Don could address his letter without letting on where it was going and who it was going to.

'You'll have to tell us, Don,' said Michael when he finally gave up trying a tech fix. Don shook his head. He was a stubborn old man, and no mistake.

Kathy looked at the time and said, 'Curfew, Michael. Don't want Faye on your back again, do you?'

The guests had to earn the privilege of being at large after ten o'clock. To be precise, they were allowed to go to the shivering gallery or the guest lounge; they were certainly not allowed in the Abbey itself.

'Night, Don. I'm sorry,' said Michael. 'I'll see you at breakfast, chef.'

'Night, Michael.'

In Kathy's eyes, Michael's rehab wasn't going brilliantly. Sure, he'd graduated to the Continuity Group, and that meant less therapy and more activity, but had he *really* accepted his future? It wasn't just the restlessness which made her wonder; it was the lack of tears.

Everyone did it eventually – broke down over something trivial. The bankers and hedgerow managers were the worst, because they were born thinking they were masters of all they surveyed, and it's a long way down from up there. When she saw them crying over Peppa Pig, or dropping tears as they folded the laundry, or swept the courtyard, it was then that she knew they had accepted their future. They were usually nicer to her afterwards as well.

The next morning, she came straight out and asked, 'How long are MI6 paying to keep you here?'

'Four months. I've got just over a month left unless something changes.' He shrugged. 'Why the interest? Are you going to miss having a sous chef?'

She tipped oats into the boiling water. 'Yes I am. I hope.' She put the jug down. 'I'm not allowed to offer therapy, but I'd say you're a way off being ready to graduate yet. For one thing, you haven't left the Abbey once since you came, and that's not a good sign.'

He shrugged and glanced at the clock. Too early to warm the griddle yet. 'Nowhere I want to go. No one up here I want to go with.'

'I'm surprised that Faye hasn't been on your case.'

'She has. Told me I need to go on a visit next week. Otherwise, I'm going to be under the spotlight, and no one wants that, do they?'

'You can drive, right?'

'I can. And I know all about the guest car. Faye put me on the insurance for it.'

'Then we can go to Leeds on Tuesday. Faye lets me chaperone.'

Michael started the griddle and focused on the slick surface rather than meet her eye. 'What do you want?' he asked, in the voice of a man who knew he was about to be used for something.

'I've an appointment with the Social, then an assessment with a psychologist. Couple of hours. The trains just don't work out that day, and I can't afford to stay the night. Faye thinks I'm going shopping, so she'd have no problem with you tagging along.'

'You trust me?'

'No. Not completely. I'll know if you get in trouble, though.'

'Leeds it is. Shall I tell Faye, or will you?'

Third Eye

'I work here, and it's my day off. For you, it's therapeutic, so you tell her.'

Part Four — Dearly Beloved

Chapter 22 — The Ellipse of Life

'And you *promise* not to schedule anything for next week?' said Mina, with an *I dare you* look on her face.

One day, I will tell her that coming so close to the phone when we Facetime is not a good look. Effective, but not her best side. With that weird telepathy thing, she placed the phone down.

The Elvenham library appeared in the background, and I knew that she was sitting at her side of the partners desk we share, and almost certainly resting her phone on the little stand I bought for her so that she could have both hands free to gesticulate, like she was doing now.

'I mean it, Conrad! You will keep your diary clear for next week or … or I will tell Myvvy that you don't need Ben's spare room after all.'

That was a dire threat indeed. The wedding is ten days away, and from next Thursday I shall be staying with Ben to give the girls quality time in Elvenham. You may think that four nights of quality time is a bit excessive, but you have to remember that the wedding itself is only going to last a day, so I reckon I've got off lightly. On the other hand, if I can't have Ben's spare room, I may end up pitching a tent on the village green.

There was a bark in the background, and Mina's eyes flicked away to the right. 'Oh no, I forgot to fasten the door,' she moaned.

The microphone picked up a skittering of claws on wood, and I couldn't resist it. 'Here boy! Come here!'

'Arff!'

'Scout! No! You…'

Paws appeared on the desk as Scout followed the sound of my voice, and his weird eyes took Mina's place. He's a strong lad now, and she was caught off balance. My faithful hound bent his head, and then a big pink tongue licked the camera. I just caught Mina's wail before the connection broke. I got busy with my thumbs and sent this: *Meeting about to start. Will call from the road. Don't be too hard on Scout. See you v soon. XOXO.*

I put my phone down and limped through to the Haven kitchen. In a corner were three suitcases of stuff which Mina had forgotten to take when she decamped from Middlebarrow last weekend. Since she left, I've spent the week going through records, making calls and generally digging into things. Up to now, my responsibilities as Deputy Constable have been more about action than administration, and I don't miss the near-death experiences one bit. I'm calling it my Peace Dividend. Evie was elsewhere, so I made a pot of tea and took a mug back to the study to wait for a call from the President of the Manchester Alchemical Society.

The Chief of Clan Blackrod in Lancashire has been a busy little Gnome. Since I pitched the idea to Lloyd, and Lloyd dropped a few hints, the Blackrod Chief has been pushing at an open door in Manchester and, as I predicted, Seth Holgate has started his campaign to include the Creatures of Light in any "Community of Magick."

My phone rang, and Seth got straight down to business.

'I'd love to chat, Conrad, but I need to see one of the coven leaders before we start. Listen, are you really going to go public on this?'

'I don't normally do politics by phone, Seth, but I've been talking to the Constable. This is embargoed, okay?' I found the note and continued, 'The Boss, Iain Drummond and I have agreed a joint personal statement, and if you mention any of this in public or private before we announce it, I'll be most disappointed.'

'Mmm. Why do I think that *disappointed* is a code word for something unpleasant? You can trust me, Conrad.'

'I know. Have you checked your phone?'

'Yes, I have. And this call is encrypted. What have you got?'

'We're going to say this. *The King's Peace extends to all creatures of magick, whether or not they choose to embrace it. We believe any reforms which do not work to include all of them are not in the interests of Peace.* There you go.'

He thought about that. 'Interesting angle. I like it. What was the other thing you wanted to discuss?'

'I'd like to formally request that you allow the Dual Natured Commission to sit at Malchs, in the reception room.'

He almost purred with pleasure, which for a guy his size sounds more like a lion than a tabby cat. 'Better and better. Anything we can do to assist the Commission?'

'Well, if the Society offered secretarial support, it would save the Occult Council sending someone up from London all the time.'

'Consider it done.'

It would also save the Commission clerk's expenses coming out of the Deputy's budget, but I didn't say that. Another side of the Peace Dividend is that I now have to watch what I spend. Good job I'm marrying an accountant.

'Thanks, Seth. Good luck with the Executive meeting, and I'll see you at the Middlebarrow Banquet if not before.'

'Can't wait. Hope everything goes well next week. Better go.'

I sat back and smiled. I could now officially clock off as Deputy Constable and get on with the business of being a bridegroom. All I needed was my transport.

Right on cue, Evie banged on the door and shouted, 'They're here, Conrad! I've let them in.'

'Thanks, Evie.'

I put my briefcase in the cupboard and locked it tight, then I picked up my gun case and my sword. I may be off duty as Deputy Constable, but the job of Lord Guardian is full time.

Evie was in the kitchen, pouring more tea and having a hushed conversation with *#TeamBride*.

'I don't know why you're whispering,' I told them. 'I can't hear you from here anyway, and the listening device in the teapot doesn't care whether you whisper or not.'

Two of the group jumped and stared at the teapot, two of them didn't understand what a *listening device* is, and the fifth just rolled her eyes before bowing to me.

'My lord,' said Faith. 'I hope you are ready?'

My faithful Fae bondswoman has seen a lot, and it takes a lot to make her flinch. 'All good, thanks. Are you fully recovered?' I asked her.

'Yes, thank you my lord.'

Faith is the leader of #TeamBride, and her crew consists of Alicia (hair), Thistle (household), Cathy (nurse), and one more somewhere. Having them on board is weird, if you think about it, and I try not to. What I will say is that the wedding wouldn't work without them.

'I'm loving the new look,' I told Alicia. Instead of the disconcerting biological replica of Mina's hair, Alicia now has something in chestnut brown. Much less nightmare-inducing. Also much improved was her "sister", Thistle, who now at least *looked* over twenty-one rather than borderline eighteen, which was how she'd been shaped for the pleasure of her previous Lord. Don't ask. I mean it: don't ask, because she'll tell you, and it's not nice.

'Welcome, Thistle, welcome Cathy. Where are the others?'

'No pass for the Wards,' said Faith. 'They're waiting by the bus.'

Alicia was squirming, something she often does. By rights, she should be deep underground, learning the Ways of her people, but Faith wanted her on the team for some reason. Couldn't get anyone else she trusted, probably. 'What is it, Leesha?' I asked.

She sketched a quick bow. 'Would my lord really spy on his own people? Is that allowed?'

'Is it bloody hell allowed,' said Evie, who was the other one who'd stared at the teapot. 'Wouldn't stop him though, if he thought he could find out what happened on the Hen Party.'

Alicia looked pleased with herself and declared, 'What happens in

167

Blackpool, stays in Blackpool.' And then she realised that she'd just given the game away. This happens a lot.

Before Faith could do something, I told a white lie. 'I already knew it was Blackpool, Alicia. Ready? Luggage is over there.'

Faith nodded and set her people to carrying the bags. I said goodbye to Evie and followed them outside and up the driveway. Beyond the Wards, an executive minibus waited, as did the rest of the party.

'Morning all,' I said cheerfully.

When Faith is a Queen, she will have a Guard, and just as Alicia and Thistle are auditioning for senior roles in the Court, so is the strapping specimen of manhood who calls himself *Robbie*. If you could see those pecs and those shoulders, you'd understand why Sophie Wilson wanted to date him. He bowed quickly and went to grab the cases.

'Could you not have found a less attractive bodyguard, Faith?' I asked her. 'Robbie here is going to show up all the men in Clerkswell. I dread to think of the effect he'll have on the women. And Reynold from the Inkwell.'

'Feeling insecure, are we?' said Faith. 'Looks aren't the only part of Robbie's … package. He is well endowed in other areas, too. Like with the blade. And in the saddle.'

Robbie tossed the last case into the back of the bus and came across with an eager expression on his face. Poor lad.

I put my arm on his shoulder and said, 'You shouldn't let them objectify you like that, Saerdam Robert.'

'Sophie said that, too. I told her that I only need to look like this for a few decades, then I'll go for something with more of an edge.'

And there you have it, ladies and gentlemen: they are like us, but they are not us.

'One minute,' I said, lighting a fag and going to meet the other two non-humans: Mannwolves to be exact.

Maria and her daughter, Lottie, had hung back, almost hidden by the bus, and Lottie was almost hidden by her mother. I grabbed the door and lowered myself gently to her level. 'Hi Lottie, how is your first trip outside the Lakes going so far?'

She gripped Maria's kilt a little tighter and looked up.

'You did brilliantly,' said her mother. 'Didn't you? Did you cry?'

'No, my lord,' said the little girl. 'Mummy said I was ever so brave.'

'Are you excited for the wedding?'

She let go of Maria's kilt and nodded her head vigorously. 'I am, and Mummy said there's going to be lots of girls for me to look after, and I get to see Scouty again. I've missed him.'

Maria beamed, like any mother would. 'Thank you for letting us spend so much time away from Birk Fell, my lord,' she said with a bow.

'I'm just thrilled that there's no full moon before the wedding. Worked out nicely. Everything well with the Pack?'

Faith is the Pack's Madreb, their day-to-day keeper. I could have asked her, but she would just say *Yeah* and move on. Maria is devoted to Faith, but she's even more devoted to me. And Mina.

Maria touched my arm. She is that rare thing, a Mannwolf with some conscious power over magick. She made the Silence and said, 'The Pack is excited. Our Guardian arrived at first light, and that means special time. I almost wish I'd stayed.' She gave me a mad grin. 'Especially when we passed the Guardian's woman on the way to Pooley Bridge.'

If Karina could hear Rebecca described as *her woman*, she'd be outraged. Becca, I think, would be flattered. I am, however, not going to put that theory to the test.

Maria had more, and spoke in a whisper, dropping her head to mine (I was still squatting). 'Could be *another* wedding! I might even live to see it.'

I forced a smile. If you saw Maria at the school gate in some parallel universe, waiting for her daughter, you'd think her Lottie's big sister. In fact, she doesn't have much more than a decade of life to look forward to. Robbie will probably still be channelling the Dreamboys by then.

Why do I look at Robbie and immediately think of strippers? Is Faith up to something? Is *Mina* up to something? Best not to ask.

'Can you help me up, Maria?'

'Of course, Lord Protector. Do you have a wound or is it age decay?'

'Just the weather, that's all.'

Maria once saved my life by, amongst other things, licking a wound with healing saliva. Once again, they are like us but they are not us.

Safely restored to the vertical, I shook out my leg and put my butt in the ashtray. 'There's a game we single-natured play in cars, Lottie. It's called *I Spy*. Shall I teach it to you?'

'Ooh, yes please!'

It was always hard to tell how rich the guests *really* were. Addiction often leads to debts, as Kathy knew only too well. Part of her rehab had been facing her debts and consolidating them into a single, enormous loan. It was where a huge chunk of her wages went every month.

The privately funded guests could be rich or poor, it was hard to tell. A gambling addict could go through the family finances like the combine harvester did to the Abbey Farm fields. Michael's addiction was drugs, and he wasn't a banker, so she had no idea. A truly rich banker would think nothing of buying an iPhone, accessing their profile from the cloud and then chucking it away an hour later.

Would Michael do something similar? If that was all he did while Kathy was with Social Services, she'd be happy to turn a blind eye.

He dropped her at the Council block after checking the paper where she'd written directions to the car park one last time. She waved him off and took a deep breath. She could do this.

Two hours later, she took a fag break and went back inside to meet the Senior Case Worker and get the results of her assessment. She hadn't met this woman before, and didn't like the look of her, either. When she heard a southern accent, Kathy nearly bolted rather than get the bad news.

The woman met her in reception and took her to an empty counselling room, all soft pastels and beanbags, with just two adult chairs and a small table. 'I'm Maddy Turner,' she said. She pulled one chair away from the table and gestured to the other. 'Have a seat.'

Kathy sat down and so did Maddy (the chair creaked a lot when her big arse hit it), and Maddy kept the files on her lap rather than rest them on the table. 'Thanks for waiting, Kathy. It doesn't seem like a good use of a day's holiday, I know, but we have to fit in with other agencies.'

'No problem!' said Kathy as eagerly as she could. 'Happy to fit in with whatever.'

Maddy smiled, and she looked almost like a normal person instead of a social worker. 'I know you are, and it's a great sign. You wouldn't believe the number of clients I've seen who can't turn up to an appointment no matter what's at stake. In fact, your previous case officer, Ms Hepple was annoyed that I decided to do this interview, because we all get jealous of good news.'

Kathy wasn't sure where this was leading, so she just said, 'Oh yes?'

'Yes. Believe it or not, the best days for us are when children go home and when we *know* they're going to a better place.'

That sounded promising, so Kathy looked down at the table rather than give anything away. Anything like *hope*, for example.

'You've come a long way, Kathy. That's great. And I can see the end of the road now. We just need to help you get there. All of you.' She opened a file and took out a piece of paper. 'This is from the foster family. I'll read it out. *Both girls talk positively about their mother now, and the younger one asks almost every day when she can see her again.* That's also not as common as we'd like.'

Kathy's heart squeezed in her chest. Could this be the beginning of the end?

Maddy shuffled papers and closed the file. 'You've done everything you can, Kathy. The assessment was just a formality, really, after Doctor Swift's report. You are now eligible to apply for custody, and I see that your solicitor has been in touch.'

Was it Kathy's imagination, or had the temperature just dropped a fraction. Probably all the sweating she was doing. Shouldn't have worn the thick tights. She smiled to show that she'd heard what Maddy had said.

Maddy smiled back. 'This chat is now informal, you understand?'

'You mean off the record.'

'I wouldn't put it quite like that, but yes, it is. For example, I'm not saying that we wouldn't allow your older daughter to move schools *again*, but that might be a factor.'

'Cherry. Her name's Cherry.'

'Cherry loves her school, and it has a great reputation. A lot of parents would fight like mad to get their kids in there. And the neighbourhood is a good one. I've checked your file, and you have no connections there. Another good reason to keep Cherry in Saint Michael's and let her sister join her.'

Kathy fought to control her breathing. The only way she could get through the next part was to reach into her bag and touch the letter. That would make her strong. She touched the envelope, then took out a tissue. 'Excuse me.' She blew her nose. 'Sorry. Yeah, Cherry loves that school. And her teacher. Mind you, Beckthorpe has a brilliant school, too. Outstanding, in fact.'

Maddy gave the social worker's smile, the one that says they have the law on their side, only this time Kathy knew better. Her barrister, her secret weapon, had written it down in the letter. *At that age, a move to Beckthorpe school would not be seen as a barrier.* What Kathy tried not to think about was the next paragraph: *Unfortunately, Ms Metcalfe's accommodation at the Abbey is not suitable for a family.*

'Looks like I'll have to start looking, then,' said Kathy.

'With these references, you'll be snapped up,' said Maddy, who clearly thought Kathy would be looking for a job. She wouldn't: she'd be looking for a house. In Beckthorpe.

'Is there anything else?' asked Kathy.

'I don't think so. The next few visits are arranged, I see, so we'll leave the ball in your court, and I'll let you get off. The trains are terrible to Thirsk, aren't they?'

'They are. Thank you so much.'

They stood, and Maddy showed her out of the building. It had taken a lot more than two hours, but Michael had insisted on having a plan. He couldn't wait near the offices, but he would drive past the entrance to the park next door every fifteen minutes. She lit a cigarette and took her time to finish it before she went to wait for him.

She took out her phone and Googled the estate agents again: still nothing for rent within walking distance of the Abbey. Maybe she needed to think outside the box about this. She hitched her bag on her shoulder and headed to the park. Michael turned up two minutes later, and he had the biggest grin on his face. 'How did it go,' he asked first. 'I've been worried about you.'

He had, too, underneath whatever it was that he was bursting to tell her, he really cared. 'Pretty good, really, but it's a lot to take in. I'll tell you later, if that's okay. What have you been up to?'

'Wait and see. There's a Costa Coffee up the road. I bet you could murder a brew.'

'Mind reader. I'll have a fancy cappuccino with an extra shot, if you're buying.'

He was buying, and he got the drinks to go. She stood outside the car while she waited, and when he sauntered towards her, the grin was back. 'We've got ten minutes, haven't we?'

'We've got all day.'

'Good. Download an app called *Ulabelit* while you drink your coffee.'

She hesitated. 'How do you spell that app?' He sounded out the letters, and it clicked in her head. *You-Label-It.* When the app finished downloading, she had a pretty good idea where Michael was going, but she still couldn't see how Don would be able to use it.

Michael reached behind her seat and took out a bulky plastic bag from Office Outlet. He opened the bag and said, showing her the items, 'One Bluetooth label printer, one robust keyboard, and one Lightning-USB cable. You don't need me to show you how to set this lot up, do you?'

'No, I don't, but...'

'...But how can Don use a keyboard if he can't even hold a marker pen? I've saved the best till last. Here.' He opened a plain brown box and took out something like a surgical torture device. 'Give me your right hand.'

She held it out dubiously, and he slipped it into a fibreglass half glove, then fastened it with several Velcro straps.

'Well I'll be,' she said.

The rigid fibreglass, together with the straps, controlled a steel rod about six inches long that ended in a little plate. She tested it, trying to imagine how much Don's hand shook. It might take a while, but it was worth a go. He was in with a shout here.

'Well? What do you think?' he asked, like an anxious little lad.

'Good work, Michael. Good work. We'll give this a go on Friday night, shall we?'

Michael took the stuff and packed it away, then put the Abbey's postcode into the Satnav. On the way back, she gave him the edited, positive highlights from her encounter with Maddy the social worker.

'Well, I think that was a good day all round,' he concluded when they turned off the A19. He paused. 'I also really enjoyed getting out. Much more than I thought I would. I even saw a concert advertised next week that I might try to get tickets for. Will I need a chaperone for that?'

The guests were allowed radios in their rooms, and you often heard them blaring out of the windows in warmer weather. Michael was *not* allowed near the kitchen radio's control knob, though. 'If it's that rubbish you listen to, then you'll need a deaf chaperone.'

'Tchaikovsky is not rubbish.'

'Matter of opinion. If it's a classical concert, I doubt they'll be overrun with dealers, so you should be fine now you've realised there's a world outside the Abbey. You should choose somewhere else first, though. Get some practice in.'

'Where would you suggest?'

They chatted about possible days out for Michael until they got back to Beckthorpe. When they arrived at the Abbey, Kathy took firm control of the Office Outlet bag and its contents. 'This is contraband, Michael. You have no use for it. I'll take it and get some practice ahead of Friday night.'

'Yeah. Sure. I haven't had a surprise room inspection for a couple of weeks now, but better safe than sorry.'

Chapter 23 — Decisions, Decisions

'Can you have themed weddings?' I mused while we waited for our guests to arrive (not that we didn't already have enough *guests* running round the place).

'Themed weddings? Themed Weddings?' spluttered Mina. 'Are you going senile, Conrad? You know what, next year the Bank Holiday is on May the fourth, so if we'd waited, we could have had a Star Wars themed wedding. I could put you in a Wookie costume and shut you up.' She warmed to her theme. 'In fact, Chris would make an *excellent* Darth Vader. Shame that Roly Quinn is dead, or he could have been Obi Wan Kenobe. Shall we cancel this wedding – which is Asian Fusion themed, by the way – shall we cancel it and re-schedule for next year's Star Wars Day?'

'I didn't know you were such a fan,' I said mildly.

'I'm not! I hate it and I would rather die than dress up as Princess Leia again.'

'*Again?* When was the last time?'

'Figure of speech. Why are you interested in themed weddings? Has Chris said something about proposing to Eseld or something, because her I could definitely see insisting on a theme.'

After my late-night faux pas, I was not going there. 'I was thinking more abstractly. *Reunions.* Something like that.'

'I know you haven't been to many weddings, Conrad, but I think you'll find that *reunions* go with the territory. Is that them?'

The black minibus crunched up the drive, Faith at the wheel, and stopped so that the sliding door faced the tower of Elvenham Grange. We stepped outside the arch, and I stood back for Mina to welcome the person who is, to her, the most important guest. Way more important than the Elderkind.

Buff Robbie (as I've heard him called) jumped out of the front passenger seat and slid back the door. Two tweenage girls got out first, mouths slightly agape at their surroundings. Robbie held out his hand, and helped Mina's cousin, Anika Desai, out of the bus. Robbie turned and pointed to the dragon over our door, and Anika became the latest person to greet the stone carving whilst she no doubt wondered just how mad we all are for insisting on it. She had barely stood up when Mina leapt into her arms for a hug of truly Indian proportions. It was still going on when I arrived to shake hands.

The reason that Anika (or *Anika Ben* as Mina calls her, *Ben* being the term for a female cousin) is such an important guest is that she is the only link to Mina's Indian heritage who doesn't bring a trailer load of emotional baggage. If Mina could have persuaded Anika Ben to give her away at St Michael's church on Monday, it would have been her cousin walking her down the aisle and not her brother, whom I'd had to bribe to turn up at all.

Anika may not have much emotional baggage, but she did have a lot of *actual* luggage, and Robbie was busy unloading it. He would be a while with that, so I turned to the girls. 'Namaste. You must be Jivika, and you must be Jiyana. I'm Conrad.'

'We know,' said Jivika, the older one. 'Mummy has shown us all the videos.'

'*All* the videos? Including the one with the cheese?'

They grinned at each other. 'We have watched that one a *lot*,' said Jivika.

Jiyana had a question. 'There is a moment where there is no sound. The little man says something, but we can't hear him. What did he say?'

There is a very good reason why she can't hear: Lloyd's remark about the consistency of soft cheese has an 18 rating. I deflected her by saying, 'That's my friend Lloyd. He's the strongest person I know. Even stronger than Robbie over there. Wait until you meet him. How was the flight? You must be tired.'

'They were like two demons until they fell asleep,' said their mother.

'Shall I show them round and get them something to drink?' I offered.

'Good idea,' said Anika.

I whistled loudly, then said, 'This way, girls.'

'Mummy was right, it *is* cold in England,' said Jiyana. 'Why couldn't Mina Ben get married in Dubai or something?'

'Arff!' said Scout as he bounded round the corner, followed at a distance by Lottie.

Jiyana might be the younger one, but she has more front. She was the one who intercepted my mad dog (who has become increasingly delirious as more people have arrived), leaving Jivika to stare at Lottie, then whisper to me, 'Why does she have no shoes? Can her family not afford them?'

Having a junior Mannwolf around mundane children was a risk. A calculated one, but a risk nonetheless. They share a lot with each other in the Pack Hall, and I've heard one small child say to another that venison blood is very musky compared to sheep's. To avoid this scenario, I had insisted that Faith enrol Lottie in an activity club up at the Rheged centre, *and* that Faith send Thistle in the guise of a big sister. Fingers crossed, it had worked (and Lottie has a drama certificate to prove it. Not that she can read). We even had a cover story prepared for the inevitable question: *where do you go to school and what do they teach you?*

'That's Lottie,' I said. 'Her family are sustainable farmers who live on my land in the mountains. She does *have* shoes, but she spends a lot of time on the fells. Her grandmother does home-schooling up there.'

'What is a *fell?*' asked Jivika.

'I'll let Lottie explain. If you need your mother, ask one of the grown-ups. They'll take you straight to her.'

'We don't need mother,' said Jiyana. 'We often play alone with the servants' children. Where are you going?'

'To the pub. We have other guests who are staying there and I need to meet them.' I gave Jiyana a sly grin. 'Only the *special* guests get to stay at the house.'

I left the madness behind and strolled up Elven Lane to the village, then turned left and headed to the pub. My next batch of guests weren't staying at the Inkwell, but they had rented the private dining room there and wanted to meet me for some reason which I could guess at but not be certain. Time to find out.

I approached the Inkwell from round the back, whistling a happy tune and feeling rather good about things. The tang of malted barley from their microbrewery hit me, and I thought of the barrels of Inkwell Bitter already racked up at home, ready to be tapped, starting tonight if I was lucky.

You may think, "No wonder he is happy if he's gone to the pub leaving all the work to the women," and there is some truth to that. Then again, most of the hard work was being done by the Fae, and who provided them, I ask you?

I wiped the silly grin off my face when I saw who was waiting by the private, rear entrance to the function room. What was Juliet Bloxham doing lurking around? Oh. She was waiting for me.

Somehow, in some twisted turn of fate, Juliet and Stephen Bloxham have rented their home, the biggest, oldest house in Clerkswell, to the Mowbrays. I know. Who'd have thought it? The Mowbrays are the ones waiting inside, and I also know that Juliet is supposed to be cooking them all dinner at the Manor tonight, so…?

'Hi Conrad,' she said, taking out her car keys and clearly ready to clear off. 'Glad I caught you. Something's come up, and we're going to Tenerife tomorrow. We won't be back until after the wedding, I'm afraid.'

'Oh? That's a shame. I know that Mina was looking forward to having the whole ladies cricket team in one of the pictures.' It was left unsaid: I had no interest in Stephen being in *any* of my wedding photos.

'I know, and I really am sorry.' She rolled her eyes slightly. 'I'm sorry about the wedding, but at least it means poor Ben won't have to decide who's batting eleven on Saturday.'

She was wrong there. Ben would rather give up cricket than drop me for the opening match of the season when it was two days before my wedding. 'Every cloud and all that.'

She took my words with the ambiguity I'd intended and added something more unexpected. 'We've also had a really amazing offer to rent out the place we've decamped to. Eseld said you'd know them: the Hardistys?'

'Aah. Yes. I do know them. I wondered where they were staying.'

'Well, seek them at the Allingham Rectory from tomorrow afternoon. I really hope it all goes off amazingly, Conrad. I really do.'

'I know you do, Jules. Thank you. And good luck feeding the Mowbrays tonight. Rather you than me. And keep Eseld off the port.'

She gave me a funny look and left me to find out for myself what was going on. I climbed the stairs to the private room and remembered the last time I'd been invited here on anything other than cricket club business: my birthday.

The room is one of those intermediate spaces. Just big enough for a proper party, but not big enough for the boys to rent it out for weddings, and not exactly intimate, either. When I went in, I could see that *something* was up, and the focus, for once, was not on Eseld, but on her mundane brother, Cador. I noted that, then ignored him because I wanted to see whether their sister had made it up from Cornwall in one piece.

She had, and she had an armchair all of her own in the corner, the others being sort of clustered around her. Her hair was as wild and red as it had ever been, and her skin had the maternity glow of someone with a growing bump and rampant hormones. 'Hello, Conrad,' whispered Morwenna. 'Scuse me if I don't get up.'

'You're sounding a lot better,' I observed, bending down to give her a kiss.

You'll notice I said *sounding*, not *looking*, because Morwenna had her vocal chords slashed almost to destruction by the first Count of Force Ghyll. She can use magick to sound normal, but prefers not to.

'I am,' she replied. 'The last operation was a great success. That's it for now, though.' She grinned and zipped her lip.

The Mowbrays should have all arrived by Smurf this morning, and one was missing. 'Where's Ethan?' I asked, after giving his Tyrolean fiancée, Lena, a hug.

'He gets you a beer. I think you are needing it.'

'Oh?'

'*Oh* is right,' said Kenver, youngest Mowbray and heir to their massive estates.

What on earth? I looked at Eseld, and she shook her head, asking me to wait.

I took a seat near Morwenna and Ethan returned with a tray holding two and a half pints of Inkwell Bitter: the other Mowbrays were all on coffee or tea. Ethan is quiet, dour and serious. He placed my beer, gave the half to Lena and took the other pint for himself. Mission accomplished, he sat down and raised his glass. 'Cheers, Conrad. Been looking forward to trying this for a long time.'

He settled back and continued, 'This is Cador's show, not that I don't want some answers, too, mind. I told him it should happen here because I want to leave it behind when we walk out.'

Now I was really worried. Not too worried to ignore the beer, though. 'Good health, everyone.' Pint sampled, I sat back and crossed my legs.

Cador went to stand up, then remembered he wasn't in court. If the Mowbrays had all started with zero inherited wealth, Cador would be the richest because his lawyer's brain is sharper than my sword. 'Hello Conrad, sorry about this, but I've got some concerns about this scheme you've cooked up with Eseld, and before you say anything, let me finish.' He paused. I drank. 'When the Bloxhams said that Cora was staying in their house from tomorrow, Eseld finally told me why. Apparently Eseld has suggested, on your urging, that Cora should become the founding Dean of Mowbray College.'

'Good,' I said. 'I'm pleased that Cora has said yes.'

'She's said *maybe*,' Eseld interjected. 'She's come up early with Mike and the kids so we could talk.'

'I'm still thrilled,' I told her, then turned to Cador. 'This was something that needed maximum discretion.'

'On its own, yes,' said Cador. 'However, when you couple it with the stand that the Manchester Alchemical Society have taken, and with the rumour that Merlyn's Tower agrees with them, I see a lot of trails leading back to you, Conrad. I see a conspiracy to sink the new Warden's plans before her ship leaves port.' He ploughed on. 'What I don't want is for my family to be dragged into your battles. We have enough of our own.'

I'd been watching Eseld out of the corner of my eye. She was itching to join in, so I took another drink and let her fill the silence.

'Go on, Cador,' she urged. 'Tell him your mad theory. Tell him why you think we have our own *battles*.'

Cador and Eseld are full siblings. Cador actually talks to their mother and has done for years; they can wind each other up in ways they wouldn't dream of using on their half-brother and half-sister, Kenver and Morwenna.

'It's not a "mad theory",' Cador responded, complete with air quotes. 'It's fact. Dad did it deliberately, and it got him killed! I don't want history repeating itself.'

'And neither do I,' added Kenver. 'This is not Morwenna's problem.'

Eseld turned and looked at me, injecting her voice with sing-song sarcasm. 'Cador thinks that Dad never forgave Isolde for walking out on him. Cador thinks that Dad created the Mowbray College Foundation to spite the Daughters in Glastonbury, and Cador thinks that Dad put Morwenna in charge to show that Aisling's children are the more important ones. Cador thinks that you're trying to use us to fight your battles and that you're putting us in the firing line. That's what he thinks.'

Lena banged her (almost empty) half pint glass on the table. 'I do not like your tone, Eseld. Just because Conrad and Mina and Rachael are almost family, that doesn't mean we behave like children in front of them.'

Lena likes wearing traditional Austrian dress – dirndls and so on. Today she was in jeans and looked very fierce. Eseld opened her mouth to have a go back, then, to her own surprise thought better of it and shut up.

I took another drink and swirled the glass around, then I looked at Morwenna. 'Has Cador explained Cloister Probate to you?'

She nodded and raised her eyebrows to say *where are you going with this?*

As you might expect, the world of magick has a lot of wealth that simply *can't* appear in the mundane world. To the best of my knowledge, for example, Dwarves do not have National Insurance numbers. Fair enough, you might think. The government thinks otherwise.

As well as crime, the Cloister Court also deals with the magickal equivalents of income tax and death duties, the latter being known as Cloister Probate. And who better to look into it than the Peculier Auditor…

'The Mowbray Estate is Mina's first Probate case,' I told them. 'If you hadn't guessed, you'd find out from her report when she's submitted it.'

'Is this allowed?' said Lena, who had just pointed out that we're almost family. It wouldn't happen in Austria.

'I'm not surprised,' said Cador. 'Normally it would go to Clan Isarn for audit, but I can see that they'd use Mina to do the hard work, then get the Gnomes to double-check it. What does the Probate have to do with this?'

'Mina hasn't shown me any figures,' I said, 'but she has had to ask me some questions and discuss some timelines.' I turned to Ethan. 'When did Lord Mowbray tell you that he would one day release Kellysporth from the overall trust?'

Ethan looked guilty. He had grown up in a property belonging to the big trust: Lord Mowbray's last act before his death had been to break up that block to prepare his heirs for the future. Alas for him, instead of decades, they had a couple of hours to get used to the idea. Today's argument is another chapter in the fallout from that.

'On my thirtieth birthday,' said Ethan, to everyone's surprise except Lena's – the break up of the Trust had been big news to the family, especially Lord M's fiancée. It was one of the reasons she conspired to kill him. 'Not long after my father was first diagnosed with cancer,' added Ethan.

Next, I turned to Kenver. 'You've just won the tender for that Ley line job in Derbyshire, haven't you?' He nodded. 'So, you'll have a good idea of how much your father used to earn from contracting.'

'I suppose.'

I looked round the group. Whenever families come to discuss money, they quickly forget everything else – like the fact that their father was indeed murdered. 'It's like this,' I told them. 'As far as Mina can see, the estate was suffering when Arthur took over. He worked non-stop for decades to rebuild the estate fortunes, to build Pellacombe, to buy more land and make the estate what it is today. At first, every penny was reinvested in Cornwall. I think his plan to become Staff King of Kernow was with him from school.'

'I think you're right,' said Ethan. 'He never said out loud, but that's what I reckon.'

'And when he'd secured the estate, he started to invest *outside* Cornwall. He bought the ruin of Ethandun Palace. He made investments in London and elsewhere. He poured money into the Mowbray College Trust. Yes, he wanted Pellacombe to be a Staff King's palace, but he wanted more. He wanted the family to become national players. I think you're wrong about the personal dimension, Cador. Your father had moved on from Isolde. However, I won't argue that he wanted to disrupt things, and we'll never know quite how big his ambitions were.'

While they were still absorbing this, I looked at Eseld. 'He might even have wanted you to be Warden one day. That's my interpretation, for what it's worth.'

Eseld snorted with laughter, of course, and the others smiled at what they thought of as a joke. Morwenna didn't. She frowned and kept her peace.

I downed my pint. 'When Morning joined the conspiracy to kill Lord Mowbray, she did it because her power-base at Glastonbury was threatened. She thought that Mowbray College would replace her empire of student Witches. Her replacement isn't a homicidal maniac, but the basic truth is the same. If you want my advice, you'll make Mowbray College strictly post-graduate. There's room for that. And don't forget, if you abandon the idea, you can't just dissolve the College Trust and pocket the cash.'

'Thank you, Conrad,' said Ethan in a tone which meant he was closing the meeting. 'That's the sort of perspective we needed to hear.'

'Yes, thank you,' added Kenver.

Eseld and Cador were staring at each other, until Ez snapped out of it. 'I'll walk you out,' she said. 'I need a fag and there's something I have to tell you.'

I stood up and winced. The stress had done nothing for my leg. 'Enjoy dinner chez Bloxham. I look forward to reading the TripAdvisor reviews.'

'I do not like the sound of that,' said Lena. 'Are they bad cooks?'

'Sorry. There's me telling you not to be biased and letting my own prejudices get in the way. I have never heard anyone say a bad thing about Jules's skills as a hostess. Put it that way.'

I limped downstairs and lit two fags. Eseld was a few seconds behind me and accepted one gratefully.

'I am only gonna say one thing about what happened upstairs, right?'

'Go on.'

'If we have to negotiate with the Daughters, I won't accept it if they put forward my mother as go-between.'

'The new Dame of Homewood will lead the negotiations,' I told her. 'And at her side will be Isolde. If they think it's a weak point on your side, they'll try to exploit it. Suck it up, Ez, and play them at their own game.'

'Have I ever told you what a bastard you can be.'

'More times than I can count.' I paused. 'Was there really something else?'

'Oh. Yeah. News from Ireland.'

Morwenna's story is a long and complex one, and *why* she is having a reunion with the Irish side of her heritage is too much to go over here. Suffice it to say that Oighrig Ahearn is coming down from London and Fiadh and Cathal Ahearn are coming over from Ireland more to meet Morwenna than to attend my wedding. I'm not taking it personally.

'They're still coming, aren't they?' I asked.

'Oh yes, and Fiadh is bringing a "friend". I've a message for you: *have you been practising your Fae Chess?*'

'Portarra.'

'Duchess of Corrib these days. She's waiting for a Changeling so she can become Prince, and while she waits, she's been showing Fiadh around the fleshpots of Galway. And Donegal. And Dublin.'

Portarra is a Fae bruiser, right hand to the Noble Queen of Galway.

'Is this an official visit?'

Ez grinned. 'Better order an extra flagpole.'

'Extra? I don't have any.'

'If you get married, and the Noble Queen's flag isn't flying alongside all the others, she'll consider it a snub of epic proportions. Fiadh told me to pass on the message. I'd better get back upstairs.'

'And leave me to tell Mina!'

'Better get used to it, Conrad. You chose Mina when you could have had someone easy-going like me. Laters.'

I was still digesting this disturbing news as I wandered out of the pub and headed for home, which was why I didn't see my mother coming.

'Conrad! What are you up to? Have you been *drinking*? At this time of the day?'

'Hi, Mum. The Mowbrays had some business, that's all. I'd better get back and drag Mina away from Anika before they call the vicar and ask for the service to take place in Gujarati.'

'She got here safely? Mina must be thrilled. And talking of arrivals, *that woman* is on her way. Do make sure she gets settled in and let me know when it's safe to go to Elvenham. I thought that was why you'd gone to the pub.'

Any guesses who *that woman* might be? Too easy. It could only be Mercedes, the mother of Sofía. *My* mother has no problem with Sofía's mother being here, it's just that Mercedes is also, by definition, one of Dad's old lovers. There had been a long debate about whether Mercedes should be invited. In the end, I'd suggested to Mother that if Mercedes didn't get an invitation, she'd make life in San Vicente very uncomfortable for them.

Mother had thought this over for a second, then said, 'You're right, Conrad. And there's no way she can steal the show, is there? Mina wouldn't allow it. One condition, though: she can visit Elvenham, but can't stay there.'

Which is why Mother thought I might have been going to the Inkwell on Mercedes' behalf: she has the single room there. In the attic. *Making trouble in San Vicente* wasn't the real reason I wanted Mercedes here, though. Tomorrow night she was going to perform a Tarot reading on our wedding, and I was keen to see the results.

You'll note that I said a Tarot reading for our *wedding*, not our *marriage*. That's none of her business, or if it is, she's not getting our co-operation in making it.

'Don't worry, Mum. It's all in hand.'

She shook her head and raised her eyebrows. 'Ben's mother had a good description of it, Conrad. *A Three Ring Circus* she called it, and she's not wrong. I hope the stress of the wedding doesn't put a strain on your marriage.'

She was looking at me with concern in her eyes. You never know when Mother is going to turn serious, and it's easy to get in trouble if you don't return the favour.

'It was my biggest worry,' I told her. 'We talked it through last year once the novelty of my proposal had worn off. It's one of the reasons Mina wants the simple church ceremony for the legal wedding, to separate the occasion from the purpose. Now, where can I get some flagpoles at short notice?'

'Have you lost your mind?'

'No. Come for coffee and I'll explain.'

We started walking and I outlined my latest diplomatic nightmare. Mother took me seriously, because she takes most things seriously, then stopped at the gates and said, 'How many flags must you have?'

I ticked them off. 'Mine, the Valknut, the Noble Queen's, the Northern flag of Caledfwlch, and something for Ganesh if I can scrounge it.'

'Why can't they go on that *ridiculous* Maypole you've insisted on putting in the meadow?'

Yes, we do have a Maypole in the meadow, near the bonfire which we're going to light on Saturday. Buff Saerdam Robbie has been gathering fallen branches from the woods in his downtime for some days now.

'That was my first thought, but the VIP guests will arrive up the drive, not park in the field, so it needs to be where the VIPs can see it.'

She pointed up at the squat tower. 'I can see five crenelations. One each, with yours in the middle.'

I went to give her a kiss, and she closed her eyes to accept it. 'You're brilliant, Mum. Thank you. I'll get Lottie on it right away. You wouldn't believe how nimble her fingers are.' A sudden thought struck me. 'Where's

Dad?'

'Gone looking for a wedding gift. Excuse to look up old flames if you ask me. Now, have you found a place for that nice Francesca Somerton to stay?'

I hadn't, and it was next on my to-do list.

'Why are you grinning, Conrad? It's not funny. How much beer did you drink?'

'Just the one, Mum. I'm grinning because it's nice to have some decisions that don't involve choosing who has to die. You know what I mean.'

She sighed and, miracle of miracles, she put her arm round my waist. 'Yes, Conrad. That's the problem. I *do* know what you mean.'

Nika the part-time paid carer was only doing a couple of nights a week with Don now, because she had taken a job at a pub in Easingwold which paid twenty percent more than the Abbey *and* was within walking distance of her flat. This meant that Kathy had to wait until Thursday night to catch Nika, accidentally on purpose, when she took a break.

'You still taking taxis to get home?' Kathy asked innocently.

'Yes. I look at cars, you know. All the ones I could afford were heap-of-shit bad.'

Kathy sighed dramatically. 'I'm not sleeping so good, Nika. How about I do the last hour tonight, then you can catch a lift with Paolina.'

'Really? Why?'

'Is Don still on that science book?'

Nika rolled her eyes. '*DNA Demystified*. Yes. I *hate* it.'

'That's because you tried to listen. I find it's the best thing to send me sleep *ever*.'

'You sure?'

'I'm sure.'

'Deal. I owe you one. See you at nine.'

After they'd done their swap, Kathy waited until curfew had sounded, as it did discreetly every night. She'd already paused the book, because the book had sent Don to sleep well before ten o'clock. All the better, because he'd be wide awake after a nap, and Kathy needed to know that she'd be on her own. She fretted on her phone until twenty past ten, then tiptoed outside and listened. All quiet. No sounds of Dr Simon dictating notes in his office. All

183

dark. Good.

She went back into the room and made tea. Something to perk him up, even if it meant an extra trip to the loo. Tea made, she woke him gently and chatted for a couple of minutes. She could see in his eyes that he was wondering what she was doing, so she got down to business.

'Right, Don. It's like this. Michael has come up with this thingy that I reckon will do your address label. We're gonna have a go tomorrow night.'

Don went almost still, his eyes focused on Kathy.

'I like Michael,' she said. 'Of course, he thinks I'm thick, and he's not wrong. He also thinks he knows all about me, and he *is* wrong about that. And wrong about just how thick I am. I know enough not to trust him.'

Don frowned.

'I trust him not to tell anyone else, yeah, but he's just too *nosy*. Know what I mean?'

Don nodded.

'He'll show you how to use the delete key and stuff, but I know him. He'll shake my phone and undo the delete. It'll only take him a second. He'll think he's doing you a favour. He'll squirrel it away and later on, he'll look into it. He can't help himself. It's what he does. Do you want that?'

Don shook his head violently.

'Thought so. Thing is, Don, I had some bad news off the Social on Tuesday. They've said I can apply for custody of my girls, but only if I live in some posh part of Leeds or if I rent a house up here, and you might not know this, but rents for a garden shed near here *start* at a grand a month.'

Don's eyebrows shot up.

'I'm not even joking. Michael's going to this concert next Monday in Leeds. I'll come back and do your label, and I swear on Cherry's life that I will *not* look. But I'll need some proper money, Don. Not now, and not next week, but I need to know you've got it. Maybe enough for a deposit on a house or something. What do you say?'

He put his double-handled mug down slowly and pointed to one of the pictures, the most depressing one. It showed some big black bird in a bare tree and Kathy always tried to sit with her back to it. She brought it over and Don motioned for her to sit next to him.

The picture was covered in glass, and the light made it difficult to see from certain angles. Don held out his right hand and touched his left to the picture. He waited until she got the message, and she took his right hand in hers. He grunted in pain, and his left hand spasmed. Was it a trick of the light, or something else, because how come she could see a signature where there was none before? *John Gould* it said.

Don collapsed back, panting, and Kathy hastily restored the picture, lining it up carefully with the dust marks. Bloody cleaner. She did a quick Google and swore when she saw the prices.

'Don, are you serious? You'd give me that?'

He nodded, resolute and suddenly looking ten years younger. The surprise made Kathy feel weak at the knees, and she stumbled into her chair. She might even have nodded off for a second. When she'd shaken herself awake, she took Don's hand in hers. 'Thank you, Don. I won't let you down.'

Chapter 24 — Beltane Eve

'I'll bet you're glad to get away from the chaos for a bit of peace,' said Ben as we leaned on the old roller at Mrs Clarke's Folly, home of Clerkswell Cricket Club.

'Keep your eyes on the gate, Ben,' I replied. 'The chaos will be following me down Winchcombe Road soon enough, and don't let them hear you call it *chaos*.'

'Point taken.'

It was nice in the sun, warm but not hot, and as peaceful a spot as you could wish for. 'I've been thinking, you know.'

'Dangerous.'

'I know. I was thinking about what *Peace* – with a capital *P* – should be like in the world of magick.'

'*Should?* Is there such a thing as *should?* Makes it sound like you're trying to play God, Conrad, and that's a bit much even for you and Mina. Well, you at any rate.'

'Mina has no aspirations to divinity, Ben,' I told him gravely. I could see that he wouldn't want to talk about it, or not today at any rate. We have more important things on our minds, specifically the figure in a blue tracksuit inspecting the wicket.

Ben pointed as the figure turned and jogged towards us. 'Here he comes. Do you think he's going to be up to it?'

The *it* in question is the first match of the cricket season, and a particular challenge for us men of Clerkswell (the women's season doesn't start for another month). We were promoted to Division One last year, and today we are hosting the upper tier's runners-up, Cheltenham Spa Second Team. They're tipped to win this year, and it's going to be a tough game – their Firsts play in the rarefied atmosphere of the semi-pro league.

One of our genuine stars is a young lad called Ross Miller, a fast bowler of some promise. I emphasise *promise* because he's only seventeen and coming to the end of a first year apprenticeship in arboriculture. Being young, we'd sent him to inspect the wicket. They need to burn off energy at that age.

'What do you reckon?' Ben asked him.

Ross looked at me darkly. 'It's your fault. We haven't had rain for a week now.'

I stood up straight. 'Me, Ross? I have influence in many places, but not over the weather.'

'That girl at your place, Thistle, she said your wedding has been blessed by the gods. At least I think that's what she said. Hard to tell with that accent.'

Ben and I looked at each other. 'When did you see Thistle?' I asked Ross innocently.

'Oh, she's around. Running errands and stuff. We were just chatting, like.'

Ben and I were both teenage boys once. We knew where this was heading. 'Did you ask her out?' I suggested.

He kicked the roller. 'Said she was too busy working. I thought she was single, that's all.'

I heaved a sigh of relief. 'Thistle *is* single, Ross, but she's also working for Mina. She won't have a spare minute until she's back home in the Lakes. Now, what about the wicket?'

'Way too dry to get a decent swing on it, and too flat to spin. It's dead.'

'You'll be fine, Ross.' I nudged Ben. 'I still think you put them in to bat if we win the toss.'

'So do I,' Ben replied. 'Let's get warmed up. Ross, go and dig the others out of the dressing room.'

When the *chaos* turned up, the whole of Mrs Clarke's folly stopped and turned to stare. Faith led the charge, driving the minibus and with Myfanwy at her side and Anna behind them. It's a five minute walk from the Grange, but in Myfanwy and Anna's condition, they were saving their energy for wild cheering. Probably.

The rest of the bridal party followed the bus chanting *Go Wizards! Go Wizards!* in a totally un-ironic burst of enthusiasm. They even had a cheerleader.

'Tell me that Maria isn't gonna wear that getup all through the match,' said Ben despairingly.

'Doubt it. I expect it's a Glamour,' I suggested. And I was right: she shook her pom poms menacingly at the opposition, then jogged round the back of the bus, re-emerging in something less eye-catching.

Also arriving were the party from the Manor. The Bloxham's historic home backs on to Mrs Clarke's Folly, and they have a gate through from their grounds. Instead of Stephen or Jules, today it was the massed ranks of the Mowbray/Ahearns.

I was surprised when they accepted the invitation to watch the match. None of them has the least interest in cricket, or so I thought. It was Portarra – sorry, *Countess Corrib* – who told me that Ethan had ordered them to attend, as a way of making the late Aisling's relatives play nicely. Apparently, the family reunion hasn't been all sweetness and light, and that was all that the Fae would tell me. It was noticeable that Fiadh and Cathal were steering clear of both Morwenna and Oighrig, and Morwenna had put on a Mowbray Blue cardigan, along with the rest of the Cornish contingent. Even Ez was being tight-lipped about things.

I suppose that Oighrig could have been on her own because she had the Bloxhams' golden Labrador, Floss, on a lead. Apparently, the Mowbrays had seen what a gorgeous dog she is and insisted that looking after her was no trouble at all, and that putting her in kennels for the weekend was cruel and a waste of money. Scout, on the other hand, was tied up in his hut. That dog is constitutionally incapable of seeing a ball and *not* chasing it. He is banned from Mrs Clarke's Folly.

The Countess Portarra herself was off to the Forest of Arden to spend Beltane-Eve with the Fae Prince who lives there. 'I wouldn't cramp your little handmaid's style,' she'd told me. I didn't tell Faith that she was being referred to as a *little handmaid*.

Before we went in to put on our whites ready for the match, the Spa captain came up to Ben and looked unhappy. Ben shrugged and pointed to me. What now?

'It's Conrad Clarke, isn't it?' said the opposition captain, without offering a handshake.

'How can I help?'

'Ben says that the woman photographer is in your bridal party.'

I could pick him up on the fact that there is no male photographer, and the bridal party is not mine, it's Mina's. No sense in winding them up, though. 'Yes. Sapphire. She'll give you a link to her exhibition when she's finished, if you like.'

'Sod that. It's intrusive. She shouldn't be approaching us during warm-up.'

'Sorry.' I whistled loudly and waved for Lottie to come over. She was standing in the nets, wielding a bat like a club and being introduced to cricket by Anika's girls. Apparently Faith had been sent to Tesco to buy the girls something they could wear to get dirty in.

I turned to the Spa skipper. 'Please excuse Mrs Gibson. She's from the Lake District. Lottie? Will you tell Sapphire that she needs to leave the other team alone. Thanks.'

'Yes, my lord. On it!' she exclaimed, then hurtled across the grass.

'Why did she …? Never mind,' said their skipper.

Ben won the toss and the Spa Seconds showed us exactly why they'd nearly won the league last year: not only could they play, they were dab hands at the dark art of sledging. If your first thought was a snowy hillside, think again. *Sledging* is the tactic of holding a loud conversation with the intention of undermining the opposition. Normally the fielders do it to the batsmen, but the two Spa Seconds at the crease started saying loudly that, *The spotty kid* was *more wooden than an oak tree.*

That would be Ross. Poor lad. At some point before the next game, Ben would no doubt tell him that he may have gained upper body strength during the close season, but that he's lost a lot of accuracy. During the match, that wasn't an option, and Ross lost it big-time. In one over, they knocked him for fourteen runs, and Ben tossed me the ball. 'Bowl as flat as you can, Conrad. Let's try and take the sting out.'

As soon as he saw it was me up to bowl, the Seconds captain said, 'No need to worry, mate. This one's mind is on other things, and he's due a blue badge or a pension soon.'

I just grinned.

Instead of trying to tempt the batsmen into risky shots, I pitched it up on the leg side and tried to frustrate them. And it worked. After I'd got my eye in, I bowled two maidens and their run rate dropped. Their skipper took a huge swing at a ball that was nipping in, missed, and I couldn't help myself: I used magick to let out an enormous shout of *Owzat!* which they must have heard in Cheltenham. The umpire flinched back in alarm, then raised his finger.

'Nice one,' said Ben. 'Keep it up.'

I did, and they didn't run away with the game. And once their skipper had left the field, the rest of the team dropped the sledging. Much more civilised. As we headed back to the pavilion, their last man observed to me, 'At least we won't have to face this circus every week.' He gestured at the unusually huge crowd. 'We never have that many except for the cup game. And they're wicked, too. Do you know what that Welsh girl called our captain?' He shook his head. 'Never heard the like before closing time, and if it didn't mean repeating what she'd said, he'd complain to the County. I know who she is, and I know that the … erm, the Indian girl is your fiancée, but who are the two in the deck chairs? And who's the man-mountain bringing them all the drinks?'

It was too good a chance to miss. 'The older lady has just retired as head of research for MI5. It was her who tipped us off about your captain's *other* business. The one his wife doesn't know about.'

'You what?'

'Straight up. Ask him about *Eulalie* if you still don't believe me. Or you could just go up to Francesca and say, "Excuse me, Mrs Somerton, but I believe you used to be a librarian." As for the other one in the deckchairs, that's Hannah Rothman. She was married to the heir of the Tsar of all the Russias, but don't mention *that*. He died in mysterious circumstances. The big lad is a bodyguard.'

'She has a bodyguard? For real, Conrad?'

'Oh no, not her. Hannah can look after herself. I can't tell you who Robbie is guarding, but I can tell you this: if one of the girls tries to chat you up, pretend you're not interested or you'll have Robbie on your case, and you do not want that.' I thought of something. 'Oh, there is one. See the two women at the opposite end of the crowd to my parents? One in jeans and the other in a red dress?'

'I don't know who your parents are, but yeah, I see the two women … are they related?'

'That's my half-sister, Sofía, and her mother, Mercedes.'

He grinned, 'Which explains their relative location.'

'Quite. Mercedes is from a long line of Spanish Gypsy fortune tellers. She would be more than happy to Divine your future, and she'll go much further than telling you that you're about to lose.' I leaned in a little closer. 'But watch out. If she refuses to do a reading, check your life insurance, because you're destined for an early grave.'

He stopped in his tracks, twenty yards from the boundary rope. 'You're winding me up.'

His voice said he didn't believe me, but his feet had a different message. They weren't moving at all.

'Try Googling some of the girls and ask yourself why they have zero online presence. You may not face this circus every week,' I added, 'but you are about to eat the best cricket tea of the season. Enjoy.'

When it was our turn to bat, the girls got properly stuck into the Pimms, and Mina had to tell them to *shush*. I have no idea whether the Spa eleventh man had said anything, but when the opposition took to the field the long way round (avoiding the circus), several of them were giving their skipper a funny look and whispering to each other.

Their bowling showed that it wasn't only us who were rusty, and we made steady progress by our standards. Unfortunately, it wasn't steady by their standards, and Ben had to try and push the pace, which led to a sudden collapse. Before he could steady the ship, Ross threw away his wicket, and I was in: last man and still thirty runs behind.

As I headed for the pitch, Faith came up and touched my arm, making a Silence. 'Don't forget what we practised. You can do this.'

I smiled and nodded and strode out as best I could. On the way to the crease, their skipper piped up with, 'Here he is, lads. Last lamb to the slaughter. We'll be on our way soon.'

When I'm bowling, I only need to run for a few steps, then all the effort is in the wrist. When I'm batting, the sheer lack of mobility in my bad leg makes quick movement all but impossible. I took guard and planted my feet.

The umpire gave me a funny look. 'Are you ready, batsman? Is that your stance?'

'Yes, sir.'

'Then play.'

Losing my wicket is sad, losing my life would be a tragedy. My bad leg makes swordfighting a challenge, and Faith has been coaching me on how to compensate. For the last week, she's been applying it to cricket, and when the first delivery fizzed down the wicket, I leaned in, left my bad leg where it was and thumped the bat down in a forward defensive. Clunk. Cue frown from the bowler.

And again for the next three balls, until he was done, and Ben had the strike for the next over. The Spa Seconds got very frustrated after that, and their spinner graciously gifted me an easy shot for four runs. We won with two overs to spare.

The opposition ran to clap us off the pitch, apart from their spinner, the one I'd been winding up at tea time. He was collecting his sweater from the umpire, and said, 'You were telling the truth about one thing, Conrad: the food was amazing. That big Cornish bloke was saying something about a party tonight, but I couldn't quite work out his accent, 'cos it sounded more German than anything.'

'He probably said *Walpurgisnacht*. Also known as Beltane-eve. Yes, there will be a big party, because tonight we will burn a wicker man, and tomorrow, the Queen of the May will lead the village maidens in a werewolf-Bollywood fusion dance around the Maypole.'

He shook his head, and I held out my hand. 'Twenty quid says there will be a video on Facebook of both events,' I offered.

He stared at my hand, then took it with a look that spoke of determination not to be bluffed so outrageously. 'Why do I think this might be the easiest twenty quid you'll make all weekend?'

I clapped him on the back. 'Because, to quote Marlon Brando, "One of these days in your travels, a guy is going to show you a brand-new deck of cards. Then this guy is going to offer to bet you that he can make the jack of spades jump out and squirt cider in your ear." And for you, today is that day.'

'How do you know that Don wants to come to the bonfire?' Faye stood in front of Kathy, blocking the door and radiating suspicion. 'We've been doing it for five years and he's never expressed an interest before.'

Kathy was an accomplished liar. Most addicts are. 'I finally got him off that DNA book, that's why.'

Faye was wrongfooted. 'What DNA book? What does that have to do with the Spring Bonfire?'

'He's been listening to some book about DNA. Or trying to. He was nodding off so much, I switched to this fantasy story, and he perked up no end. Even made me listen. And when they got to the Feast of Saint Whatshisname, I looked it up. He got very excited when I put two and two together and figured out your "Spring Bonfire" was all about some witchy stuff. It doesn't say that on the tin, does it?'

And now the Fragrant Faye was on the defensive and didn't ask how Don had made his wishes clear. Instead, she half shifted to one side and said, 'It's about connecting to Mother Earth. It happens all over Europe in different ways, it's just that ours is not specific to any religion, that's all. And who doesn't love a bonfire and barbecue?'

'Me, when it's on me night off, that's who.'

Faye seized the initiative again, or thought she had. 'Which is why we offered you double time and a day off in lieu for doing the food tonight, Kathy. Never mind, won't be a problem again.'

It was Kathy's turn to be off balance. 'What do you mean?'

'We need to talk about your contract soon, don't we?'

'I am not changing my overtime rates,' said Kathy. 'With deductions for board and lodging, I'm only just over minimum wage as it is.'

'Of course. No one's going to ask that. We still need to talk, though.'

Faye turned and went back towards the private rooms which she and Doctor Simon shared. Kathy carried on towards the kitchens, where Michael was already well on with the home-made coleslaw.

'I've been thinking,' he said after greeting her. 'Do we really have the right to send Don's letter?'

Kathy stopped buttoning up her jacket. 'You what?'

Michael put down the knife (he was safe enough with coarse chopping). 'It's been a bit of a game up to now, I'll admit. It's just that when you showed me the pictures of your girls the other night, I couldn't help thinking about them. And me. And how much trouble we'd both be in if things went wrong.'

'What could go wrong?' she asked. 'They're not gonna come and assassinate him, are they? If they were gonna do that, he'd be in the ground, not trapped in a nursing home.'

'It's not Don I'm worried about,' he replied. 'It's you and me. If that letter *does* get to wherever it's going, the first thing that will happen is a phone call to Simon, and the next thing that will happen is you and me on the carpet.'

He kept saying things like that. 'On the carpet?'

'In trouble. In the headmaster's office. They could fire you for this, Kathy, and I could get a really negative report.'

Her fingers fumbled the buttons. Michael was making a good point here, damn him. But if she didn't post the *real* letter, Don wouldn't give her the picture, and no picture meant no home for her and the girls. No proper home at any rate. She stalled for time by asking, 'What do you suggest we do, then?'

He looked eager now, as if he'd been waiting for her to come round to his way of thinking. 'I think we should say we've posted it, then after a couple of weeks when no one comes, we ask him to tell us what's going on. It's up to him then whether to ask for Simon's help officially or whether to forget about it.'

She sighed. It was a real dilemma, and one she'd have to go through again in a couple of days. 'Alright. I'll put the envelope in the bonfire tonight. That way we'll preserve his privacy.'

'Thank you, Kathy.' It was Michael's turn to sigh. 'I got so caught up in the mission that I forgot to think it through, and that's a weight off my shoulders. Go on, cheer me up: tell me what Long Lenny would say.'

It had become a game with them. In some difficult or unusual situation, Michael would ask what Long Lenny would say, and if Kathy couldn't remember something suitable, Michael would have a go. He was usually spot on.

'I know just what he'd say,' she told Michael. '*You're damned if you do and in the dustbin if you don't. Just remember that the dustbin doesnae have hellfire burning in it.*'

'Of course he did,' said Michael fondly.

'Why?' said Kathy. 'Have I said that one before?'

Michael jerked. 'What? No. I don't think so. It's just that you've described him so well. How much of this coleslaw do we need, you reckon?'

They moved on, and Kathy gave a grim smile to the fridge. After her prompting last night, Don had watched Michael carefully and, yes, when Kathy's back was turned, Michael had indeed glanced at her phone to clock the address that Don had typed so laboriously and pointlessly.

Coleslaw and food all prepped, she watched with satisfaction as Michael wheeled Don out of his room to enjoy the warmth of the bonfire. The old man's face was alive in the firelight: this little bit of new age nonsense clearly meant something to Don that she would never understand, and she turned happily to supervise the grill.

Later, just before Faye decided that Don was getting tired and cold, Kathy caught Don's eye again, and he winked at her. His left hand jerked towards the fire, and sparks shot up into the air. Was it her imagination, or did they make the shape of a bird? A big bird. She shook her head. Trick of the light.

Her final performance in tonight's show took place in front of the residents and guests (minus Don). Everyone was supposed to let go of the past by burning something symbolic, some part of their history which was no longer useful. When Kathy fed the folded envelope into the flames, she had to lie, and so she said that she was letting go of something which she'd been encouraged to let go of again and again in therapy.

'I no longer need to search for my father to be my own person,' she intoned.

There. That should keep everyone happy.

Part Five — With These Rings

Chapter 25 — A Beltane Blessing

You wouldn't think we'd won, so quickly did Mrs Clarke's Folly empty out. The reason is the Walpurgisnacht celebrations, which are only a few hours away, and there is a lot to get ready. I am in charge of checking the meadow, and after dropping my kitbag, I summoned my faithful hound, then limped through the gardens to take a look.

Elvenham Grange used to be a large monastic farm with chapel. After the Black Death, the monks left, and my ancestor, William the Clerk, bought (or stole) the farmhouse and a chunk of land. When James Clarke became a rich lawyer, he sold off all the farm except a five acre meadow which has its own gate to Elven Lane, very handy as a car park and place to light a bonfire.

The first thing I checked was that the contractors had laid the ground protection matting in the right places while I was winning the Man of the Match award. They had, and I didn't need the farmer next door to be on standby with his tractor to pull cars out of the mud. Not that it was muddy – as Ross observed, it has been very dry lately. Unusually dry for April.

After the matting, I checked the water (running), the temporary power supply (intact and active), and then I checked the bonfire. There isn't much vandalism in Clerkswell, but we are out of the way here, and the temptation to light a bonfire early might be too much for the local tearaway (who lives at 14 The Spinney).

Faith had hidden the wicker man with a Glamour; he isn't very big (they had to fit him in the minibus), and I dispelled the magick prior to chucking him on top of Robbie's mound of dead wood and sawn off chunks of fallen tree.

Once I'd stopped Scout trying to wrestle a large branch with a view to taking it back to the house, I brushed moss off my hands and realised that my pocket was vibrating. I checked the screen and took the call. 'Hi, Stewart, thanks for the messages.'

Stewart knew I was playing cricket, so he'd rung Mina a couple of times with updates on her brother's progress at the symposium, and he'd messaged me to say that Arun had acquitted himself very well.

'A pleasure, Conrad,' said Stewart. 'I mean that. Today has exceeded every expectation, and Arun had them eating out of his hand. Once they understood his sense of humour.'

'I didn't know he had one. And you're back at the Roost?'

The Cherwell Roost is Hawkins HQ, and Stewart had invited Arun and Saanvi to stay the night. 'Just about to leave. The drinks reception has gone on longer than I expected.' He paused. 'You don't know them very well, do you?'

'Never met them.'

'Hmm. I just wondered whether Mina had said anything about Saanvi to you?'

My mind was boggling. Saanvi grew up in India, then America, and it was there that she was matched with Arun. Her parents followed her brother when he moved to the UK, and Saanvi's mother is looking after their children tonight. 'I've seen pictures, and I've seen Mina ignore her calls a few times. I thought that was just because she's been so busy.'

He sighed. 'She's probably just nervous, that's all. I'll let you go, then. No doubt you have a virgin to sacrifice or something.'

'Jest not about that which you do not understand,' I announced.

'Okaaaay. That was way too convincing for me, Conrad. Don't forget I grew up in a God-fearing Scottish Presbyterian family. I'll see you tomorrow.'

'You're sure you don't mind giving them a lift?'

'Of course not. I love a gander around people's homes.'

Oh dear. I pinched my nose and took a deep breath. 'Let me guess: you've been liaising with Saffron about this, haven't you?'

'Yes. Why do I not like the sound of that?'

'Because Saffron can twist you round her little finger, and you won't get angry with her for not telling you that tomorrow's Maypole dance is women, girls and small boys only. Men are barred from the Grange from dawn onwards.'

'Little minx! She's got me driving all the way to Cheltenham and I can't even cast aspersions on wee Mina's taste in soft furnishings when I get there. Are there no exceptions for old queens like me?'

Stewart is a bit of a chameleon, and he can switch from the Highlands to high camp to high table in an instant.

'You're welcome to join the stag party for a football match. Lots of nice young men…'

He snorted and didn't dignify my suggestion with a response. When he spoke again, it was something like the real Stewart McBride. 'I am a little annoyed with Essy, though. She knows that this is one of Solly's big weekends, and I do like to support him.'

Stewart's husband runs the Hawkins home as a mundane tourist attraction, and Bank Holiday Weekends are big business. I could see his point, and wondered if I could talk Dad into it.

'I'd better go, Conrad. Don't worry, I'll sort it. You have more than enough on your plate, and I really am very grateful for today. A couple of hacks from the broadsheets turned up and were most taken. See you tomorrow.'

'Thanks, Stewart.'

Of course, while my back was turned, Scout had gone back and dragged ten feet of tree up to the gate, where he was waiting for me to open it. Bloody dog.

'Arff?'

'No chance, pal.'

I took a tennis ball out of my pocket and lobbed it towards the well. He looked at the branch for a second, then shot off after the ball.

There was more event matting all over the lawns, and that had been followed by the marquee erectors. I am not in charge of that, so I passed by unconcerned and went to wait for the security team.

You might think that it would take a small army to besiege Elvenham Grange, given the firepower staying here, and you'd be right. The security team were here to stop the non-Entangled from disturbing our Walpurgisnacht, Beltane and Wedding ceremonies, not that I'd used those words in the booking.

Beltane is a flexible feast, though not usually put to the purpose we had in mind tonight. All these jobs and checks were a way of putting off thinking about what was to come. I shivered, and looked at the sun dropping in the sky. It was getting cold now, and that was only the universe's way of letting me know that things would soon be hotting up.

That would happen at dusk, and really will be no place for the mundane, which is why Nell Heath from the village shop is having Jivika and Jiyana for a tea with their new friend, Nell's niece, and why my father has been sent with the Mowbray minibus to collect Lloyd's children (and his mother) from Worcestershire.

When Anika learnt about the world of magick, she was adamant that her girls should *not* be exposed when they're over here, and a full-on Mage-led festival could actually damage my father's brain. For once that's not the cue for a joke: it could give him a serious haemorrhage.

The van rolled up, and four guys in navy sweaters got out, Hi-Viz jackets over their arms. 'Mr Clarke?' said the leader, after he'd escaped Scout's interrogation.

We shook hands, and I pointed out the gates and what their job was to be: other than the faces on the printout I supplied, only the two food trucks were to be allowed in, and someone had to watch that the truck owners didn't try to leave the meadow towards the house.

'How hard should we try to stop them?' he asked. 'I'm sure they'll be busy cooking, but you never know.'

'As hard as you need to. Anything short of fatal is fine with me.'

'I see. Anything else?'

I showed him a picture on my phone. 'Do not allow this man to enter the property *at all*. Even if he says he's my father.'

'Who is he?'

'My father. He can't come in until *after* the bonfire is lit. If he does turn up, escort him to the pub and buy him several drinks.'

'That's … that's fine, sir.'

'Good.' I pointed to Scout. 'If this hyperactive hound gets loose, just ignore him. If you try and catch him, he'll think it's a game of chase, and believe me, he'll win. Once the show's on the road, you'll be on traffic duty and you're all welcome to a free bar and free food. Until then, thank you.'

And then it was time to get ready. I summoned Scout and headed for the house. The detail-oriented amongst you may be wondering why my mother simply didn't take Dad out for a meal tonight. I'll give you three guesses…

And if you said, 'Because Mercedes will be there,' you'd be right. Once Mother had gathered the significance of the procession and the offerings, and the potential for cosmic upset, she was all in, even though she hates the world of magick. Mother would walk behind me as I led the procession out of the house, and nothing was going to stop her.

And what a procession it was. From eight o'clock onwards we had been gathering even more people, each with their own reasons for joining in. For the Clarkes and Clarkes-to-be it was about my wedding; for the Fae, it was about us honouring them (which we would), for Lloyd and Sapphire it was about Mother Earth paying tribute to Mother Nature, for the assorted Mages it was about marking the seasons and following their own traditions, and that left two. For Lucy Berardi it was something she wouldn't miss for the world, and for Tom Morton it was about making sure Lucy was okay.

We gathered in the hall because there were so many of us, and I looked behind me to check that we were ready. Rachael was in position, carrying the box, Mother at her side, and Mercedes behind them, trying not to look put out. I took Mina's hand and asked, 'Ready?'

'Yes. Let's do it.'

Ben and Lloyd pulled open the doors and stood to one side, and I tried to resist the urge to march rather than walk out. I turned left, going through the garden gate, and I took us up the slope to the edge of the woods. With my Third Eye, I could see the Ley lines glowing brightly in the dusk, radiating from the well to the house, to the boundary fences, to Myfanwy's Herbal garden, and to the stables, with one more of special interest. It was short and branched, and at either end of the branches was, appropriately, a tree.

Off the right branch was a healthy young sapling, which last year had been a stick, and had begun life as part of the Homewood Oak in Glastonbury, seat of the Daughters of the Goddess. The stick (staff, really) had been a gift from

198

the Eldest Daughter, and both its presence and its rapid, magickally assisted growth was a blessing from the Goddess herself.

I've been *in her presence* once, and She is not like the other Elderkind, if She's one at all. It is also rare for her to be unambiguous, and that thriving Homewood Oak could easily be a blessing on Myfanwy rather than me. I was not expecting her to appear in the near future, unlike the author of the other tree.

Ringed and protected from damage, a tiny yew was struggling to establish itself. The fencing around it was also to protect *us*, and Myvvy had put a note saying *This is NOT Rosemary!*

We passed the trees, and I took up a post some distance from the well, allowing the company to form an evenly spaced circle. Myfanwy took a coolbox from Ben and stepped forwards. As a practising Druid, she is the nearest we have to a spiritual leader here. Yes, I know I'm the Priest of the Dyfrdwy Altar, but that's up north and dedicated to Nimue. Tonight is not her night.

Myfanwy took a fertilised egg and placed it on the rim of the well. 'As we are given life, and carry life within us, accept our offerings for the Spring and return them multiplied. So mote it be.'

She stepped back, and the ceremony continued. Everyone either took something from the coolbox or laid down their own offering, spreading them round the well. Some spoke aloud (the Mowbrays and Erin amongst others), some knelt (the Ahearns), some prayed in silence (Hannah), and some spoke in their own language (Mercedes, Anika, Lloyd), and some let others speak on their behalf (Mother, Lottie and Tom Morton. Oh, and Sapphire, who joined Lloyd and Anna).

The only two who didn't place an offering on the well were Mina and I. We had another job to do, and it began by collecting a big, heavy box from Robbie (I wasn't going to carry it up here myself, was I?).

The box's contents thumped a little, but I couldn't hear broken glass, so I knew it was intact even though it was still sealed. I took the box, stepped back, then moved to his right to stand in front of Faith.

I lifted the case to show her the writing on the side, then placed it on the ground. 'My lady, I would have peace between my people and your people. Here is an offering of good faith.'

Faith and the other Fae had dressed up for tonight way more than anyone else; it was their night off, after all. Their Queen-to-be was wearing a gown of light green gauze over dark green silk, and her hair glowed and cascaded down her bare shoulders. She parted her ruby lips and said, 'What is your gift, mortal man?'

'From far away, from where the sun warms the ground. A case of fine wine from the vineyards of St Georges. It is unfit for mortals today, and will mature in the years to come, as I hope the peace between us matures.'

She inclined her head. 'It is fitting. Let there be peace between us, Lord Guardian. As a sign of this peace, take your offering and place it in your cellar. I will return and share it when it the time is right, whether I share it with you or with your heirs, only time will tell.'

I bowed again. 'My lady is gracious.'

'I also have a gift,' said Mina. 'This cheese was made of milk from cows sacred to my lord Ganesh. I have offered part to him, and part to you that we may dwell in peace.'

Faith accepted the muslin wrapped package and passed it to Alicia. 'Let there be peace between us, and let us all enjoy Mother Nature's bounty.'

Mina made Namaste, and it was time for the penultimate act of tonight's drama.

Tamsin Pike had made her offering in turn with the others, asking Mother Nature to be generous to her children in a quiet voice that I could barely catch. When Mina and I had returned to our places, Tammy stepped up to the well and drew on its Lux.

She didn't speak, she just spread her arms and swept all our offerings on the well up and away to the Spirit Realm. She turned and bowed to me, then rejoined the circle, where she stood at Faith's right. It was time.

Mina and I moved to the well, and Rachael picked up the chest she'd brought from the house. She opened the lid and offered me the contents, a rather nondescript tankard which a friend of Dad's had given me on my eighteenth birthday, and which had languished unloved and banished until one memorable night last year.

I took the tankard and felt it throb in my hands with suppressed magick. I placed it carefully on the rim, and Mina dropped a clean water sampling bottle on a new rope down the well, counted to three then pulled it up.

The tankard was starting to glow, and a faint green script appeared on its side. I took the sampling bottle and carefully filled the tankard. I was either about to make a huge mistake or I was about to owe Mercedes a huge favour. My sister's mother's words had been ambiguous at first, then crystal clear: *Your wedding will be blessed by the elephant, the king-wolf and the raven. Each must have their season.* So with Ganesh to come on Monday, the Allfather to come when he pleases, that left a small window to fit in the raven.

I took Mina's right hand in my left, grasped the tankard and lifted it. 'Great goddess of field and battle, hear your name. Morrigan, I drink this to you.'

The tankard never made it to my lips: simply saying her name was enough. In a flash of light, the world of Elvenham Grange disappeared, and we were standing at the threshold of the Elven Sídhe, raised to a higher plane. Mina's nails dug into my hand and she gasped.

I bowed low, out of respect and to protect my eyes from her form. The Morrigan is hard to look at. 'My lady, you honour us.'

Her rich Irish brogue rang out. 'Well met, mortals, and you, Princess.'

Princess? Was that a dig at Mina? I risked looking up, and the Morrigan had not brought us here alone: standing behind us were Myfanwy and Faith, and both had taken a knee.

I risked a glance around the home-within-a-home that has shared space with Elvenham Grange since time immemorial and which I was seeing for the first time in my life.

The hills and woods that backed on to the well in Midgard, our realm, were replaced by a gentle slope and by large, healthy specimens of Fae trees that were in full leaf, as they always are: collecting Lux is a year-round job. They formed a ring around us, making a beautiful grassy glade, replete with ancient spring flowers.

Behind the Morrigan, I caught a glimpse of an old, wooden door set into the slope. I had expected it to be a ruin, but it was still doing its job, still barred against intruders. The well was here, of course. That thing probably exists all the way up to Asgard, and ranged around its rim were our offerings. Was …? No. It was time to look up and meet her gaze. If I didn't faint first.

She is terrible to behold, as you would expect from the goddess of battle. Today she was wearing a gown of white, full-length and long sleeved, with a blood-red sash at the waist and a great sword dangling from her hip. Around her neck, the necklace of emerald skulls glittered in the glow of Lux from the well. I finally met her terrible, terrible gaze: emerald eyes that matched her necklace set in a face of angles and planes and surrounded by a black halo of hair. The lips were deep scarlet, the colour of fresh blood, and they split into a smile. Odin preserve me.

'You made a wise choice, Dragonslayer. It is a fitting day for me to bless your union, and you have good company down there. Apart from the Diggers, of course, but hey, it's a holiday.'

I glanced at Mina, and I could see the naked terror in her face. I could also see her determination.

'Can't hang about,' said the dread queen, 'so lets get on with it. First, there's the small matter of *loot*.'

Loot? Is that an Irish word?

She lifted a finger towards me. 'You took something from the Fair Queen's bower, Dragonslayer, am I right?'

I took several things, including the jewels in Mina's engagement ring. But they were a trade, and the only thing I took without asking was … aah. The yew cutting. *Morrigan's Tears*, the Fair Queen had called it: a yew tree which flowers.

I bowed. 'She was gone, and such beauty should be remembered, my lady. Forgive me if it was not there to be taken.'

'It was there to be taken, alright, and fitting, too. But it won't grow down there.' She lifted her gaze. 'Druid, come here.'

There was a groan from Myfanwy, and not in terror. 'Faith, can you give us a hand, cwch?'

The Fae Princess leapt to help Myfanwy to her feet, and held her hand to steady her as they approached the well.

The Morrigan pointed to the equivalent spots in Midgard where the Homewood Oak and the tiny yew sapling grew. I was shocked to see that in *this* realm, the oak was a foot taller and had broad leaves already. It's very, very unusual for plants to exist in more than one realm; Hedda had been very generous when she gave me her staff. On the other branch of the Ley line was nothing: no yew tree.

'Princess Faith, a test for you. Reach down and bring it back. A Queen should be able to reach between realms.'

Faith bowed, followed the Ley line and gritted her teeth. She didn't reach down into the ground, she reached *down* into Midgard, and plucked the sapling whole from its bed of compost. I cannot imagine how you would begin to keep one part of your body in this realm when another part is elsewhere. She held the yew up, then held it out towards the Morrigan.

'Give it to the Druid,' said the Elderkind. 'She is blessed by Mother Nature, and she can plant it. It takes around fifty mortal years to flower. Maybe you'll see it, maybe you won't. Give her a hand, Dragonslayer. Don't want her breaking a nail, do we?'

I reluctantly released Mina's hand and joined Myfanwy. We picked a spot where it wouldn't have to compete with other trees, and I dug into the soft grass to make a hole. Myfanwy planted the shoot, taking great care with the roots and working magick I'd never seen before. 'I think we'll both need a hand up now,' she smiled. And she was right.

Faith had watched the digging and planting, but she'd been whispering to the Morrigan in the Fae tongue. She dashed over to help me up, and Mina did the same for Myfanwy. We stood and watched the mutant tree for a second, then turned back to the dread goddess.

'I've two more gifts and a blessing for you,' she announced. 'Druid, you might need to get on the phone. You've until sunset tomorrow to get two beehives.'

'Two, my lady?'

'That's right. There will be a swarm near the well, a healthy one, and you need to capture it. A colony of bees will complete your garden, I think. The other hive needs to be here. Princess Faith and her mortal assistant are going to make you a nice step up to this glade, and I name you its custodian.'

'I ... I ... My lady is very generous.'

My sense of smell isn't wonderful, at least in its mundane manifestation, but when it comes to living creatures of magick, it's sharp. You don't need to know what the Morrigan smells like (it would put you off your cocoa), but you do need to know that when Myfanwy stammered her thanks, a waft of something entirely more wholesome and ripe wafted from the Elderkind, and

I was taken back to Lunar Hall, to a dark night where I'd felt something touch my skin.

I'd been wrong. The Goddess *had* been here. Was still here. And She was with the Morrigan, or the Morrigan was with her. I nearly missed what was said next.

'… swarm is a special one. Close your eyes, ladies. All three of you.'

They did as she asked, and the Morrigan's hands glowed with the perfect silver of mercury. She held them cupped, then opened them and released a giant silver bee. I've seen one before, released from the sídhe of the Fair Queen, and it has something to do with the Fae. The Quicksilver bee flew lazily and drunkenly out of her hands, then picked up speed and headed for a brilliant yellow gorse bush.

'Open your eyes. One more thing and I'll be gone. Little child of Ganesh, I would speak with you. Druid, Faith has a job for you both, and Dragonslayer, I'd take the weight off your leg for a while.'

'Y…Y… Yes, my lady,' said Mina with a nervous swallow.

Mina stepped cautiously away from the well, Faith led Myfanwy towards some flowers growing at the margin of the glade, and I went to park my backside on the edge of the well, after I'd cleared a space…

Oh. My instinct before was right: some of the offerings were gone. I'd say they never made it up here, but Tammy is too good a plane shifter to make that mistake, and the bara brith was half eaten. I dropped that rather disturbing information into my Larder of Unfinished Business, sat down and stared intently at Mina.

She was listening, clearly under a Silence, and she nodded her head a couple of times, then said something to the enormous Elderkind, who towered over her. And over me, it must be said.

Over by the trees, Faith and Myvvy had plucked some of the white flowers and Faith was showing Myfanwy how to make something small, with bending and twisting. When they'd finished, they carried whatever it was in their hands, much as the Morrigan had carried the Quicksilver bee. I stood up, and the others were finished, too; Mina looked excited, nervous and guilty all at the same time.

We assembled, and the Morrigan came much too close for comfort. So close, I could see that her fingernails were painted – or stained – like dried blood, in contrast to her lips. She stooped and picked up the abandoned tankard, then swept her hand into the well and filled it again. 'It's been a while since I conducted a greenwood marriage in person,' she observed. 'Princess?'

Faith offered me her cupped palm, and I saw the flowers and grass had been twisted into a small circle. 'Take it and put it on Mina's ring finger,' she said.

Mina nodded, now more excited than anything, and I took the flower band and slipped it past her engagement ring. It was almost snug, and the stems had clearly been bonded with magick of some sort. Myfanwy offered her hand to Mina, and Mina slipped a matching floral ring on my finger. As it passed down, I felt the pulse of something very strong, and it gripped the flesh below my knuckle.

'Mother Nature, bless this couple, and take them to your heart. Cheers!'

The Morrigan drank, wiped her lips and as it had been on her last visit, the well water became transformed, not into blood this time, but something yellow and sticky. She turned the tankard, an egg-cup in her great fist, and offered the handle to Mina.

My bride in nature took it gingerly and drank, then offered it to me. Flowers and the earth hit my nose as I lifted it up. Strong mead, sweet and rich. It slipped down my throat with a warming glow that started spreading outwards until it joined the tingle in my ring finger. A fitting toast.

'It's safe for your witnesses,' announced the Morrigan. 'You're too far gone to be bothered by a drop of this, Druid.'

Myfanwy drank, and her eyes nearly popped out of her head. 'Mmmm. Mm Mm.'

When Faith drank, she turned her head slightly so that Mina couldn't see her wink at me. Good job I've been practising my poker face. She placed the tankard on the well and stepped back. We all turned to face the Morrigan, and she smiled. Instinct made me grab Mina's hand, and hers had been looking for mine.

'Don't be scared, mortals. I'm going to bless your union with a kiss.'

The blood-red lips and sharp teeth descended from the sky and planted themselves right on my Third Eye. A shiver of nerves and numbness ran all the way down to my boots, and Mina squeezed my hand. The Morrigan kissed my bride in the same place, and Mina flushed almost red. Even her fingers heated up.

The Morrigan stepped round us and offered a ruby ring on her right hand for Faith and Myfanwy to kiss, and then she stared at me. At my Third Eye. 'One day, you will have a difficult choice to make, child of the Clerk's Well. Good job you've had plenty of practice.'

I glanced at Mina, and in the length of that glance, the Morrigan was gone.

'Oh my days!' said Myfanwy. 'I was not expecting *that*!'

'Neither was I,' said Faith, with an almost human lack of understatement.

'What just happened?' said Mina.

Faith shook herself back into being an alien Princess. 'Conrad will explain it, and we'll explain your absence. Come on, sister, let's leave them to it.'

She took Myfanwy's hand and disappeared, just as Mina was saying, 'Explain what????'

'Let's go over there,' I suggested, putting my arm round my love's waist. 'That grass looks soft enough.'

'What in the name of all your freaky gods is going on, Conrad?'

'I thought the Morrigan was telling you, under that Silence.'

The flush in Mina's cheeks had abated a little, and came rushing back as she put her arm round me and nestled her hip next to my thigh. 'That was women's talk. And why did we have to close our eyes? What did I miss.'

'I'll tell you when you tell me. Later. Right now, I'm going to explain the concept of *greenwood marriage*.'

'Will it take long? It will be time for the bonfire soon.'

I answered her with a kiss on the lips and pulled her body into mine, lifting her kurta with my hands and running my fingers up her spine.

'Are you sure no one else can see it?' asked Mina, staring dubiously at her hand.

'Anyone with the Sight can see it. That's the whole point of having the Morrigan's blessing, love. No one else will see a thing. You can only see it because she allowed you to.' I paused.

She lifted her hand and tilted it in the light of the downstairs cloakroom. 'Hmm.'

At some point, up there on the spongy grass mound while we were consummating our greenwood marriage, those bands of twisted stems and flowers had merged into our fingers, leaving us with the feint green mark we'd carry for the rest of our days. When we returned to Midgard, Mina had needed to get changed, and I'd been for a smoke. Fag finished, I'd found her combing her hair and staring at her finger.

Her brain was slowly coming back online. 'If everyone with the Sight can see it, they must know what we've been doing all this time!'

I coughed. 'Well, even if they don't have the Sight – like Tom and Anika, for example – I'm sure Myfanwy will have told them *exactly* what we were doing, possibly with page references to the *Kama Sutra*. You know what she's like.'

Mina closed her eyes and sighed. Then she grinned, fluttered her eyelashes at me and held out her hand. 'Let's party.'

Chapter 26 — Relatives' Values

'Since when is your dad an expert on beekeeping?' asked Ben the next morning, while we waited for my father to turn up.

'He's not. He knows as much about beekeeping as I know about double-entry book-keeping. What he is an expert in is *sourcing* things, usually from dubious blokes he's met at the bar of an antiques fair. Somewhere, there is an apiarist who has fallen on hard times and had to sell up, for cash, no questions asked.'

Ben reflected on this for a moment. 'Sounds about right. I'll never forget the day he turned up with a fairground carousel.'

I shuddered. It was a day I'd never forget, either, but for entirely different reasons. Dad's plan had been to cut the poles off the carousel rides and turn them into genuine antique rocking horses. I was down by the old stables, saw in hand, when a van load of big men from a circus family turned up and threatened to use the saw on *me*. I was only fourteen.

Ben looked up and looked around. 'Would you listen to that! They're coming here!'

He stared around in wonder while I, of course, couldn't hear a bloody thing. Until I could, and then I ducked instinctively because we were suddenly at the epicentre of a swarm, a mature queen bee and half a hive full of workers, in search of a new home.

The other half of the workers have stayed behind, nurturing a bunch of virgin queen cells. And you know what the first queen to emerge will do? She will sting her unborn sisters to death, then fly off to mate. You can see where the Fae get it from.

We dodged out of the way of the swarm, just as Saerdam Robbie bumped down the track from the meadow on the quadbike with two beehives wedged into the trailer, my father perched behind him, and Scout as an escort. We'd have done the haulage ourselves, but we've only been allowed as far as the well today, for reasons I'll come back to.

When Scout came to say hello, I grabbed his ruff and held on tight. If left to his own devices, the mad dog would consider the swarm an invasion and try to eat it. I do not want to spend the day at the vet's.

'Robbie, take Scout, will you? We'll manage the hives.'

The massive Knight stared at the woods in awe. Excitement, even. 'Has the swarm appeared?'

'Yes it has.'

He carried on staring, and I think that any second now there might be drool.

'Dad, take the dog! Ben, text Faith and tell her to get up here.'

What we didn't have was beekeeper suits, so Ben and I settled for leaving the hives at the edge of the woods, with help from Robbie after he returned to planet earth. Faith *wafted* up the garden in something light and floral that would have a human shivering in no time; a more suitably dressed Myfanwy sailed along next to her.

'Don't I need to bond with them or something?' asked Myvvy.

'Not this lot,' said Faith. 'They might have been drawn here by the Morrigan, but they're just bees. The other lot, in the Elven Glade are another matter.' She appraised the swarm, gathered in a great beard of bees in the fork of an oak tree. She pointed to a shady spot and ordered, 'Robbie, put the hive just there. Myfanwy, I'll deal with this lot.'

'Tell me where Elven Glade is again?' said Dad, who had managed to subdue Scout. I keep forgetting that I didn't inherit my disintegrating hearing from him. Damn.

'Erm, through the woods a way. So they don't compete too much with each other or something. Look, Dad, could you pass Scout on to one of the girls?'

He gave me the exact look I used to give him when an American tourist walked into the shop: *You're up to something, and you want me out of the way so I don't tell Mum.* It was only many years later that I was forced to admit that he used to get rid of me far more often when it was a single female tourist rather than a couple. Them, he used to fleece in public.

Nevertheless, he dragged Scout away, and Faith went up to the now partly dismantled hive. 'Sorry, Conrad,' she said. 'I keep forgetting.' She gave Myvvy a look. 'And asking me about a *bond* when Alfred was here didn't help, did it? Right, here we go.'

Faith had brought the Morrigan's vessel, aka the tankard, and she dipped her finger in the dregs of last night's mead. She took out a frame from the brood chamber and, with a burst of Lux, wiped her finger on it. 'There. Should do the trick.' She replaced the frame and, with no regard for the storm of bees flying around, she stepped back and let the scout bees get to work.

I couldn't swear to it, but this is what I think happens. Scout bees who've found a suitable home return and do a waggle dance in the swarm. When enough scouts come back and do the same dance, the swarm, queen included, will go and check it out. I'm not sure whether Her Majesty gets a veto or not.

It didn't take long before the beard of bees split open and they descended on the hive; with the lid off the brood chamber, they soon disappeared. Faith shooed the guard bees away and put the queen excluder on top, then left it for Robbie to reassemble the rest. 'I'll take it from here,' she told us.

Ben wasn't happy leaving Myfanwy to disappear to the Spirit Realm, and seeing his reluctance reminded me of the sacrifices Mina had to make to embrace the world of magick. Except that being a man, it came much harder to Ben. He's getting there, though. I took his arm. 'Come on, Ben. We have a rendezvous to keep.'

He let me lead him away, and we cut round to the front of the house, where Rachael had somehow ended up on leash duty. Dad always could get her to do things mother and I couldn't. Mind you, Rachael could talk him into things I wouldn't *dream* of asking, such as taking her all the way to Darlington for a tennis competition. 'Thanks, Raitch. Have an amazing day.'

'You, too. Lucy is purple with jealousy, and I still think she might bolt.'

'Just tell her there's no seats on the bus.'

She grinned. 'That would be an excuse to sit on Tom's lap.'

'I don't think Maggie Pearce would be entirely happy with that. You know what a stickler she is.'

'Here you go.' She handed me the lead and added, 'He could do with spending time in a less stimulating environment.'

'Arff!'

She wasn't wrong.

Ben, Scout and I took a last look at the Grange (or last sniff, in Scout's case), and we turned our footsteps to Elven Lane and the road to the Inkwell. After my talk with Stewart McBride last night, he'd torn a strip off Saffron and told her in no uncertain terms that she was to hang around the pub until he got there, and that's where we found her, nursing a coffee in the beer garden.

'They'll be here in five minutes,' she announced.

That would be Arun and Saanvi, with their children coming later, along with Saanvi's mother and Mr Joshi, the priest who'll be officiating at the Hindu part of our wedding tomorrow. Of all the logistics and desperate seeking of beds that have gone on, finding a berth for Mr Joshi had been surprisingly easy. He's staying with the vicar.

There are more and more people turning up today, and the seams of Elvenham Grange have finally burst. Along with the camp beds in the dining room, there will be blow-up mattresses in the cricket pavilion tonight. Rather them than me.

A gleaming purple Toyota Prius bounced into the Inkwell car park, and I gathered the troops. I *think* the Mowbrays are richer than the Hawkins, but not by much because the Hawkins have more London property. Either way, if the Mowbrays can have a blue helicopter, why can't the Hawkins have a small fleet of purple cars with Cherwell Manor signage? Very tax efficient, I'm sure.

Arun got out first, and looked nervously at the approaching welcome committee before opening the rear door to release Saanvi. I've seen photos of their deceased older brother, and a handsome devil he was, too. Arun and Mina are different from Sunil, and where Mina is a pocket whirlwind of energy, Arun looks … I suppose *ascetic* is a good word. I bet he got called *weedy* when he was a kid, though. Stop it, Conrad. He'll be your brother-in-law come tomorrow night.

The boot opened of its own accord, and Arun went to get a big case still adorned with Virgin Atlantic labels and a small overnight bag which looked *very* expensive and chic. I'll bet Stewart lent it to him.

'Namaste and welcome to Clerkswell,' I said. 'This is my best man, Ben, and this is Saffron Hawkins. I'm sure that Stewart has told you all about her.'

'Arff!'

'And the one trying to make friends is Scout. Ignore him.'

Before we could get closer for hugs or handshakes, Stewart lowered the window and said, 'I won't get out if you don't mind, Conrad. If I can get turned around now, I'll be back in time for the afternoon rush.'

The last part was delivered with a glare at Saffron, and she blushed and shuffled her feet. 'Sorry,' she muttered. 'Should have said.'

I stuck my hand through the open window. 'Cheers, Stewart. I owe you for this.'

He returned the handshake and held on for a second. 'We'll see. I wish you both all the very best, Conrad.'

We all stepped back from the car, and he drove off. Arun stepped forwards and shook hands very formally, as befits the man who's standing in for his late father. 'Nice to finally meet you,' he said.

When Arun went to greet the others, Saanvi stepped up, and I decided that she needed a kiss. Poor woman looked scared half to death. She is almost as tall as her husband, and sturdy with it. The biggest shock came when she looked around and said, 'This is like *sooo* British! Downton Abbey last night and Miss Marple this morning! Wow.'

The American accent was a shock, I'll admit. 'Did Stewart explain…?'

She bobbed her head. 'That I have to go with Essy. Sorry. I mean *Saffron*. I'll have plenty of time to change, right?'

She looked like she was wearing what she'd had on for the Transatlantic flight – baggy tunic, leggings and gold trainers. 'You do, but you might want to stick with that. It's very informal today.'

'Come on, let me get that case,' said Saffron. 'It's only five minutes from here.'

Saanvi was dumbfounded. 'You're gonna *walk*???'

'Blame Conrad. It's what I do for most things. Do you know what? He's posted me to *Yorkshire*. Think *Northern Exposure* but with totally incomprehensible accents…'

Saffron marched off, and a bewildered Saanvi cast a longing glance at her husband, then jumped to follow her.

Arun nodded as if he'd had some prejudice confirmed, then spoke to Ben. 'You're the cereal agronomist, right?'

Ben was taken aback. 'Yes, I am. Makes a change from being known as *Myfanwy's fiancée* or *Conrad's best man*.'

Arun looked from Ben to me, and I got the message. 'Ben, have I got time to buy Arun a ... a coffee before the bus leaves?'

'If you're quick. Don't make me set Lloyd on you.'

Ben left us, and I handed Arun the lead. 'I can't take him inside, I'm afraid. Won't be long.'

'Does he bite?'

'All dogs bite. He won't bite you, though. Here, give him one of these and you'll have a friend for life.'

I jogged into the pub, where a harassed Reynold gave me a filthy look. They may be making a lot of money out of my wedding, but they're busier and spread more thinly than they have ever been. He paused in taking a breakfast order and said, 'Why are you still here?'

'Two coffees. Mina's brother's just arrived.'

'One sec,' he told his customer, then slopped coffee into two cups and shoved them over the bar. 'Have a nice day.'

I picked up the cups and bit my tongue. Out in the garden, Arun was talking to Scout as if he expected an answer; Scout was looking at Arun as if he were mad. The human looked up and said, 'I hope they weren't expensive. I don't really want any more coffee, but it is very kind of you to get them.'

'They were on the house, as it happens, so no harm done. Do you mind if I drink mine?'

'Of course not, if you say we have time.' Arun's voice had shifted east, back towards England, and he knew he was being too polite. He shook himself and said, 'Mina says you are very easy-going, Conrad. I suppose you must be, to put up with her.' He smiled and took a pair of glasses out of his top pocket. Within seconds, the lenses had turned opaque in the sunshine. 'I'm allowed to say that, of course.'

'Wait until you meet Rachael. She can give masterclasses in being an annoying little sister.'

He gave a thin smile and braced himself to say what he really wanted to say, whatever it was that had made him want Ben out of the way.

'As soon as Mina told me who she was dating, I looked you up. And all the other people she's mentioned. The Chinese secret police have a bigger online presence than you and your friends. They're easier to hack, as well.' He raised his hands defensively. 'Not that I tried to hack the MI7 website, of course. No point. It's a total fabrication. Like that story about the shootout in Oxfordshire. And the recent serious incident in the Lake District. There one minute, almost completely erased the next.'

I lit a cigarette to cover my surprise. 'You're good, Arun. No wonder Stewart was impressed yesterday.'

He waved away the flattery. 'Perhaps, but I'm not as good as the people you have working for you. I am scared, Conrad.'

'You're quite safe, Arun. Safest place in England right now is Clerkswell. And it's not *people* who hide things, it's one person. Li Cheng, and he's coming up tonight. I'll introduce you.'

'I do not *want* to be introduced. I want to know that Mina can marry into your family and that *my* family can keep their distance. I do not want anything to do with whatever you and your kind get up to.'

I put my cup down. 'Shouldn't be a problem, Arun. You've had a lot of practice at *keeping your distance*. Starting when Mina was in hospital.'

'I was looking after Maama-ji! She was in pieces.'

It was about the worst thing he could have said. 'Not as much as Mina's jaw.'

'I tried! She won't believe me, but I tried! That … that man Miles wouldn't let me see her.'

'Bollocks, Arun. I knew Miles. He was a good man. Better than me in a lot of ways. He would never have stopped Mina's brother going to see her. Come to that, how could one man stop you visiting someone *in hospital*.'

He looked down. Guilty of something, but not lying, I don't think. 'What did you say to him? Did you lay the whole *betraying her family. Disgrace to the community* thing at his door? If you did, it shows what a good man Miles really was, because he didn't break your legs for it.'

He shook his head. 'I shouldn't have brought it up. I'm sorry. I had really hoped to see Mina tonight and make my peace with her, but she's cooked up this monstrosity.' He made a vague gesture to go with the description *monstrosity*.

'Sorry?'

'Saanvi says that Mina's wedding is a *fusion*. I would prefer to characterise it as *fission*. Particles exploding everywhere and setting off further reactions.'

I couldn't help it, I'm afraid. I know this may sound Geekist, but I burst out laughing. 'I think you've just hit on the perfect metaphor there. A chain reaction is exactly what she wants. I'm sorry you can't get to spend quality time with her, Arun, I really am. You've got a lot of ground to make up, and, like Miles, I wouldn't stand in your way.'

I stubbed out my cigarette and nodded slowly to him. 'I'm not going to apologise for who I am or where I come from, and if you can set that aside, you might find that Mina carries the name Desai with more pride than you think, in spite of everything that's been done to her. And if you give her half a chance, she'll be touting your CV round every philosophy department in Britain as a guest lecturer so that she can see more of you.'

The last statement was a lie, but the rest was true. Arun looked up sharply, and his eyes blinked behind the photochromic lenses. 'What has Stewart said?'

It was my turn to be taken off balance. 'About what? He's said you were great, but that's all. And he meant it, too.'

'Oh. Look, please don't tell anyone, especially Mina, but he said there might be a new post coming up at Oxford, or something else.'

'That's a big ask, Arun, the *not telling Mina* part. Then again, this is your story, and I'm honoured you mentioned it to me. Good luck, if that's what you want. We'd better go, I'm afraid.'

We stood and headed for the rendezvous at Mrs Clarke's Folly. 'Are you into football?' I asked hopefully.

'Oh, yes. Will you keep another secret? I'm a Gooner.'

'Good job Michael Hardisty's not coming today… Oh. I spoke too soon.'

I had stopped just by the village green and seen Cora dropping off her husband and son, and their places in the car were taken by Eseld and Lena. Interesting. Cora turned left into Elven Lane – even more interesting: she was off to the Mayday picnic.

As soon as he spotted me, Mike gave an enthusiastic wave.

'Him?' said Arun. 'He's in the Yid Army?'

Ouch. Double ouch with brambles.

'If you say that again,' I hissed. 'You will find your gonads being served on sticks by my boss, who is not only a Spurs fan but is *actually* Jewish, and has broken more men than you've solved differential equations.'

Arun was going to object that he solves differential equations instead of counting sheep until he saw the look on my face. 'Oh.'

Mike and ... Josh? Yes, Josh. Mike and Josh were jogging towards us, and Josh looked excited. If you're not up on the tribal affiliations of English football, Arun is an Arsenal supporter – a *Gooner* – and Mike Hardisty has the cockerel of Tottenham Hotspur tattooed on his arm. Arsenal fans are proud to support the Gunners, and, more controversially, the hardcore Spurs fans identify as the Yid Army. How long they'll carry on doing so is a question they refuse to answer.

'Hi Mike,' I said. 'This is Arun Desai, Mina's brother. He's a Gooner, but don't hold it against him. Arun, this is Mike and Josh. Mike is a great grill chef, for which he is justly famous. He's also married to the Principal of Ironmongers' College.'

Mike got the reference: *This man is not Entangled*. Arun knows (or should do) that Ironmongers' College, the cover name for Salomon's House, is as fictitious as MI7, even if Arun wouldn't know why. Mike runs a construction firm, and he still handles bricks, something Arun discovered when they shook hands.

'Neutral ground today, and neither of us want Trafford to win, do we?' said Mike in an inclusive, welcoming tone of voice that urged Arun to agree with him, which he promptly did.

'Our enemy's enemy is our friend. Good to meet you, erm, Mike.' And so we arrived at the bus with peace prevailing, though I couldn't help being glad that I prefer cricket and that I come from a county whose best football team is usually eighty places below the ones we'd be watching today. In a good year.

Ethan Mowbray stepped out of the crowd of men and came to say hello and be introduced to Arun. 'Doctor Arun Desai,' said Ethan with a booming roll of the Rs in *Doctor Arun*. 'Honour to meet you.'

Arun was suitably impressed (and a little intimidated). Ethan turned to me.

'Any chance we could grab the back seat for a chat with Mike, Conrad?'

I should have seen this coming. 'Erm, hang on.'

I scanned the group. Who could I trust to be nice to Arun? Not Lloyd, clearly. Chris was here, having dropped his girls off with their mother (he was with *his* mother at the Foresters last night). No. Too risky, and he was already in deep discussion with Cador. Barney had already been assigned someone to look after, and Ben's suffered enough. Alain would be a good bet, but he's not here. The last man came round the bus. Of course. Perfect.

'Arun, I'd like you to meet Tom Morton. He's a devotee of the oval ball, so you should be safe sitting next to him.'

The men shook hands, and Arun said, 'And how do you know Conrad?'

Tom gave me a funny look. 'I'm the one who arrested Mina. Didn't Conrad say?'

Arun's face froze, span around and settled into a picture of consternation.

'Lots to talk about, I'm sure,' I told them. 'Excuse me. I need to pass this daft dog on to Ben's father for the day.'

When I got on the bus, the expression on Tom and Arun's faces told me that they were trying to decide if I were their enemy and that they should therefore be friends. I grinned and moved swiftly to the back of the bus.

Maggie Pearce, resplendent in her Mowbray Estate polo shirt, walked slowly down the aisle, checking that we all had our seatbelts fastened. 'Aren't you gonna count us?' asked Lloyd. He was fired up today, and wearing *his* colours: the old gold and black of Wolverhampton Wanderers, whose Molineux ground was our destination.

Maggie gave him a disdainful blink. 'I know who's on the bus that I need to get home. The rest of you can do as you like. And if you so much as lift both buttocks off that seat while we're moving, you'll be hitching a ride from the nearest motorway junction.'

Lloyd zipped his lip and tried to look like a choirboy. Didn't work.

Once we'd crawled out of the car park, Ethan placed a Silence around the back of the bus, locking himself, Kenver, Mike Hardisty and me into our own little world. Then he looked at his cousin and said, 'Go on, Kenver.'

Kenver licked his lips. 'I thought Cador was doing this.'

'He's the adviser, you're the Mage. I'm the Staff King of Kernow and Boar of Kellysporth. You're the one who needs to run this in Eseld and Morwenna's absence.'

Kenver should still be studying. Kenver should be having some fun. The Universe has other ideas. He breathed in, breathed out and turned to me. 'We had Mike and Dean Hardisty round for the day on Friday.'

See? I told you he should still be studying. Calling Cora *Dean Hardisty* is a bit of a giveaway. Eseld would have rolled her eyes and interrupted at this point, but Ethan just kept his peace.

'How did it go with Cora?' I prompted.

'She's provisionally accepted an offer to become the Founding Dean of Mowbray College.' He glanced nervously at Mike and me. 'Subject to some conditions.'

'They wouldn't give me a blank cheque,' said Mike, to move things along. 'Don't blame them. They wouldn't give the Kellysporth Marina…'

This time Ethan did interrupt. 'Conrad isn't bothered about the Marina project.'

Am I not? I didn't even know there *was* a Kellysporth Marina project. I shrugged to agree with Ethan and made a mental note to look into it one day soon.

'Sorry,' continued Mike. 'It's fair enough: the Estate want to do their due diligence on me, and they've delegated that to your sister, Conrad. She's not just a pretty face, is she?'

'None of the women I know are just a pretty face, Mike.'

He grinned. 'I thought you'd say that. If I can show the Estate that I can handle the project by the summer, Cora's going to announce her retirement at the August barbecue, and Eseld's provisionally booked the Mercers Hall for the Bank Holiday Monday to do the launch.'

I spluttered. 'Tell me you're joking again, Mike. I can forgive the everyday sexism, but this is a bit close to the bone for humour.'

Kenver shuffled in his seat. Ethan folded his arms and said nothing. Finally, Kenver broke the silence. 'I thought you knew my sister quite well, Conrad.' He looked up. 'Not as well as Chris Kelly, obviously.'

I ran my hand over my head, trying to run my fingers through hair that just isn't there any more. 'Are all three of you in on it?' I tried as a last resort. Ethan's face told its own story, and I sighed. 'Only Ez could do this.'

'It gets worse,' said Ethan, in much the same tone as I'd heard Lord Mowbray use about his daughter, only he had some control over her.

Salomon's House is known to the mundane world as *Ironmongers' College*, partly because it has a mundane entrance on Ironmonger lane. That door is squeezed in next to the very real and very public Mercers' Hall, the home of an ancient City livery company. Talk about parking your tanks on someone's lawn: there is no way that Salomon's House and the Invisible College wouldn't take this as a direct insult.

'How can it get worse?' I asked.

'You have to be on the board, and you have to be at the launch.' Mike let that sink in for a second, then he looked at the two Mowbrays. 'Look, Conrad, I wasn't happy when Cora told you what she'd done. No one likes having their private life discussed like that, but you did me a solid, and I owe you. Cora won't go for Mowbray College if you want to stay neutral, and it's enough for me to know that she *would* go for it. Cora tells me the guy from Napier in Edinburgh would jump at the chance to be Founding Dean. You can back out if you want.'

Strictly speaking, there was nothing to back out of because I hadn't agreed to anything yet. On the other hand…

'I'm in. Subject to Mina getting a consultancy role.'

'Already pencilled in,' said Ethan. He narrowed his eyes. 'Why do I always get the impression that you're backing two horses in every race, Conrad? Have you suddenly discovered an angle I haven't seen?'

'Yes. Of course I have. But it's as personal to me as Cora's is to her, if you don't mind.'

'Fair enough.'

'And I have my own conditions: Eseld runs everything past me before August. I am not buying a pig in a poke.'

'You what?' said Kenver. 'What's one of them?'

Ethan nudged Kenver. 'Go on then, lad. This is the point where we all shake hands on the deal, starting with you.'

We did, and when it was my turn to shake with Mike, I said, 'I might have the perfect job for you, starting soon. Might help you pass due diligence.'

'Is that right?'

'It is. I need to talk to a couple of people first, though.'

Kenver frowned. He had the central seat and could see down the aisle. 'If it didn't mean getting dumped at the side of the road, I'd suggest you went and rescued Arun. He looks like he might pass out. And I think they might be singing.'

'Singing?'

Ethan cancelled the Silence, and Kenver was right: Lloyd was trying to get Josh, Tom, Arun, Ben, Barney, Chris, Cador, Ross Miller (with a note from his mum), George Gibson and Alex to celebrate their new-found love of Wolverhampton Wanderers and their undying hatred of West Bromwich Albion. With patchy results, it must be said.

And if you said, "Alex?" to yourself, then let me confirm that we are taking an *actual* wolf to watch Wolves. Yep. He was very excited when he heard. Not too excited, I hope.

It took ages to get Ethan alone at the match. Lloyd had twisted a few arms and called in some favours, and the Clerkswell Stags Redux were being hosted in a very expensive executive box. The game – Wolves versus Trafford Rangers – was a scrappy, end-of-season affair, and very tense. It meant more to Trafford than Wolves, and the Manchester team bottled it. Molineux erupted at the only goal, and Ethan slipped out to find the Gents. I slipped out behind him.

'Tell me,' I said. 'Did the atmosphere at Mrs Clarke's Folly yesterday come about because you pitched Mowbray College to Oighrig?'

Ethan stopped in his tracks. 'Bloody hell, no. And don't dream of mentioning it to her. To *anyone* in fact. I should have spelled that out.'

'Then what was it?'

He looked as if he were about to shut me down, then leaned in to whisper. Maybe the Banks's Mild (pleasant, but not a patch on Inkwell Bitter), had softened him up.

'Sorry, you'll have to repeat that,' I told him.

He grimaced. 'It was about the Ahearns in general and Aisling's sister in particular.'

Aisling was Morwenna and Kenver's mother, and she died when they were tiny children. 'I thought that Éimear had disappeared without trace.'

'She did, and the Mowbrays want nothing to do with finding her, which annoyed the Ahearns a great deal. Even Kenver said that Éimear was welcome in Pellacombe and that was the limit of his concern. Given how much Kenver idolises the mother he can't remember, that was quite something. Now if you'll excuse me…'

Arun and Tom spent the afternoon as far apart from each other as they could, and Arun had started to look left out and lonely. I was sorely tempted to ignore him, purely for what he's done and said to Mina in the past, but this weekend is about the future. I was gritting my teeth to take him a drink when I saw suddenly him deep in conversation with George Gibson, of all people. Being a Gnome, George was after something, but I have no idea what, so I let them get on with it.

After the game, we lingered for another beer, to let the traffic die down, then headed outside to wait for Maggie Pearce. The whole bus was very grateful when Lloyd fell fast asleep after one final chorus of the Molineux version of *Those were the days, my friend…*

And when we got back to Clerkswell, Dad was waiting with Scout, two hip flasks and my outdoor coat. 'This is it, son,' he said. 'Last night of metaphorical freedom. Do you want to go now?'

I did. I said goodbye and thanks to everyone, and that I'd see them in the Inkwell later, then I swapped my coats, took Scout's lead and set off with my father.

We took the path from the western edge of the village, and we took it slowly, switching back and forth a little until we hit the top of the scarp, then we sat down. Dad is in good health, really, but he knows he needs to take more exercise. 'You should get yourself a dog,' I told him. 'You can always borrow this one.'

'I don't think I could stand the pace, son.' There were sheep in the field, and Scout was on a very short leash. That meant that he stood on guard with the wind ruffling his fur for a few seconds, then lay down and went to sleep.

We took the top off our hip flasks and toasted the future. 'It's been a funny few days,' he observed. 'We've both been relegated to visitor status, haven't we?'

'It's what she wanted, Dad. Gujarati weddings – all Indian weddings really – are focused on the bride's home. After all, they're preparing to say goodbye to their daughter forever. Mina wanted to keep the spirit of that idea alive, even if she left home a long time ago.'

'Fair enough. Look, normally the bride's family would pay for all this, and presumably you're on the hook? You haven't asked for help, but all this must have cost a fortune.'

'Sometimes my job has perks, Dad. I can't say any more than that I'm allowed to collect bonuses from some of the grateful parties we protect.'

'Bit rum, that. If you're sure…?'

'I'm sure. We're good.'

He breathed a sigh of relief. 'Your mother and I had a long talk before we came over, about whether we should think about moving back permanently. This Brexit business has spooked her a lot.'

'No news on whether you'll get resident status?'

'We should. We'll just have to hope that Juan gets re-elected as Mayor of San Vicente. We're staying in Spain for now, and don't worry, we won't be asking to move back into the Grange.'

'You mean you don't fancy the sound of Myfanwy's twins.'

He laughed. 'Have you had the discussion with Mina yet?'

'We have, and we're going to wait at least a year. Perhaps longer, but not much.'

He passed me a very fine cigar and we watched the sun sink towards the horizon. You could see the hills of Wales today, and the clear sky meant we should have good weather tomorrow, even if it would be a bit cold for bare midriffs. Still, all that Indian dancing should keep everyone warm.

A couple of minutes later, he looked away from the view and said, 'This is the moment I'm supposed to pass on my fatherly wisdom about marriage. I think I blew the chance of that when Sofía turned up and the scales dropped from your eyes.'

'Discussing my father's infidelities the night before my wedding was not top of my to-do list, Dad. You've made your peace with Mum, and that's that as far as I'm concerned. It wasn't me and Raitch you betrayed, it was Mum, and if she's put it behind her, then who am I to drag it up?'

'Thank you. That means a lot. And the way you and Rachael have taken Sofía under your wing has … well, I'm not ashamed to say it's touched me, you know.'

We smoked a little more, and made further inroads into the Laphroaig. 'Go on then, Dad, you're dying to pass on your wisdom. I'd rather you did it now than stand up and make an impromptu speech tomorrow.'

'Why aren't you having speeches? Not that I'm sorry Arun won't be making a substitute father-of-the-bride speech. Ben messaged Carole while you were at the match and he said that Arun is hard work.'

'He's alright, really. No, we're dodging the speeches because there's so much going on that we didn't need them to put the seal on things.'

'Fair enough. Well here goes.' He rested his cigar on a lump of moss. 'Some of these you've heard before, and they only work if you don't mention them to Mina. First, it's a cliché, but never let the sun go down on a quarrel. We didn't sleep at all the night that Mercedes told me I had *two* daughters, but we got through it. Second, always, and I mean *always*, let Mina have the last word.'

'I'm with you so far.'

'You know the *Does my bum look big in this?* line. Well, it never applied to Mary, and it won't apply to Mina. With your mother, it was *Does this make me look like a traffic light?*'

'And with Mina, it's *Do I look like Niði?* And before you ask, Niði is a bona fide little person. He also has an extravagant beard, so I never have a problem saying *no.*'

Dad chuckled. 'Same with me. Your mother never actually wore a red blouse, yellow skirt and green tights, or at least not at the same time, so my conscience was clear.'

'I still think you should have said something about the outfit she wore to collect her CBE.'

He shook his head. 'I was in the doghouse at the time, and her chum from GCHQ insisted it was flattering. Anyway, I've saved the most important until last.'

'Hit me.'

'Always remember that your partnership, with or without children, is more important than *anything* else. We were lucky, son. I inherited a nice house and your mother didn't need to move to get promoted, but if they'd relocated GCHQ to the Outer Hebrides, I'd have put Elvenham House on the market as soon as the estate agents opened for business.'

I turned to look right, where the now-renamed Elvenham Grange nestled out of view behind the woods. If they *had* relocated GCHQ, I think my ancestor would have done something to stop them moving, but that's fate for you. For four hundred years, the Clarkes have been tied to the Grange, and now we're free.

'Thanks, Dad. Want a light?'

'No thanks. My bum's getting wet. Shall we go?'

Chapter 28 — Get me to the Church

The Church of St Michael in Clerkswell is a bit of a mish-mash, architecturally. As the village grew, they needed more space but never had the money to pull it down and start again. As a result, there's a low nave with very wide aisles, a tiny crossing, small transepts and a huge chancel and apse, and the chancel was where the Worcester Belles String Quartet had set up, until Libby the Vicar reminded them that this was a religious service, not a music recital, and could they move to the South Transept? They could, and that's where I found them when I turned up for my wedding.

My mother and Ben's mother, under direction from Miss Parkes, had done the bare minimum with the flowers (because the usual team, like the organist, had a "prior engagement"). There were columns of lilies near the altar and garlands of bright marigolds at the ends of the pews, but not a lot else. It wouldn't bother Mina, and what doesn't bother Mina generally doesn't bother me.

'Sorry you had to move,' I said to Alexis, the first violin and leader of the quartet. All the girls were wearing puffer jackets over their sleeveless purple evening gowns, and I didn't blame them: we had decided that heating the church for a short service was money better spent elsewhere. Alexis looked absurdly young to be leading an ensemble, but then again I will be forty next year.

'My bad, Conrad.' She looked up. 'My god, you really are in the RAF. Do you wear that getup to the office?'

'No, this is Number One Dress uniform. I only wear it when I'm in trouble, getting a medal or for weddings and funerals.'

'Neat. Why is the sword over your back? You look like someone from Game of Thrones who got given the wrong costume.'

'It's too long to wear at the hip, and it's like having ... I don't know, it's like having a Stradivarius. You make special arrangements. Are you all set?'

'We've got half an hour, haven't we?'

'Doors open at nine sharp.'

'Great. We might need to move the timpani. Bit too close for comfort here.'

Libby emerged from the vestry, adjusting her white and gold stole and checking to see if her trainers were peeking out of the bottom. Mr Joshi followed her, and they appeared to be having an animated conversation about something. Good to know I was playing my part for ecumenism, but hang on guys: priorities.

'Everything okay?' I asked.

Libby blushed. 'Oh, sorry. Yes. Never mind me, how are *you* Conrad? And if you tell me you aren't nervous, I won't believe you.'

'I'm not nervous. I'm *very* nervous.'

She came and took my hand. 'Imagine how Mina feels.'

Ben arrived at that point, and we started putting Orders of Service on to the pews. Anything to take my mind off things. I kept checking my phone, and there had been no update since Vicky announced that everyone was awake and that all was on track. I think Ben might be getting sneaky messages, but I'm not going to ask.

Chris and Lloyd were next, and Ben took over completely at this point. 'Now remember, Chris, your main job is to stop Lloyd making remarks during the service.'

'Oi! What are you trying to say?' said Lloyd indignantly.

'I'm trying to say that you forget how loud your voice can be, Lloyd. We don't want a repetition of the TGV, do we? Shouting *Look at the size of that arse* is bad enough on a train, thank you very much.'

'Don't worry, Ben, I've got this,' said Chris with a meaningful look. 'I've also got coffee. Want one, Conrad?'

I could have kissed him. I probably will, later.

At that moment, we all jumped. Great rolling waves of sound from the drums crashed down the nave, and the trumpeter joined in. We beat a hasty retreat, and I took the disposable cup outside and went round to the north side of the church for a sly fag. And to say hello.

Thomas Clarke and his Alice, are buried in an out-of-the-way plot where the sun doesn't shine. I think they chose it so that no one would recycle the grave, and the seventeenth century headstone still marks their last resting place. 'Big day,' I told them. 'I really think this is the end of the story that William started, you know, back in the Plague Years. I hope it is, anyway. Cheers.'

There was a handy bin where I dumped my cup. I put my cap on and went to stand by the south door just as Ben and Chris cranked it open. Game on.

Mina had ordered the ushers *not* to wear morning dress ('A total waste of money,'), so #TeamGroom were in a variety of lounge suits, as were the male guests. The women had dressed up, though, and not a head was unadorned by hats and fascinators (or in two cases, *hatinators*, or so I'm told). I must confess that things started to pass in a blur at that point as I shook hands and tried to remember some of the names. I even found myself asking where Alain had got to.

'You shook his hand five minutes ago and asked where Manon was,' said Chris.

'Where is she?' I said, panicked. Had I really forgotten that?

'Already inside. She was scared and didn't want to run the gauntlet,' said Lloyd. 'Shame. I was hoping she'd have the leather outfit on.'

Dad, who arrived with Ben's family, gave me a huge hug and wiped away a tear. 'Glad you're getting married first,' he said. 'Gives me a chance to rehearse how I'll feel when Rachael ties the knot.'

She has a flat in Mayfair, a huge business and friends in high places. Doesn't stop her being Daddy's Little Girl, though.

I felt an arm on my shoulder, gentle but firm. Ben was holding out his phone. 'Time to go inside, mate. They'll be on their way soon enough.'

Ben and I walked up the aisle and took our places. When I planted my feet, the quartet struck up with some Schubert while people settled in. I glanced round a few times, and I knew it was getting close when Mother slipped in and took her place next to Dad, then came the bulk of the bridal party. I got thumbs-ups and big grins from Myfanwy and Saffron as they sat on the bride's side of the church. Rachael and Sofía joined the Clarkes and Raitch said, 'You got this, big brother,' in a stage whisper. Not long now.

Tom and Lucy had argued about which side to sit, and I was trying to spot them when Lloyd delivered the one line we'd allowed him to say: 'Eyes front!'

The Belles switched from Schubert's Rosamunde to Fauré's Dolly Suite, and behind me the children processed up the aisle. It was time to practise some magick.

All week, I've been trying to Enhance my hearing, and if ever there was a moment, it was now. I did my best, and I caught a bewildering melange of *Gorgeous! How cute! Is that real silk?* And I promptly cancelled the Work. Sweat was pouring down my back from expended Lux. And nerves.

A lingering waft of sound came through: Alexis saying *Three, four...*

The drums thundered, the trumpet rang out, and the strings soared into *The Princess of Clerkswell's March*. She was here.

Chapter 29 — I Do

On a signal from the vicar, I turned and saw her: my bride, my wife, my future. Mina, radiant and glowing was standing there with the biggest smile. Suddenly, it was going to be okay. Nothing to worry about. I let out a sigh.

She was four inches taller than normal, and perfectly poised. Her hair was up and retained by a modest tiara, if silver jewellery studded with emeralds can be called *modest*. More emeralds dangled from her ears, and there was a shock when I realised that she had a tiny emerald nose stud. *That* wasn't there on Saturday night, not just the stud, the piercing, too.

She turned and handed her bouquet of cascading spring flowers to Vicky, and then I noticed her arms. Every centimetre from her biceps to her fingers was covered with henna designs of wheels, swirls, and images, too much to take in until she turned her right palm up and a smiling Ganesh *winked* at me. A deep intake of breath from my right said that the vicar had seen it, too, and was no doubt wondering if she'd had too much to drink last night.

The henna tattoos gave way at her shoulders to a high-necked ivory silk gown that clung to her all the way down to her hips, and from there it spread into a slinky sheath with about a metre of train behind her. 'You're beautiful,' I blurted out. 'Stunning.'

She lowered her head slightly. 'And you are the reason, Conrad.'

Vicars have a special altar voice that doesn't carry into the nave, and Libby said, 'He's right. You look amazing, Mina. Are you both ready? Good.' She looked out across the church. 'Dearly beloved…'

We had opted for the Alternative Services Series One. You don't get much choice in the Church of England: you're only legally married if the priest follows one of three prescribed orders of service. The room for negotiation is tiny, thinner than one of Eseld's cigarette papers, and is usually limited to the woman not saying "obey" as part of her vows. We had two stipulations that Libby couldn't get her head round, though, and it was only by wearing her down that I got to amend my vows to say that I was *forsaking all other men and women*.

When the day comes, and I have to keep my promise to Faith, she won't be a woman any more, if she ever truly was.

Exchanging rings was the other sticking point: I put Mina's on the bible and took it back to place on her finger after the blessing. Technically, only the bride's ring has to go through this, and Libby had finally relented when I'd asked, "Who does it hurt?"

When Mina's ring was on her finger, she carefully removed the Troth ring from my right hand and placed it on my left. With my Third Eye, I could see the tiny Valknuts pulse red when she let go, a sign that my vows had been made in the sight of more than this congregation. Whether Saint Michael or his boss made a similar note of the proceedings is a question I've been trying not to ask myself. At least he didn't strike me dead on the spot.

And then, when the rings were exchanged, followed by this pronouncement: *they have declared the same by giving and receiving of a ring, and by joining of hands; I pronounce that they be man and wife together.*

'In other words,' said the vicar, 'you are husband and wife. I strongly recommend that you seal it with a kiss.'

So we did.

Chapter 30 — *Signed, Sealed and Sirens*

When I saw the video later, there was a standing ovation during our kiss. Didn't hear a thing, and I had my eyes closed, too. When we turned to face the congregation, I *did* wonder why they were all on their feet, though. Libby coughed and pointed to two chairs. We sat, still holding hands and she rattled through the prescribed words of Psalm 128 as if no one was listening or cared. We looked over the congregation, making eye contact and smiling and giving little waves.

On the bride's side, Saanvi, Anika and her daughters stood out as beacons of primary colours. With no mandated bridesmaids dresses, #TeamBride had mostly gone for pastels, except for Vicky and Hannah who, in a bizarre twist had opted for matching lilac suits. I'm sure it was a good idea at the time, but they looked like either unbranded cabin crew or a mother and her adopted daughter.

I scanned towards the back, to where the general throng of Clerkswell had come to see what was going on. I'd waved to the congregated Mowbrays and Ahearns, and assumed that Eseld (who had driven Mina and Arun from the Grange in a horse-drawn carriage) would have snuck in at the back. It's what she'd said she'd do, but there was no sign. Probably went for a smoke and got too nervous to come in.

Libby finished the psalm and came to stand at the front. 'We now have some paperwork to sign, and while we do, the Worcester Belles are going to play …' she glanced at the order of service, '… something borrowed from Odin, and some Dvořák. If the witnesses would like to step forwards.'

We stood up, and as there was movement below, I whispered, 'I hope that wasn't a Freudian slip, Reverend.'

'Sorry?'

'*Borrowed from Odin*. It's actually *Borodin*. His String Quartet Number Two. To the best of my knowledge, the Allfather doesn't compose chamber music.'

'Allfather. Right. Silly me. Why are so many people coming up here?'

There was a desk at the back of the apse, to one side, and a motley crew were heading our way. 'About that, Reverend. I'm afraid that our status is a bit complicated, so we need extra paperwork.'

We hadn't let go of each others hands since Libby had joined them, and now I did so, pulling out the chair for Mina to settle into. When she sat down, I got to see the back of her dress, or lack of it.

The front was a diamond of silk, designed to cover her swastika tattoo, and it was held up by a collar, hidden at the back by her hair. Below the collar at the back was a matching diamond of bare skin, all the way to the dimples at the bottom. It was all I could do not to run my fingers up her spine. I must look up whether having the vertebrae as an erogenous zone has its own special name.

I took Great Fang off my back and laid it down on the table; Libby's eyes bulged but she said nothing about that, and instead pointed to Lloyd and George Gibson who had taken up a position facing the congregation.

'Is it me or do they look like bodyguards?' she asked, trying to cover her nerves.

'They're actually using noise cancelling technology to give us some privacy,' I told her. 'Shall we start with the most important bit?'

'Yes please.'

Mina and I signed the register, then turned it round for our witnesses.

Libby tried to keep the tone bright. 'This is an honour. I've never had an actual *Dame* as a witness, and a colonel to boot! I couldn't believe it when Conrad told me your full name, Dame Hannah.'

The Boss smiled, uncomfortable at being the centre of someone else's attention. She'd opted for a red headscarf today, with black trim, and I was slightly disappointed she hadn't used the *Oighrig Ahearn* Glamour she'd sported at the Hen Party. Given that the actual Oighrig was on my side of the church, that would have been a sight to behold.

The Matron of Honour and the Best Man signed as witnesses, and Libby completed the ceremony by signing as Celebrant. If you've ever wondered, that was the exact moment we actually became married.

Sapphire Gibson almost shouldered the vicar aside as she manoeuvred people to get pictures of us holding fake pens to re-enact the signatures, then she posed the Boss and Ben for another few shots. She checked the screen on her camera and nodded. She turned and headed back to the nave, pausing to give George a little peck on the cheek. I think that was the first time I've seen them be affectionate in public.

'What now?' said Libby. 'I presume you're all here for a reason?'

'Wills,' said Cador, opening a monogrammed document case. 'New wills needed. Who's witnessing these?' He slipped two bundles of heavyweight paper on to the table, one each for Mina and me.

'I am,' said Chris.

'And me,' added Vicky. 'Though I'm a bit gutted, like, that me Uncle Conrad has asked me to be a witness, 'cos that means I can't be a beneficiary.'

'She is not his real niece,' said Mina, before Libby could ask awkward questions. 'I have asked her to stop calling him that, because it makes the age gap between my husband and I sound a lot worse than it is.' She grinned. 'I win! I was the first to call him my husband!'

We signed the wills, and I stated as a matter of fact that there was no change, really: Elvenham Grange will go to my firstborn child, if he or she exists, or to Rachael if the Grim Reaper gets me first.

'Now the more complicated part,' I told Libby. 'I have to make a Disposition.'

'A what?'

The figure lurking at the back spoke up, making the vicar jump. 'If you have a glance at this, it explains things.'

The Honorable Mrs Justice Bracewell handed the vicar a note, and Cador handed the judge a truly hefty piece of Enchanted Parchment.

Libby struggled to read, gave in and took out some glasses. '*By the order of His Majesty King Charles the Second, be it decreed that all holders of Peculier Offices on the Privy List shall, on their marriage, renew their Occult Dispositions under licence of an Ordained Minister.*' She looked up. 'What have I let myself in for here?'

'It's because I'm in the secret service,' I said soothingly. 'That's all the *Occult* thing means. They should update it, but you know what they're like. I have to make a sort-of secret will. I should have done one last year, but I never got round to it.'

'And it needs to be witnessed by a judge,' added the woman who may or may not be called *Marcia*. 'But that's not why I'm here. I'm also Mina's boss, so I couldn't say no.' She glared at me. 'Even if it did mean seeing someone last night whom I've gone to a lot of trouble to avoid. And see them again today.'

Well, she didn't see *me* last night. Who on earth could she mean? I looked at the signature page of the Disposition, and there it was: *Full Name of Witness*. I met Marcia's glare and returned it with a grin. Everyone knows that her initial is *M*, so… 'Margaret? Margot? Millicent? Mary? Mungo? Midge?' I suggested.

'None of the above. It's *Mélisande*. And if that leaves this conclave, you can whistle for your next injunction, Mister Desai.'

The last eye-bulging moment for our poor celebrant came when Hannah used magick to melt some wax, and I upended Great Fang to put the seal of Caledfwlch next to mine and Mélisande's signatures.

'Are we done?' asked Libby hopefully when Cador had re-fastened his case.

By way of an answer, I stood up, put Great Fang on my back and held out my hand to my wife. I love saying that.

The legal party dispersed, and Libby led us back to the altar for a final prayer and the blessing.

She lifted herself on to her toes, lowered back down and raised her voice. 'Before the happy couple leave to begin their married life together, let me remind you that the gates of Elvenham Grange will be open to everyone from two o'clock, and that the dancing will begin at five. I very much look forward to seeing you after my shift at the hospital, though whether I'll have any energy is another matter. I now give you the bride and groom. May they go with the Grace of God.'

Alexis lifted her bow and cued in the trumpeter. Handel's *Réjouissance* from the Royal Fireworks rang out. The congregation stood, and I walked my wife down the aisle. It was later pointed out that she'd instinctively stood on my left, unusual in weddings, but all too necessary in our life: she didn't want to obstruct my sword hand.

Family fell into place behind us, and we left the church to stand blinking in the sunlight. I looked to the Lych Gate, expecting to see Eseld and our carriage waiting. Nothing. A tiny frown crossed my forehead, then people streamed past us. George Gibson was under orders, and used his Gnomish lungs to order different groups to form in front of the church so that his wife could get to work.

Mina had said she didn't want random shots of the two of us in the churchyard, so without further ado, George gathered the Clerkswell Wizards and the Clerkswell Coven, the men's and women's teams, and they formed a guard of honour, raising their bats in an arch. We walked through it as the guests rained rice and biodegradable confetti on our heads.

I looked up, and there was *still* no carriage. But in the distance, coming up the Cheltenham Road, was something else.

'Why have you stopped?' said Mina. 'Oh. Is that a police siren?'

'I'm afraid it is. What are the chances it's passing through?'

'Zero.'

The whole churchyard turned and looked as a Wessex Constabulary 4x4, lights flashing and sirens screaming, hurtled round the corner and sped off down Elven Lane towards the Grange.

'Ez!' shouted Chris Kelly. He started running, fumbling his phone out, then picking up speed. He was followed by Ethan and Kenver. They went as fast as they could, but they weren't going to catch a Senior Long Distance champion.

'What shall we do?' said Mina.

'For once, I'm doing nothing,' I told her. 'Do you know what the new Clerk to the Watch said to me last week?'

'Sheila? What did she say?'

'She said, "It's not a proper wedding if no one gets arrested or goes to hospital." I can't see any smoke, so I'm not panicking. Shall I ask someone to get you a chair? I'd suggest we sit on the Danvers tomb, but it's a bit mossy.'

'And that's your *only* reason for not spending your wedding day sitting on a grave? It's a good job I didn't expect marriage to change you, that's all I can say.' She shook her head. 'Yes, please. A chair would be nice.'

And that's where the Police Sergeant found us, twenty minutes later.

More chairs for the ladies had been fetched, and Mina had my RAF jacket draped over her shoulders. I asked if it might rub off the henna, and Mina replied, 'You are going to be looking at these for a *long* time, husband. Especially the one with the cricket bat mandala. Myfanwy said she used *special glue* for that one.'

We'd heard within seconds from Chris that there were no casualties, but the police weren't letting him on to the property. 'There's this bloke with a submachine gun blocking the way, so I'm hiding behind a tree,' were his exact words.

I was standing with my back to the west door, so I saw her coming. She stopped at the gate and looked at the crowds, and I distinctly saw her square her shoulders and put her best foot forwards.

'Here we go again,' I said.

'Again?' asked Libby, who was lingering protectively, standing between the seated Mina and Hannah.

'Do you remember the night the tree came down?' I asked her.

'Yeees?'

Myfanwy certainly remembered it. It was also the night we'd been ambushed by the church and forced to clear up a dead Pyromancer. 'No!' said Myvvy. 'Is that the one you asked out on a date when you were eighteen? The one who gave you the number of the Chinese takeaway?' She turned to Mina and said something only she could get away with. 'Look, Rani, if only she'd given him the real number, she could be sitting where you are now! Just think of that!'

Mina crossed one leg over the other and the silk of her wedding dress rippled like the water that flows through Nimue. Mina stuck out her foot from the bottom and admired the unexpectedly blue sandals, red toenails and even more henna on her feet. 'I don't think this dress comes in her size,' she observed. 'Perhaps she *did* give him her real number, and the gods changed it.'

The guests stepped off the path and let the sergeant make her way up to the door. I stepped down to meet her, and her thumbs remained firmly hooked in her stab vest, so I didn't offer to shake hands.

'Sorry to intrude, sir,' she began. She looked uneasily around at what must be over a hundred people, then she looked up. 'Reverend Hauxwell, could Mister Clarke and I step inside the church.'

'Yes, of course. Please do.'

Mina stood up, slipped off my jacket and handed it to me. I stood back to take her hand, and we followed the sergeant through the door. She stepped to one side, away from prying eyes and ears and relaxed a little, dropping her hands to her side. Mind you, that put them closer to her PPW (or gun, if you prefer).

'Is everything – and everyone – okay?' I asked.

The police are trained never to answer questions at the beginning of an interaction, thus keeping control of the situation. 'Did you know your house has been temporarily re-classified as a Grade One protection target, Mister Clarke?' she asked mildly.

'No, sergeant. As it happens, I didn't,' I responded.

'Well, it was. I got a briefing yesterday that it was hosting several judicial and security related assets. We were also told that protection should be discreet and responsive, which is why I've been stuck in the layby on the old road since eight o'clock this morning.'

That must have been Hannah's doing, and it was just like her not to burden us with the knowledge. 'And I'm very grateful. I genuinely had no idea, or I'd have sent someone with refreshments.'

'Very funny, sir. Almost as funny as responding to reports of an aggravated burglary and finding three people tied up from head to foot in ribbons with a little Scottish girl dancing round them and poking her tongue out at a border collie. Care to say anything, sir?'

I was too stunned to respond. Not so my wife.

'I hope that the others were getting ready for the next stage of the wedding, officer. I'm surprised they let Thistle out of the kitchen.'

The sergeant's eyebrows did the talking for her, then she shook her head, took out her phone and read from the screen. 'A lady identifying herself as Eseld Mowbray said that it was all a mistake and that you wouldn't want to press charges on your wedding day. At the moment, my colleague is keeping an eye on them, as best he can.'

I looked at Mina, and she just smiled and, in an act of gross provocation, fluttered her false eyelashes at me.

'No, sergeant. If Eseld says that it's a misunderstanding, then I'm sure it is. In fact, now that we're done at the church, there's no further need for protection. I'll get someone to call Security Liaison and cancel it.'

She pushed the button on her radio and identified herself. When her colleague acknowledged, she said, 'No further action. Come and pick me up from the church, will you?'

This time she did extend her hand. 'Congratulations, Mister Clarke. I wish you all the very best.' She turned to Mina. 'Is it Mrs Clarke?'

'It's Mrs Desai for most purposes, but I shall change my passport.'

The sergeant shook Mina's hand. 'Can I say you look beautiful? Because you do. I hope you're very happy together.' She nodded to me. 'Take care, sir. I'll be off now and leave you to it.'

She hooked her thumbs back in her vest and left the church. I already had my phone out and was calling Eseld. It went straight to voicemail. Mina took the phone off me and shoved it in my back pocket, giving my bum a squeeze as she did. 'Let's carry on where we left off, shall we?'

We went to leave, but a red-faced Arun blocked our way. 'What is going on?' he hissed. 'Why are my family being exposed to this? Are we in danger?'

Mina gave a sharp response in Gujarati, he answered back, and she said, 'No. You can live with it or go home and stay away. Up to you.'

He turned and stormed out of the church. 'Give me a moment,' said Mina. She composed herself, and we exited the church for a second time.

The police sergeant must have stopped to talk to someone, because she was still half way down the path. She passed Lloyd, and he said something to Anna (who clearly didn't mind getting moss on her maternity dress, because she was perched on the Danvers tomb). Whatever he said, it caused her to take a swing at his groin. He dodged that, and she counter-punched into his thigh. Ouch.

The police 4x4 sped off, and I caught the clatter of iron-shod hooves approaching. I led Mina down the path, and we walked through the Lych gate as a genuine farm cart, pulled by two shire horses, began to turn round by the village well. I say genuine farm cart, but this one had been painted – or Glamoured – a vivid Mowbray Blue, and blue fabric had been laid in the back, covering straw bales. A grinning Eseld had the reins, and she winked at me as she pulled up the horses.

'Eseld said that I would make an impression in this,' observed Mina. 'And yet again, I do not know whether to be grateful to her for such a wonderful gesture or annoyed that she's tried to upstage me.'

'Let's go with grateful, shall we?'

'Agreed.'

Maggie Pearce was sitting next to Eseld, and both of them were wearing Mowbray Blue frock coats and matching top hats. Maggie jumped down and ran round to put some steps in place. I handed Mina up the steps and joined her in the back. More rice was thrown, and Eseld told the horses to walk on.

My parents were married in Lincolnshire, my grandparents in Gloucester, so goodness knows the last time that a Clarke brought his bride home on their wedding day. Most of the Fae and my faithful hound, were lined up by the great front doors to welcome us, and they bowed low as Eseld turned the cart. We weren't far ahead of the guests, and the crowd began streaming through the gates behind us.

We dismounted, and we first bowed, then made Namaste to the Dragon. Sapphire insisted on a couple more photos outside the Grange, then I turned to look at everyone.

'This is the only speech I'm going to make,' I told the throng. 'And it's going to be very, very short. I am today, as I am every day, the luckiest man on earth. Having Mina in my life has completed it in ways I hope you either already understand, or soon come to do so.' I looked at my watch. 'I believe that there will be snacks served in the marquee, but I wouldn't know because I'm not allowed them. I have to carry on fasting until the completion of the next ceremony, which will begin in an hour and a half. I shall see you all at noon.'

At that point, Alicia rushed up to stand near us. 'I'm here for the dress,' she said.

Mina put her hand on my arm. 'What she means is that when you pick me up to carry me over the threshold, she is going to make sure you don't trip over,' said Mina. 'That would not be auspicious.'

I kissed my wife again (because I could), and braced myself to sweep her off her feet.

Chapter 31 — Reception

Faith was waiting for us at the back of the hall, carrying a tray of freshly poured chilled champagne flutes. She did something only a Fae could do, and bowed without spilling a drop.

'My lord and lady, welcome home. Please take a glass.'

I scooped up two, passing one to Mina. Anika took one and put her arm round my wife's waist. 'A quick toast to the happy couple. May your lives be long and full of love.'

We raised our glasses and drank, then Anika started propelling Mina towards the stairs. 'See you under the mandap at noon. Or thereabouts. We are on Indian time now, Conrad.'

Women started nudging their men towards the doors: we had to get changed in the marquee. I lingered for a second, then grabbed another glass and took the shortcut through the morning room before it was officially declared out of bounds. I found Eseld exactly where I'd expect her to be: up at the stables. What I hadn't expected was to see Rachael edging away and clearly bent on avoiding me. How she managed to get up here so quickly in those heels is a secret known only to the sisterhood.

Eseld had carefully hung her blue tailcoat on the back of the door, and she was about to bring the two shires in to wait for their owner to collect them. She watched me every step of the way up the slope, then at the exact moment she could be sure I'd hear her, she said, 'Congratulations, Conrad. I can't say anything about what happened, though.'

I closed the gap and handed her a glass of champagne. 'Thank you. Why not, pray?'

''Cos I wasn't there, and Rachael agrees we should wait until Alicia can tell you herself.'

'*Alicia!* What on earth? Where was Faith?'

'Having a lie-down, I think. The past few days have been tough on her, even though she doesn't show it to you or Mina.'

'Are you being serious?'

'Yeah. I am. Sorry, but you're gonna have to leave it. I don't know who, what or why, but Leesha dealt with it, and only she knows the full story.'

I got a strong sense that Eseld was telling me *half* a story here. I'd stake a lot of money that she at least knew the *who* of the matter: the question is, how hard would I have to press her to get an answer? Eseld can be *very* stubborn. Just look at the way she's treated her mother for nigh-on twenty years. I weighed it up and decided that I'd have to press so hard that it would ruin the day for both of us. On the other hand…

'I'll let it go if you answer two questions. First, was there any risk to any of

Mark Hayden

the human guests? Any risk at all?'

She shook her head. 'None at all. They were not planning an ambush. I give you my word on that.'

'Fair enough. Second, how come the police turned up?'

She snorted. 'Blame Maggie. After we dropped Mina and Arun at the church, Maggie said she was bursting to pee. I knew they'd be ages sorting Mina out before she went into the church, so I brought us back here so Maggie could use the lav out back while I turned round in the meadow, only she saw something, or heard something. Next thing I know, she's running back from the stables shouting that there's burglars but not to worry, 'cos the cops are coming.'

'And she thought the police could stop them when Saerdam Robbie couldn't?'

'Well, she's never met Robbie, thank the gods, and she thinks that Shear Magic are just that: hairdressers. She's not used to the Fae, and we thought it'd be easier all round if she didn't know. That's why she didn't come on Walpurgisnacht.'

It sounded plausible. Maggie was possibly the only person who *would* have dialled 999 rather than send Eseld into the fray. I looked at the Grange: conveniently for Ez, Alicia was going to be closeted with #TeamBride for quite a while.

'Fair enough. For now.' I lit two cigarettes and passed her one to show we were good. 'Thanks for dealing with the police, by the way. I'm sorry you didn't get a chance to see the wedding. If you wanted to, that is.'

In a rare moment of self-reflection, Eseld said, 'Mina said that she wanted me to see you married for myself, and she said it in that way where you can't tell whether she's joking. Just so I'd got the message. I think she said it in revenge for me draping the carriage in Mowbray Blue. And for everything else. Not that there ever was an *anything else.*'

That sounded exactly like Mina and exactly like Eseld. 'As soon as the police mentioned your name,' I told her, 'Chris legged it from the church at warp speed. Your safety was his first and only thought.'

'Was Tamsin's face a picture?'

'That's unkind. I may be the only person who can say this to you, but if you don't feel the same about Chris as he does about you, then you should let him down gently.'

'He's a great dad. He had the kids last weekend, and Tamsin finally agreed to let me meet them. Amanda's a real case, in't she?' She smiled. 'I dunno, Conrad. You know that he's one of the Peculier Appointments, right?'

It was a factor I hadn't considered. There are some offices in magick that go back before the establishment of Salomon's House: the Constable, the Keeper of the Esoteric Library, the Royal Exorcist and the Earthmaster. The monarch no longer chooses them personally, but their appointment is outside the control of the Warden and the Inner Council. In theory, Chris could resign from the Inner Council and keep his job, his house and most of his salary. Sod that.

'If you want to spend the rest of your life with someone, the politics are something you can work out. If you *don't* want them, every molehill is a mountain.'

She sighed. 'Yeah. My therapist said the same thing. Cheeky cow asked if I was *afraid of repeating my mother's desertion.* I think Chris might be waiting to see where Moodyface decides to park herself long term, once her job for Faith's done. Amanda will start school next year, and Chris is adamant that she's not home-schooled. We'll see.'

We were interrupted by a visitor at that point, padding through the garden and looking for someone to play with. When he caught my scent, he broke into a doggy-jog and came to congratulate me on my wedding. Or that's my interpretation, anyway.

'Hello, boy. You look happy.'

Eseld gave me a dark look. I got the feeling she was about to leave something else out of her account of the morning. 'We tried tying him up to stop him raiding the buffet, but he howled like a banshee, so I just put a Ward on the food and let him get on with it.'

I grabbed his spare lead from the stables and said, 'You're not off the hook yet, Ez, but thank you for everything you've done for Mina and me.'

She shook her head and looked down. 'Yeah. It's what you do, innit? Besides, I haven't had this much fun in years.'

'I'm off to wait for the VIPs. See you later.'

'Come here, Conrad.'

We had a big hug, and I headed for the main gates, overexcited hound in tow. On the way there, I checked to see if Ez had done anything to have the last word — such as leaving a Mowbray Blue stain on my uniform. She's more than capable.

I took the long route to the front of the house. Today has already been a lot to take in, and there's a lot more to come. I was married. Married! A husband! I flexed my left hand for the umpteenth time and admired the gleaming Troth ring which also showed my unending commitment to Mina.

Did it make me feel any different? I think it *will.* In days to come. Right now, I'm just riding the crest of a wave, carried along on a wedding tsunami. I tried to wipe the silly grin off my face, then gave up. If you can't sport a silly grin on your wedding day, when can you?

I checked in to the marquee (busy and under control), and to the mandap (the Indian wedding canopy, supported by elephants) which had been erected outside the great tent. Two of our dining chairs had been covered in red brocade and raised on a platform, ready for us to take our seats, and in front of the mandap, Mr Joshi was making sure the sacred fire was ready to be lit. 'Ah, Conrad,' he said. 'I have not had the chance to congratulate you. I thought Reverend Hauxwell coped very well in the circumstances.'

'You two seemed to be getting on like a house on fire. Good night last night?'

Mr Joshi grinned like the Cheshire Cat. 'She was most hospitable. Thank you for arranging for me to stay there.'

I gave him a dark look for a second, then looked over the mandap. 'Is everything in order? Are the auspices suitable?'

He stepped over and patted my arm. 'There is much superstition in all religions, Conrad. Does Ganesh have an opinion on whether the taking of four pheras is more pleasing than seven? I doubt that he does.' He gave me a sly look. 'I think that Jesus might be a little more put out that you and Mina used one of his churches to enact a civil wedding with added prayers. Then again, some say that the recognition of society and the law trumps any prayers or turns around the fire.'

And that's what you get for asking a Hindu priest a simple question. I should know better by now.

'Thank you, Joshi-ji. If you'll excuse me…'

'Of course. The co-celebrant will be here shortly, and the smell of those bhajis is making my stomach rumble. I didn't have much breakfast this morning.'

I'll bet he didn't. Did he and the vicar *really*…? I shuddered. 'Come on lad, it looks like everyone's getting some today except you and me.'

'Arff!'

'That's what I thought.'

When we originally planned the Gujarati part of our wedding, Mr Joshi was acting solo, but Mina told me a couple of weeks ago that she wanted someone who Anika knew to be here as well. Damini is a ground-breaking woman, one of the few female Hindu priests, and she is here in the UK. When Mina said that Damini could make it to Clerkswell and back in a day, it seemed perfect. I grabbed a camp chair and headed round to the front of the house.

The first VIP to arrive did so on foot. She is both the most important and least powerful of the three I'm expecting, and she only wanted two things: to see her lady's favour flying and for there to be a free bar. Some people are easily pleased.

'Countess Corrib. Well met and welcome to Elvenham Grange. You honour my home on this day.'

The Fae bowed to the dragon, then to me. 'Well met, Dragonslayer. The honour is mine. Did all go well at the House of the Crucified God this morning?'

I wish they wouldn't call it that. There are a lot of people here who take a dim view of that sort of thing. I trust Corrib not to let it slip, but Alicia…

'Splendidly, thank you.' I showed her my newly relocated Troth ring. 'It's official: I'm hitched.'

She shook my hand. 'Congratulations. In the name of the Noble Queen, I wish you all the happiness a mortal can possess and all the fortune the gods dispense. She renews Her favour and hopes that the grass will grow not long before you meet again.'

'And I am honoured to have her favour. My door is always open to her and her People.'

'Never mind the door, is the *bar* open? I've a thirst after wandering your queer little village all morning. Mind you, I did see something I haven't seen in a long time: a real life steam train.'

'Good! The bar is in the marquee, but it's beer only until after the ceremony. You can get changed there as well, if you like.'

'Sounds like a plan. Catch you later, bridegroom.'

She strutted off through the gate, seconds before the front door of the Grange opened and Lucy slipped out, still in the yellow dress she'd worn to the church. She must have had a message from our next VIP.

'Tara's just passed the Inkwell,' she announced, fiddling with her hair and shifting nervously from foot to foot. 'Are you *sure* she won't have a strop because Faith is here and because that "Cute Irish hoor's" flag is flying?'

'Did Tara really call the Noble Queen an *Irish hoor*? Good grief, Lucy, when did that happen?'

'*Cute*. Don't forget *Cute hoor*.' She shifted her footing again. 'I think Faith bothers her more. Alicia told me to engineer their first meeting somewhere private, that way no one but me sees Tara being obliged to curtsy.'

'How come? I thought that didn't happen until Faith becomes a Queen Proclaimed.'

Lucy looked from left to right. 'Don't ask me. I just want to get through today with my business and my boyfriend intact. Oh, and for you and Mina to be okay.'

Any further questions were forestalled by the Bentley sweeping into the drive. It didn't take long for Tara to emerge, along with a surprise: her four year old daughter and a nanny. Oh. What do I do now? I'm not sure that the full Fae greeting would be appropriate in front of a child who will never know her mother is both more and less than she seems.

Tara answered the question for me by flinging herself into my arms, saying, 'Conrad! Congratulations! I can't wait to see the bride! Hiya Lucy, is Mina still in her dress, or have I missed it?'

The relief in Lucy's body was palpable. 'Someone opened champagne, so yeah, she's still in her first dress. They've started on her hair, though.'

'Come on then, let's get going,' said Tara enthusiastically. The only hint that she wasn't a multi-million Insta followed celebrity was a throwaway, 'I

237

believe there's someone you want me to meet.'

With a brief nod to the dragon from the adults, they disappeared inside, the small girl still asleep in the nanny's arms. And I hadn't said a word. Just goes to show, doesn't it?

I messaged Lloyd: *Any chance of a cuppa round the front???* And sat down again, as did Scout. It's been an epic morning for both of us. Ross Miller sauntered round two minutes later with a mug of steaming (English) tea, and I was about to start checking my phone when Ross looked up at a noise and said, 'Is this Tara Doyle? She had a Bentley last time.'

'No, she's already here.'

'Who's coming in a Roller then?'

Who indeed? A gleaming black Rolls Royce rounded the trees and slowed down to less than a crawl. The back of my neck started to prickle, and Scout levered himself upright. The front passenger door opened and a whole rippling mass of hired muscle, complete with earpiece got out. He scanned the surroundings, his gaze lingering on the quaint locals, and having decided we were no threat, he went to open the back door.

I didn't get my enhanced sense of smell for magickal creatures until well after my last encounter with one of her kind, but something must have embedded itself in my Mage-memory, and although he's never smelled one, it sent Scout ballistic, too. I didn't need to see the brown skin or the sleek black hair or the shimmering ruby on her forehead to know that the woman getting out of the Rolls was a Nāgin, a Dual-Natured snake-woman from India. What in the name of Odin and the Morrigan is Pramiti doing turning up to our wedding?

Oh. Scratch that. *Not* Pramiti. Definitely a Nāgin, though. Younger in seeming, slightly taller and with slightly fewer curves. And more modestly dressed. For now. I'm guessing that the fuchsia pink athleisure wear is temporary.

She stared at me, and I stared at her. Scout gave a running commentary by growl, and it took the other hormonal adolescent to break the standoff.

'Should I know her, Chief?' whispered Ross. There was no point whispering. Snakes have *superb* hearing.

'Is a hand to the blade any way to great a guest?' said the snake woman. She was right. My right hand was over my right shoulder, fingers firmly gripped on the hilt of Great Fang.

I lowered my arm. 'An unexpected guest,' I told Ross.

My thoughts turned to the poem *Grímnismál*, where Odin tests whether a young host is genuinely hospitable. It would be entirely within keeping for the one-eyed trickster to turn up like this. 'My home is always open to those who come in peace,' I told her. This could get very tricky very quickly. 'Ross, can you go and tell Chris that we have a visitor.'

Ross looked dubious about leaving me, then did what he was asked. I took the first step, and the snake woman moved towards me. I bowed, she made namaste to me and then turned to do the same to the dragon. She was clearly nothing if not well briefed, I'll say that. She also looked up towards the upper storey, where there was no doubt much Prosecco flowing and magick being done.

She turned back to me and tossed her hair so that it rippled down her back. 'Do you always do as your mother tells you, Conrad?' she asked.

'Yeeesss. Mostly. If I know what's good for me. How do you know my mother, if you don't mind me asking? Bridge tournament, perhaps?'

She gave me a wicked smile and pursed her lips, then remembered that it was my wedding day and that today was not a good day for flirting. 'Wise words. My mother said much the same: that if I knew what was good for me, I would greet your dragon. She also said that my arrival should be a surprise to you. On that matter, I think she may have been teasing me.'

Unpick that, Conrad. I didn't know where to start. Scout turned his head left, and I looked to see Chris loping over the gravel. Our guest got in first.

'Ah, you must be Christopher, Tamsin's ex. I have heard much about you.'

'Have you? How come! Sorry. Yes. Conrad? What's going on?'

'You are Damini?' she nodded. 'Then other than our unusual guest's name, I haven't a Scooby, as Vicky would put it.'

Damini looked from me, to Chris and finally at my faithful hound, still at the alert. 'I am sent by Ganesh to bless your wedding, amongst other things. My mother would have come, but she is otherwise occupied.'

Chris isn't slow when it comes to the important things. 'Is her mother who I think she is?'

Damini nodded. 'Pramiti. Yes.'

Chris can also keep his trap shut when necessary. He didn't add that I'd had Pramiti deported and barred from the country. We all knew that, and we weren't going to mention it.

I made a stab in the dark. Metaphorically speaking. 'I take it that your arrival won't be a surprise to everyone?'

Her security guard had stood impassively behind the Rolls Royce throughout the exchange. She turned to him and said, 'Could you get my bags and put them on the steps by the front door? Thank you.' To me she said, 'No. I have met most of the girls, and if you will excuse me, I will join them and see you at the ceremony.'

I weighed things up. If Damini were telling the truth, my wife's magickal sisters would have checked out her story, so it looked like Ganesh was being literal when he said that he would be blessing our wedding.

'Of course. Will your driver and your … assistant be staying?'

'No need.' She frowned. 'They will drive to Gloucester and return tomorrow. For some reason, there were no decent hotels near here with availability. Aah. I see that Saffron has been sent to welcome me.'

Bags were passed and carried. Damini disappeared into the house and the car drove off. 'You had no clue, did you?' I asked Chris.

'No I effing didn't. Does this change anything?'

I stared at the front doors for a moment. 'Yes. I need Cador Mowbray. And Erin. And I don't know whether or not I should be worried that our guest was wearing an outfit from Tara Doyle's Signature range.'

'Eh?'

'It could be a coincidence, but I doubt it, somehow.'

Chapter 32 — The Road to Hell

After the fireworks of Saturday night's bonfire and barbecue, the Abbey settled back into its routine, and it was only the absence of the wholesale delivery van which reminded Kathy that it was bank holiday Monday. She was prepared for that, as you'd expect; the Abbey kitchen was not going to run short on *her* watch.

Just to be sure, she double-checked the fridge. Good. The pork belly was where she'd left it, marinading in one of the few recipes she'd clung on to from her days at the FE college: Subtle Szechuan Ginger Pork. Every time she drew her knife through the finished dish, she remembered the tutor who'd taught it to them. Sometimes she gave the blade an extra-vicious twist because he was the bastard who'd tried to force her to get an abortion and walked away when she refused. And sometimes she drew it lovingly through the crispy layers because he'd given her the greatest gift: Cherry.

She closed the fridge, comforted that her menu for the day would go ahead as billed. You wouldn't think a slab of belly pork would be a target for theft, but you never know. If Kathy had her way, the fridges would have locks on them, but even after the incident with the surgeon and the rib-eye steak, Dr Simon had been adamant.

'We do not lock away healthy things,' he'd said patiently. 'There are too many in here who see a locked door as a challenge, even if there's no contraband in there. Remember Sergei? Hmm?'

Now there was a man who truly couldn't help himself. Sergei had made her laugh, though. Really laugh. He was short and wiry and could have come from anywhere between Dublin and Vladivostock (according to Dr Simon). He had nimble fingers that moved faster than the eye. And they were light fingers, too. Very light-fingered was our Sergei.

The CCTV in the Abbey didn't cover the inside of any rooms, but was otherwise pretty comprehensive. That's why Sergei had broken into the consulting room via the window, and she knew that because he'd told them the next morning. 'What sort of place has a *two pin* lock on their pharmacy cabinet! Insulting! And there was no Oxy in there anyway. Waste of time. I have seen where Ducktor Simone he keeps his files, and they have much better security. I think Simone has something to hide in there.'

He'd told them his findings in the shivering gallery, and Kathy had been the one to tip off Dr Simon. 'He wants you to know,' she'd said. 'He'll deny everything if you ask him, but he wanted you to know.' She'd paused. 'Apparently there are a lot of videos on the net about picking two pin locks. See you.'

The new (high security) cabinet was installed that week, and Sergei was asked to leave the Abbey the week after. The final straw had been the spirits cupboard at the village shop, which the Abbey owned and where guests could work as part of their treatment. The shop was managed by a man who didn't trust the Abbey guests, and after five years of nothing, his illegal but highly effective cameras had finally caught someone. Rumour has it that the cameras are still there. Maybe Kathy would ask where he got them from and put one in the kitchen.

She decided to put the rice on nice and early to be fried later, and she was carefully propping up the sack when Michael wandered in looking bored. 'Sure you don't need a hand?'

She didn't look up as she said, 'You have to have a day off and join in the fun, Michael. Your "employers" won't like it if you hide in here all the time.' She poured the grains into the pan and looked up at him when she'd finished. 'And I'll get in trouble, too.'

He blushed. 'Sorry. You're right. It's just with going out tonight, I didn't want to shirk, you know?'

Faye Langley had clearly been listening, and showed herself from behind the archway to ask, 'Shirk what, Michael?'

'Helping me,' said Kathy on his behalf.

Faye shifted the weight off her right foot, preparing to leave, then shifted it back and stepped over the threshold. 'That might not be such a bad idea, Kathy. Just for once. It means we can have a word while it's quiet. Do you want to brief him and make yourself a brew? I'll see you in the shivering gallery in five, shall I?'

She stepped back and pivoted on the ball of her foot as if she were an ex dancer instead of a burnt-out London lawyer who'd discovered yoga, inner peace, and Dr Simon's bank account.

'Must be bad,' observed Michael. 'If Faye's willing to expose herself to the gallery, you must be in trouble.'

They both stopped and stared at each other. 'I've said nowt to no one,' said Kathy flatly.

'Me neither,' said Michael.

'That's alright then, in't it? This rice is for frying tonight, so don't overcook it and make sure you keep the lid on tight. You can prep the spring onions, too.'

'Yes chef.'

Kathy poured water on to her teabag and muttered, '*Make yourself a brew* indeed. If Faye had to drink a proper cup of tea instead of caffeine-free herbal dishwater, she'd come down with a fit of the vapours.'

'I heard that,' said Michael. 'And if I can hear…'

'Yeah.' Kathy zipped her lip and went upstairs to get her coat. Apparently it was sunny and warm all over the west of England for bank holiday (lucky bastards), but on this side of the Pennines there was a thin wind blowing a chill.

Michael had made her tea just how she liked it and she found her mug by the door when she got back with her coat. She pulled open the outside door, collected her tea and went to see who'd rattled Faye's cage, only Faye wasn't there. Bloody typical. She found a patch of sun and squinted up at the sky, letting the rays warm her face.

'Here I am!' said Faye from under the shelter. 'Sorry. Had to send a message before I came out.'

The Abbey's Therapeutic Lead was wearing a birthday present from Dr Simon. If you needed proof positive that he was much older than her, you could see it in the Tara Doyle branded padded training coat. Only a wannabe influencer in her twenties would dream of buying such a thing, and Faye needed a rear-view mirror to see her twenties.

Faye caught Kathy looking at the signature running down the arm and said, 'Hideous, isn't it?'

'Not for me to say.'

Faye laughed. 'Kathy, your eyes are speaking volumes. Simon bought it online over a *month* before my birthday, so I can't return it. I thought about selling it on eBay until I saw the look on his face.'

It was the most human Faye had been for ages, and it was thinking about Dr Simon that had done it to her. He has that effect on people. Then she ruined it by adding, 'In his eyes I'm much better looking than Tara Doyle, which says more about his eyesight than his last visit to Vision Express ever could.'

'It also says what a gentleman he is,' added Kathy. She lit a cigarette and said, 'Are all the guests busy or something?'

'All bar Michael and a couple of others are down by the stream looking for signs of otters or something. Not my idea.'

Kathy shook her head. Another thing they agreed on: outdoor activity should be worthwhile for its own sake, not just as a way to pass the time. That was what the TV was for.

They'd spent long enough being nice to each other, so Kathy said, 'What's up, Faye?'

The other woman nodded, accepting the limits of their bond, and set her face in concerned neutral. 'I don't like springing surprises on people. Not when it concerns their future.'

'What's this, then, if not a surprise?'

'It's an early warning. We'll talk properly at your review, and when we do talk, I want you to be open to the idea that it might be time to leave the Abbey.'

'I think it's exactly the wrong time to leave the Abbey,' said Kathy, fighting hard to be assertive and not angry. 'Another thing that might come up in the review is that I'm getting very close to regaining custody of my girls.'

Faye pretended to be pleased. 'Wow! That's amazing, Kathy. I'm thrilled.' She paused. 'You know they can't live here, right?'

'They can't even *visit* me here,' spat Kathy. 'The Social made that very clear. *Not a positive atmosphere*, she said, and yes, if I get custody, I will be leaving. My room, that is. I certainly won't be leaving my job. It's not your decision, anyway.'

Faye didn't bat an eyelid. 'Which is why I wanted to mention it today, when nobody's deciding anything. It simply wouldn't have been fair to spring it on you at the review. I'll leave you in peace.'

Kathy forced herself not to mutter *bitch* at the retreating puffer jacket, and instead focused on what she could do about the situation. By the end of her second cigarette, she'd realised two things. First, that Faye had most definitely decided to get rid of Kathy and would be working on Dr Simon non stop until he gave in. Second, that Kathy would have to start fighting dirty. Starting tonight, in fact.

Chapter 33 — Dharma, Artha, Kama and Moksha

No one cares what the groom wears (except his parents), so I'll skip straight to the bride. To say *saree* doesn't do it justice. The Desais have been a big noise in their corner of Gujarat for hundreds of years, and I'm told that there is a special cupboard full of sealed boxes in the family seat, each box containing a unique Patan Patola saree brought by generations of previous brides. We'll get to that in a minute.

Naturally they kept us waiting. I'd briefed #TeamGroom to circulate and make sure that people didn't hang around like they were in a church. 'Tell them they'll know when the show starts, and by all means give them a drink. Or several.'

The first I knew that things were about to kick off was when my mother appeared, looking more confident in her yellow saree than I'd expected. That's Mum all over, mind you: nothing if not adaptable. She's had to be.

'Is that alleged priestess another of those *creatures*?' she asked me. Adaptable, yes, but also straight to the point.

'Damini isn't human, Mum, but she's not Fae. Apart from that, is there a problem?'

Her face *adapted*. It changed from *you associate with demons* to a look which said *it's my only boy's wedding day*. And she meant it.

'That colour really suits you,' I told her.

'Liar. It makes me look like a canary. A rare, priceless canary, but a canary nonetheless. Even Anika, who is *so* lovely, even she couldn't hide her dismay when she came to fold it and what have you. Did you know there's a Gujarati phrase meaning *my not-birth-sister's husband's mother*?'

Classic mother: she'd buried the most important part of what she said in the middle: *Anika is so lovely*. 'Do you reckon I've married the wrong Desai, then?'

She gave me the wink, the one she used when I'd spotted the trick question in my maths homework. 'Oh no, dear. You and Mina were destined for each other from the day she was born. It was written in the cosmos, you know, and I have that on good authority.'

'You're wittering, Mum.'

She sighed. 'I know, dear. It's just that I caught a glimpse of Damini through the door, and she was anointing Mina, and Mina looks … well, I just can't wait for you to see her, that's all. I think …' She trailed off, looking over my shoulder. 'Good lord, Conrad, who *is* that woman? She's … Well, I'm not the tallest female here any more, that's for certain.'

I didn't need to look round. 'That's Vicky's new BFF and Rachael's new client. Georgina Gilpin. She's a Hawkins, really.'

Mum took my arm. 'Is it me, or does she look like a banyan tree that's uprooted itself?'

I wasn't going to answer that, was I? A shifting black and white shadow gave me a distraction. 'Do you think Dad would like a puppy for his birthday?'

'A puppy! You're the one who's wittering now. Look, here come Rachael and Sofía. Not long to wait, I shouldn't think.'

My sisters, in co-ordinating red and gold sarees, sashayed down the red carpet arm-in-arm. (oh, have I mentioned the red carpet? Well, there is one, and it runs from the morning room to the mandap.)

'You look…'

'Amazing. We know,' said Rachael. 'Not a patch on Mina, though. Pass me your hip flask. The one with brandy in it, not that disgusting whisky.'

Of course I had two hip flasks: one with Laphroaig, the other with a present from Mercedes: Gran Duque d'Alba brandy, aged in sherry casks. Rachael barely had time to get the top off before Dad mysteriously appeared and relieved her of it. 'Cheers, Raitch. I must say you're both looking gorgeous. Are we nearly ready?' Drummers answered the question. A jaunty, up-beat rhythm announced the arrival of the V-est of today's VIPs.

Whether you're into celebrity or magick, Tara Doyle / Princess Birkdale was always going to be a strong candidate for centre of attention, especially as she was leading #TeamBride down the red carpet.

'Is she a secret Wanderers fan, d'you reckon?'

It could only be Lloyd. Yes, technically Tara was wearing a black and gold saree, but no, you wouldn't consider her a Wolves supporter. A few seconds later, he twigged: *What creatures are normally gold and black…?*

The women fanned out to make an arc, and the drummers slowed down their beat to something more regal. Something more suitable for a Rani.

Damini came first, the Tara Doyle Signature outfit exchanged for a modest combination of loose trousers and tunic in bright orange. Damini walked smoothly, not hurrying, but not hogging the limelight either, then she took her place behind me, next to Mr Joshi.

Then came the flower girls, still firmly under Lottie's command and now including Tara's daughter. Away from the church, they could go wild, and they did, scattering petals and turning the red carpet into an explosion of oranges, whites, yellows and purples.

Arun knew what was good for him. He walked one step behind Mina so that all eyes could focus on the bride, and I felt my jaw ache with a mixture of joy, wonder and (for the second time today), euphoric anticipation.

The Patan Patola saree was mostly blue, with a gold and red border. Her hair was piled high and threaded with rubies which winked like fireflies, and joined more rubies adorning her ears, and studding the fae jewellery on her arms and at the centre of the nath dangling from her nose. Mina turned to look around, camera flashes going wild, and then she lowered her head as Arun took her hand and led her up to the mandap.

'You look more beautiful than I thought humanly possible,' I told her.

She looked into my eyes and smiled. She didn't need to say anything.

'Let us make puja to Ganesh and call the spirit of Agni to the fire,' said Damini.

She spoke the prayer to the little statue of the elephant-headed god, and I laid gifts at his feet. Puja complete, she took a little disk of red paper and touched it to Mina's forehead. A shimmer of magick followed, and I flexed my fingers, but Mina smiled her happy smile and looked at me again. When Damini took her finger away, I'd expected to see the bindi, the red dot of blessing, but no. Nothing. Mr Joshi called on Agni, the god of fire, to witness our wedding, and he lit the sacred flame with more prayers.

A proper Gujarati wedding goes on for days, of course, and is based on the principle that the groom is coming to take the bride away from her family. Mina had talked me through which parts she was keeping and which parts either made no sense or which she wasn't happy with. 'No one will be washing your feet, Conrad,' she'd announced. 'Except yourself. In the shower. Hopefully.'

The core of the ceremony was still there, though, and it began with Damini announcing, 'Bring forward the Jaimala garlands.'

These are long but simple garlands of flowers, in our case a mixture of hothouse imports and local flowers gathered and woven by Myfanwy. Lottie stepped up, her little arms struggling to present them to Damini.

When the priestess/Dual Natured snake woman took the first garland, half of the congregation gasped and murmured when the flowers sparked off colours that only those with a Third Eye could see, and for now, in this moment, that included my wife. 'How…?'

Damini offered me the garland, and I took it gingerly from her hands. Magick pulsed around the wire holding the flowers together, and it stayed contained, so I couldn't sense what was going on. Marriage is about trust, and if my wife trusted Damini, then who am I to dissent?

I placed the glowing wreath around Mina's neck, and she did the same to me. Both garlands still pulsed with restrained magick. 'Please, hold out your hands, Conrad,' said Mr Joshi.

I laid them open, and Arun laid Mina's heavily hennaed hand in mine. *Kanyadaan.* Giving away the daughter. From the look on his face, I could tell that this time he believed it. When he'd done the same thing in the church, he was acting the part. This time it was real, and it meant two things. First, that he was letting her go, and that it was not done unwillingly. Second, and more importantly, it meant that he had accepted her back into the family, because we cannot give away what is not ours to give.

For the Hasta Milap, the joining of souls, Mr Joshi read the Sanskrit blessings and his co-celebrant tied the end of Mina's saree to my sash. Damini stepped back and said, 'Now make your commitment to the goals in life, to Dharma, Artha, Kama and Moksha, and do it with Agni as your witness.'

We walked round the sacred flame, accompanied by drumming, chants from the priests, cheers and more assorted confetti. As we took the fourth circuit, I could feel the magick building, and when our footsteps had crossed the finish line, the Lux in our garlands discharged itself, down and through the tied knot which joined us together. *That* was Ganesh's blessing.

For one split second, I saw what Vicky saw. We both did. I have no clue what it meant, but for a fraction of time Mina's Imprint – her atman, her soul, her spirit, her whatever – for just a moment it was revealed to me, and mine to her, and so was a tiny golden chain that ran from her nose to mine.

'The vows,' said Mr Joshi. And the moment disappeared in a flash of gold. 'I have them here,' he added with a smile.

He passed us note cards and made one final blessing on the bride. 'As Sachi to Indra, as Svaha to Agni, as Rohini to Chandra, as Damayanti to Nala, as Bhadra to Vivasyat, as Arundhati to Vashishth, as Lakshmi to Vishnu, may you be to your husband.'

We took the Saptapedi, the seven vows (re-written in slightly less patriarchal terms – for some reason Mina wasn't keen to take charge of the home and all household, food and budgetary responsibilities), and then it was time for the final blessing, the Sindoor Daan.

There is nothing remotely erotic in a Christian wedding ceremony, and not so much in a Hindu one, except for this. Damini handed me a bowl of vermilion paste, and I slipped off my wedding ring, the Troth Ring, and dipped it in the bright red sticky goo. There was a tiny parting at the front of Mina's hair, underneath the mass of plaits and curls. I drew the sindoor daan down her hair and just on to her skin, and then I leaned down to kiss her on the lips, just brushing them with a promise of what was to come.

When I was done, both priests stepped back and we turned to the congregation.

The mandap had been built in front of the marquee, and we looked out on the back of Elvenham Grange, with all family, friends, colleagues and, yes, our *people* ranged in front of us. Some sat, most stood, and all but a handful had bought something Indian to wear, or rented it from the *Go Saree Go!* Pop-up shop. I waited until the applause had died down and phones had been lowered, then I spoke up.

'Thank you again for coming, and thank you for witnessing the happiest day of my life so far. You don't need a speech from me to know what your eyes are already telling you: that I have just married the most beautiful woman in Albion.' More applause. 'And that is now going to be recorded in numerous photographs by Sapphire Gibson. If you want to get in one, then hang around, if not, amuse yourselves for a while. When we come back, the food will be served, and there will be a bowl here to wash your hands on the way in. There will also be a display of the work done by Mina's cousin, Anika Desai. We said in the invitations that gifts should go to those who need them, and the girls helped by Anika's charity need your help more than we do. Please give generously, and, yes, Anika has brought a card reader!'

When the applause died down again, I finished by saying, 'I have one small announcement from Tara Doyle. She is more than happy to have a selfie with you, provided that you do it here, and that you make a donation. And that's it. Positively no more speeches from me.'

Sapphire broke ranks and began to snap away, and for some strange reason Alicia had become her assistant, marshalling relatives and ticking groups off the list.

The final pictures were taken at the well, where so much has begun for me. For us. There were even red brocade cushions to sit on, and the bees from the new Grange Hive steered well clear of Alicia. Even when she ran off to get a reflector, they avoided the well. Convenient.

Finally, Sapphire put the cap on her lens and nodded to us. 'I'm done. And starving. I'll leave you in peace until the first dance.'

'What dance?' I said. 'You said you didn't want a First Dance.'

'For you, no. I know you *can* dance with that leg, but it would have meant lessons and rehearsals and time we couldn't afford, and there is enough going on anyway. You will be a spectator at *this* first dance. Can you reach the box down there? I got Alicia to leave it.'

I stretched our joined sashes to their limit and found a long jewellery case. I passed it to Mina and she took off the heavy nath hanging from her nose and the chain hooked to her ear. She placed them carefully in the box and put in a simple nose ring with a single ruby. 'Better. You can kiss me without risking serious injury now.'

Even by Mina's standards, she barely ate anything when we sat down at the family table. I was still debating whether to go back for more chicken paneer or try a pot of Anika's Undhiyu when Mina got up and said, 'Let's circulate while everyone's in one place.'

I wiped my hand and got up. 'You just want to hear everyone say how beautiful you look.'

'Of course! That and to check that they're having a good time. That's the most important thing.' She looked almost tearful for a second. Almost. She pulled down my head to whisper, 'Because I am having such an out of body experience, Conrad, that it would break my heart if they weren't.'

'In that case, we should start with the one person I know you *haven't* met before. And I've only met her once.'

Manon Roussel had found herself on the M40 table – the one that connected London (Vicky, Desi etc.) with Oxford (the Hawkins clan). I wouldn't say that Manon was intimidated, but she was definitely bewildered. Georgina Gilpin has that effect on most people.

'I have never seen anything like this before in my life,' declared Alain's Plus One. 'I had no idea.' She shook her head. 'And now that I have seen you all, I wish that I had let him make me wear *un sari.*'

Vicky looked at my wife (still not tired of saying that) and said, 'Rani, is there any chance that there's a spare kurta knocking about? Mebbees that green one with those leggings Leesha had on the other day…?'

'Oh yes! You would look amazing, Manon. Leesha!'

The Fae Knight flew across the room and almost skidded into her mistress. 'My lady?'

'This is Manon. Take her inside and help her try on Anika's green kurta with your disco pants.'

'Have you had enough to eat?' I asked the poor kid in case she wanted an out. Or in case she was still hungry. I certainly was.

'Mmmmm,' said Manon, eyes starting to bulge.

Alicia led her away, and Vicky turned to jab a finger at Alain. 'You are in *soooo* much shit, pal.'

'It was not my fault!' he exclaimed.

'I should flippin' arrest you, I should.'

GG looked up. 'Ooh, please do arrest him! I love to see a man in handcuffs. Fnah!'

'I don't know who is worse,' observed Mina. 'Her or Lloyd.'

'Oh, Lloyd. Definitely.'

'And then you could strip search him! Ooh yes!'

'Scratch that, love. It's a draw.' I edged closer to Vicky. 'What's Alain done now? Is he late with the rent?'

Vicky snorted and hitched the shoulder band of her black and white saree back into place. To emphasise her point, she jabbed Alain in the kidneys. 'You don't change, do you? You keep forgetting that Manon may be a stunner, but she's got a flippin' *brain*, too.' She jabbed him again and turned to me. 'Poor girl's seen so much weird shit today that she nearly freaked out. Every time Alain should have stood her with the village guests to deflect the magick, he forgets and plonks her next to someone with no filter.'

To emphasise the point, Vicky turned to Georgina. 'And you haven't helped matters, have you?'

Georgina may not know the meaning of guilt, I don't think. Remorse, possibly, but not guilt. 'Bound to happen,' she declared. 'I couldn't let the use of an Imprint Bridge pass unremarked.' She saw the look on my face. 'When your scarves were joined, the serpent made an Imprint Bridge between you. I wonder what they call it in Sanskrit? Maybe… Ow! Vicky! That hurt.'

'It was meant to hurt, you great buzzard. You'll never guess what Alain said next, Uncle C. He said that we – the Mages – were all part of a Top Secret government agency. This to the woman who thinks *Star Trek* is a documentary series from the future! I've half a mind to get Cheng over here and wipe her memory.'

Mina placed a calming hand on Vicky's shoulder. 'Alain's punishment will be to enjoy an exclusive, monogamous relationship with her until she bores of him and goes back to France. He will have to keep her satisfied in other ways to keep her distracted.'

'I wouldn't mind distracting her,' said Georgina wistfully. 'Oh! I've been meaning to ask, Conrad. Is your wicket keeper single? I'm sure he winked at me in the queue for the samosas.'

'SHUT UP GEORGE!' chorused the entire table.

'What?'

'Come on, Mistress Desai of Elvenham Grange,' I said, offering her my hand. 'Shall we head over to the Salomon's House table?'

'Please. Oh! It isn't time already, is it?'

Damini had been talking to Rahul and Priya, the Bollywood Dance team who also provided the drummers (where from, I have no idea). The Nāgin made a sign to Mina, and my wife dragged me to the middle of the marquee. What?

Mina clapped her hands several times until she had everyone's attention. She cleared her throat and said, 'Honourable Guests, Ladies and Gentlemen. It will soon be time to clear the tables, so tuck in while you can. I am going to get changed in a moment, but there is something I have to do first. Faith?'

Faith, who was wearing a hand tailored take on a butler's outfit, walked slowly out carrying a tray covered with a gold cloth. She stopped next to Mina and whipped off the cloth. The tray was our "antique" silver salver, polished until it was almost a mirror. On the bright surface lay a dagger, curved and sheathed in a tooled leather holder. It looked ancient, and more than that, it looked well used. The dagger's pommel was silver and engraved but not jewelled. It also stank of magick.

'This is a gift from … from someone in India. Faith will keep it in a safe place for later, and there is more.' The salver was lowered and Mina took a bulky envelope from underneath the dagger. 'You can open it in a moment.'

She passed me the envelope and brushed her fine hand down my face before turning to look round the room. 'Let's go, girls.'

Mina lifted the bottom of her saree and strode towards the red carpet. #Teambride, or most of them, fell into step behind her. I noticed that Hannah and Myfanwy were still seated, and that Faith was still by my side while Tara Doyle and Thistle tagged along with the mortals. They disappeared into the house, passing Manon on the way.

I turned to Faith and stopped her walking off. 'I think you've got some explaining to do. What's going on?'

She gestured to the dagger and the envelope. 'About those, yes, but about the Ladies in Red, not so much.'

'Ladies in Red?'

'You'll see.'

'Fine. Put a beer on that tray and I'll see you in the stables in two minutes.'

Chapter 34 — The Third Ring

As soon as I left the marquee, I turned into a magnet, dragging the iron filings of smokers (and dogs) behind me. And why was the Boss tagging along?

Sofía and Mercedes were first, and Mercedes gave me a formal embrace. 'I wish you a long and happy marriage, Conrad.' She turned and rattled off some Spanish to her daughter.

'Mama says that for once her wish comes from here. The heart. Your future is hidden from her, so she does not have to … fake the truth?'

'Dissemble,' I suggested. 'Good word, that.'

Others arrived – Eseld and Dad, and my father offered me a King Edward cigar. 'Congratulations, son,' he said. 'You're one very lucky boy.'

'There is one thing I would like to know from the future,' said Mercedes. 'Your mother is the second tallest woman here, and your new wife is the second shortest. If you have children, who will they look like?'

'That depends how lucky they are,' said Hannah. 'If they inherit their father's good fortune, then they will closely resemble their mother.'

Everyone laughed except Mercedes. The logic of that didn't quite translate, I don't think.

'Ah. Faith. Thank you.'

Dad rushed to help her. Not because he was trying to chat her up, but because he was the only one who didn't know that she was physically the strongest here. She let him help her, and offered me a pint of Inkwell Bitter. 'I saw your crew, so I brought us all a drink,' she said. 'Including me, if that's acceptable.'

'Why wouldn't it be?' said Dad. 'And it's a damn good job you did, because I'm going to toast my very lucky boy. To Conrad!'

We all chatted for a couple of minutes, then I put my cigar down and waved the envelope. 'Well, Faith?'

She focused her mind for a second. 'I'm to tell you that it's an expression of thanks from those who can't pay the debt in other ways. And you had something to add, Madam Guardian?'

'Yes,' said Hannah. 'Don't break it. You won't get another.'

I raised my eyebrows and fished inside the envelope. I pulled out a set of keys wrapped in several sheets of paper, and on the keyfob was the Airbus logo. Eh?

I unfolded the papers, and the top sheet had clearly been written by Erin. Or Jay Hawkins. No, definitely Erin. It was a list of people and groups running down the centre of the Parchment, many of whom had a logo instead of a name. At the top was the Mowbray Boar.

'It was my idea,' said Hannah. 'Mine and Eseld's, really. All the people on that list have chipped in to buy about half a helicopter. And the Watch will cover the repayments on the loan so long as you remain Deputy Constable.'

I didn't know what to say. I stared at the keys, and at the papers. 'Was Mina happy to have that sort of money going on a chopper?'

Hannah smiled. A genuine, non-ironic smile. 'She was. She said that it would save lives one day. Hopefully yours.'

'In that case, thank you. Thank you all.'

I glanced at the transfer document, and saw that I was now the proud owner of 60% of an Airbus EC 120 Colibri Hummingbird. Wow.

'It's somewhere in East Anglia,' said Ez. 'Collect at your leisure.'

Part of me wanted to scan the mechanical report right now to see when the engine had been overhauled, but I folded the papers and shoved them back in the envelope and handed it to Faith. Just to make me feel good, I dropped the keys in my pocket: a physical reminder. I looked at Hannah and said, 'You'll make the repayments while I'm Deputy, eh? I call that naked bribery.'

'How dare you! It's modestly dressed bribery.'

'Excuse me,' said Faith. 'I think I'm needed for clearing the tables.'

'And I'd better get changed,' I added. 'Mina wants me to keep this outfit as clean as possible. Thank you all. Again.'

It was Mercedes who took my arm. 'I have never been in a helicopter, Conrad. Perhaps one day you will take me and your father. When no one is watching.'

I like Mercedes. She is a kind-hearted (if devious) woman, and her daughter is a tribute to her essential goodness. I didn't break Mercedes' hold on my arm as we walked back down the path, but I did say, 'My mother does not have the Sight, Mercedes, but from her height, believe me, she sees everything. One day I will take you and Sofía for a special trip.'

When I got back to the marquee, Ben shooed me away from clearing the tables. 'We got this, Conrad. You look like you could do with a moment.'

'I could do with some more food, Ben. Thanks.' I was still the host, though, and after grabbing a pot of undhiyu, I went to say hello to Rahul and Priya.

At our Bollywood party last year, the young married couple had provided the sound system, yes, but more importantly Priya had led a tent full of enthusiastic yet wildly clueless guests in the basics of Indian dancing, and, for the record, there was a forfeit if anyone were caught unscrewing a lightbulb or patting the dog.

Rahul had been rushing around since we got back from the church, but Priya had been either absent or sitting outside. When I went to talk to them, I guessed why: the green tinge to her skin and the hand over her abdomen were a dead giveaway.

'Congratulations!' I said. 'I'm thrilled for you.'

Rahul grinned, but Priya said, 'I'm sure I will be thrilled again when this morning sickness stops. Urrp. Excuse me…'

Rahul went to follow his wife, then hesitated and stopped. 'There is nothing I can do,' he said, shifting uneasily. 'I think it will be like that until the birth. The *nothing I can do* part.' He smiled. 'It is us who should be congratulating *you*, Mister Clarke. And the food was superb.' He looked towards the kitchen door. 'Even though proper food doesn't agree with her at the moment.'

'So does that mean you'll lead the dancing? I got the impression that it was Priya's thing, not yours.'

'Oh no, I …' He clammed up. 'It is in hand, Mister Clarke.'

Another surprise. If I weren't in such a good mood, I might be the tiniest bit annoyed. No. Not really: living with Mina means living with surprises. 'I look forward to it,' I said.

I left the poor man to choose between his wife and his sound system and headed to where Anika was counting the cash, ably assisted by her daughters. 'A good haul, I hope?'

'Yes, thank you. This will do more good to more girls than you would believe.' She held up one of many twenty pound notes. 'This is two weeks' wages for a casual worker.'

'And you can't buy lunch in the Inkwell for that. Unless you're Scout, of course. He's a cheap date.'

'What is this?' asked Jivika, holding up a Scottish ten pound note. 'Is it real money?'

I frowned. Who on earth did I know who'd been to Scotland recently? Never mind. 'Yes it is,' I told her. 'Sort of. Don't worry, though. We're paying the money into the bank for you, so it doesn't matter.'

'And it is worth a full ten pounds?'

'It is.'

'Then we are finished. Can we go and get changed, Mama-ji? *Please?*'

'Off you go.'

I tried to find out what was happening from Anika, but her lips were sealed, so I grabbed a coffee and carried on circulating. It turns out that the drummers were from a cultural centre in Leicester and had answered an advert on Facebook. Their day job is in a travel agency specialising in pilgrimages to Mecca – the Haj. 'We don't often get paid for this,' their leader observed cheerfully. 'And thanks for the food.'

Lloyd appeared and said that the security team were in place for traffic management, and shortly afterwards they opened the gates to let in anyone who fancied a free pint and a Bollywood boogie. I was going to greet them when a flickering image on the big screen stopped me in my tracks, and I was confronted by Mina and my good self writ large, posing in front of the mandap earlier in the day.

'Why?'

Sapphire shook her head as if I were dense. 'Because the newcomers will want to know what she was wearing, of course.'

Silly me.

'Very thoughtful of you, Sapphire.'

Is it the same everywhere? Give away *free beer* and people complain that there is no free wine. Probably. And it was only a minority of one (who shall remain nameless).

I was starting to think that I'd better ease off on the Inkwell Bitter when Faith gave me a ten minute warning, and I found a chair next to Mum to rest my leg and get a good view of whatever was going to happen. People wandered in, saw the slideshow on the big screen and looked around. When they couldn't see the bride, they ignored me, shrugged and followed their noses and tried not to be disappointed when they saw the sign saying that food service was suspended until six o'clock.

After that, they got a drink and started swapping stories. I heard at least three groups mention the words, *police*, *sirens* and *only to be expected*. Mina had only been gone an hour and I was already missing her. There were more children than you see at a lot of weddings these days, and they were running around, forming and breaking up groups and generally having a ball.

As I'd said to Dad, we've had The Conversation, and Mina wants to wait until next year before thinking about starting a family. 'Not too long,' she'd said. 'I don't want you to be too old and decrepit when there are nappies to be changed and school runs on the horizon.' Her face had turned serious then, and she'd added, 'Our marriage will be semi-long distance with you up north and me working for the Court. It's a factor, Conrad.'

It is a factor, and not one I was going to brush under the carpet. When Sapphire appeared with a serious looking video camera, my mind started to boggle. With good reason.

The music started. Quietly, then louder. Smoke drifted out of the speaker stacks and wafted over the dancefloor. Two spots came on and bathed the marquee in dim red light. The drummers took up position along the red carpet and set up a syncopated, spiral rhythm that ratcheted up the tension even more. Then they stopped. And when they re-started, it was a driving beat that almost drowned out the sound system.

The girls skipped out of the house, barefoot and bursting with energy. Mina led the parade, and just behind her was Tara Doyle, then Damini, then the rest: Vicky, Saffron, Erin, Lucy, Tamsin, Rachael, and bringing up the rear, Alicia and Thistle. The Ladies in Red. Red sequinned crop-tops and red Indian skirts.

They skipped on to the dance floor and spread out and launched into their routine.

Mina did a short solo, facing me. Her skirts swirled the smoke around her and the jewels on her body flashed and glinted. As soon as she began, I stood up to watch, and I was going to embrace her when the music finished with a crash, but she sketched a quick bow and backed off, rejoining the girls.

Then the professionals joined in: Tara Doyle won *Strictly* for a good reason, and it was obvious that Damini had been drilling the Ladies in Red for a while. Mina, Tara and Damini had energy, synchronicity, rhythm and sinuous moves that got a standing ovation when the other girls joined them for an ensemble piece.

'You'll catch flies,' observed Mother. 'Shut your mouth dear or Sapphire will film you drooling.'

There was another climax, the lights went out and more wild applause. This time, Mina skipped over and I lifted her in a swinging embrace. 'You are amazing. Utterly amazing,' I told her, then put her down for a long kiss.

'I am also exhausted,' she finally said. 'Dancing with two Creatures of Light is more exercise than I have ever had in my life. For once, I actually need some of that Inkwell Bitter.'

I returned to our table with a glass of Mike and Reynold's finest brew – and joined the queue. There were a lot of people wanting to talk to my wife.

'Pass that to the bride,' I said to Thistle. 'You can get in underneath.'

'I'm not always going to be short, you know,' she replied after carefully taking the drink. 'I think I might copy Doctor Gilpin. She gets *loads* of people looking up to her, and none of them hitting on her. I like that idea.'

'I don't think she's entirely happy with that, but never mind. Mina looks thirsty.'

'My lord.'

The drummers came to say goodbye and head off, then as I was crossing the dance floor, Chris and Eseld stopped me.

'I've got him for an hour,' said Ez. 'Tamsin offered to let him off child-minding duties so long as we stuck to the shadows.'

'I told her to stuff it,' said Chris. 'I'm not sticking to the shadows with Ez.'

Eseld took his hand and grinned. 'I thought there was gonna be World War Three for a second, then Tamsin picked up one of the twins and said, "Where's the changing bag?" I almost felt sorry for her.'

Chris frowned. 'Yeah. She said something weird, too. She said, "Tell Conrad I want to see him when I get back. I've fulfilled my side of the bargain." What's she on about?'

'A job I got her to do in the Particular,' I lied. 'She wasn't happy, but she must have come through on it. Thanks for passing on the message.'

I intercepted Tamsin and two of her daughters outside the marquee as they returned from the scullery. I think the oldest girl, Amanda, is in love with Lottie and hasn't left her side since the church service. The twins were fast asleep in their double buggy, the special model with a Silence Work built in to the frame. Handy. Tammy looked around and said, 'Right. Tell those bastard toadstool botherers to give me back my property. Now.'

Gnomes do not generally like the Fae. Their preferred term of abuse is *cockroach*. In return, the Fae either call them *rockheads* or something with a reference to garden gnomes. As you can gather, Tamsin has nailed her flag firmly to the Fae mast. I let it pass, though, because this was personal.

When their marriage collapsed – and let's not forget, it was Chris's infidelity to blame – Tamsin had tried to force Mina to take sides by banning Eseld from the wedding. I don't blame Tamsin for that, but I certainly wasn't going to let her drive a wedge between Mina and me, so one day I snuck into the basement of Earth House. Hidden away in an old lumber room was a locked, sealed and Warded filing cabinet which went back to Tamsin's life in her first body. That was what she wanted back.

I'd gambled that there were things in there which she *really* didn't want others to know, so I'd kidnapped it and suggested to her that she and Chris should have a truce until after the wedding. And, yes, she's kept her side of the bargain.

'Clan Octavius never had it. I wouldn't give your property to Gnomes, Tammy, no matter how much I trust them.'

'But you showed me a picture! They were loading it on to a furniture van!'

'They were loading *a* cabinet. Yours never left Earth House. It's hidden in the main Ley line room, right next to the wall behind those shelves. I will admit to getting help with a little Glamour, but I doubt that Chris has been back there since he refurbed the cellar. Not if the dust is an indicator, anyway.'

She fumed and bristled, and hit out at the only thing she could latch on to. 'Did eSlag Mowbray do the Glamour for you? Was she there?'

I don't often do this, and I wasn't happy doing it on my wedding day. I held out my left hand and showed the ring. 'I give you my word that no one but you and I know what happened. Eseld has no clue. It was Cordelia who made the Glamour template, and she thought it was for a prank. That's it.'

She looked down at the twins (still asleep), and she adjusted the elastic under her armpit. Then she tried to subdue the vermilion dance skirt and gave up because those things aren't designed to sit still. 'Mina is the best friend I've ever had until I met Faith. I might not be alive if it wasn't for the way Mina clung on to me to stop me going over the edge. If you ever do *anything* to hurt her, Conrad, I'll be first in the queue to make you pay. Got that?'

'Message received.' I paused to show that I'd taken her as seriously as she meant me to, then I said, 'Faith is not your friend, Tammy. Thank you for everything, and by the way, you have great moves. It's a toss-up between you and Lucy who's the best human dancer. After Mina, of course.'

She shook out her hair, lifting it away from her neck. 'Not bad for a mother of three, am I?'

I smiled back, leaving her have the last word. I carried on into the house and used the bathroom. When I got back, a pre-recorded video of a much healthier looking Priya was playing on the screen.

'… so don't get worked up about following me. Just let the music take over, and Damini will be there to show you as well. This first one is really easy…' As you'd expect, 90% of the dancefloor was female, including Mina, and I went to join her for the first round. I reckon my leg had that much in it.

She was holding out her hand for me when I saw Ben waving frantically from the back of the marquee. He had a radio in his hand and a frown on his face. Mina saw him too, and hurried over with me.

'Security have got in touch,' said Ben. 'They say that two blokes have turned up to fix the new doorknocker and that you're expecting them.'

'Ask for a name and description.'

Ben did, then turned up the volume so that I could hear the response.

'The van is branded as *Wayland Ironworks of Shropshire*. Two IC1 males, one looks like a blacksmith and the other looks like his father. The older male has an eye patch and asked where the Inkwell bitter was.'

'Is that…?' said Ben.

'Yes. Come on, Mrs Clarke, we're wanted.'

'We may be wanted, but I am not meeting the Allfather with no shoes on. That gravel is *very* painful in bare feet.'

I couldn't argue with that; Rachael actually has a small scar on her left foot which proves her right. I cast about for the shortest woman with shoes on. Thistle. The junior Fae had got changed after the show, and I shouted her over. 'Mina needs your trainers.'

They were orange. Even I could see that they clashed with Mina's dress as the Knight slipped them off and got to one knee.

'Put a Glamour on,' hissed Mina. 'Or I may never forgive my new husband.'

While Thistle sorted out my wife's footwear, I spoke urgently to Ben. 'Tell security we're coming, then get Lloyd, Alex and Cara to follow us round. And tell the Boss what's going on, will you?'

I grabbed a tray and jumped the queue to fill four tankards, then set off round the house to meet what I hoped would be our last non-human guests of the day.

I checked out the van as we crossed the gravel to the front door. I couldn't see magick, so it looked like there really was someone driving around calling themselves Wayland the Smith. He was wearing green overalls, standing next to our front doors and examining the wood. A variety of tools and objects were strewn around him on the steps; even without fully opening my Third Eye, I could see flashing lights drop from his fingers like metal sparks in a forge.

Odin was wearing matching but much older overalls and standing chatting to the security guard. They appeared to be sharing a joke about something, and the Allfather waved when he saw us. He patted the guard's arm, and my hired help drifted off towards the gates, where he probably found himself asking what had just gone on.

We converged on the stocky figure at the steps, and we were joined by an audience which included three women who were trying (and failing) to look like they weren't jealous of Mina's trainers as they crossed the stones barefoot. There was one woman and one man who weren't bothered, because Wolves don't wear shoes. Dimly by the garden gate, I saw the back of Eseld's Mowbray blue kurti as she faced the marquee and kept the non-Entangled away from the danger zone.

I bowed. 'Once again, you honour what is now *our* home, my lord. Would you accept our hospitality?'

'It is me who is honoured by your invitation, Mister Clarke. Congratulations. You have made a good match.'

'I know. I'm a very lucky man.'

'Put down the tray. We will drink a toast in a short while.'

I did so, and his one eye glanced at the Smith. 'As you can see, I brought a Plus One.'

'You also honour me,' I told the alleged Greatest Artificer; he nodded in return.

Odin glanced at the tray of beer and licked his lips. 'I will relish that. After I have offered you my gift. Volund?'

He pronounced the Smith's name as *Foorlunth*, not *Wayland*, and who was I to argue? There are so many conflicting stories about the Smith that I don't know what to tell you. Whether he was a hero or a villain, he was standing there, and he held up an elaborately sculpted wolf's head, made from iron and with rubies for eyes. It had a simple iron ring dangling from its jaws, about twelve inches in diameter. He held it up to the right hand door, in the centre of the upper panel.

'Lower, please,' said Mina.

He dropped it a few inches and made a mark with the pencil he'd taken from behind his ear. He put four screws in his mouth, picked up a cordless screwdriver and motioned for the Allfather to hold the piece still. In seconds, the doorknocker was in place and a striking plate had been added at the bottom to save our door from battery. Job done, the Smith stood back, admired his handiwork and nodded his approval. I was dying to ask him a proper question, just to hear him speak. I didn't.

'A toast,' said Odin. He picked up the tray and passed tankards to the Smith, to Mina and to me. 'May Mother Earth and Mother Nature bless your home, your hearth and above all your hearts.'

We clinked the tankards together and drank. Is the Smith of the

Elderkind? He certainly has their appetites, because he beat the Allfather to the bottom, wiped his lips and put his tankard back on the tray. I had a good go, but I'm only human; Mina did what she could, then frowned at the lipstick stain on the rim.

'Every home should have a Troth Ring,' said the Allfather, 'and this is my gift on your wedding.'

'Is that like your ring?' asked Mina. She's read the stories, and she's an accountant; she would absolutely check the teeth of any horses offered for nothing.

'Mine is for one. This is for two or more,' I told her. 'Any bond or bargain made with hands holding the ring become binding.' I frowned a little and glanced at Odin.

'Your Sight has improved much since our first meeting,' he said. 'Yes, you are correct. At present it has no power, no magick. Let us charge it.'

He opened his arm and ushered Mina to the top step.

I touched her bare, bejewelled and hennaed arm. 'Shall we?'

'Of course!' she replied with a smile. 'Why would I say no?'

Mina's tiny hand grasped the steel, and it was joined by three hairy men's fists.

'It will feel hot, but it will not burn,' said Odin to Mina. 'Close your eyes and repeat my words in your head. Both of you.' He paused and continued slowly, the heat of Lux in the Troth Ring building with every word. '*Let this bond echo our bond. As we plight our troth, so do those who follow.*'

As soon as I'd sounded the last syllable in my head, brightness burst around me. I opened my eyes and all I could see were swirls of rainbow, the seven shades of mundane light and the two of magick. Nothing was solid and all the world had become colours.

With a great burst of Mother's Red, the light dimmed to the spots and sparks of afterimage, then resolved into darkness and a shaft of sunlight. Mina stifled a scream and let go of the great iron ring hanging from the stone pillar. Instinctively, she grasped my waist, and I moved to shield her, because we weren't in Clerkswell any more.

'Welcome to Asgard,' said Odin. 'There's something I'd like to show you.'

Part Six — Sanctuary

Chapter 35 — A Bargain

There was enough warmth in the sun for Kathy to work up a sweat during the afternoon's Tai Chi session. She was getting the hang of it now, and it seemed to be doing something to her core that went beyond muscles. Good job, too, because tonight she was going to take a huge gamble, not just with her own future but with her girls' futures and with Don's, too.

She wheeled the old man back to his room and winked to him. 'You've got me tonight, Don. Nika's doing a shift at the pub, and my date cancelled on me, so I won't be going to the ball.'

He gave a slight smile to show he sympathised with the ludicrous idea of Kathy having a date of any description, never mind one who might take her to a ball. What was a ball, really? A club night for posh people, she supposed, but with long dresses and crap music.

She put the kettle on and moved back into his line of sight. 'Have you ever been to a ball, Don?'

He raised his eyebrows slightly and nodded to her. He struggled to raise his hand and showed three fingers. His grin got bigger and he pointed to the letter wheel. Kathy unfolded and spelled out two words.

'You met your wife at a posh ball! You dark horse, Don. All this time and you've never said you'd been married.' The implications struck home to Kathy, and she frowned at him. 'Was she alive when you were put in here?'

He looked down and shook his head. A few months ago, Kathy would have pegged that as sadness, but she knew him better now. Whenever Don wanted to hide something – to lie, to change the subject, to leave something out – then he looked down. He *did* look very sad, though. Whatever had happened to his wife, he'd clearly loved her.

'Did you have kids, Don?'

A short sharp shake of the head, still looking down. So, he *did* have kids. Maybe they'd been the ones to put him in here. Not her business. Kathy made the tea and settled down. Don glanced at the iPad, expecting an audiobook, but she put it away and said, 'Did you enjoy the food? You certainly cleared your plate.'

His grin was genuine, and he brought his curled, useless fingers to his lips in a sign of approval.

'D'you mind if I tell you how I learnt to cook it, and who the chef was who taught me?'

He nodded approval and picked up his two-handled cup, then made himself comfy. To begin the story, Kathy found a picture on her phone and held it up for him to have a good look. 'That's Cherry. Would you say she looks half Chinese? She is, you know, and let me tell you about her father. I met him the second time I got properly sober, when I signed up to do catering at the local college. I was ten years older than all the others, you know. They started calling me *Auntie Kathy* 'cos I wouldn't go out clubbing and drinking with them.'

By the time she'd finished telling Don her story, she could see that he was running out of steam, so she left him to have a nap and went for a break. On the way back from the shivering gallery, she picked up the holdall which Nika had dropped off yesterday, dropping the keyboard and label printer into the bag as well.

She helped Don to the toilet and made more tea. When he was comfy, she pulled her chair in front of him. 'It's like this, Don. That first envelope didn't go in the post last week. It went into the bonfire on Saturday's Walpie-Night thingy.'

Don's eyes narrowed and drew up the power of a much younger, much angrier man. Kathy held up her hand protectively. 'It were Michael who convinced me to do it. He got cold feet. Said it could wreck all of our lives. I didn't want to go along with him at first, but I did.'

The cold fury in the old man's eyes didn't abate, and Kathy found herself sweating profusely, and her own eyes were watering. She stood her ground, though. 'I would have told you in a week or so. Swear down I would. But something's changed, Don. I want to do it and do it properly this time.'

He motioned for her to get on with it, and she continued, 'Faye wants to sack me. I can deal with that, but I need security. I need a home for the girls. I need that picture, and I need it now. If I get it, that letter will be in the post tonight. I promise. I swear on the girls' lives.'

The heat ratcheted up another notch, and Don pointed his fist at her, holding it steady and trying to get some message over. From somewhere in her head, Kathy heard the word *again*.

'I swear on my girls lives that if you give me that picture, your letter will be in the post tonight.'

He lowered his fist and slumped into his chair, panting. 'You okay, Don?'

He nodded and rallied, and Kathy set up her phone. 'I'm gonna record this, okay? Just in case I'm accused of theft or something.'

He shrugged, and in a touching gesture of normality, he tried to straighten his sweatshirt before she started recording.

'This is Kathy Metcalfe talking to Donald Bell at Beckthorpe Abbey on

Monday the second of May. Don, if you understand me, can you nod three times.' He complied and she pressed on. 'Just to prove you're compost mentis, who's the prime minister?' Don blew a raspberry. A very eloquent raspberry. 'Correct answer! Seriously, can you nod once for Theresa May, twice for David Cameron and three times for Boris Johnson.'

Don snorted at the mention of Boris Johnson's name, then nodded once for Theresa May. He confirmed that Donald Trump was the US President, then Kathy got down to business. 'Do you wish me to have that picture of the raven?' When he nodded, she moved the phone to show the picture, then put it back on Don. 'Is it valuable?' He nodded vigorously. 'Is this to help me provide a home for my girls?' Another nod. 'Have I done you any favours other than be here for you?' A firm shake: *no*. 'Have you seen the report from Social Services explaining why I need the money?' Another nod, more grave this time.

'One last thing. Is the picture yours to give away, Don?' A firm nod. 'Thank you so much. I promise that if it doesn't work out, I'll give you the money back.'

She ended the recording and took down the picture. 'I don't know what you did, Don, but I need everyone to see that signature. Is it like some trick with the glass?'

It took a bit of sign language before she realised that she had to hold the picture in one hand, near his chest, then hold on to his shoulder with the other hand. She stared at the glass as the artist's name revealed itself, then it went blurry and dark, and she felt herself slipping. She let go of the picture and everything went black.

When she woke up, the picture was perched precariously on Don's lap, held by his left hand, and she was on the floor with a bruise coming on her hip. 'What the fuck happened there, Don?'

He shook his head impatiently and tried to lift the picture. She crawled to her knees and took it off him, then slumped into a chair. When she'd got her breath, she stowed away the picture, now clearly revealed as a signed John Gould original. She put it in the holdall and took out the junk shop print which Nika had picked up for a fiver. There had to be *something* to cover the empty space, and … oh shit. *Fucking centimetres.*

The new print was much smaller than the raven. Ah well, who would *really* look? Dr Simon was probably the only one who would notice, and he rarely came in these days, preferring to have Don wheeled to the treatment room.

Swap made, she set up the label printer and went through the routine again. Before attaching the label, she saw Don peering at the stamp. 'It's a Large Letter stamp, Don, 'cos this is an A4 envelope. They don't put the prices on any more, neither. Do you know this stamp cost a quid! One pound and one penny.'

He frowned, struggling with both concepts: a stamp with no value on it

265

and a stamp which cost one whole pound. 'I'm not joking you. A quid for a letter. No wonder no one writes them any more. I just need to send someone a message which will cost me nothing, then one last cup of tea and I'll get you ready for bed.'

Chapter 36 — Jenga

Tom Morton stared at the front door of Elvenham House as the rainbow colours swirled and dispersed into the air, for all the world as if they were made of vanishing silk and not light. Not *light*, of course, they were made of *Lux*. Had he actually seen it for the first time in his life, or was it just a side-effect? And was he wondering about that because it stopped him thinking about the fact that he'd just seen an actual *god* whisk away the Happy Couple?

'I'll go to the foot of our stairs,' said an unmistakable Geordie voice from behind him. 'Ow, these bliddy stones are … ow! Me foot!'

Tom shook himself and took one last glance at the doors. The workman in the green overalls was whistling a happy tune at a job well done as he packed his tools. Presumably all in a day's work for a jobbing immortal.

Half a dozen of the most magickal guests had charged like soldiers when word had got round about the visitors, and Tom had joined in because his nose for trouble had told him something was about to happen and he wasn't going to let Lucy face danger on her own. Not that he could have helped in any way; it was just the way he was.

He glanced behind him, where Chris Kelly and Eseld Mowbray were standing guard at the garden gate, then took in the fact that Hannah Rothman had begun an argument with Tamsin Kelly. He caught the tail end of it, with Tamsin saying, '…Know what I'm talking about, and they've made a vertical *and* a lateral Transition. They'll be thousands of miles and hundreds of levels away, because we both know where they've gone, don't we? And we both know that by the time whatever the Gallows God has in store for them is over, we'll all be back home.'

Hannah looked as if she didn't *want* to believe Tamsin, but that she had no choice in the matter. 'Only he could do this,' she muttered. She looked up and around, and found everyone staring at her. 'In Hashem's name, don't look at *me*! I'm not in charge.'

Vicky coughed. 'Sorry, Boss. I think you are, actually. You and Ben. And maybe Chris?'

'And you!' said Hannah, pointing an unhappy finger. 'Definitely you, Captain Robson. As your CO and the Matron of Honour, I am ordering you.'

'Me and my big mouth.'

Tom had a sudden thought: if he wasn't careful, there would be eyes on *him*. He looked at Lucy. Like Tammy and Vicky, she was still in her dance costume and looking anxiously at the sharp stones of Elvenham.

It was a day for grand gestures, so Tom swept her off her feet. 'I'm only doing this as far as the garden path,' he said through gritted teeth.

'Hey! I'm not that heavy!' she responded. She also put her arms round his neck and clung on, then whispered, 'Thanks, Tom. I think I've cut my foot, and Vicky's definitely bleeding. I'll need the first-aid kit.'

Eseld stepped aside, and Tom put Lucy down. He may have escaped a seat on the emergency committee, but he'd swapped that for centre stage in the gathering group outside, with Conrad's poor parents and Mina's brother centre stage.

'What is going on!' demanded Arun. 'Why did everyone run off?'

'I think it was a special surprise,' said Tom. 'Conrad's boss is going to say something in a minute. If you'll excuse me, I need to fetch the first-aid kit from the scullery.'

He returned in time to see Chris Kelly carrying Vicky, whilst Lloyd performed the same service for Chris's soon-to-be ex-wife. Tom grinned: so how had *that* worked itself out? Had Chris glanced at Eseld and realised he couldn't offer? Given that Tamsin hated Gnomes almost as much as her Fae employers did, had she been tempted to put her foot down? As it were.

The music had stopped and Hannah found herself facing almost the whole wedding, which now of course included most of Clerkswell's residents. She cleared her throat and said, 'Ben has something to say.'

Nice swerve.

Ben did not look happy, but most of the eyes on him at least knew who he was. 'Ahem. Ladies and gentlemen.' He paused. 'Do we have any lords? No? Right. Ladies and gentlemen, the whole point of a surprise is that the, err, the recipients…'

'He means *the victims*,' chimed in Lloyd from the back of the emergency committee.

Ben's fingers flexed and he nearly made a fist. 'Whatever you call them, the happy couple have just been swept off on a surprise honeymoon! Nothing else has changed. The dancing will continue in five minutes, and the bar is still most definitely open. Any questions, the Matron of Honour, Dame Hannah, will answer them.'

The Matron of Honour glared at the Best Man, and her glare turned from ice to fire when someone did indeed have a question.

'Where have they gone?'

'It's a surprise. They won't know until they get there.'

'I was in the house,' said the woman from the village shop. Nell, was it? 'And Mina didn't take any luggage. She didn't even have a coat and she was wearing Thistle's trainers!'

'All part of the surprise,' said Hannah through gritted teeth.

'Ooh, someone will pay for that,' said a man who Tom didn't know. And Tom was inclined to agree with him.

'As Ben told you,' said Hannah with a voice that would close any meeting, 'the bar is still open. Thank you.'

Tom handed off the first-aid kit to Lucy and went in search of a drink. Having grabbed a pint of Inkwell, he was waved over by a woman he'd heard about but only seen this morning during the ceremonies at the wedding: Judge Bracewell.

She was on her own at a table for four, and Tom asked her if she wanted a drink.

'Not right now. Have a seat, Inspector Morton.'

He sat. 'It's Tom.'

There was a pause. She knew he knew her nickname, and after a moment she said, 'And I'm Mel, as it's a celebration. Did I hear right? Has the One-Eyed Lord whisked away the bride and groom?'

'I believe so. They're not expected back any time soon, either.' Tom risked a joke. 'Will Hannah post him AWOL, do you think?'

Judge Bracewell (whom Tom was a long way from thinking of as *Mel*) was in her late forties, he supposed, and somehow managed to make the aquamarine salwar kameez look like a uniform. She shifted the scarf and sighed. 'Believe it or not, there is case law on this. He – and Mina – will have their leave counted on their clocks, not ours.' She leaned forwards. 'I've read your report on the Irish business, Tom.'

He took a swig of the Inkwell Bitter. He could forgive Clarke an awful lot for bringing this into the world. 'And every word I wrote is true.'

She snorted. 'It should have come with a dozen blank pages to show what you'd left out.' She shook her head. 'You've known him a long time. What do you make of our Deputy Constable?'

Tom hesitated. 'With respect, he's *your* Deputy Constable, not mine. I'm only a guest in the world of magick, not a paid-up member.' He paused for a second to let the message sink in. 'If you were to ask me what I thought of Conrad Clarke, I'd have to say that if I owned a tent, I'd very much want him inside. Even if he does snore.'

She laughed. 'Well put. I like that. Does he snore?'

Tom put on a grave face. 'He does. But not as badly as Lloyd Flint. Are you on your own this weekend?'

He knew fine well she was, but it was a fair question.

'I am. When my husband heard that it was a wedding with Mages and cricket playing villagers, he opted to stay at home by the phone.' She whispered conspiratorially. 'I'm about to become a grandmother. And unlike my name, that's a secret I'd like kept.'

So why had she told him? Had she been on the Elvenham Punch? 'Of course.'

She sat back and frowned to herself, then smiled. 'I've seen Sir Thomas in action. Before he joined the bench full time.'

It wasn't a surprise. Tom's father was a judge in the High Court, Northern Circuit. He nodded.

'We need another Recorder in the Cloister Court, Tom. For the Hawkshead Sessions. I think you'd do a very good job.'

He nearly spat out his beer. In the English courts, a *Recorder* is a part-time judge. 'My certificate to practise law lapsed a long time ago, though I'm very flattered.'

'And Mina Desai's barred from being an accountant because you arrested her for money laundering, yet she does a good job for me as Peculier Auditor. The ship of magick is going to be hitting stormy waters, Tom, and we need good people like you on the bridge.'

The judge looked over Tom's shoulder. 'I think Lucy has finished her ministrations and is looking for you. Nice meeting you, and think it over.'

He stood. 'Nice to meet you, too. And thank you.'

One corner of the marquee had become a Bollywood field hospital, with three women putting their weight on dressings to see whether further dancing was an option or, Tom presumed, whether they'd have to settle for getting steaming drunk.

'Alright love?' he asked. 'Shall I take this?'

Lucy nodded. 'Thanks. All sorted. Could you bring us a drink when you've dropped off the first-aid kit?'

'My pleasure.'

Lucy stood up on one foot and put her arm on Vicky for support. 'What did Marcia want?' she whispered.

'Tell you later.'

On the way to the Elvenham scullery, he thought about the Honourable Mrs Justice Bracewell's suggestion. It was a totally mad idea, of course, but no less mad than being attacked in a field by a pack of w*r*w*lv*s. His thoughts went back to Lloyd's impassioned plea at the art retreat in France: that Conrad make a stand for the rights of non-humans. From what he'd heard, Clarke and Hannah were doing just that.

He dropped off the kit and headed for the bar, grabbing a bottle of Prosecco and four glasses. If the ship of magick was going to need sturdy foundations, he wasn't sure he wanted a ticket to ride on *that* train.

He dropped off the wine and went to retrieve his beer just as Damini stood up on a table. 'Hello Clerkswell!' she said, her voice cutting through a dozen conversations. 'Now that the parents have gone, it's time to party I think!'

He didn't get round to telling Lucy what Marcia had wanted until several days later, as it happened. Between the dancing, the Prosecco and trying to stop the Mages organising a midnight cricket match ("Magickal floodlights are dead easy!"), Tom never quite got the chance. By then, he had other things on his mind.

It was dark when Kathy slipped out of the Abbey and headed for Beckthorpe village. She passed the empty spot where the guest car lived, and she wondered what Michael was making of his concert. The walk down to the village was a very pleasant one if you cut through the small wood at the edge of the grounds, and there was just enough light for Kathy to see the path through the bluebells. She wasn't afraid. Not here on a night like this. It was a different matter in winter, with the wind blowing through the trees and noises from the undergrowth on all sides.

She dodged through the kissing gate and turned right at the Old Rectory into Beckthorpe's one and only street, narrow and a right pain for lorries and vans heading to the Abbey, a fact that every driver reminded her of when they were late.

There was a small widening of the street when she came to Yorkshire's smallest village green, barely large enough to hold the war memorial, itself a budget model with only eight names on it. Beyond the grass oval was noise and laughter from the Red Grouse pub. She turned her face away from temptation and walked slowly towards the full size pillar box which stood outside the Old Post Office. That building was now a holiday cottage, and the village's postal needs were met three times a week in the church hall. Could have been worse: some villages had their post office in the pub.

The village shop was across the road, a sea of darkness and shadows at the front with LEDs from the fridges glowing deep beyond the glass like fireflies in a coalmine. Did you get fireflies in a coalmine? Probably not.

Her footsteps slowed to a crawl as she passed the tiny school, and her shoulders were hunched up around her ears with tension. Twenty yards. Ten.

'Kathy!'

She span round, and the shadow detached itself from the darkness around the shop. It was Michael, and he ran across the road, passing her and stopping in front of the postbox.

'I thought you were in Leeds,' she said flatly.

'I couldn't. Not when I heard you were subbing for Nika tonight. Don can be very persuasive.'

'It's between me and him, now. Nothing to do with you. As far as you're concerned, the envelope went up in flames on Saturday. Leave it, Michael. You'll go back to your world soon, and I'll be left here in mine. It might be a game to you, but for me it's real life.'

'And that's exactly why I want to stop you, Kathy. I care about you. You know I do. Maybe it was a game at first, but it's not now. It's like real life Jenga, and I don't want you to bring the tower crashing down, because posting that letter could get us all in trouble.'

'I'm already in trouble. This will help me get out of it.'

He reached into his pocket, and she flinched for a second until she saw a wadge of paper. Cash.

'I don't know how Don persuaded you, but I'll bet there's money involved. Somehow. And not a promise, either. I know you, and you wouldn't do this for anything but cash in advance. I have no idea where Don got it from, but I'll match it up to a thousand pounds. It's all I've got.'

She wanted to see how far Michael would go. 'And if he gave me more?'

'I'll have to take his letter from you and tell Simon. But I don't think he did.'

'You're right. He had some gold coins, and I sold them in Leeds for two hundred and fifty quid. Most money I've had since I robbed me cousin.'

Michael split the money in half. 'Yours. The extra is to get the printer and keyboard off you.'

'What's to stop me buying another?'

'The same thing that keeps you from buying a bottle of vodka. If you haven't got the printer in your room, I don't think you'll go out to buy one.'

She nodded and slowly took out Don's letter. She checked to see if there was anyone in the Old Post Office, but the curtains were open and no lights shone in the house. With a flick of her lighter, the paper started to burn, and she held on to the corner until she had to drop it. Michael held out the money, and she stuffed it away.

'Thank you,' he said. 'Do you want a lift back to the Abbey? I'm parked in the Red Grouse.'

She turned to face the street light and opened her coat to show it was empty. 'I'd rather walk, but you could do me a favour though. Can you nip inside and get me a bottle of Appletiser? I fancy a drink before I go.'

'Of course.'

'I'll be on the bench with my back to the pub.'

He did as she asked, and handed over the bottle without offering to join her, though he did double check that she didn't want a lift. He drove off and she waited until she'd seen the headlights appear higher up the hill in the Abbey grounds. When she'd finished a cigarette, she got out her phone and messaged Nika. *You can post that letter now.*

Michael thought he was clever. And he was. Maybe he could break into embassies or kill people with his bare hands like they did on the telly. Whatever it was he did for the Spooks, it clearly hadn't involved dealing with people like her. People who always made sure they had an alibi. Or an excuse. Or someone else to look after the stash.

Nika didn't ask questions. Nika wouldn't dream of unfolding the letter to read the label. And at half past eleven, when Kathy was safely back at the Abbey, she got a reply. *Put in big post office Easingwold. Collection at 0730. X.*

Kathy took a brew outside for a last smoke after Nika had confirmed that the job was done. She counted the money: four hundred and forty pounds. Neat. 'Jenga my arse,' she muttered towards Michael's window, high up in the guest block. 'This is poker, Michael, and I've just cleaned you out.'

Chapter 37 — Tumbling Down

Two days after the wedding and Tom was back in his office at the Cairndale Division of the Lancashire & Westmorland Police. He'd taken Tuesday off for obvious reasons, and they'd travelled back on Wednesday morning. Lucy was gearing herself up to take over the lease on a coffee shop in the little village of Byford and was rushing around in anticipation. She was also, for some strange reason, judging a baking competition on Saturday. He shook his head and looked up when he heard a knock on the door frame (he was true to his word, and his door was only closed when confidentiality demanded it).

'Morning sir, and May the Fourth be with you. Oops! Sorry! It's afternoon, isn't it?' said Elaine Fraser with a grin.

Tom had two Detective Sergeants who were both excellent officers, and both of whom he trusted, but he had brought in Elaine (a Detective Constable) because he needed someone who knew him and his foibles and who would make allowances. The fact that Elaine was also an outsider in the claustrophobic world of Cairndale didn't hurt, either.

She put down a steaming mug of strong tea on his desk and leaned against the door. 'Good to have you back. Finally. You should have seen the state of Barney when Erin dropped him off this morning. Still looked hungover. And Liz has showed me a whole bunch of pictures. Looks like it was an epic weekend.'

'It was. Oh, thanks for the tea.'

Elaine hadn't finished. 'Is it right that Conrad and Mina just *disappeared*?'

'They did. Destination unknown.' He sat back and laughed. 'Mina left behind everything but the clothes she stood up in. She also left behind some unfinished business. At midnight, the bridesmaids rebelled.'

'Sounds ominous.'

'Erin insisted that as Mina's nearest relative, her sister-in-law, Saanvi, should stand on the stage and throw the bridal bouquet over her shoulder.'

'You're joking. What happened?'

'It was carnage. Half of them tried to use magick to blow the bouquet towards them, and the other half used elbows. One of them ended up with a black eye and another will be limping for days.'

'Really?'

'Really. It was lucky no one got seriously hurt.'

'So who caught it?'

'That's only the start.' He lowered his voice. 'As one of the Entangled, you'll know who Tara Doyle really is. Well, she and this…'

They both jumped when Tom's phone burst out with organ music. He had set it up so that only three people could interrupt him when he wanted quiet: Commander Ross, Lucy, and his mother.

From long acquaintance, Elaine knew that Vidor's Toccata meant his mother, so Elaine detached herself from the doorframe and walked off.

Tom took the call. 'Not interrupting, am I dear?' asked his mother.

'Not at all. Everything okay?'

She sighed down the line. 'I'm afraid not, Tom. I'm sorry but your grandfather has had a fall. Not good. He's being rushed to hospital. Now before you say anything…'

'…I'll come up tonight.'

'You don't need to do that.'

'Yes I do. Ross owes me plenty, and he understands. How bad is it?'

She sighed again. 'He's in his eighties. He's broken his hip and his femur.'

Tom hadn't spent long as a uniformed officer in the City of London. Even so, he'd attended a lot of falls and bangs as First Responder. The chances of a happy ending for his grandfather were not good.

'I'll let you know what happens,' said his mother.

'And I'll go to see the Commander.'

One week on from posting Don's letter and the old man was starting to flag. With every day that passed, there was no news and no sign that the letter had been received. In all the time Kathy had known him, he'd always been patient; Dr Simon called it *stoic*, whatever that meant, and something she'd heard in rehab came back to haunt her: *It's always the hope that kills you.* She tried to cheer Don up, but he'd lost interest in everything except staring out of the window. Waiting.

It was a quiet Monday. Two guests had left before the weekend, and no one had replaced them yet. Kathy settled down in the kitchen with a stack of delivery notes and got ready to compare them against the invoices, to see which bunch of chancers was trying to rip off the Abbey this week.

'Hello Kathy,' said Dr Simon. 'I don't mean to interrupt, but could we schedule your review for this week? Does Wednesday sound good? Two o'clock.'

'Yeah. Fine. No problem.'

'Then I'll leave you in peace. Thanks.'

Wednesday did not sound *good* to Kathy. No day would sound good for what was coming up. Unable to concentrate on the paperwork, she got her phone out and looked at the list she'd put together. A list of art dealers.

The previous week had seen everyone who was anyone go in and out of Don's room, including Dr Simon and Faye. None of them had noticed the change to the artwork on the walls, or if they had, none of them had said anything to anyone. She could risk trying to flog the painting now.

'Hello? Could I talk to someone about a John Gould original … Oh no, I want to sell one … Yes really … I'm Katie Marsh … Of course I'll hold.'

'Have a seat,' said Dr Simon on Wednesday afternoon.

They were in his office. His *study*. Sometimes he treated patients in one of the beige consulting rooms, but mostly they came here. At least he didn't offer her the patient's chair, the one facing the blank wall. He stood behind that one himself, offered Kathy an armchair, and Faye parked herself on the large couch.

Kathy's chair faced Dr Simon's desk and the bookcases behind it. She'd never sat here before, and it changed the way you felt about the room completely.

'Tea?'

'Just had one thanks.'

Dr Simon sat down and passed Kathy a piece of paper with her name, the date and the title *Annual Contract of Employment and Treatment Review* in big letters. There was also an agenda.

She put the paper down on the coffee table without reading it and sat back in the armchair.

Dr Simon took off his glasses, rubbed his eyes and put his specs back on. 'You know me, Kathy. A lifetime of meetings has wrung me dry, so I'll get straight to the point. You're a great cook, a valuable member of the Abbey community and above all, you're a very special person who's come a long way. In fact, you've come so far that it's time for you to move on.'

'No,' said Kathy.

Fragrant Faye was wearing something floaty today. Way too young for her, really. And too thin for Yorkshire at this time of year. *Ne'er cast clout while May be out.* Up here, even Global Warming meant that you shouldn't take your big coat off until June.

Faye straightened up, ready to speak, but Dr Simon beat her to it.

'What did I tell you in our very first session, Kathy? And at the beginning of every session for several weeks?' he asked.

She couldn't play dumb to him. She owed him too much for that. 'You said that change is the hardest thing in life.'

'It is. The Abbey is a sanctuary. An asylum. All of our guests arrive here as diminished people. Shrunken from their full potential. It's time for you to leave that sanctuary and grow. Your children need their mother. You know that.'

This time Faye did put her two pennyworth in. 'And the Abbey is no place for children. You know that, too.'

'But Beckthorpe could be!' said Kathy, unable to keep the desperation out of her voice. 'There's plenty of ways of sorting it so they can live in the village. The school is Outstanding, for one thing, *and* it's got spaces. Two more kids might mean it can keep going with all these cuts going round.'

That got her nowhere: both Dr Simon and Faye had their Caring Faces on them, the Face that says *I hear your pain, and I acknowledge it, but tough luck.* It was the face they used before kicking out transgressors.

It was time to unleash her secret weapon. Well, Michael's secret weapon to be exact. Once he thought she'd destroyed Don's letter and handed over the printer, he was mega-friendly, and Kathy was happy with that. She needed someone to talk to about the shit she was in, and Michael was used to dealing with things without losing his rag.

'If I go,' she began, making sure that Dr Simon and Faye were both listening. 'It'll have to be quick 'cos the Social will need time to check out my new situation. I can't afford any delays.'

Dr Simon understood straight away. He was a *proper* therapist. Not like Faye. He said, 'We'll give you an excellent reference that should more than compensate. After all, it's going to take you a few weeks for you to sort out a new job and a new place to live.'

She shook her head, determined to get this right. 'I'm on a week's notice, and I've got contacts in the trade.' She pointed to a hole in her jumper. 'Have you seen me spend owt on meself these last years? No. I've a deposit saved, and with your excellent reference, I'll be good.'

Fragrant Faye finally twigged what was going on: Kathy was threatening to leave them without a cook on a week's notice. Faye could also see that no agency worker would do the job for Kathy's wages, and recruiting a permanent replacement could take weeks, if not months. And in Kathy's absence, who would end up chained to the kitchen sink…?

'What are you suggesting?' asked Faye. Dr Simon frowned.

'We all need security,' said Kathy. 'You and me both. How about you extend my contract for another year and we find a way to make it work with the girls? I'll swear on their lives, that if it isn't working, I'll go. We'll go.'

'It's a very tempting suggestion,' said Dr Simon, 'but it would be bad for everyone, in my opinion.'

'On the other hand, it's something completely new, in its own way,' said Faye with sudden enthusiasm.

Dr Simon looked at his partner with shock. He was not going to have a row in front of Kathy, so where did that leave them? Kathy dug her nails into her palm for courage. Not that it hurt: she had no fingernails. Unlike Faye, who had very elegant nails, buffed in fortnightly trips to Northallerton. Those nails wouldn't last five minutes in the kitchen.

'How about this?' said Kathy. 'We'll take it that I've given my notice for the end of next week, and you think about what I've said. If you want me to stay, we can all carry on.'

'That sounds like a good idea,' said Faye. 'Simon and I do need time to think this over.'

Dr Simon agreed, and the meeting broke up. When she got back to the kitchen, Michael was waiting. 'How did it go.'

For the first time since they'd met, she put her arms round him. 'Thank you, Michael. That was ace advice you gave me.'

He stiffened a little at first instead of returning her hug, then he melted. 'I'm thrilled, Kathy. Thrilled. And it was you who did it, not me.'

She backed off. 'And now I've got a week to *really* look for somewhere, because if Doctor Simon wins, I'll be out.'

'Faye will talk him round,' said Michael reassuringly.

'We don't know that. Not for certain.'

Tom got the news while watching the news. The BBC regional programme *North West Tonight* was looking at the potential impact of Brexit on the extensive Polish community in the Lake District. Lucy had a lot of them working for her already, and if she lost Lilianna from the Cairndale branch, she'd be in serious trouble. The reporter was going round the houses to say that the situation was 100% uncertain when Tom's father called, and that could only mean bad news.

'He's had a stroke,' said Sir Thomas. 'A bad one. The doctors have told me that it's only a matter of time.' He paused, and Tom was reminded yet again that although his grandfather was seen as just that – *Granddad* – to his many grandchildren and great-grandchildren, he was in fact Sir Thomas's father.

'I'm sorry, Dad.'

His father sighed. 'We've known this could happen since his fall. Doesn't make it any easier. Can you come over? Your mother's been telling me about this business with Lucy and the murder.'

It was a Northern thing: *Come over.* He meant *Come over the Pennines,* the small but hugely symbolic mountain range which divides Lancashire and Westmorland, where Tom now lived and worked, from the Mortons' home county of Yorkshire in the east.

'I'm not involved in the investigation,' said Tom, 'and Lucy's working flat-out on the new business. I'll come over alone in an hour or so.'

'Thanks, son. I'll call Fi and Di now.'

'How's Grandma?'

His father managed a small laugh. 'As you'd expect. Stiff upper lip on the surface and cut adrift underneath. Your mother's with her.'

His father disconnected the call, and Tom sat back to let it sink in for a moment, then he stirred himself and went upstairs to get changed and to pack a case.

It was no betrayal of Lucy and their future together to say that, for the very last time, he was *going home.*

On the long journey over, he wondered if he'd make it before his Grandfather passed away. He did, and saw him on Thursday afternoon. He passed away on Thursday evening.

It was Filey which tipped things over the edge. Everyone whom Kathy had known growing up, and most of the people she'd met since, had had at least one holiday in Filey or the other static caravan parks along the North Riding Coast. Some rented a basic box for the weekend whilst others would take a big van in one of the full-service parks for most of the school holidays. After all, there were pools, shops, kids clubs and entertainment on site. What's not to like?

It wasn't one of the mega-camps who came through for her; it was one of the smaller places, and they needed a cook-manager for the onsite café almost as much as the Abbey did. It was when they threw in a two berth caravan that she said yes. Her daughters would absolutely love it. She closed her eyes and tried to pretend that it was a long-term solution rather than a summer contract, then went to see Faye.

As soon as Faye saw the email on Kathy's phone, she set her mouth in a fixed smile. 'I can see the attraction, Kathy. If you can get custody at the end of the school term, your girls will have new friends on tap all summer. And you've shown here that you can manage the most difficult people, so a staff of six should be no problem.'

And there they were. It was a perfect stepping-stone for Kathy. So much so that Faye said, 'And you'd still rather stay here?'

Kathy put her phone away. 'If the van didn't have summat wrong with it, they'd rent it out, and those places are dismal in the rain. Folk go stir crazy. I'd rather have my girls run round the woods and start at Beckthorpe school come September.'

Faye nodded with approval. It was a good argument. 'I'll talk it over with Simon over the weekend. Or maybe Monday – those two new private guests are arriving tomorrow, and that's always a challenge, and there's no need to overload him.'

'Good plan,' said Kathy. 'We'll all be busy at the weekend; there's hardly anyone booked to go out, either.' She looked Faye in the eye. 'I were talking to Michael this morning. A problem shared and all that.'

Faye's eyebrows rose a millimetre. Faye was not stupid, and she knew that Kathy didn't like her. They might be allies at the moment, but she wasn't expecting this. 'A good idea, Kathy. I've found Michael to have very strong empathy. With everyone but himself, of course.'

It was a step towards common ground. Kathy took another. 'I know what you mean. Has he still not opened up about what sent him here?'

Faye shook her head, unwilling to speak even a hint of a clinical confidence. Kathy nodded in return and continued, 'Michael said that if I *did* stay on, I should take more responsibility. Maybe I could reintroduce the guest cleaning rota. I know that Doctor Simon did it at the beginning.'

This time, Faye looked *very* interested. When STAND was founded, guests were supposed to do almost all domestic chores on a rota, but supervising them was taking up so much of Simon and Faye's time, and Mingey Mora had refused to join in, so they'd started with contractors. If Kathy brought it back, it could save them a packet without them having to lift a finger.

'The therapeutic benefits for guests, and the chance for you to grow your role make that a compelling argument,' said Faye. She lowered her voice conspiratorially. 'And we'll pretend it was your idea, not Michael's shall we?'

Kathy zipped her lip. The women nodded to each other and went their separate ways.

Kathy knew exactly when Faye and Dr Simon started discussing her case: she could hear it when she passed the study on her way to see Don. At least she assumed they were discussing her case, because there were raised voices and both of them sounded like they were digging in for the long haul.

She was tempted to press her ear to the door and listen. If there wasn't a carer on duty with Don, she might have done so, but you could never tell when someone might appear magically and catch her in the act, so she passed on by and knocked on Don's door before breezing in.

The old man seemed slightly different today. She hadn't seen much of him recently, partly because she'd have felt obliged to let him know what was going on, and she didn't want to add to his troubles.

The room was just the same, except the milder weather had meant the outside door was propped open. The carer today wasn't a carer, she was a nurse from Africa, come to give him a routine checkup. 'Hi, I'm Kathy. I cover some of the evening shifts.'

The woman didn't give her name. Probably thought she was above that sort of thing, especially as Kathy wasn't wearing a uniform. 'Ah good. You can help me find something.'

Sweat prickled Kathy's hairline. What was she looking for? Surely not the painting. She stalled for time. 'Yeah. How is he? Passed his medical has he?'

It was the nurse's turn to be put on the spot. 'As far as I can tell from the notes, there's no change.'

Kathy translated in her head: *I've never seen him before and I have no real clue, but he probably won't drop dead today.*

'Good. Glad to hear it.'

'He keeps pointing to the wardrobe, but I have no idea what he wants.'

Translation: *I have no intention of forming a bond with this man because I will never see him again.*

'Let me. There's only clothes in there. Does he need fresh ones?'

'If you're asking whether he's had an accident, then no.'

'Good. Right, Don, are you wanting to dress up for dinner?' The old man pointed outside. 'Breath of fresh air? Something a bit warmer, then.' *Imperceptible nod.* 'I have the very thing.'

The nurse stepped aside and Kathy rooted through Don's limited selection. Ninety per cent of his wardrobe was mid-range loungewear: easy to take on and off, robust and ideal for the Abbey's washing machines. It also made him look like a long-term convict sometimes. Perhaps that's what he was.

She selected a pair of baggy trousers in a subdued tartan. They looked awful, but they were all wool and good cloth. She also picked a dress shirt with buttons. And a belt. No elasticated waists today.

Don nodded approvingly, and Kathy was going to leave the nurse to it, but the woman said, 'If you want him to go outside, you'll have to do it yourself. I'm only here another half an hour.'

Kathy blinked. 'I think it's *Don* who wants to go outside, but if it's too much trouble … how about you make him a brew and I'll get him changed and into the wheelchair. I've an hour before my real job starts. His is the two-handled mug, and he likes it strong. So do I. That's my mug at the back of the tray.'

The two women didn't speak again until they had to work together to get Don into his wheelchair. When he was strapped in, the nurse said, 'I'd better write up my *medical* notes.'

Kathy ignored the jibe and wheeled Don outside. He took a lot more interest in things today, pointing and gesturing until she picked a sprig of bay leaves, of all bizarre things, and put them in the pocket at the back of his chair.

Half an hour later, the sun went in and a breeze picked up. 'Time to go back, Don.'

The old man looked around with a smile, then nodded. The nurse hadn't even said goodbye.

There was silence from Dr Simon's study, but that didn't mean much. They could have finished rowing or they could be continuing to argue at a normal volume. Kathy noticed that both of them avoided her over supper, neither of them talked to each other, and they didn't linger beyond the absolute minimum of time with the guests.

When Kathy went to bed, there was a light on under Dr Simon's door. Not unusual in itself, but she could hear music, and that was very unusual. She looked over her shoulder as she mounted the staircase, and it took ages to fall asleep.

She didn't know what had woken her, but she knew that *something* was wrong. Very wrong. She lay still, trying to hear every sound inside and outside the Abbey. Quiet. Nothing. There was still something wrong, though. Reluctantly, slowly, carefully, she sat on the edge of the bed, put her feet in her Crocs and grabbed a sweatshirt. And her phone. Wasn't going anywhere without that.

She peeked through the curtains, and a low moon washed a little light on the grounds. Nothing moving. No torches or other weird lights in the trees, but there was something… How could she see the roses? She couldn't normally. Oh. There was a lot of light coming from downstairs, either Don's room or Dr Simon's study. She knew she'd never get back to sleep, so she nipped to the loo, then slipped out of her room and tried to move as quietly down the stairs as her kitchen footwear would let her.

Silence in the corridor. Silence from the study, but the light outside must have been coming from here, because it blazed from under the old door. Dr Simon often worked late, but rarely after ten and *never* at three o'clock in the morning, which was what it was now.

She pressed her ear to the door. More silence. She moved from one foot to the other and wished she could have a smoke in here. Another of Dr

Simon's mantras came back to her: *When in doubt, ask what the worst case scenario might be. It's never as bad as you think.* It was that mantra which had helped her get over her first day as Abbey Cook. And other days. So what was the worst case scenario tonight?

If Dr Simon was with a patient, he'd tell her to go away. Ditto if he was with Faye. Otherwise, he'd let her in and be nice. And thank her for her concern. She breathed out and knocked assertively on the door. Nothing. She counted to twenty and knocked again, and followed that up with an ear to the wood. Still nothing.

He'd probably left the light on. That's all. If the door was open, she'd know he was coming back; if it were locked, there was nothing she could do anyway, and it was only a few coppers in electricity. She knocked one last time and turned the handle. It opened, she stuck her head in, and immediately wished she hadn't.

Part Seven — Fragmentation

Chapter 38 — In Pieces

Technically, Tom was not on compassionate leave. Not yet. Technically, Commander Ross had said, 'Take yourself over there, laddie, where you're needed most. Put in for official leave when you've a date for the funeral.'

And therefore, technically, he was still at work, which was why his phone was next to the bed and not muted. He groaned, checked the time (twenty past three), and took the call from the unknown number.

'DCI Morton? This is the duty inspector from North Riding Control.'

Tom sat up in bed and as there was no Lucy to disturb, he put the light on. 'This is Morton.'

He was worried, and part of him wanted to ask what the problem was, because clearly there was a problem *somewhere*.

'Sorry to disturb you, sir. Cairndale Division said that you were away on a family matter but not on leave. Can you talk?'

'I can talk, and no, I'm not on leave.'

The inspector sounded relieved. 'Right. I got your name from John Lake.'

John Lake. Security Liaison Officer in Whitehall and also known by Elaine Fraser as *The Angel of Death*. Great. What now?

'I bet he was even less happy than I am to be disturbed. Go on.'

The inspector slipped into operational mode and continued. 'At three oh five we got an emergency call to a suspicious death at Beckthorpe Abbey. Do you know it?'

'I know Beckthorpe, and I've seen the Abbey. What is it now? Some sort of hotel?'

'You could say that, sir. It's an addiction and rehab clinic. And it has a security level four. As soon as the call handler put the address into the system, all sorts of red flags were raised.'

Tom sat up straighter. Level Four was only two levels below calling in the SAS. No wonder the inspector was desperate to find someone. 'Do you not have anyone in North Riding?'

'We do. One is on the sick and the other is in London. I called the Liaison desk and they gave me three names. When I found out that you were actually in York, I thought it was worth a try. You're only twenty minutes down the road.'

'If I drive like a traffic patrol, then yes I am.' He stood up and went to the dresser, opening the drawer and reaching for clean underwear. 'Give me the situation.'

'As it happens, our nearest unit was actually the Armed Response Vehicle. They were patrolling the A19 and got there in five minutes. According to the officer, there has been a serious incident. At the moment, the whole place is still asleep apart from the woman who called it in. The control room are organising a crime scene manager and more uniformed officers, but John Lake didn't want any further local involvement until you've assessed the scene.'

Tom had put the inspector on speaker while he continued to get dressed. His childhood home, the Cloister, had very thick walls, so no one would hear anything. He was up to fastening his shirt when he said, 'I'm on my way. Get on to Cairndale Division and get them to contact DC Elaine Fraser. She's got security clearance. Tell her to set off and call me when she's calmed down.'

He slipped on his waistcoat and grabbed his jacket and his coat.

The inspector stifled a chuckle. 'Will do, sir. Do you have a radio with you?'

'Sorry, no. It can be a surprise when I get there. I take it that your officers have done a sweep of the area?'

'A preliminary one. The scene looks like the offenders were long gone, put it that way. I'm on duty until eight, so call me on this number if you need anything.'

'Thanks.'

Tom disconnected and sent texts to Lucy and to his mother. *Been called out. Will call later.* And then he slipped out of the Cloister and had the satisfaction of seeing no lights come on. Good.

'I'm calm. What's up?' said Elaine when she called. She sounded anything but calm: half asleep, grumpy or annoyed, definitely. Calm, not so much.

'The Angel of Death came to me in a vision.'

There was a pause. 'Is this magick related or has John Lake been on the phone?'

'According to Doctor Somerton, there is no Angel of Death. At least, that's what I think she said. It was quite late and we'd both been at the sherry. Anyway, I'm on my way to a little village on the North York Moors. It's a Level Four target, but I didn't have a secure comms link, so I've absolutely no idea what I'm heading into other than a suspicious death. Not even a name.'

'Right. So why am I driving up the Lune Valley in the middle of the night?'

'Because you're too good to leave in bed, that's why. I'll be there in two minutes, and if you're not needed, I'll call straight away.'

'And I can go back to bed? You are joking, aren't you?'

'You could go for a run…?'

'Ha ha. If I hear nothing in five minutes, I'll put my foot down.'

They disconnected, and Tom passed through the sleeping village and on to the driveway which led to the STAND buildings. It swerved a couple of times as it rose even higher, then bent round to reveal the Abbey in all of its mock Gothic glory. The headlights of his BMW didn't pick out much, and he was more interested in the two police vehicles and the reflective flash of a HiViz jacket. Good. Reinforcements had arrived. He did get a fleeting glimpse of something in red brick at the back of the old building and filed that away for later, but for now, an appreciation of the architecture could wait.

Before he got out of the car, he checked his phone for messages. There was one from his mother: *Take care*, and another from a very surprising source: Conrad Clarke. The missing groom had Whatsapped the whole Wedding group to say *We're back. Will be in touch.* That was it. Nothing else. Tom shrugged to himself and got ready for action.

The shock started to wear off when the second lot of coppers turned up. The first two through the Abbey's front doors had been like something from a science fiction film, all helmets and guns and, 'Stay there! Do not move!'

And Kathy had stayed there, not moving, gripped by memories of Dr Simon's *broken* body. And the horrible bloodstain high up the wall. And the metal cabinets torn open like packets of crisps at a toddler's birthday party, orange folders strewn on the floor like crumbs. And the duvet on the floor. And the pillow.

Taken together, it was more than her brain could cope with, and she must have slipped into a daze for a few minutes.

'Hiya love, are you Kathy?'

She blinked and tried to focus. The shape in front of her had the HiViz jacket, but no helmet and, reassuringly, no gun. It was also female. Kathy nodded.

'I'm Police Sergeant Oldroyd. Call me Jen. Is there somewhere else we can go? The building's safe, so maybe somewhere with a kettle?'

'Kitchen,' said Kathy her dry mouth mangling the word. She coughed, swallowed and tried again. 'The kitchen. Down there.'

'Do you need a hand up?'

Kathy was on her knees behind a sofa in the hall, and she definitely needed a hand up. The reassuringly solid copper hauled her to her feet and stuck close as they went down the corridor to Kathy's domain. She was shivering in the pre-dawn chill, and grabbed her coat when she put on the lights.

'Where's the kettle?'

'Let me. I'm the cook.'

'That's right,' said Sergeant Jen, bizarrely. 'You're Kathy Metcalfe, cook in residence. Yes?'

'Domestic Lead, but yeah.'

'Go on then. I'll be next to you.'

Kathy got to the sink without wobbling and filled the kettle.

'You think the victim is Simon Swift, correct?'

'It is. That's Doctor Simon, or what's left of him.'

'Try not to think of that just now. It's hard, I know. You said his partner lives in? And another resident?'

'Faye. Faye Langley. In their quarters. Further down the corridor where he … where his study is. I think … I think they must have had a row and he was kipping in his study. They've only got one bedroom in the flat. It's my fault.'

'What's your fault, Kathy?'

'Me. They were rowing about me. If they hadn't, he'd be tucked up safe in bed.'

'And there's someone else?'

'Donald Bell. He's here on a care basis, not rehab. He's had strokes and stuff. His room is next but one to the study? Is he okay?'

'No other lights on. If he's asleep, he's better off there for now.'

The kettle was nearly boiling, and Kathy was putting out mugs on autopilot. 'But he's vulnerable. If he's seen the lights, he could be panicking.'

'We'll stick our heads inside in a minute, okay? And how many in residential block out back?'

She told her, and Sergeant Jen started repeating things into her radio. Kathy found herself staring at the mugs. How many residents. How many mugs. Not enough mugs. *Pull yourself together, girl.*

She counted out four for the coppers and one for herself, then poured the water into the big teapot.

The radio crackled into life. 'Confirm that an SIO is en route. Dawson, check private quarters for access and signs of forced entry.'

'Dawson receiving. Copy that.'

'Is Doctor Swift's private flat normally locked?' asked Sergeant Jen, and Kathy nodded her answer. 'Confirm that the private flat is normally secured,' the copper told her radio.

Kathy got the milk and sugar, but Sergeant Jen took them off her. 'I'll do this bit. You sit down. And I'm putting sugar in whether you like it or not.'

Another message came through saying that there were no signs of forced entry and that the flat was indeed locked. Sergeant Jen put two mugs on the table and didn't take out a notebook, like they did on the telly, but some sort of iPad thingy. She tapped a couple of times, then said, 'Drink up, Kathy, and tell me what happened. I'm going to record what you say. Okay?'

'Whatever. Where do you want me to start?'

'Last night will do.'

Kathy looked at the policewoman properly. She was probably mixed race, and her hair was tightly bound in a bun that must hurt. There was a hardness around her eyes that was softened by a generous smile. When Kathy started to tell her story, Sergeant Jen nodded and opened her eyes wide, but she didn't interrupt.

Kathy had got as far as wondering about the light under Dr Simon's door when the radio announced, 'Vehicle arriving. Looks like the SIO.'

'That's the one in charge,' said Sergeant Jen. 'But I'm guessing you knew that. He or she will probably want to have a look round first then come straight here. I know I would.'

'Then we can stop, yeah? I need a fag. I really do.'

Sergeant Jen's eyes lost focus as she calculated things. 'Yeah. Go on. Is there somewhere close?'

'Shivering gallery. Just outside.'

When they stepped outside, Sergeant Jen started asking about Kathy's past, and Kathy said, 'I'll save you the bother, yeah? I've got a record, alright? Fraud, theft and assault when I was drunk. I've been sober for a long time now.'

'And you're doing really well on it. I can tell that.'

What the hell did she know about it? Whatever. Kathy was going to light another cigarette when Sergeant Jen said they'd better go back inside, and she said it in her copper's voice, so Kathy nodded and went to wrestle with the door again.

The three extra mugs were unused, and Kathy was thinking about biscuits when she nearly jumped out of her skin.

'Is that pot fresh?' said a posh voice.

'Jesus! You gave me a shock,' said Kathy, and it looked like Sergeant Jen had got one, too.

'Sorry. I'm DCI Morton.' He looked at the policewoman. 'I'm from Cairndale Division in Westmorland. Sergeant Oldroyd, is it?'

'Yes sir.'

Kathy had expected someone much older and with a much cheaper suit. Who wears pinstriped suits with waistcoats *at four o'clock in the morning*? Not only that, he had a posh coat on, too, which he took off and draped over a chair. She took some small satisfaction in noting that his hair was sticking up at the back. 'May I?' he said, pointing to the teapot.

'It needs fresh,' said Kathy. 'I'll do it.'

Morton's eyes flicked around the room. 'Thanks. Sergeant? A quick word while we wait?'

Kathy put the kettle on and the two coppers slipped into the corridor. As soon as the kettle started to make its racket, she slipped her feet out of her Crocs and padded over to the archway.

She had discovered a long time ago that the acoustics of the old corridor and the archway meant that there was a sweet spot where you couldn't be seen, but you could hear. It was how she'd heard that Dr Simon was putting his foot down about treating a sex offender.

She focused on the police officers, and Morton was saying, '…team will be here soon, we're also waiting for your ACC to allocate a Yorkshire SIO, and basically I'm only here until MI5 send their own forensic specialist and case officer. In other words, I'm babysitting the filing cabinets and supervising the scene.'

'That was quick, sir. What now?'

'The sooner we hear Kathy's statement, the better. Then I can allocate actions. And I get tea, which…'

Kathy slipped away, and when they returned, there was a pot of tea waiting. 'Let's give it time to brew,' said Morton, 'and you can tell me about what you do here.'

He listened attentively for a couple of minutes, then ushered her into a seat and asked Jen to pour.

When the mugs landed in front of them, he put his phone on the table and said, 'Thanks. Sorry to say this, sergeant, but I think we need to check on Ms Langley, even if it means getting the battering ram out.'

Kathy didn't know what gave her the courage. Maybe it was the way the detective hadn't thrown his weight around. 'And Don,' she said. 'I'm right worried about him. He could have a panic attack, and maybe another stroke. He can't get out of bed on his own.'

Something in what she said about *another stroke* made the detective flinch, and he rubbed his upper left arm, then looked at Sergeant Jen. 'If you could stick your head into his room on the way, sergeant? If he's asleep, leave him, if not, then come back here, okay?'

'Sir,' she replied, and left them to it.

'Biscuits are excellent for shock,' he said with a smile.

Suddenly, Kathy didn't want to get up. It seemed like someone should be running around after her for a change. 'In the larder, but it's locked. Spare key. We have a spare key, and it's behind that file on the shelf.'

Morton looked at the shelf. 'Let me guess: it's the VAT file.'

'How did you know?'

He grinned instead of answering, and got up. He'd found the key and was unlocking the larder when Sergeant Jen returned at a fast walk. 'Are you sure

Mister Bell couldn't have gone somewhere? His bed's empty.'

Kathy gasped and blurted out, 'They wouldn't do that!'

Two pairs of police eyes fixed themselves on her, and Morton's flashed red in some reflection, maybe of the dawn. 'Who, Kathy?' he said in a firm voice. 'Who wouldn't do what?'

She slumped back in her chair, and tears started to gather in her eyes. She was in so much shit. All her plans were collapsing. Like the bricks in Jenga. Like Michael said they would.

'What's going on, Kathy?' asked Morton, leaning towards her and drawing her in to his space. 'Could Don have done this?'

She dragged the tears away from her eyes. 'No. Course not. He can't even get out of bed on his own. That's why he needs a chamber pot at night.' She lapsed into silence, and Morton carried on staring at her. She looked round the kitchen. Would this be the last time she saw it before they took her away in handcuffs?

She shook herself. *Come on, girl. You've got one chance.* 'They – that's Faye and Doctor Simon – they think that Don's got nothing upstairs,' she said with a sigh. 'And for ages, he hadn't, but then he changed.'

'Changed? Changed how? You said he's been here a long time. Just tell me what happened.'

'It sounds daft.'

'Just tell me and let me be the judge of that.'

'Back in February it was. He suddenly got control of his hands and his head. I learnt to speak to him. Like with a Ouija board.'

'Suddenly? What did you do, Kathy? Did you give him something?'

She shook her head violently. 'Not me. It just happened. I've told you: you won't believe me.'

'Just tell me everything. The reason I'm here is that my job is to keep an open mind.'

Kathy had been questioned many times over the years. By good cops, bad cops, bored cops and once (memorably) by a detective who was off his face on speed. Never had she met a detective who had all the time in the world despite being in charge of a dead body and now a missing patient. If she told him the truth, maybe they'd think she was mad and not bother to charge her. Being arrested she could cope with, but if they charged her with anything, she'd never live with her girls again.

'A load of lights came over the field, and it was, like … like his chains had come off. After that he could communicate, and he got us to write a letter.'

Sergeant Jen shifted in her seat, clearly desperate to shut her up and get on with giving her the third degree. Not Morton. He went from being patient to being utterly motionless. Like a statue. Like Don's bust of Homer. Then Morton rubbed his left arm again and looked away from Kathy to his colleague.

291

'Sergeant, as this is now a North Riding case, I'd like you to call in a potential kidnapping, and then go and see Ms Langley. As soon as the crime scene manager turns up, tell them to add Mister Bell's room as an equal priority. Okay?'

Sergeant Jen stood up and backed away. 'Yes sir.' She was on her radio before she'd left the kitchen.

When Kathy looked back, Morton was staring at his phone. He keyed something, then paused and looked up. 'I believe you, Kathy. I'm going to call an expert.' He looked down and thumbed the screen. It only took a couple of seconds before it was answered, and Kathy heard a loud man's voice boom over the speaker.

'Tom! What are you doing up at this hour?'

Morton flinched and put the phone to his ear. Didn't matter, because Kathy could still hear the other bloke.

Morton cleared his throat. 'Conrad, I'm in Yorkshire, and I may have a situation.'

There was a crackle on the line and it sounded like this Conrad was talking to someone else for a second. 'Really? Oh.' It came back to the speaker again. 'Tom, I've just heard about your grandfather. I'm so sorry.'

'Thanks. Look, will I be able to get hold of Saffron easily?'

Saffron? Was that a code name for something? For someone?

'Never mind Saff, you can have me. Could save my marriage. Where exactly are you?'

Morton winced, torn between getting up and moving for privacy or staying put and getting the call over with. 'I'm in a place called Beckthorpe, by the North York Moors. More to the point, where are you?'

'Perfect.' There was another rustling. 'I need to drop into RAF Cranwell, if they'll let me, then twenty minutes to you. Text me the exact location and sort me a landing zone.'

Morton was showing that he was a normal man now, and he was looking almost as pained and bothered as Kathy was feeling lost and in deep shit. 'You've got the Smurf?'

'Better! I've got the Wasp. I take it this is serious? If not, I'll get Saffron.'

'It's serious, and if you really can get here, then I'd be grateful.' Morton looked up and made eye contact with Kathy. 'Grateful and embarrassed, but I think this is one for you. I'll be in touch by message.'

He disconnected and sat still for a moment. 'Can you give me any names, Kathy? Anything which I can use? If you can, it will make a huge difference. If Mister Bell is in danger…?'

'If I could help, I would. Seriously. But Don made sure we never knew the names.'

'Who's *we*, Kathy?'

It was bound to come out sooner or later. Better for her if she got it out of the way sooner. She sighed. 'Michael the spook.'

'Who would that be?'

'He's a guest. He's one of the spies or agents or whatever.'

'He told you that did he?'

'Didn't need to. I can tell.'

Morton nodded slowly. 'And he's in the block out the back?'

'Yeah.'

'If you give me your phone, and give me your promise to stay here, I won't arrest you or restrain you.'

She slid her phone across the table. 'How much trouble am I in?'

'We, Kathy. If there's trouble, I'm in it, too.'

It was a strange thing for a copper to say, but Morton was clearly a very strange policeman. 'Is true what that bloke said? About your grandfather?'

'Yes. He passed away last Friday. How will I find Michael, and will his door be locked?'

'In my room I've got a master key for all the guests, for cleaning and in case we think they're trying to top themselves. If you come with me, I can give it you.' She hesitated. 'And maybe put some clothes on? You can watch. I've nothing to hide any more. Nothing.'

She did have something to hide, of course, but if Morton got to nose around her room and saw nothing obvious, he might not be inclined to ask forensics to look behind the old fireplace, where she'd put the painting.

Chapter 39 — Do Ravens Come Home to Roost?

Back in the kitchen and now properly dressed, Kathy drank her tea. Morton had told her to hurry, checked her bathroom and told her to get changed in there. 'Mind if I look around?' he'd asked.

'Course not,' she'd replied, and no, he didn't look behind the fireplace, but he did leave her wadge of cash on the desk to show he knew about it. Bloody hell, he must have a real coppers nose to have found that in the time it took her to pull on a sports bra, leggings and sweatshirt. Oh, and to grab a scrunchy.

She was just beginning to wonder whether *stay here* could be expanded to include the shivering gallery when Morton strode back in, posh coat flapping and police radio pressed to his ear. He came in to the kitchen and gave her a very hard stare.

'Michael is also missing. I think we need to go somewhere more private and start at the beginning, don't we Kathy?'

She looked around the kitchen and grasped at the only straw she could think of. 'I'll be needed on breakfasts soon, and it were Michael who helped me.'

'I don't think you'll be doing any cooking for a while,' said Morton. 'Let's go.'

She started trembling. 'I am in such a deep hole of shit,' she muttered to herself.

Morton seemed to have an unerring instinct for Kathy's weak spots, so naturally he chose one of the small counselling rooms. It was the one where she'd had some of the most difficult sessions when she first arrived.

It was simple, just a couple of abstract pictures and a view of nothing but the top floor of the guest block to look at. Two padded chairs were separated by a coffee table, where a box of tissues and a carafe of water were all the suspect/patient had to call their own; a less comfortable observer's chair lurked behind the client's seat.

Kathy sighed and plonked herself down. Morton hung up his coat and placed his radio and phone on the therapist's side table and said, 'The beginning, Kathy. I know you want to help find out what happened to Simon, and where Don and Michael have got to so just tell me everything.'

'I get bored at night,' she began, 'and that's why I started doing care shifts with Don. And I needed the money. Before you say anything, I'll get round to that cash you found.'

'I'm sure you will,' he replied in a neutral way that left her trying to guess whether his posh voice was menacing or sarcastic or just stating a fact.

Things got even worse when someone told the police about the Abbey pool car, and a quick check found that it was missing and had been since before the police turned up. All Kathy could suggest was that maybe the sound of the engine was what had woken her in the first place.

Morton frowned a lot. He clearly wasn't happy with what he was hearing, but he wasn't aggressive, which was fine until *she* turned up.

Morton left the room a couple of times to take or make calls, and he frequently stopped to type a message. When he opened the door, the sound of voices, radios and thumping feet burst their little bubble of confession. After half an hour or so (she had no watch or phone to tell the time), he let her have a smoke break, with Sergeant Jen keeping a close eye on her. When she was escorted back to the room, Morton had a friend with him. Friend? More like his pet Rottweiler.

'This is DC Fraser from my team in Cairndale, Westmorland.'

The woman was wiry and younger than either Kathy or Morton, and her black jeans ended in well-worn Doc Martens. She took the observer's chair, the high-backed one, and placed it to the side of Morton, but not so close that Kathy could look them both in the eye. They were clearly used to working together, and Fraser got straight into it.

'I believe that you're currently trying to regain custody of your children. Is that right?'

Morton hadn't asked a question that had gone remotely near Kathy's circumstances. Maybe he'd been saving it for Fraser.

'I am.'

'And according to Ms Langley, this has been a source of disagreement between you and Doctor Swift.'

Kathy had learnt something from her police interviews, even without the cheapshit legal aid solicitor to look after her: never respond to a statement, only to a question. Kathy stayed mute.

They waited long enough to realise that she wasn't going to cave in, then Morton said, 'Did you argue about it?'

'Not about the girls, no.'

'But you did argue, didn't you?'

'Not really. He didn't want to renew my contract.' She turned to stare at Fraser. 'But Faye did. *She* wanted to keep me, and it was *them* who argued, not me. Doctor Simon would never argue with me.'

Fraser ignored her and looked at her phone before asking, 'What was your relationship with Mister Papadakis *really* like?'

'Who?'

'Michalis Papadakis. The patient who's gone missing.'

'Guest. They're *guests*. And his name's Michael, and that what you said sounds Greek. Michael's Spanish.'

She looked at her phone. 'Mister Papadakis is British. What was your relationship with him *really* like?'

Kathy felt part of herself closing down. First Don, now Michael. She'd trusted both of them, and they'd lied to her. Typical bloody men. Typical of the bloody men she chose, anyway. She took refuge in Dr Simon's words and said, 'Our relationship was therapeutic. I was helping Michael recover from addiction, and he was helping me *stay* in recovery. Which I have done.'

'I'm sure you have, Kathy,' said Morton. 'But you've been very frank with me so far. The less you keep back now, the more I'll believe that you're telling me the *whole* truth. Why did you tell me that Michael was in the secret services when he was …?'

'A private client who worked in finance,' supplied Fraser.

'Private client?' said Kathy with genuine surprise. 'It costs a fortune to come here. Usually it's on their firm's health insurance.' She shrugged. 'He played the spook. Right from day one.'

The detectives looked at each other, and Morton shook his head at something. 'Let's go back to Don. I…' He stopped to check his phone. 'Wing Commander Clarke will be here in five minutes. We'd better head outside. You shouldn't need your coat, Kathy.' He gave a smile. 'And I suspect you'll be glad of one thing: the first thing Conrad will want to do is conduct an in-depth interview in the shivering gallery.'

They emerged from the counselling room into a whirlwind of activity. Men and women in white paper suits were going in and out of Dr Simon's study and Don's room, via both the corridor and the french doors to the gardens. She knew this was happening because Morton had taken her the long way round so she saw as little of the Abbey as possible, but he couldn't hide the slew of police vehicles which now occupied almost all of the car park.

Morton and Fraser were deep in conversation, but kept enough distance that she couldn't hear a word. When they got to the edge of the lawns, she coughed. 'Did you say this Conrad bloke is a Wing Commander. What does that mean?'

'It's a rank in the RAF,' said Morton. 'He used to fly helicopters in Afghanistan. Now he works for a specialist branch of the security services.'

Morton looked up, away from the trees and towards the open fields. A few seconds later, Kathy heard it, too. They fell mute as the high pitched rat-tat-tat of the helicopter drowned out everything else.

The machine seemed to pause, looking at them and twisting slightly as it hung in the air, then it swung its tail and almost backed down on to the lawns without a bump, landing just like its namesake; Conrad Clarke had promised the *Wasp*, and here it was, bright yellow-orange and deep black.

Seconds later it started to calm down and get quieter. As soon as it did, one of the doors opened and an RAF cadet got out, a teenage girl with long black hair. She marched towards them, and as she got closer, Kathy realised that she was of Indian or Pakistani heritage, and that she was not a girl at all but a woman. Didn't they have a height restriction in the RAF these days?

Her uniform was a bit baggy and she clumped along in her boots. A scrawled patch on her chest said *Desai*. She did not look happy, and barely glanced at Kathy before shaking hands formally with Fraser then taking Morton by the arm as if she were his sister or something. From the way that Morton nodded and pressed his lips together, she wondered if the Desai woman were giving the detective her condolences about his grandfather.

Then she pressed him to step aside, and Morton allowed himself to be led away, bending to have an urgent conversation. The noise stopped completely, and Kathy expected some James Bond type to appear, not the great long man in camouflage uniform who tumbled out, like he was drunk. He hopped around and straightened up, then limped over the grass carrying a kitbag. He didn't seem to be in a hurry.

Morton and Desai turned, and Morton looked at Kathy before saying, 'Of course she does. I've seen it with my own eyes.'

'Then that is settled. Give me some money. You can get it back from Conrad.'

With a bemused smile, Morton handed over two twenties, and the little woman marched up to Kathy and held out her hand. 'Hello, Kathy. I am Mina Desai.'

Kathy didn't know what to do, so she shook hands and said nothing. Mina looked at Conrad Clarke and said, 'The other three have a lot of catching up to do. You are to come with me until then, and you can do me a big favour by taking me to your room and allowing me to buy some makeup off you.'

Kathy felt like she was in a personal helicopter all of her own, being thrown around. 'Buy makeup?' was all she could say.

'Well, you have no reason to offer it to me for nothing because we have never met before. Oh, and please do not try to run away or talk to anyone.' Mina turned her face and Kathy realised that she hadn't seen that side up to now. A network of scars criss-crossed the woman's jaw. 'Please.'

'Follow me.'

They stepped away, and Kathy said, 'Does your boss normally allow you to do makeup on operations?'

Mina tipped her long, pointy nose in the air. 'That man is not my boss, he is my husband, and he would be in the doghouse if he did not love his dog more than he loves me and we didn't own the largest dog kennel in England.'

There was absolutely nothing Kathy could say to that, so she forced herself to look at Mina's ring finger. Bloody hell. How had she not noticed *that*? As well as a gleaming, ruby studded wedding ring, Mina's engagement ring had the largest diamond that Kathy had ever seen in the flesh. She shook her head and went into the Abbey via the fire doors.

Once in her room, Kathy breathed a sigh of relief and said, 'I'll just nip to

Mark Hayden

the loo. Help yourself to whatever you want and I'll be out in a minute.'
She was desperate for a moment to herself, but Mina followed her and leaned against the door, only looking away when Kathy sat on the loo. When Kathy had finished, Mina said, 'My turn. Helicopters always go straight to my bladder.'

Kathy had no problem taking advantage of people, especially when it became obvious that Mina was having trouble with the camouflage uniform. But what could she do? Kathy didn't have a second phone or anything, and even if she did, who would she call? Nor could she run or hide anywhere. Or even move that bloody picture.

Mina swore as her trousers dropped to the floor, and not only did Kathy's minder need makeup urgently, she was wearing bright red lycra gym knickers.

Kathy coughed. 'Are you actually in the army or anything?'

'No. I am an accountant, and if my husband had not whisked me away to a "Honeymoon" without my phone, I would show you pictures of our wedding.' She struggled into the uniform again and ran the tap. 'Right. Show me what you've got.'

Kathy pulled out the chair by her desk-cum-dressing table, and Mina set too with blending foundations to match her skin tone. 'Tell me about yourself, Kathy. Not about today. I'm sure you've talked about that more than enough. Tell me about your children. You have two, I believe?'

Kathy didn't want to go there. Not with this young woman who could be absolutely anyone and was quite likely to have the Social's number in her phone. 'Are you really an accountant?'

Mina held up a loaded sponge for examination. 'Yes and no. I qualified as an accountant, but I'm not allowed to audit any more, so I do advice and analysis. How about you? Are you a qualified cook, and if so, do you like real Indian food?'

'Chinese. I prefer real Chinese.'

'Go on. I'm listening.'

She did end up talking about Cherry. Couldn't help it, could she?

Mina opened the breast pocket of her combat jacket and took out a pair of ruby earrings. 'You're not joking, are you?' said Kathy. 'You really did get whisked off on your honeymoon straight from your wedding. Was it in that helicopter?'

'No. In something even faster. Do I look less like a squaddie now?'

'I don't think anyone would every mistake you for a squaddie, Mina. That's good. I love the way you've contoured your cheeks.'

'I have had a lifetime of trying anything but surgery to hide my nose.' She touched her jawline. 'I have had enough surgery, I think.' She took one last look in the mirror. 'Let's find the boys and Scarywoman.' She grinned. 'Don't tell anyone I called her that. Lucy will kill me if she finds out.'

'Lucy? Is that Fraser's name?'

'Goodness me, no. Lucy is Tom's girlfriend. Let's get some tea on the way.' She turned to Kathy. 'Have you eaten *anything* today?'

Suddenly, Kathy realised that she hadn't.

They wouldn't let her anywhere near the kitchen, of course, and they had to clear the shivering gallery, but five minutes later, Kathy found herself huddling in her coat, devouring a sausage sandwich while Mina rattled on about never having been to Yorkshire before in her life.

Kathy wasn't huddling from the cold: she was huddling away from the prying eyes of all the guests in the Abbey, who were now confined to their rooms. She saw a forensic technician emerge from the guest block at one point, and assumed that he'd been in Michael's room.

She was just about to light a cigarette when Conrad Clarke came out of the Abbey with Morton, and they were both carrying mugs of tea. She felt slightly offended that Morton was using *her* mug, then surprised when he turned it and offered her the handle. 'Yours, I believe.'

She was accepting the tea, so missed what Clarke said to Mina. His wedding ring looked weird, and was similar in design to Mina's, but had some sort of engraving on it.

Mina came over and said, 'My driver is here. I'm taking an airport taxi home. To Clerkswell in Gloucestershire. Here.'

She passed Kathy the two twenty pound notes and wouldn't take them back. 'Good luck. My husband may be in the dog house, but he's a good man. You can trust him.'

'I…'

But she was gone, off with her new husband to say goodbye out of sight.

'Bit of a whirlwind, isn't she?' said Morton.

'You can say that again.' Something shifted inside Kathy. She had liked Mina, and wanted to trust her, but how could she believe *anything* about this morning? 'Inspector, show me a picture of Lucy.'

He glanced at where the newlyweds had gone. 'Why? What did Mina say?'

'Please. Just show me.'

Without another word, he opened his phone and showed her the first picture he came to: a girl with wild brown hair, pointing at the camera, laughing and with eyes full of love.

'Thank you.'

He didn't ask why, he just put his phone away. Kathy sighed. She had her answer now, because if Mina were telling the truth about Lucy, then this nightmare was all too real.

Conrad Clarke marched towards her with only a trace of the limp he'd shown when he got out of the helicopter. Now he was close, Kathy could see that he was a good ten years older than Mina. And tall. So tall. She stood up, and he smiled at her. And offered her a very firm handshake.

'How d'you do, Kathy? Call me Conrad. And please feel free to smoke, because I fully intend to. Would you mind if we sat down?'

The bench was very crowded with him on it. Long arms, long body and great long legs, the left one stretched out straight. 'Do you think she'll forgive me?' he asked with a smile.

Kathy considered the woman who'd pitched up, raided her makeup table and blown away like the wind. 'I think she's already forgiven you. Doesn't mean she won't get her own back, though. Taking a girl on *honeymoon* with no makeup or phone. That's got to be worth at least a ruby bracelet to go with the earrings.'

He snorted. 'She's got one with her. Didn't she put it on? Probably didn't want to overawe the driver. He twisted slightly and smiled the smile of a man newly married. 'I think another trip to the jewellers is the least of my concerns. Thank you, by the way. You didn't have to do that. Now, DCI Morton tells me you've seen some strange things, Kathy. Is that right?'

Morton hadn't left them. He was leaning against one of the shivering gallery's supports, standing behind Kathy as if he were more interested in watching Conrad than in her. She nodded and said, 'That's right.' Then she lit a cigarette.

He did the same, taking his time and using an old Zippo lighter with a weird picture on it. When he spoke, his voice was softer, less of the parade ground. 'This question is very important, Kathy. Not to me, but to your girls. Okay? Can you tell me whether you had really bad nightmares when you were a teenager?'

She flinched, the truth surely written all over her face. She nodded to confirm it and dragged on her cigarette.

'And did anyone come to see you? Maybe said they were from a special clinic or something?'

This time she gasped. 'How do you know that?'

'What did they say?'

'They said I had this rare condition. I could go to this special school where they'd treat it, or I could take this medicine and make the nightmares go away.'

'You chose the medicine.' It was a statement of fact, not a question.

'Mum didn't want me going away to school. I didn't fancy it much, neither. I'd have stuck out like a sore thumb there, all them posh types. No offence.'

'And did the medicine work?'

She took a deep breath. In all the years of therapy, counselling and pleas of mitigation in the courtrooms of Leeds, she'd never said this before, because Conrad Clarke was the first person who ever looked like he might believe her.

'It were alright at first. Then it stopped working and I discovered that cider works just as well. Lots of cider.'

She was used to sympathy, and it meant nothing, even if it were genuine. Conrad didn't look sympathetic: he looked pained. And sad. 'That's such a shame, Kathy. Such a shame. You deserved better from us. So do your children.'

It was the most deeply buried fear in her swamp of anxiety: that this nameless *condition* she had would be hereditary. 'What can I do?' she whispered.

He looked thoughtful, then looked over her shoulder at Morton. 'I have a dangerous job. I really might not be around in ten years, but if I am, then I will personally make sure they get proper treatment. If they need it. There's a good chance they won't. And if I'm not here, then whoever has my job will do it, and I know they will because Tom and Mina will make sure they do.' He paused, and when he spoke again, a little shiver ran down Kathy's spine. 'I give you my word.'

When it came to her children, now that she was sober, Kathy was like a terrier. 'How will I find you?'

'Google. Have a look for us after we're done and you'll see what I mean.'

She turned to look at Morton, and he nodded reassuringly.

'Good,' said Conrad, slapping his bad leg. 'Tom's told me that you never saw the real address.'

'I did not. I swear it. And neither did Nika. She's really good at turning a blind eye is Nika.'

'And I believe you. But you and Mister Bell made a decoy address, I believe?'

'Yeah.' She looked over her shoulder at the detective. 'I told you.'

'This is one of those moments when you need to tell us again,' said Conrad patiently.

'Only I didn't see it! Only Michael saw it!'

'But you must have seen the letter. You made three, I believe?'

'I did. And I wrote them all because we didn't have any way of printing them. They were all the same, though. And they were all on headed paper. That's easy enough to nick.'

'And what did they say.'

'They had the date and they had this: *Rumours of my death have been greatly exaggerated. For the sake of Legacy, seek me here. D.* That was all. Michael told me that Don stole the first bit from some American writer called Mark Twain. I said to Don that they might not have a clue who it was, but he put his foot down: anything else would be too much of a risk.'

Morton spoke up. 'Did you ask what the legacy might be?'

She didn't turn round to answer him. 'Yes. He refused to answer, but he did ask me to write it with a capital "L".'

'And that's why we ask you to go over things again, Kathy. It could make all the difference.'

Conrad looked at Morton, then said, 'Let's go to Donald Bell's room before you tell me the rest, Kathy.'

She flinched. 'Will I have to … to see Doctor Simon?'

He shook his head. 'No. I've already done that part, and you have nothing to tell me about *that*. I've avoided Donald's room because I want to see it through your eyes. Are they ready for us, Tom?'

They were, and Morton led them round the Abbey again after returning their mugs to the kitchen. As they approached the little garden, Conrad stopped and looked. 'Who planted this?' he asked.

'Me and Don. I did the hard work. It were after he learnt to communicate, he could tell me what he wanted.'

'I see. Carry on.'

He might see, but Kathy certainly didn't. She moved slowly towards the french doors, then turned and said, 'The night the lights came, they came over that way. Through the trees. They were bare then. The trees, I mean.'

'Really? Could you be exact?'

She stood on the steps and brought back the scene. 'That way,' she said, extending her arm.

Conrad stood in front of her, following her gaze. He said nothing for a while. 'Interesting. After you.'

The room looked the same, but with added fingerprint powder. Ugh. She hated that stuff. Even when they switched to doing it digitally, the greasy paste was a bugger to shift. Total nightmare.

'His wheelchair's gone,' she said straight away.

'That's what the Polish carer told us,' said Morton. 'She had a look round and said she couldn't see anything else out of place. Faye didn't want to come in, so we asked Nika.'

'Faye wouldn't know,' said Kathy without thinking. 'I mean, because Don wasn't getting treatment from her.'

'Of course,' said Conrad. 'You knew him better. Anything else strike you?'

'His statue thingy. *Bust* Michael called it.' She straightened her shoulders. 'It was where he kept his gold sovereigns. The ones he gave to me to buy the printer.'

'I see,' said Conrad. 'I don't suppose you know the name of the person whose statue it was, do you?'

She gave a mirthless laugh. 'Makes sense now. Michael recognised it straight away because it was some Greek bloke, and if Michael really is Greek, then that explains it. *Homer.* I had to look him up, 'cos I had no idea there were two Homers.'

Conrad's eyes hadn't stopped roaming the room until this moment. He stopped and looked at her. His poker face was good, but not that good. She could see that something had changed inside him, like a dog that gets a scent. His voice was still mild, as if he didn't care, but he eyes had narrowed a fraction. Just enough to make her realise that this man wasn't just large, he was scary. 'As far as you know, Don brought that bust with him. Correct? What else here is his personal property?'

'The paintings are his.'

Conrad went to the little bird and examined it closely. 'A skylark,' he said to himself. Then, to Kathy's horror, he went and looked at the substitute. It took him about five seconds to turn around and raise his eyebrows. 'When did you swap the other one?'

The shame was intense. It burned. She shook her head, unable to speak.

'This is important, Kathy. We can sort out what happened to it later, but for now I really do need to know what was in the picture.'

'Can I have my phone?' she said to Morton. 'I'll show you.'

Morton got her phone from his back pocket and passed it to her, standing next to her as she unlocked it. When she'd flicked to the picture, he took it from her and passed it to Conrad.

When he saw the image, his poker face vanished completely. The picture of the raven clearly meant something very serious to him. Something that scared him.

'I need to take this upstairs,' he told Morton. 'Not to Hannah, but as far upstairs as you can go.'

He turned back to her. 'You've had a lucky escape, Kathy. Very lucky. Excuse me while I go outside. I might be a few minutes.'

He left the room, and Morton said, 'While he's gone, we'll go and retrieve the picture, shall we?'

'How do you know it's still here?'

'We haven't analysed your phone because your not under arrest, but we've traced your calls, including several ones recently to art galleries. If you'd sold the painting, the pile of notes on your desk would have been a lot higher.'

She *tsked* to herself. 'So that was a pantomime, was it? Conrad knew about it before we came in here?'

'Oh no,' said Morton. 'He figured that out for himself.'

Chapter 40 — Scales of Justice

I stood outside the room where "Donald Bell" has spent the last umpteen years. I stared at the line which Kathy had pointed out to me, a line which led across the plains to the Pennines, and over the Pennines to the Lakeland Particular, and it looked very much as if the Peace I'd celebrated at the Vernal Equinox was about to be shattered.

I flexed my fingers, itching to take out my fags. Not here, though. And not now. I turned to face North, where Asgard lies and where Yggdrasil towers over the nine worlds. Then I took out my phone. It was time.

The Allfather had told me that one day I would find him, the man who created the giant Witch, Raven, and I knew that it was the missing man because he also had a picture of a Skylark on his wall. That is *not* a coincidence, especially when you add in the late Warden's warning to beware *Homer.*

It still gives me the shakes when I bring up Odin's contact details. Makes me want to look over my shoulder in case the men in white coats come to take me away. Or lock me up here in Beckthorpe like Donald Bell.

I thumbed the message: *My lord, I have tracked down the man who created Raven to a place called Beckthorpe Abbey in Yorkshire, possibly under sedation or confinement and the pseudonym Donald Bell. I am there now and he has been liberated or kidnapped. He also created Skylark Wilson of Grange over Sands, but she is completely ignorant of magick and has no Gift.*

I had sensed almost no magick in Don's room, but outside was another matter. The hard work put in by Kathy had, in a very rudimentary way, created a collector of Lux, just enough to make it stand out. Like a candle in a forest. That fact alone told me that Bell must have been a well educated Mage even if his powers have shrunk or been bound.

Apart from that, my Third Eye told me almost nothing about his room, and there was certainly no magick in the picture of the innocent skylark, and talking of birds…

My skin crawled a little, and my Troth ring pulsed as a dot appeared high in the sky, grew bigger, then smaller, and finally became a raven. It spread its wings and soared above the Abbey, circling majestically in defiance of mundane aerodynamics, then it tilted and headed for the trees, taking a perch on the top branch of an oak. As it folded its wings, my phone pinged.

Thank you. I shall pay a discreet visit to Sophie's mother. I presume you will be hunting the author. Go well.

Okay. He does like to bowl googlies does my sponsor. *How in the name of Mother Earth does he know Sophie????* And does it matter?

The ways of the Elderkind are strange, and I don't claim any great insight other than this: Skylark Wilson may have had an extraordinary conception, but she is in no danger from the Lord of Valhalla. Unlike "Donald Bell", who I think deserves to be known by his nickname from now on. Did you notice that I didn't tell Odin about *Homer*? What? Well, he doesn't tell me everything either.

I returned to Homer's cell and found Tom and Kathy both staring at her phone, with a rather beautiful picture of a raven perched on a chair next to them.

Tom pointed to the painting. 'This is the original. Have a look and then I've got something to show you.'

I picked up the framed image and my right hand got a tingle of residual magick, just where the artist had signed it. 'Is this valuable?' I asked.

'Yes. Very,' said Tom. 'Does that make a difference?'

'It explains why Don or someone else hid the signature.'

'How did you know that?' blurted out Kathy.

'He knows these things,' said Tom. He turned to look at the Abbey's resident cook and said, 'Kathy has volunteered to share this with us.'

Kathy nodded rather than speak. Even though she once had a Gift, there's barely a trace now. The brutal Suppression Tincture she took as a teenager and the years of alcohol abuse have erased almost everything, leaving her just enough to see what happened to Homer that night and be there as a human battery when he did his little Works, like revealing the signature.

Kathy is a fighter, though, and she's keeping her head above water today. Just.

'What's that?' I asked.

Tom pressed play on a video, and I flinched: there he was. There was Homer.

I watched him gurn, blow raspberries and nod to the camera as Kathy confirmed that he was gifting her the picture. 'Again, please, Tom.'

This time I concentrated on his aged, withered face, and I could see the determination in his eyes. The herb garden showed that Homer was not done as a Mage, and if he had been rescued rather than kidnapped...

Time to worry about that later. 'Is there anything else you can tell us, Kathy? About Michael in particular?'

'I wish I could. I still can't see him hurting Doctor Simon, though.'

'How was he around Don? You implied that Don outwitted him. With help from you, of course.'

'I dunno. I got the impression that he wasn't really *that* interested. I know he fooled me about being a spook, but he never took any real interest in Don.

Didn't ask questions about his past or nothing.'

'Did you ask questions?'

'I tried a few times, but he just shook his head. Beyond saying that it was his family who put him in here and that they separated him from his wife, I got nothing other than that he loved her. Still does.'

If I were locked up in the Abbey, Mina would not rest until she found me, so either Homer's wife is also imprisoned or she is dead; the look in Tom's eye said that he'd come to the same conclusion.

'Thank you, Kathy. You've been very helpful.'

'What happens to me now?' she asked. Her thin features were twitching with nerves, because Kathy Metcalfe is very astute. She knew that her usefulness to me was over and she was back in the hands of the police. She flicked her eyes to Tom, then looked down.

'I'm going to hand you over to Sergeant Oldroyd,' he told her. 'You never finished making your formal statement, did you? After that, the new SIO from Northallerton may want to interview you again.'

'So you're not arresting me or nothing?'

'No. Ms Langley may sack you when she finds out what you've done, but that's up to her.' He gave our witness a disarming smile. 'Between you and me, though, if you make yourself indispensable, you should be safe. Faye may not be in a fit state to continue running the Abbey for a while, and the young Doctor Swift, Simon's daughter, has never had executive responsibility.'

Kathy managed a crooked smile that wasn't quite a grimace. 'In other words, keep your head down, your nose clean and you might get off.'

'I couldn't possibly say that, Kathy. If you could wait outside.'

'Yeah.'

She left us, with one lingering glance at the room rather than Tom and me. He got on his radio and gave instructions, and a tired looking woman appeared to escort Kathy away. 'Well?' said Tom.

'Do you remember the Witch, Raven of Glastonbury? Also the former partner of Cordelia Kennedy?'

'Yes.'

'Donald Bell, or whatever his name is, he created Raven. The Allfather is not happy.'

'And if we find this man, will he just disappear, like you and Mina did at the wedding?'

'I have no idea, Tom. I'm fairly sure that Don didn't kill Doctor Swift, though. Is the crime scene ready?'

'Let's see.'

I had been allowed to view the poor Doctor Swift where he lay, to confirm what Tom had begun to suspect: that the owner of Beckthorpe Abbey had been killed by a Blast of magick which had lifted him off the floor and slammed him into the wall hard enough to shatter most of his bones. The total lack of noise or signs of a break-in were also indicators to Tom, but he hadn't been certain until Kathy had started telling him about lights in the night.

Elaine Fraser was waiting for us, already suited and gloved, and with spares for us. 'The new SIO will be here in half an hour, sir,' she informed Tom. 'The MI5 examiner will be another couple of hours yet.'

'Thanks. Police surgeon?'

She rolled her eyes. 'Finally been. The crime scene manager has covered the body now, but won't move it until later. Shall I clear the room?'

'Please.'

While we got ready, Elaine politely asked the forensic team to vacate the study. They grumbled a bit then decided that a break would be good for them and left us to it, with strict instructions for us not to disturb anything.

'Not as scary as Tracey Kenyon is he?' I whispered to Tom.

'Shh!' hissed Elaine.

The good Dr Swift must have another store-room somewhere, because although there were dozens of personal files strewn on the floor, the Abbey must have had hundreds of patients through its doors over the years, way more than these three metal cabinets could contain.

'The mess has been photographed multiple times,' said Tom. 'We can start examining it if we want, but…' he looked theatrically at his watch. 'I presume that time is of the essence now you're certain that this is a magickally enabled crime.'

'It is. What do you suggest, then?'

'Look at those files, up there.'

The top left of the first cupboard appeared to have been undisturbed.

'Armstrong, Ashcroft… Aah. I see where you're going, Tom. The files are in alphabetical order, and they're intact up to "B" for "Bell".'

'Yes. And I think they wanted Donald Bell's file, but didn't know what name it would be under.'

I peered down at the discarded folders. Some of the few pieces of information on the front cover were dates – of birth, of admission, of discharge. Homer would be easy to spot. I was about to confirm to Tom that I was on the same page when there was an urgent knocking on the door and a shout of, 'Sir!'

'I'll get it,' said Elaine.

She opened the door a crack and had a whispered conversation, then jerked her head. 'You need to hear this, sir. And you … erm, Wing Commander.'

We returned to the corridor, and a young Asian man didn't know which of the several bits of kit he was carrying to show us first.

'This is our digital specialist,' said Tom, in case I was in any doubt. 'What is it Imran?'

'I found something before, but I wasn't sure, but now I've found the other end. It's definite,' he announced in a broad Yorkshire accent.

Tom had obviously worked with him earlier in the day, and held up a hand to slow him down. Naturally, he used me as an excuse. 'Start again, Imran. Wing Commander Clarke here has only just arrived and you need to bring him up to speed.'

Imran seemed to see me for the first time, and took in the bits of my uniform visible under the boiler suit. 'You're in the army,' he said. 'No. Wait. You're a wing commander. What are you doing here?'

'The same as you,' said Tom. 'He's assisting a murder investigation. So what can you tell him?'

Imran looked as if he didn't want to tell me anything until Tom folded his arms. That's Tom all over: I normally have to draw a sword to have the same effect on difficult subordinates. And not even that works with Scout.

'Right. Okay. I found a well-concealed audio-visual surveillance device in the study. I thought it could be the shrink taping his patients.'

Imran didn't see Tom wince at the use of *shrink* and it didn't bother me. The digital specialist held up a small box. 'Then I found this in Michalis Papadakis' room. It's a receiver, and they're the same make. I checked and the Abbey network has had a load of security levels removed recently. *After* he arrived. I reckon he planted it. Oh and yeah, I double checked. Whatever it fed to is gone. Probably a laptop.'

Tom was ahead of me with his next question. 'And what about Mister Bell's room?'

'Nothing. I haven't found no others, neither. Then again, it's a huge place, and I haven't even started on the other inmates' rooms.'

'Imran, they are patients. Guests. What about Ms Metcalfe's?' He shook his head. 'Go and do that one now, but get her consent first. You don't need to tell me if it's negative.'

'Right,' said Imran, then he bustled off.

Tom's hand ventured towards the flesh and blood scar on his arm which stands in for the mental scarring he got from a near-death experience. An experience for which I was partly responsible. Responsible by association, I should point out.

'How's Faye Langley?' he asked Elaine.

'Probably asleep. I had no choice but to allow the police surgeon to see her, and she gave her a happy pill of some sort then told me she'd need to be assessed before being interviewed again, however informally. Right pain in the arse she was. The doctor, that is.'

'Fine. In that case, let's look under *P* for *Papadakis* in that mess in there.'

'Could I leave you to it for a moment?' I asked. 'I need to tell my earthly boss about this. And summon Saffron.'

'And you need a smoke,' added Elaine. Hah! I wouldn't allow

insubordination like that. Who am I kidding? I get it all the time. At least Elaine didn't try to kick my bad leg.

I stripped off the suit and followed my nose to the kitchen, where Kathy was restored to being queen of her domain, assisted by a wide-eyed black woman. Kathy passed me a mug of tea with a smile, and I went outside.

He probably thought I wouldn't notice, but young Imran took a picture of me from upstairs. I tend to notice when people are focused on me. It was something I'd mention to Tom when I'd had a difficult conversation with Hannah. And a smoke. Not going to deny it.

It took seconds to find Michael's file. Tom spent a few moments staring at the photograph pasted to the cover of a man around his own age with a tentative smile and, yes, a definite Mediterranean look to him. 'Take this and commandeer the office photocopier,' he told Elaine, handing over the folder. 'Three copies. Don't let anyone see whose file it is and set Conrad on to them if they get arsey.'

'Right.' She hesitated. 'What are your plans for this? The whole thing, I mean.'

'Good question. We've got Donald Bell's DNA, but that will take days and only be any use if he has a close familial match on the system, which is unlikely, so Michael is our only lead.'

He pointed to the file. 'If he *is* involved, he can't be a main player, because his file would be gone, too. I am now going to check on everyone's progress so I can write a report and then have a very difficult conversation with the local SIO.'

'I thought they've been very good, so far.'

'And so they have. I doubt that attitude will last once I tell him that I'm keeping Michael to myself. Ourselves.'

Tom was taking notes from the Family Liaison Officer when Elaine strode out from the Abbey office with a worrying frown and pointed outside.

'Thanks,' said Tom to the FLO. 'Excuse me.'

Elaine was clearly not happy and strode at a pace to a quiet spot in the yard, well away from the shivering gallery, where Conrad was still glued to his phone.

'It's fake,' she announced. 'There is no Michalis Papadakis with this date of birth or address. The company he's supposed to work for is nothing but a skin deep website, and even his GP is fake. Do we need to go back to the Angel of Death? Could Michael or whatever his name is be an agent under the deepest cover.'

Tom felt the urge to rub his scar more strongly than since he'd realised that there was magick involved. 'Not yet. Let's dig a little deeper first, then I'll let North Riding do it. No point in doing John Lake's dirty work for him, is there?'

'Very devious, sir. I like it. How are we going to dig, then?'

'You didn't mention his detox clinic. I would have thought Doctor Simon unlikely to take a client without talking to them first.'

Elaine opened the folder and found the report. She stared for a second, then grunted with surprise. 'It's an NHS trust in North London. Surely that must be real.'

Tom sighed. 'I'm sure it is. And I'm equally sure that an overworked, underfunded public body would also be easy to fool.'

Elaine was still skimming the notes. She was good at that. She could find a nugget twice as fast as Tom. And then she'd hand it over for him to read properly. If he had a bigger Ego, he'd worry that it should be the other way round.

'His drug use isn't faked,' she observed. 'These printouts have even been annotated by Doctor McNair. *Mingey Mora* according to Kathy. Michael was close to overdosing on cocaine when first admitted.'

'Cocaine? Never mind. Looks like Conrad's finished. He can join us over here.'

Clarke had limped over to join them. 'Hannah is bemused and checking the records,' he announced. 'Saffron is on her way. Should be here in half an hour. You?'

Elaine waved the folder at Conrad (she'd never got round to photocopying it), and she told him what they'd discovered. 'Is there anything you can do to find either of them with magick?' she asked.

Tom had tried to explain what he understood about magick to Elaine, but she never quite believed that there were limits to it, and he spoke up before Conrad could say anything. 'Doesn't work like that, unfortunately. I'm afraid that there's only one certain way we're going to track down Michael.'

Elaine sighed. 'Yeah. I know. Follow the money.'

'Which will take time,' added Tom. 'And probably need search warrants.' He took a half step backwards, just so he didn't have to look up quite so much when he spoke to Conrad. 'Even if the King's Watch wasn't involved, even if this were just a mundane abduction and murder, we'd be in trouble.'

'It's a very serious matter, yes,' said Conrad, unsure where Tom was going but too polite not to show he agreed.

'Michael has paid a lot of money to be here, and everything points to a premeditated plan. Eventually the money would lead back to him. Eventually isn't soon enough.'

'No,' said Conrad looking frustrated, then a light dawned. 'You've got something, Tom, haven't you?'

'Me? No. Elaine is going to take a copy of the file, then I am going to brief the new SIO. I'm going to tell him everything we know that's not magickal and offer to help him tracing the money.' He paused. 'It's *you* who is going to follow our only lead.'

'Me?'

'Yes. The only person Michael talked to was Kathy. She's the only way we're going to find out what he was really doing here.' He held up a hand. 'I know he didn't confide in her, but he must have given her some indication.'

'I'll do my best.'

Conrad and Elaine headed off on their missions, and Tom allowed himself a smile. *How has it come to this? That the least scary member of the team is the killer in combats?* He returned to the counselling room and started putting his notes in order. When he'd finished, his mind drifted back to the wedding and to Mrs Justice Bracewell's suggestion that he join the Cloister Court.

However it was that Donald Bell had ended up here, he definitely had questions to answer about the birth of Raven. Tom couldn't help thinking of Don Giovanni at the end of Mozart's opera, or Dr Faustus: both of them dragged down to Hell. Tom had no choice but to believe in the existence of the Allfather – he'd seen him at Clerkswell – but Tom did not want to be part of any system where divine punishment was a prelude to stamping *Case Closed* on the file.

Elaine knocked and came in. 'Ready, sir? The local SIO is here. And Saffron Hawkins is waiting patiently at the perimeter.'

'Right. Keep Saffron away from Conrad for now. You can tell her everything. I'll see you when I'm done.'

He took the original of the Michalis Papadakis file and headed out, past uniformed officers taking statements from the guests, past the FLO trying to contact Simon Swift's daughter, past Mora McNair arguing with a very tired Sergeant Jen Oldroyd, past umpteen crime scene technicians, and finally to the crime scene, where a battle scarred detective chief superintendent was looking at his phone.

Tom introduced himself and got a grunt. 'We have a leak,' said the DCS. He showed Tom his phone. It was a picture of Conrad striding around the shivering gallery, and he was named underneath on social media. 'Does this matter?'

'Not really. He's quite good at hiding in plain sight.'

The DCS grunted. 'Fine. He's not my responsibility anyway. Right. What have we got, and what are you not going to tell me?'

Chapter 41 — Long Lost Lenny

When Conrad walked back into the kitchen, Kathy reached for a mug. How many teas had she made since Sergeant Jen first let her put the kettle on? Hundreds. At least. She had no idea that the police could possibly consume so much. Some of the coppers and civilians had looked longingly at the Abbey's cafetieres when she'd offered them instant coffee, but she wasn't going to squander a month's supply of best beans on that lot.

Dealing with the police was like dealing with builders: it was just part of her job, along with trying to organise lunch for the guests and deal with the aftermath of Paul taking charge of the kitchen for breakfast. Bastard.

She'd get her own back for the state of those pans. Probably when his botoxed bitch of a wife came to visit him next. Definitely. It was about time she learnt about his trip to Bradford, followed shortly by his visit to Mingey Mora to get antibiotics. No. All of this she could deal with; it was when the great lanky streak of Camouflaged Conrad Clarke reappeared that she was forced to confront the truth again: Dr Simon was dead. Don was gone. Michael was a snake in the grass.

'Is there somewhere comfortable and private we can go, Kathy?' he asked mildly, as if he was her new therapist.

'That's a laugh,' she said.

'Sorry?'

She shook herself. 'It's me that's sorry. Yes. Of course. You can choose between the gardens or my bedsit, and I'm not allowed to smoke up there.'

'The gardens it is. I'd bring your coat, though.'

She filled two mugs and backed dJulie into a corner. There had been a tremendous change in dJulie since the winter. A *Quantum Leap* Dr Simon had called it. 'We are having soup and only soup for guest lunch. Okay?'

'Yeah. Right. Whatever.'

'And if Paul turns up, tell him he's barred. Chef's orders.' She waited until dJulie nodded. 'Good.'

She led Conrad out of the courtyard, giving the front of the Abbey a wide berth. This meant crossing the lawn, and she said as they passed the angry looking aircraft, 'What's it like to fly a helicopter?'

He stopped and looked like he wanted to stroke the metal. 'Hard to explain. This might sound strange, but it's not like flying a plane.'

'You're right. That does sound strange.'

'It's more like riding a galloping horse, only scarier and more exhilarating.'

'I wouldn't know. I've only ever been on a donkey. Not likely to ride any sort of horse. Except in my dreams.'

'And I once thought I'd never walk again, yet here I am. Are we heading for that bench with the roses round it?'

'Yeah. It's pretty sheltered.'

'Good.'

They sat down and she waited for him to get on with it. She sneaked another look at his wedding ring and saw weird triangle thingies. Must be a family crest. And the lighter. 'What's on the side of your Zippo?' she asked, as a good way of avoiding the subject.

'A copy of my first present from Mina. Before we started properly dating. It's Ganesh, her patron god. Here.'

She examined the brightly coloured elephant headed image. 'Why a copy?'

'Because the first one got damaged saving my life, believe it or not.'

She returned the lighter and said, 'I still haven't got me phone back. Could you put in a word with Morton?'

'Just ask for it. If you're not under arrest and he hasn't got a warrant, he can't keep it.'

'I know that. This isn't my first close encounter with the law, and I don't want to push him.'

'Leave it with me.'

'None of the guests have phones, so I still haven't been able to Google you.'

He took out his phone without a word, and found something. He turned up the volume and passed it to her. She watched entranced as Mina, dressed in bright red, danced with … surely not.

'Is that the real Tara Doyle or a lookalike?'

'Watch the finale.'

Kathy's eyes were on stalks. It was real enough. This was Tara Doyle, Strictly winner, playing second fiddle to Mina Desai. 'And was that Morton's girlfriend doing the shimmy?'

He chuckled. 'Yes it was. Don't let on to him that I showed you.' He took back his phone, thumbed it to another picture and showed the happy couple outside a church, him in his posh uniform and Mina in a gorgeous dress which clung to curves which Kathy hadn't seen when Mina dropped her trousers in the bathroom. Padding? Photoshop?

'Show me your dog.'

He looked surprised, but didn't say anything. He found a picture of a manic looking border collie with different coloured eyes, then said, 'I didn't think Mina was up there long enough to get round to our faithful hound, but there he is.'

He made sure she'd seen, then locked his phone and slipped it into his jacket.

'Now what?' said Kathy. 'If I had my phone, I'd show you pictures of my kids, but I can't, so shall we get on with it?' She didn't give him a chance to answer and pressed on. 'No, there's nothing I've not told you. All the hints he ever gave about his past were lies. Totally made up.'

Conrad didn't seem bothered. 'You don't know that for sure, Kathy. I've had a lot of practice at lying. I'm quite good at it. Some of it has to be the truth.'

'Duh. I know that. If I had a month I could write it all down. Christmas Day on Copa Cobana Beach. Learning to cook pasta on holiday in Italy.' She frowned. 'Actually, he's better at pasta than I ever was, but he could have learnt how to do that in Batley not Bolognese.'

'See what I mean? You know more than you think.'

'I doubt that very much.'

'Did he ever talk about his parents?'

'Only vague stuff. Like how his mother wasn't a great cook.' She looked up and met his gaze. 'And he made a point of saying that his parents didn't know where he was and that he wasn't going to tell them until he was better. That cut that avenue off. And he said he was an only child.'

Conrad sat back. 'Did he?'

She reflected. 'Actually, I think he might have been. Just a feeling.'

'Excellent,' he said, way too keenly, then he realised she was giving him a funny look. 'It might be significant that he doesn't have a sister. Might be.'

'Whatever you say, Wing Commander.'

He snorted. '*Sir* will do. Should you ever find yourself in the RAF, that is.'

'I'll give that some serious thought.' She paused. 'I'm too old for helicopters, right?'

'Sadly.'

'Then it'll have to be the cavalry. They're the ones who ride horses.'

'I'll put in a good word for you.'

They shared a look, and Kathy knew that they were both visualising her trying to vault on to a horse.

'You might know something else, Kathy,' he said, breaking the spell. 'Tell me truly, do you think Michael was an addict?'

She opened her mouth then closed it in shock. It was like Conrad had unzipped a part of her brain that she didn't know was closed. 'You know, that's a very good question, as Doctor Simon says. Used to say. I dunno.' She leaned her elbows on her knees. 'We all have a hole in our lives here. The addicts. Michael had one, too. Mine's shaped like a bottle. I can feel it. Now you've asked me, I don't think Michael's hole was shaped like a line of cocaine.' She sat back and shrugged. 'But how did he get in?'

'I think he planned it all, including taking an overdose of cocaine and being admitted to hospital with forged documents.'

'Fuck me. And you're still telling me he wasn't a spook after a stunt like that?'

'Not one of ours, and MI5 don't think he's anyone else's.'

'Then why? Why go to all that trouble to get in here? And who was paying? I couldn't afford a weekend here, never mind *months*.'

'Tom is following the money, but that takes time.'

'Shame Mina's out of it.'

He laughed at some private joke, then leaned forwards. 'I have a huge respect for Tom Morton. Huge. He does have one weakness, though. When he's stressed, he sometimes says weird things. He was briefing me before, and I asked the same question as you: Why? Why go to this trouble? And do you know what he said? *You've hit the nail squarely on the bullseye.*'

'He didn't.'

There was a glint in Conrad's eye, a bit like the look in his dog's. 'Oh yes he did. So, Kathy, tell me this: what was Michael *really* interested in? What questions did he ask? Where did he go that he shouldn't have gone? Who did he make friends with that you wouldn't have expected?'

'Me.'

'I'd make friends with you.'

'Give over. We might have shagged, and I'm sure we'd both have enjoyed it, but I doubt we'd have been friends. Not like Michael and me. He cared. He did things for me and Don, even though he wasn't from my world and we had nothing in common but cooking.'

'And a hole in your lives.'

'I have kids. I'd swear on their lives he didn't have any. Kids, that is. He definitely had a hole in his life of some sort.'

'So apart from company, what did you give him? Take your time. And could I steal one of your cigarettes?'

Conrad was patient. They smoked and looked out, he towards his helicopter and she towards the guest block at the back of the Abbey. When the answer came, it was just that: answers.

'Long Lenny.'

'I've been called a lot of things, Kathy, mostly by flight sergeants when I was training, but I've never been called that.'

'No, no. It all makes sense now. He used to ask about old guests. Those who had left. He'd dress it up like he was trying to find out what would happen to him, but now I think about it, he was just being nosy, and the person he wanted to know more about than anyone was Leonard. Long Lenny. Trouble is, once he'd got me going, I couldn't stop.'

'So who's Long Lenny when he's at home?'

'Leonard Little. He had some stage name as well, 'cos he was an actor or something, but everyone called him Long Lenny. I only know his last name because it was in the papers.'

'And how did you know him?'

'You know I first came here as a guest?' Conrad nodded. 'Well, he came when I was like in transition. I was working part-time as a cook and still doing a lot of therapy.'

'How did you get to work here at all?'

'Like Morton said, I made myself indispensable. The regular cook wasn't that interested. Kept saying his car had broken down and he couldn't get up the hill. I filled in once, and it became a habit. Next thing I knew, Faye was suggesting that it would really help my recovery if I worked here full time.'

He smiled at something there. 'I think Faye might be a woman after my own heart.'

How did he reckon that? If ever there were two people with absolutely nothing in common it was Conrad Clarke and Faye Langley. Even she and Conrad had more in common than he did with Fragrant Faye. Whatever.

'Long Lenny,' he said gently.

'He was just a big personality. Made everyone laugh. Made you look forward to seeing him again.' She looked down. 'But he wasn't here much more than three weeks.'

'What happened?'

'The first time he left the Abbey alone, he came back loaded.'

'I see.'

'No you don't. It happens a lot. Doctor Simon has a note on the door: *It's not wrong to be tempted. Hand it over now and we'll try to figure out why.* I brought a bottle of scotch back the first time, then I hammered on his door at ten o'clock and gave it to him. He said it was a good omen.'

'Did he?'

She smiled at the memory of Dr Simon in a dressing gown, hair a mess. 'He took the bottle and said that if I just wanted a drink, I'd have bought vodka. Spending the extra on scotch showed I wanted to fit in with casual drinkers.'

'He sounds like a great man.'

'He was. So was Lenny, but Lenny didn't hand it over. He had a case of wine and five wraps of speed. He hid them in the kitchen and offered me the amphetamines to keep quiet. He said so long as we avoided our demon of choice, we could party on.'

Clarke smiled. More of a grimace really, to show he understood. Then he went quiet, looking at her and waiting.

'It was me who shopped him to Doctor Simon. The taxi came for him at ten o'clock the next morning.' She closed her eyes so she didn't have to see the look of sympathy on Conrad's face. 'Lenny overdosed the same night.

Took all the speed and two bottles of wine at a hotel in Harrogate.'

She heard the rustle of cloth as he took out his phone, then the clicks as he sent a quick message.

With her eyes still squeezed closed, she said, 'Was that what you wanted to know?'

'I hope so, Kathy. I'd hate to think you told me that for nothing.'

She couldn't help but laugh, and opened her eyes. The sun was still shining and the roses around the bench were still busy blooming, and Conrad Clarke was the first person outside the Abbey she'd told this story to. She breathed out and offered him a cigarette.

'In a minute, thanks. Ah. Here she comes.'

A young woman in jeans and a leather jacket was jogging over the grass towards them. She had a shiny, healthy face and huge white hair that she was trying to keep penned in. When she got closer, she looked at Conrad and stopped. Then she *saluted*. And he saluted back.

'Morning Chief.'

'Saff, this is Kathy Metcalfe. Kathy, this is Captain Saffron Hawkins.'

Kathy was too bemused to say anything, and found herself shaking hands with the girl.

Conrad stretched out his bad leg. 'Have you brought Sammi with you?'

'Yes. And Sarah. You've not met her yet.'

'Excellent. Can you tell Tom to look into Leonard Little, former guest, and any possible connection to Michael?' He turned to Kathy. 'Do you think they could have been related?'

'Only distantly. Long Lenny was pale and Scottish, but you never know, do you?'

'Thanks. We'll be back in a minute, Saff.'

'Right.'

'Sounds like quite a team with Sammi and Sarah,' said Kathy.

'Believe it or not, Saffron is a master of disguise. They are two of her characters.'

'Right now, I'll believe anything.'

Saffron jogged away and they smoked a last cigarette in silence. By the time they got back, Sergeant Jen (who looked ready to fall asleep standing up) was waiting to take Kathy off Conrad's hands and escort her back to the kitchen.

Chapter 42 — Tribute

'Are you going to tell him what we're thinking and where we're going?' I asked Tom, nodding in the general direction of the office, where the new SIO had set up his command centre.

'I'm not,' said Tom. 'Elaine can do it. After we've gone.'

'Why me!' she moaned. 'I'll proper get it in the neck for that!'

'Because there isn't room in the helicopter?' said Tom with a twitch of his mouth. Elaine is quite capable of counting to four passengers, so she knew he was winding her up.

'Actually,' I told them. 'I'll go and tell him, because I'd rather have their co-operation and a car waiting at the LZ.'

'He'll go ballistic,' said Tom. 'I would.'

'He'll be too busy dealing with Imran.'

Tom immediately looked suspicious. He does that a lot when he's working with me. I couldn't possibly say why.

I put him out of his misery by explaining, 'I saw Imran taking a surreptitious picture of me. It must be him who posted it on social media. Or more likely a friend.'

'Candid,' said Saffron annoyingly. 'They're called *candid* pictures. Be thankful you don't wear a skirt.'

'No, you should be thankful I don't wear a skirt. Imagine having to look at my leg all day. No, I'll sort the SIO. Saffron, you can get your dressing up box and contact ATC for me? If you remember what to do.'

Of all the people who've worked with me, Saff is the only one who spent long enough as my partner to learn the basics of civilian air traffic control. Very useful. It also meant she got to sit in the front.

The Wasp is nothing like the Smurf, apart from them both being helicopters. Imagine going from a Range Rover Sport Special Edition to a bottom of the range ex-rental car. But she was mine. Mine and the bank's. My fingers were itching to get back in the air as soon as the SIO had kicked me out of the room.

Tom had very quickly established that Leonard Little's stated next of kin had been his life partner, Miguel Ortiz, born in Venezuela but who grew up mostly in the UK. After Lenny's death, Miguel's name had never been mentioned in the press, and if he was at the funeral, he had not been at the front of the mourners.

That was not surprising, given what Kathy had told me. The surprise had come from Miguel's profession: private security consultant. That explained a lot.

Saffron had got permission for the Wasp to land on the Yorkshire Showground, currently unused, and I could see the very conspicuous police 4x4 from the air. We wouldn't be using that to approach the hotel, but we'd need it to get through town.

One of the North Riding officers had been in charge of looking for the Abbey pool car ever since it had been discovered missing. I'm going to stick to the name he gave to Kathy and call our quarry *Michael*; he clearly knows a lot of tricks, and the pool car had triggered several number plate cameras, including one next to Harrogate Station, and officers had already found the vehicle, abandoned in the car park (with the keys thoughtfully left behind the visor). Until we'd learnt about Lenny, Tom and the team had assumed that this was a blind and hadn't yet allocated much resource to following it up.

I don't know if Long Lenny had been an Agatha Christie fan or whether it was just his taste for luxury. When Mrs Christie famously disappeared, she was found in a spa hotel in Harrogate. Consciously or not, Lenny had chosen to party himself to death in a very exclusive boutique hotel not far from the western gardens. More suitable for an actor, I suppose.

Tom's first thought was that this was *still* a blind, but I argued forcibly otherwise.

'He expects to be found,' I told them. 'He could have dumped the car in York before the first officer had even arrived at the Abbey. He could have gone to ground there and disappeared. No. He's gone to the Enclave Hotel to say goodbye to Lenny.'

Tom had thought about it and agreed, and so that's where we were heading. We'd brought Elaine with us, and it was a squeeze in the police car; I don't normally get that close to my partners unless it's a life or death situation.

At my direction, they dropped us in an alley two streets from the hotel. 'Why here?' said Tom when our lift had disappeared.

'Because Michael is clearly good. He may even be good enough to set up cameras on the approach and hack the hotel's CCTV.'

I saw Tom's shoulders go a little bit firmer. 'Be honest, Conrad. Do you believe he may be a threat? This isn't the First Mine or a Fae racetrack, this is a hotel in Harrogate.'

'I'm going to take precautions, that's all. My main worry is that he changes his mind about being found. I don't want him to see me coming and take fright.'

'Which is what most sensible people would do,' added Saffron. 'Sorry, sir. Couldn't help it.'

'So what's your plan?'

'Tom, turn your back. Elaine, give Saffron a hand.'

I also turned my back, and when she'd finished, Saffron told us to turn round. 'What do you reckon?'

We make assumptions about people all the time: Saffron's scrubbed look and white hair make people think she's posh and important, which she is. Sammi's ombre dye job, tight tee shirt and enormous hoop earrings make her look less like a police detective. Especially after she'd popped in a huge wadge of chewing gum. As I said, we all make assumptions, and sometimes they're wrong.

'Not bad,' said Elaine. 'You might want to get cheaper trainers next time.'

Which is why Elaine is the professional and I'm an unpaid part-timer when it comes to police work.

Saffron peered at her feet. 'Nah. He's a bloke. He won't know the difference.'

The Enclave is a hotel. If Michael was somehow watching the service entrance, Sammi is exactly who he'd expect to turn up. Even if he was listening, he'd hear a young woman ask for the head of housekeeping because she'd come from the agency about the chambermaid's job.

It was only when Saffron had made contact and accessed a unmonitored room that she would use magick and her ID card to crack open the shell into which Michael had retreated. We'd been standing around in the alley for ten minutes when my phone rang.

'He's here. He arrived at nine o'clock this morning and paid extra to have a room right away. He used his own name, too. As far as they know, he's still in there. I'll meet you at the entrance to the back yard, and once we're through the store room, there's no more CCTV.'

'Good work, Saff. We'll be there in a minute.'

'We?' said Tom.

'You and me. Saffron can do a Glamour for both of us, and you'll be waiting at the end of the corridor when Saff and I access the target's room.'

'And me?' said Elaine.

'Ready to contact the SIO at the Abbey.'

Elaine nodded. She quite rightly has strong reservations about getting close to magick again. I don't blame her. I think Tom has the same reservations, but either masochism or a strong sense of duty forces him to go there. Then again, it could just be that he doesn't trust me.

'What are you going to disguise yourself as?' asked Elaine, looking dubiously at Tom's Crombie overcoat and mirror-shined shoes.

'When it's over, check the hotel CCTV and see for yourself,' I told her with a smile. She looked even more dubious when I took Great Fang out of my kitbag and slung him over my shoulder.

'Do we really have to hold hands?' said Tom as we stood at the back gate to the Enclave's service yard.

'No, but it was too good a chance to miss.'

He gave me a hard stare. 'Now is not the time, Conrad.'

I took Great Fang off my back and held it by the hilt, parallel to the ground. 'Hold the other end of the scabbard and Saffron will cascade a Glamour out from my Badge of Office. It will look like we're carrying a roll of carpet. Oh, and look straight ahead, no matter how much your fingers tingle.'

We shuffled across the yard, over the threshold, and Saffron / Sammi beckoned us into a tiny staff lift. 'Second floor, Hideaway Suite.'

Tom let go of my sword and Saffron pressed the button. 'It's not really a suite,' she added. 'Just a big room with a sitting area and dining table. Look.'

As the much abused lift clanked up the building, we stared at a rather over-decorated room on her phone. 'Two steps and all of the suite bar the bathroom will be visible,' I said. 'You open the door, and I'll head in. Okay?'

We reached the second floor, and the doors jerked open. We stepped out on to a landing at the top of the emergency staircase; the public facing part of the building was on the other side of a door. Saffron made the Silence and touched Tom's shoulder to bring him in. It's a sign of how much he's done this sort of thing that he now knows what to expect.

'Give us five seconds, then come through the door. You'll have a clear sight of the target without being in line.'

Tom nodded, Saffron let go, and I opened the service door.

Thick carpet would have deadened our footsteps anyway, and in less than a dozen paces, Saffron was tapping the master card on the door. When the light flashed green, I put my shoulder to it and pushed hard.

Michael was standing at the window, staring at the street, his laptop open on the table next to a bottle of wine, a half full glass and scattered tablets.

Saffron cancelled the Silence. 'No Power!' she shouted, our code for Michael having no visible magick.

He jerked round and stepped backwards, banging into the window. For a second, I thought he'd go through it, but the double glazing held, and I was striding across the room. He had no visible weapon and no visible explosives, so I got a little closer and said, 'Turn around. Hands on the wall.'

'Who the fuck are...' he began, but I'd already launched myself at him, bringing him crashing into the wall, then down to a soft landing on a sheepskin rug.

His instincts kicked in, and he started to struggle, but Saffron planted an (apparently expensive) trainer on his arm, and restored the Silence so Tom didn't hear the cry of pain when I yanked the other arm behind him and put on the restraints.

'Let's take it easy, Michael,' I told him. 'We're going to help you into the chair, okay?'

He looked like he was working hard to suppress his fear, and didn't struggle when we put our arms under his shoulders and helped him to his feet. He was staring at my uniform, and it suddenly struck me that he thought we were with the killers. 'Get Tom, will you?'

'Sir.'

'Have you taken anything, Michael? Have you taken any pills? How much have you drunk?' I asked.

'What's it to you?' he spat.

Tom took in the scene and said, 'Because he's fulfilling his duty of care. Have you taken anything?'

Michael didn't know which way to look between Tom's pinstriped suit, my uniform and Sammi's rather feral grin. 'No. Just the wine,' he replied.

'Good,' said Tom brightly. 'Excuse me a moment.'

That's Tom all over: he apologises to a suspect for keeping him waiting. The reason for the delay was that he radioed Elaine to tell her that the mission had been accomplished and that she should come to the hotel's reception. 'Sorry about that. Miguel Ortiz I am arresting you on suspicion of conspiracy to murder. You do not have to say anything but it may harm your defence if you do not mention something you later rely on in court. Do you understand?'

'Who are you and who are these clowns?' he said, some of his confidence restored.

Tom, meticulous as ever, showed his warrant card and introduced himself. 'And this is Special Constable Clarke, and that's Sammi,' he added.

'I'm innocent, and you know it,' said Michael.

'In that case, you won't mind showing us the video, will you?' said Tom matter-of-factly.

'I can't. Not chained up like this. The laptop has a fingerprint reader.'

'Does it? I'll bet it also has a password, and you know yourself that the sooner we see what happened, the more chance we have of finding Don alive.'

Michael looked surprised, then suspicious. 'What do you mean?'

'Haven't you been following the news?'

'What's the point? It was only a matter of time before you found me.'

'Sammi?' said Tom. 'Show Michael the statement on your phone.'

North Riding Police haven't got round to a news conference yet, but they have issued a statement. They had to, really. It said that they were investigating a suspicious death and were concerned for the welfare of Mr Donald Bell, who was missing. Michael read it and looked genuinely concerned. 'But why? Do you think he saw something.'

'We don't know what to think,' said Tom. 'Seeing your evidence might help us understand. The password?'

He recited a long string of alphanumeric characters that must have meant something to him. Saffron typed them in and nodded confirmation.

'Thank you,' said Tom. 'Before we watch the video, tell us why you set up the cameras, what you were doing there and how on earth you knew that it was time to run? Hmm?'

He sighed. 'For the last week, I've been wondering how to get out.'

'They don't lock the doors,' said Tom.

'Perhaps they should have.' His laugh was harsh and had no humour in it. 'Who am I kidding? It wouldn't have made any difference. Not in the end.'

'Wouldn't have made any difference to what?' asked Tom, with all the patience in the world. I knew better, because he was scratching his scar.

'To Leo. Leonard. *Long Lenny.*' He looked at Tom, searching for sympathy, for understanding. Perhaps even for absolution. 'I sent him there. After detox, I made him go to the Abbey. Their success rate is phenomenal. With normal people.'

'Everyone thought that Leo was special.'

Michael shook his head. 'That's not what I meant. He *was* special, yes, but he was also a proper actor.' He tried to straighten up, but the restraints wouldn't let him. 'All addicts are actors. I sort of knew that, but I didn't realise the truth until I went to the Abbey. Addicts get away with it by pretending to be someone else, until they can't keep it up any longer. Leo was too good an actor. He fooled the detox people *and* STAND. They thought he was facing his demons, but he wasn't. He was playing a part.'

'You went looking for proof of negligence?' said Tom.

He nodded. 'And to get revenge on the people who chucked him out. Who didn't give him a second chance. He messaged me all the time he was there, you know. He'd hidden one phone in his luggage, which they found, and another where no one was going to search him.'

'Ouch,' said Sammi. Then she put her hand to her mouth.

'Yes, I was the Top,' said Michael defiantly. 'So what?' When Sammi had got the message, he turned back to Tom. 'He told me they were all do-gooders and hypocrites. He described Kathy as a *cringing kitchen maid.* They're not. She's not.'

'No, she isn't,' I murmured. Or thought I did. The trouble with losing your hearing is that you lose your benchmarks.

'You don't need to tell me that!' he snapped, then his shoulders slumped. 'As soon as I'd realised, truly realised, what a good person she is, I just wanted to get out, but that would mean admitting the truth to Simon. And myself. That they'd already given him enough chances. That Leo couldn't face being sober. Or he wasn't wired for it. Whatever.'

'That explains a lot, Michael, but it doesn't explain how you knew to get up at three in the morning and do a runner when the only other person who knew anything was Kathy, and her room's above Simon's study.'

Michael has good self-control. He was weighing us up and wondering how to spin this. Another suspect would have looked shifty. Not him. He was aiming for *confessional*, and almost succeeding. 'How much has Kathy told you about what I did?'

'Just assume that she's told us everything,' said Tom. 'It'll be quicker that way.'

'I don't want to get her in trouble.'

'As you say, she's a good person. Her only thoughts were to help us find Don and to catch Simon's murderer. Assuming you're not the murderer, then you should do the same.'

'She posted the letter, didn't she? In exchange for the picture?'

So Michael had noticed the switch and kept quiet. Tom nodded encouragingly. 'As I said, assume she told us everything.'

'I was worried about her. Something about Donald Bell stinks. I'm not saying Simon was involved, but something about Don and his situation was right off.' He glanced at me and then at Saffron. 'Is that why you're here, whoever you really are? To stop Don's story coming out, whatever the hell it is?'

I said nothing.

'The state was not responsible for Don's presence at the Abbey,' said Tom. 'Though you're right, Conrad does have an interest in finding him. Let's start with the letters. Why did you want to stop her sending them?'

'Because I knew there'd be trouble and that I'd be exposed.'

'You snooped at the first address, didn't you?'

'I did. And when it was a dead end, I knew that Kathy was doing something behind my back.'

'What was the address?'

He relaxed a fraction, probably didn't know he was doing it, but he was slipping back into professional mode.

'It was addressed to *The Akademia c/o Angel House PO Box 777, Cambridge*. Didn't take me five minutes to figure out there was no such place.'

There is such a place as Angel House. Mina's been there: it's the centre of magick in the ancient university town. I looked at Tom to show that it was important but not for discussion now.

Tom took the hint and said, 'What made you think that there was something going on?'

'There was a woman. She came last week, and I knew there was something off about her as soon as she got out of her car. I was doing some work in gardens.' He didn't pause in his story; he just assumed that Tom would follow and accept his professional opinion. 'First time visitors either stop and admire the building or scurry in like they don't want to be seen. She was different: she was looking for something. Around sixty, well dressed, drove a black Mercedes 4x4. I found out later the plates were cloned, but I've got a note of them.'

'Good,' said Tom.

'I took a break and followed her into the Abbey where one of the guests was showing her the visitors book. There's no bars on the windows at STAND, but we have it drummed into us that *every* visitor must sign in. Again, I found out later it was a fake name. Faye gave her the tour then they went into Simon's study.'

'And you've kept the recording?' asked Tom; Michael nodded. 'Forgive me for interrupting, but how much did you listen in to Doctor Swift's work?' Tom asked the question as if he were talking to a waiter, and it was very much a question I'd like answered, too. It wasn't lost on Michael.

'I give you my word that I neither listened in nor kept any recordings of therapy sessions.'

Tom acknowledged the statement with a nod, then asked him to continue.

'The woman called herself Fiona. She said that her brother was in detox and wanted to pay for him to come here. Painted a picture of a younger sibling who wasn't going to inherit the family estate and got into trouble. That sort of thing.'

'Sounds reasonable. What made you suspicious?'

'The way she kept eyeing up the secure cabinets. She even got up and pretended to admire a picture so she could get a closer look.' He tried to make himself more comfortable in the restraints (Saffron always gets carried away with those). And for the first time since we'd burst in, Michael actually looked guilty.

'I'm sorry about this, but I got it wrong,' he said. 'I thought she was either a journalist or in my game. I didn't think she'd come to rescue Don, so I said nothing.'

'And what is *your game*?' asked Tom.

'Corporate security. And corporate espionage for the right fee.'

'Aah. I see. Go on – what did you do about her?'

'I assumed she'd be back, so I put extra sensors on Simon's study.'

Michael was starting to look scared the closer he got to last night. I've seen it many times in witnesses or suspects, and so has Tom. 'What happened?'

'I got a shock when they were triggered at ten o'clock and I looked in to see a naked Doctor Swift going to bed on the couch. I closed my laptop and went to sleep. The sensors went off again at three, and I would have ignored them only the outside one was triggered first. I took a quick look.'

His mouth had gone dry and his story ran into the sand. He tried to swallow, coughed and said, 'See for yourselves. I've cued it up ready because I knew you'd be here sooner or later.'

Tom made no move to watch the video. What he did was open the complimentary bottle of mineral water and give Michael a drink. 'Why not sound the alarm? Why not call us? Why did you run?'

Michael shook his head, still trying to process what he'd seen. 'I didn't want to sound the alarm because of what he's capable of. I didn't call the police because I wanted to come here. It was always my plan to come here, to try and stand in Leo's shoes. I knew that if I called you lot, I'd be stuck. I wanted to come in my own time and say goodbye to Leo in my own way.'

Tom looked at me, and I tried to give a micro-shrug. Neither of us quite believed what Michael was saying, but breaking down that part of his story wasn't our top priority. Tom moved round to view the laptop and beckoned me to join him.

'Make sure the sound's on high,' said Michael. 'You won't believe me otherwise.'

Saffron woke the laptop, pressed Play on the video, and a greenish view of Simon's study came to life. The man himself was fast asleep and snoring like a sawmill. The buzz and drone continued for ten seconds, then it stopped. Completely. Utter silence, or should I say utter *Silence*.

The camera was mounted above the internal door, and had a wide angle lens which caught the garden doors opening, and tracked a figure moving into the room, crossing the floor and putting the light on.

The low-light cameras and his movement effectively blurred his features, but he was average height, well-built and not at all nimble. As soon as the room lights flicked on, I swore inside and Saffron swore quite audibly as she paused the video.

'I take it you know him?' said Tom drily. 'And now Michael knows that you know him, Sammi. Never mind. Keep it running.'

As soon as the light came on in the study, Simon jerked upright and the intruder flinched backwards, just as scared. Simon's mouth opened and no sound emerged. He struggled out of the duvet and stood up, backing towards his desk and still trying to speak. The other man ran towards him, there was a struggle which Simon appeared to be winning, and then it happened.

Almost in slow motion, the man pushed with his hands and Simon was flung off his feet, up and backwards into the wall. All three of us watching jumped as the mute body of Dr Simon Swift slammed into the plaster and *flattened* ever so slightly, lingered with its feet in the air, then dropped like a sack of meat to the floor.

'Oh fuck,' said Saffron slowly.

None of us moved or could drag our eyes off the screen as the intruder went to look at what he'd done, put his hand to his mouth, then ran out of the french doors.

'He comes back in one minute twenty seconds,' said Michael, his voice tight with forced levity. 'Then it gets really weird.'

We sat it out in silence until I said, 'Stop it! Go back four seconds. There. Look at the window next to the door. A shadow.'

'You're good,' said Michael. 'Took me three goes to spot that. I wouldn't bother, though, you can't see anything.'

He was right: there was nothing to learn, and I doubt that technology would help us. Didn't matter, really. The murderer returned, ran to the cabinets and peeled the locks away with his bare hands, then proceeded to scatter folders all over the floor until he came to Don's. He had his back to us, so Michael wouldn't have known that it was the file of Donald Bell which was taken.

'Show's over,' said Michael. He couldn't see what we could see, but he knew exactly when the intruder walked out. 'There's two more minutes of empty room, then I disconnected my computer and got out of there.'

We straightened up and looked at each other for a second. Tom was about to speak, but Michael wasn't finished. 'There's another reason I came here, you know. I wanted my lawyer to know where I was when I was arrested, and I wanted to transfer the video to a safe place. Just so you know. Whatever crap it is you're trying to cover up, you won't do it by getting rid of me.'

'You're quite safe with us,' said Tom automatically, then he looked at me with the most intense raised eyebrows I've seen since my mother tried to teach me bridge.

'Come on,' I said to Michael.

I lifted him to his feet, cut the restraints and let him massage his wrists for a second. 'Bathroom, please.' I pushed him gently into motion, and when he'd stumbled into the en suite, I put new ties on, this time with his hands in front of him. I placed the bottle of mineral water on the sink and said, 'We're going to shut you in. Just for a minute. Don't try to listen at the door, because I may open it suddenly and crack your head open.'

'I don't want to know,' said Michael. 'I really don't.'

I closed the door on him and pointed to the opposite corner of the room, where we gathered and where Saffron made the Silence. We joined our hands in the centre, like Musketeers, and Tom said, 'Who is it? How do you know him?'

'Do you remember the Fire Games at Cherwell Roost? The one where Georgina outed Chris's affair with Eseld?' I asked. Tom hadn't been there, nor was it something he'd read in a report. All he'd heard was second hand gossip, and clearly none of that had focused on the Hawkinses' guests, for reasons I was about to discover.

'The man's name is Richard Geldart,' I told him. 'From a family of Mages near here. A place called…'

'Blackwater Tower,' said Tom, cutting me off. 'No wonder we never got invited there.' He pointed to the laptop. 'He's a third cousin or something.'

Chapter 43 — Blackwater Tower

Saffron and I were equally bemused, and shared a shrug. Tom rubbed his scar and looked out of the window. 'You've heard me mention the *Original* Thomas Morton, First Baron Throckton? Did I ever tell you that all the Mortons are descended from his *second* wife? His first wife was a Geldart and the heiress to the Blackwater Tower Estate. They lived there with her family for some years until she became ill. When she died, all the property went to their little girl, and Thomas wasn't even a trustee. It all makes sense now.'

He looked back at us. 'They were Mages and all the money stays with the Mages. Like your family, Saffron.'

'Yeah. It does. Only more so with the Geldarts.'

'Quite. The First Baron married his daughter's governess when the child was twelve and either chose to move out or was forced to move out a year later. Blackwater Tower isn't *that* close to Beckthorpe. It's a few valleys over, much further than Throckton.'

He grimaced, pulling his face in all sorts of directions. 'We're still in touch with them, but they keep their distance and almost always come to us, and Richard's never visited, which is why I didn't recognise him. In fact, I've only been there twice, and the last time was years and years ago. The second time I went, I asked why it was called Blackwater Tower, given that it's just a big old house with a turret and that it says *Blackwater Lodge* on the gatepost.'

'Mmmm,' said Saffron. 'How much of the Estate did you see?'

'They said it was all grouse moor on the other side of the hill.'

'They only use the Lodge for mundane business. In fact, I think Richard moved in there about ten years ago. Or so I've heard.'

He shook his head and sighed. 'As if my life wasn't already complicated enough. They've already said they'll be coming to Granddad's funeral. Is Richard the head of the family?'

'No,' said Saffron. 'That's Lady Eleanor Geldart. She was probably the one who came spying last week. Richard is their fixer and negotiator. How do we know it's him and not someone using a Glamour? Because Simon had no magick, it would be easy to keep up a disguise.'

Tom was two steps ahead of her. 'We know that because we've already discovered that the Abbey's CCTV was blanked out just prior to the break-in, a fact that Michael in there has assumed we know. And Because Eleanor did her reconnaissance, she knew there was no official CCTV in the study. They thought a Silence would be enough. What are we going to do, Conrad?'

I pulled my lip, thinking through the next steps and likely scenarios. 'They won't attack the King's Watch. Would you agree, Saff?'

'Yes, Chief. They have too much at stake.'

'But I wouldn't put it past them to lie through their teeth and deny everything. We'll pay them a surprise visit by Wasp, shall we? I'd very much like your help, Tom.'

'Good,' he said. 'I need to radio Elaine.'

We broke the Silence and he contacted his partner. 'Get Reception to order us a taxi. As soon as it arrives, tell it to wait and then come up here.' He released the button and asked Saffron to make sure the laptop's password protection was completely removed. I got straight on to a navigation App to plot our route.

The Enclave must have a lot of pulling power with local taxis because Elaine appeared before Saffron had finished fettling the laptop (fettling is a word Vicky taught me. Don't worry, it's not obscene, so you can use it freely).

'Elaine, we're going to follow a lead,' Tom told her.

'And you're not telling me because then I don't have to lie,' she added, then looked around. 'Where's…?'

'In the bathroom and probably listening in. Conrad?'

I opened the door and retrieved our prisoner. I'd found him sitting on the toilet lid, staring into space and not listening in at all.

'What's going to happen to Kathy?' he asked.

'Who knows?' said Tom. 'I can tell you that she won't be facing any criminal charges.'

'What about her kids? What are you going to tell Social Services?'

'Nothing. No hidden files. No blacklist. And if they ask, I'll say she was a witness who did her best to help us.'

He seemed satisfied. 'Then look under the bed. It might be useful.'

I used to be as flexible as Saffron. Once. She bent at the waist and whisked up the valance. Bending further, she retrieved a messenger bag, looked inside and grunted, then showed us. Lurking inside one of Kathy's freezer bags was a pen. Interesting.

Tom had a message for our prisoner. 'Miguel Ortiz, I am further arresting you on suspicion of breach of privacy. You are still under caution and do not have to say anything.' He paused. 'DC Fraser is going to accompany you to the Northallerton custody centre. I would strongly advise you to say nothing until I've been in touch.'

When he spoke the last words, he looked meaningfully at me, and I folded my arms to glare at Michael. He got the message.

'What do I do when I've booked him in?' asked Elaine.

'Get a lift back to the Abbey and update the SIO.'

'I really will get it in the neck then,' she responded.

'No you won't. You'll just blame Conrad and me. It's what I'd do. Shall we go?'

By mutual consent, we got the taxi driver to stop at a sandwich shop;

breakfast in Valhalla had been a long time ago. Not that I told Saff or Tom where we'd been, although Saff was bursting to ask. There was no mutual consent to my suggestion that we needed to stop at a newsagents for more cigarettes, so I made it a direct order. Sometimes you have to show true leadership.

We ate our elevenses standing around in the showground while I updated the Boss and Saffron tried to find out what was Occluded on the Blackwater Tower Estate, and Tom had a conversation with Lucy whilst declining several calls from the North Riding SIO.

'I have found no trace of anyone called Donald Bell or any mention of a missing Mage of around his age,' said Hannah after I'd given her the headlines. She paused, then dropped her voice. 'What do you think the Geldarts will do?'

'I don't know enough about them. Or about Donald Bell. It depends what their priorities are.'

'Then may Hashem guide you.'

Saffron was about to tell me something when the Wedding March burst out. Mina was home.

'Can you talk?' was her first question.

'For a while. This is a difficult situation, but not a dangerous one. Not yet. Tom's coming with us on a short flight to track down a missing Mage and a murderer.'

'And not instigating a cover-up into a government torture centre?' she asked, as if wondering whether I wanted sugar in my tea.

'Erm, no.'

'That is not what it says on the Internet. As soon as I turned on my phone, there was a Google alert for your name.'

'Damn. Hopefully Cheng will be on the case. Could you message him to make sure?'

'I already have. Are you even still at the Abbey?'

'No. Harrogate. Is everything okay?'

'With me, yes. With Myfanwy, I'm not so sure. I think she may be getting very close to giving birth, and I am not the person to be the responsible adult in that situation.'

'Get Ben's mum round, if she hasn't already moved in.'

'A good plan. Now, if you'll excuse me, I need to get changed. Oh, and if pictures of me in uniform ever appear anywhere, I shall divorce you. Take care, husband.'

'And you, Mrs Clarke.' I disconnected and looked up. 'What you got, Saff?'

'I risked a call to Murray. He was my predecessor,' she explained to Tom. 'He wasn't close to the Geldarts, and I span him a line about a no-notice inspection. Apparently there is a real Blackwater Tower Estate, and it has a lawn which they laid down especially for helicopters.' She tilted her head. 'A bit like Cherwell Roost. The only difference is that theirs looks like a rose garden on Google Earth. Is Mina okay?'

'Yes. Are we good to go?'

'Yup.' She hesitated. 'Murray couldn't tell me about any Wards, though.'

'Leave it with me.'

I called the Boss back and said, 'Give me twenty minutes and then call the Geldarts. Tell them to take down any Wards immediately and expect a chopper. I'd rather they had a small chance to move Don out than take a risk.'

'I agree. I'll message Saffron with an update.'

'Thanks.'

'Then we really are ready. All aboard.'

This is the third Mage stronghold I've approached by air. I've seen the cutting-edge eco-friendly home of the Mowbrays in Cornwall, the Palladian splendour of the Hawkins in Oxfordshire, and now I was descending towards the home of the Geldarts in the North Riding. It lies right on the shoulder of the North York Moors, not far from the village of Pickering, and I was looking forward to something truly Gothic and worthy of powerful users of magick. Something to go with the name.

'Is that it?' I asked Saffron, pointing to where a series of grey structures were appearing through the trees.

'Yes. The navigation is spot on,' she added, worried that I might be concerned about a Diversion Work.

'Then where's the Tower???'

'Over to the … north west. It's a folly, really, on top of a hill.'

I sighed, and I have no idea whether it carried over the intercom. 'Thanks.'

They didn't have a Gothic Castle, but they did have a lake, big enough to take boats on, and with a quaint bridge at the top. Several low-rise villas made of local gritstone had frontages to the water, and there were further buildings in the woods which spread out around the Estate.

I was heading for the far side of the lake, where a meadow had been laid out. Lenses glinted in the sun where landing lights had been hidden in bushes, and they'd even turned on a landing beacon. Very civilised, as was the golf buggy crossing the bridge to meet us. I made one final adjustment for the wind and caught sight of the Tower, away and up from the LZ.

Saffron watched carefully as I went through the Wasp's shutdown, a much abbreviated process compared to the Smurf (which does have *two* turbo engines). I pocketed the key, grabbed Great Fang and said, 'This should be interesting.'

'I hope not,' said Tom, not even trying to mutter. There's no point muttering with me around. Unless you *really* don't want me to hear.

The LZ was smooth and green and would make an excellent cricket pitch. That's the rich for you. It meant that the golf cart, an eight seater, could glide effortlessly to a stop in front of us. I recognised Eleanor Geldart from the Fire Games, and her daughter was driving. They stopped just far enough away that Eleanor would have time to get down before we descended on them.

She was keeping a very straight face as I limped up. 'Lady Geldart, I am here on the business of the King's Watch under the power vested in me by the Peculier Constable.' She was only half listening to me, because she only had eyes for my male partner.

'Thomas! Is that *you?*'

'DCI Morton is my partner in a joint investigation,' I said. 'And Saffron, of course.'

'Then who is this?' she asked, pointing to Sammi.

'Me, Lady Geldart,' said Saffron.

The matriarch did a double take at Saff's disguise and turned back to Tom, who intercepted her by folding his arms and saying, 'Deputy Constable Clarke is leading this part of the investigation.' She took a step backwards, closer to her daughter, and some of the polish had already gone from her act.

I was looking forward to seeing the CCTV from the Abbey at some point, because I wondered how much Glamour she would have used to disguise her rather aggressive high forehead and battleship bosom. In the genetic raffle, I'd say that the Mortons had held the winning ticket when it comes to looks. Magick, though, is another matter. Her daughter was obviously cut from the same cloth, but thirty years younger.

'You're here about Douglas,' said Lady G, making it a statement.

Douglas? Who's Douglas? I wondered, trying not to let it show when I said, 'Yes we are. Where is he?'

Her eyes flicked upwards and behind me. 'The Tower. It's secure. I am so sorry that it has come to this, Saffron,' she said.

And why was she apologising to Saffron all of a sudden? Her next remark was even more cryptic.

'I had no idea Manny would do something so stupid or dangerous as trying to break Douglas out of that place, and yes, I'm afraid that Manny lost control of the situation. He Unbound Douglas, and before Manny could do anything, Douglas had killed that man. I can only suppose it was in revenge for his treatment. I am dreadfully sorry.'

So, Donald Bell is really Douglas Geldart. I didn't doubt her about that, but as for the rest…

'Who's Manny?' I asked, and put the question to Saffron. Somewhere under her Sammi disguise, my young partner was going bright red.

'Emanuel Geldart, known as Manny. Eleanor's nephew. We were supposed to be going on a date next week, Chief.'

'Chief?' began Lady Geldart. 'Who…'

'Take us to the Tower,' I said, cutting her off. 'We'll deal with Douglas Geldart first, then follow up the other matter.'

She made no move to go. 'I had no idea what was going on at first, and by the time I'd worked it out, the news of Doctor Swift's death had been announced. I'm afraid that when I confronted Manny, he refused to surrender to the Watch, and I couldn't detain him. He has fled.'

'But you didn't report him missing?' said Tom, speaking up for the first time.

She stared at her distant cousin, presumably they've met before at some point. 'No. And I will take the consequences of that. I also had to deal with Douglas, don't forget.' She turned her head. 'Lily? What did I say?'

Her daughter had the same, rounded vowels as her mother. She probably went to the same school and was a member of the same house there. 'You said that as soon as Douglas was securely bound, you would contact the Watch. That was only an hour ago, and the Constable called us first.'

Tom looked at me, his face inscrutable. I've worked with him long enough to know that look and that gesture: *This is bullshit of the highest order, but I'll leave you to do the shovelling.*

'He's dead!' said Saffron, blurting out the words. 'Sorry, Chief, I've only just remembered. Doug, Douglas Geldart, died twenty years ago in an accident.'

'And that is what we all believed,' said Eleanor gravely. 'Until we got the anonymous letter. You'll want to see that, of course. I've preserved it carefully. We were wondering what to do, but Manny and Lily took matters into their own hands.'

They were in such a rush to confess that they were tripping over themselves. Lily stepped forwards. 'I went to the Abbey last week and found out that it was true, that Douglas was alive and Bound there. It was Emanuel who decided to release him.'

Tom cleared his throat, loudly enough for me to hear and thereby getting funny looks from everyone. 'You must be richer than the Treasury,' he observed. 'Because you've been paying for his confinement for all that time and you've not wondered what the fees were for?'

I found out later it was a gamble. Tom knew what STAND was charging for "Donald Bell's" board and care, and he had the start of the money trail. That the Geldarts were paying was a gamble which paid off the second I saw Lady G flinch back like she'd been slapped.

'If Manny has fled, and you two are here, who's guarding Douglas?' I asked, changing the subject and hoping to get her off guard.

'Richard. You've met him, I think, Mister Clarke.'

'Good. There will be plenty of time for explanations later, but if we have a murderer confined, that has to take priority. We should all fit in the buggy.'

'Wouldn't...'

I got in the front, next to the driver's seat, and saw that there was no lock, so Lily couldn't stop us if I ordered Saffron to drive. The same thought must have crossed Eleanor's mind, and she said, 'Of course.'

Tom slid in the third row, and Lily got in the front. Saffron was already on her phone, madly texting as she risked life and limb by taking the rear gunner's seat.

Lady Geldart took her time getting in, sneaking a surreptitious look at her watch. I half expected her to tell Lily to take the scenic route, but with the Tower squatting right in the line of sight, they had no option but to switch on head off.

Blackwater Tower is shaped a bit like the rook from a chess set, with a narrower waist than top, and big bold crenelations on the roof. It was also black, which no rock native to Yorkshire has a right to be.

We discovered why as we got closer: it was made of bricks and had been painted. And it appeared to be Glamoured, because my Third Eye was revealing a swirl of magick around the place as we bounced up a less than even path. I glanced back, relieved to see that Saffron had abandoned her messages to hold on tight.

The only person who spoke during the journey was Lady Geldart. She leaned over the seat in front to say to Tom, 'I'm sorry about Alexander. He was a very good man. A lovely man. How's your grandmother doing?'

'About as well as you'd expect, thank you,' he replied.

The Three Musketeers all stopped to crane our necks up and look at the Tower when we dismounted at its base. The windows were much bigger than you'd think, and had been cleverly recessed to give the impression of a more solid structure, aided by a Glamour which made them look black from a distance.

This was more than a folly. This was a major centre of magick. I looked back down to the lake and the villas around it, and I saw little or no evidence of occult activity. As I was turning back, Saffron touched me to pass on some news under Silence.

'The Boss says that Douglas Geldart had no convictions and there is almost no record of him at Merlyn's Tower, and barely even any links to the family. Most of the references are to Angel House in Cambridge.'

'Thanks.'

'I'd better go in and make sure everything's in order,' said Lady G in one last attempt to control the situation.

'We'll be fine,' I said cheerfully. 'Lily can guard the chariot while we're inside. After you.'

The big, iron studded door was already standing open. They probably don't close it when the tower is in use, because a boring oak door was doing the hard work at the end of a short corridor. This one was locked. Magickally. Eleanor fumbled for ages to find the Stamp, finally locating it in the most obvious pocket of her coat.

She was about to open the door when I said, 'Where are they? Which floor?'

'The basement. It's quite large and a bit of a warren. I'll show you.'

In other words: *you're not going in there on your own.* I smiled and nodded.

The ground floor of the tower was a single open space, dominated by a round table set with thirteen chairs. Of course it was. I should be used to this by now.

A huge picture window gave views over the lake and towards the Vale of York, and there was very little space for the cupboards and presses which no doubt held starched linen and cutlery. Most of the wall which wasn't window was taken up by the start of a staircase which spiralled up to the top floors and down to the basement. 'This way,' said Lady G, pointing down.

'I do rather think you'd better wait outside,' I told Lily, who'd followed us inside. To reinforce the point, I touched my Badge, then touched it again to bring up my Ancile. She turned and walked out.

Chapter 44 — Blackwater Basement

We followed Lady Geldart down the stairs, and they went much further underground than one level, going below the foundations of the tower and away from the load-bearing rock. At the end was a broad landing with three doors and a passageway leading off, and further, rougher stairs going down again. All in all, a very impressive magickal bunker.

'No wonder you need the buggy,' I said. 'It's a long way from the lake when you have magick to make.'

'There's a road which leads round the back, out of sight of the holding.' She looked at Tom. 'It also goes to the Lodge. I remember you coming as a young man, Thomas, and you very nearly made it through the Wards. Perhaps there's a drop of Geldart magick in you after all.'

'Unlikely,' said Tom, 'Given that I'm not descended from them.'

'Oh but you are! Lord Morton's second wife was a Geldart, too. But she had no magick, so....'

'So she ended up as a governess,' said Tom sourly. He didn't seem at all pleased by that.

'She was more than a governess,' said Eleanor. 'You'll find out soon enough. Anyway, there are three bedrooms above ground here, and there used to be...'

She was about to launch into the history of Blackwater Tower, so I interrupted her. 'And I look forward to exploring it all. Where are they?'

'The green door on the right. Let me check that it's safe.'

She went to stand in front of the door, and I said to Saffron, 'Is it locked?'

'No, Chief.'

'Tom, you wait here.' I unsheathed Great Fang and stepped forwards. 'We'll be fine, thanks.'

With a naked blade shimmering with magick in front of her nose, Lady Geldart wisely stepped aside, but only after knocking hard on the door.

It was a substantial door, and it was metal. The sort of thing you'd see on a ship or an aircraft. It was also pulsing with magick of the kind that went right over my head (my magickal stature is still closer to the pygmy than the giant).

There was no catch, just a handle to push, so I pushed. Hard. The door swung open, and there was a scene which had GUILTY written all over it.

Douglas Geldart was lying back in something resembling an antique dentist's chair, and yes, his arms were bound. But so was his mouth, and that alone made me stop on the threshold. I have seen some grotesque things, many of them authored by the Fae, and something in the way that the insubstantial silver thread pulsed with a light that glowed into the Royal Violet made me suspect non-human magick straight away. Thinking about that helped me ignore what they'd done. For half a second.

Silver threads of magick pierced his lips, sewing his mouth shut, and Kathy had glimpsed them, but they went further: his Third Eye was partially covered with a gauze, some of which had come away, and what I can only describe as a crown of thorns was stitched into his forehead. And trying to unpick it all was Richard Geldart, holding a Blade of the Art.

It was part of their story that Douglas had to be blamed for the murder of Simon Swift, and if they'd handed over Doug's corpse with the bindings still in place, or worse, if they handed him over alive and bound – then even I would know that Douglas hadn't killed anyone.

I took all this in as I was advancing towards the pair. I also saw that this was their medical room, with an equally antique operating table also present. Was any of this licensed? Had Murray Pollard been down here to ask what in Odin's name they were up to?

'Step away from Douglas,' I said to Richard. 'And hand over the Blade to Watch Captain Hawkins.'

'But I've started,' said Richard, 'There are safety Wards on these Bindings, and if I don't unravel them soon, they could activate and kill him.'

'Step away and hand over the Blade. Saffron, check out what he says.'

'It's over, Richard,' said Lady Geldart. 'You'll have to face the consequences, I'm afraid. I gave you long enough to sort this out.'

How typically Mage. The problem wasn't that Richard had Blasted Simon Swift to a pulp. Oh no. The problem was that he hadn't practised his magick enough.

Saffron stepped closer to Richard, and was just in time to stop him stabbing the defenceless Douglas in the chest. She grabbed his arm and twisted it away, pulling him towards the dentist's chair and banging into the side, still tussling for control of the Blade. The next few moments happened in disastrous slow-motion, and there was nothing I could do to stop it.

Douglas Geldart drew on the Lux in the chair, and the ropes holding his arms burst into flames, a bright white conflagration. He ripped his right arm free and grabbed Saffron's Badge of office from its sheath. Her Mark of Caledfwlch is stamped into a knife, and Douglas Geldart shouldn't be able to touch it, let alone bypass Nimue's magick and use the Badge as a weapon, but that's what he did, and he slashed at Richard's arm. And missed.

Saffron grunted with pain as blood welled out of her forearm, and she let go of Richard. Richard stared at Douglas in shock, and I was trying to get an angle to use Great Fang without simply scything them down. Then Douglas reversed his grip, hacked at the stitches on his mouth, and when they were severed, he roared with pain and anger and hatred.

I could see that his hands were crippled with the Mage's Curse of arthritis, and he wasn't going to be doing any fine work with them: the blood running down his face was testimony to that. But he could stab. There was nothing wrong with his grip.

337

He slashed at Richard. Saffron had recovered from the initial shock and put herself in the way, trying to grab Doug's hand. The old Mage had added power to his arm, and he missed his cousin completely and smashed his blade into Saffron's chest. I even think I heard a rib crack, though that might have been my subconscious supplying the sound effect.

Saffron started to collapse, and Douglas stared in horror at what he'd done. At this range, with limited room, I had no option but to drop Great Fang and try to smother Douglas before his reactions kicked in, and I would have succeeded if Richard hadn't put himself first.

Dropping Great Fang had severed the bond which created my Ancile, and Richard tried to Blast me out of the way, using uncontrolled force the way he had with Simon Swift. As his hands came up in the same gesture I'd seen on the video, I knew that I couldn't dodge or dive, and that I'd soon be jelly. All I had time to do was reach into the reserves of Lux in my titanium tibia and try to fight fire with fire and air with air.

Two accelerated fronts of compressed air met in the space between us, and my timing had been good enough to deflect his Blast away from my head. If only I had the power to go with it.

The two fronts met with a thunderous boom, and the backwash from the concussion hit my side, throwing me across the room and into the operating table. I covered my head and my left arm hit the metalwork with a jarring crack, and then I was in a heap on the floor.

I ignored my arm, which was stretched out on the floor, and tried to focus on what was going to happen next. From my position, I could see red spreading out from Saffron's body, and the two Geldarts standing in a face off, Richard with his Blade of Art and Douglas still holding the stolen Badge of Office.

Douglas looked around, and the gauze which had been covering his Third Eye was almost gone, just tatters left where it had been stitched to his forehead. I was still trying to work out whether my arm was broken, and I realised that Doug wasn't looking at me, he was looking at my wedding ring. The Troth Ring. The one given to me by Odin.

Our eyes locked, and he knew that I knew about Raven. He groaned with a pain that went deeper than any of his torture or self-inflicted wounds, and he turned to face Richard again. He made a mighty slash that I would have dodged and riposted, but Richard leapt back and tripped over poor Saffron, landing on his arse with a bump and dropping his Blade.

Instead of going in for the kill, Douglas headed for the door, menacing Lady Geldart as he passed. You may have noticed that she had made no effort to intervene. I suppose I should be grateful she hadn't tried to help Richard.

Douglas was a different man to the one whom Kathy had described. Yes, he was old and suffering from arthritis, but he didn't shuffle, he ran with a limp and being a Geldart who'd grown up and learnt magick in Blackwater

Tower, he knew exactly where to go, and it wasn't to the staircase.

I had recovered my breath enough to roll away from my arm and try to move it. Owww! Bloody hell, that *hurt*. It also moved, as did my fingers. I pressed gingerly on the floor. More pain, but no collapse. Up you get, Clarke.

Richard Geldart also got up, took one look at me, and then legged it through the door, where Tom executed a perfect rugby tackle, bringing him to the floor and doing something I've never seen Tom do before: execute extreme violence.

Richard had hit the ground with a thump and a grunt, but he was still a Mage with deadly powers. Tom did the one thing he thought might buy him some time and grabbed the back of Richard's head before smashing his face into the stone floor. Blood burst out from his nose and there was already a huge red stain when Tom did it again.

I pointed the tip of Great Fang at Lady Geldart. 'Your nephew is under arrest. If he escapes, or Odin forbid, if he harms one hair on Tom Morton's head, then I will hold you personally accountable. Not professionally, *personally*. Are we clear?'

'What about Douglas?'

'Fuck him. I asked if you understood.'

She gave a curt nod. 'Leave him with me.'

I sheathed Great Fang as I dashed to Saffron's side. 'Bring cloths. Bandages. Anything!' I shouted.

Tom was at my side, taking off his tie. 'Do we need to tourniquet that arm first?'

'No. Just wrap it tightly. And we need to stuff the chest wound.'

Tom looked properly at her chest, then looked away. I don't blame him. Her right breast was sliced deeply, two ribs smashed and I could see lung poking out. Thankfully she seemed to have passed out. I was about to tear open her teeshirt when a different shadow loomed over me.

'Tom's watching Richard,' said Lady Geldart, tearing up a sheet. 'You hold her, I'll wrap her.'

She worked quickly under my direction, and in two minutes we'd done all we could do here. 'Give me a second, then I'll try to lift her.'

'Shall I call an ambulance?'

I shook my head. 'I'll fly her to Jimmy's in Leeds. I'll be almost there before an ambulance could get …'

The whole tower rumbled. Not with an earthquake, because nothing was moving. It was as if every crystal in the rock, and every atom in every crystal was vibrating. And glowing.

Blinding swirls of Lux shot up from the floor like flames, and they passed through the ceiling into the ground above. The Lux was coloured, mostly towards the violet and there were flickers of silver in it.

'What the fuck was that?'

'A beacon,' said Eleanor Geldart. 'We use it to make FireLux on festivals, but he's tapped our primary Ley line. That must have been visible from space.'

'Mundane visible?'

She shook her head. 'No, and there's no time to worry about that now.'

'Mum! What's happening?'

Lily Geldart rushed in, terror and then shock written all over her face.

'Good,' I said. 'You're going to drive us to the chopper then sit in the back with Saffron.'

'What? Oh. What's happened?'

'Never mind. Put your hands under her arse and when I try to stand up, lift as hard as you can. It'll take some of the weight off my back.'

'Come on!' urged her mother. 'Wake up, girl.'

I couldn't have done it without her. Saffron isn't huge, but she's a grown woman, and doing a stoop lift without help would have crippled me. I am not a Gnome.

When she was cradled in my arms, I started walking because there was still a flight of stairs to negotiate, and my left arm was already starting to throb from where I'd banged into the table.

As I passed through the hallway, I saw Tom with his foot on Richard Geldart's neck. 'Tom! Call control and tell them to expect a hot offload at Saint James's Hospital in Leeds. Then call the Boss. Then call Mina and tell her to get on to Faith.'

Lily ran in front of me to clear things out of the way and hold the door open. The jolting of the staircase stirred Saffron half awake, and she groaned with pain. 'Don't try to talk,' I said through gritted teeth. 'We're heading for the chopper. You'll get morphine in no time.'

I had to stop and stare when I got through the tower's front door. From somewhere down the slope and to the right, on a level with the underground workshops, I saw Douglas Geldart emerge. A secret entrance. Or exit.

He looked around, saw what I was doing and actually waved, then he jogged down the slope towards some trees. I forced him out of my mind and made it to the buggy before I had to drop Saffron and scream.

I knelt on the floor of the cart so that I could hold her in place on the seat. Lily drove as carefully as she could, but the downhill track was not flat, and every time we swayed or bumped, more blood escaped from the dressings and more groans escaped Saff's mouth. When we got to the flat, Lily sped us to the Wasp.

'Same again,' I told her after I'd opened the doors. 'Make sure you give me as much help as you can.'

She did, and I only staggered a little as we transferred Saffron to the cramped space behind the pilot's seat. 'Not long now, Saff,' I told her. There was blood running down her face from where she'd bitten her lip nearly through, and I think she'd passed out again. 'Try to keep her awake,' I said to

Third Eye

Lily as I chucked Great Fang in the front and got out the key.

Chapter 45 — Family Values

Air Traffic Control tried to get me to fly to York. For about ten seconds. And after that, it was just a question of whether the internal injuries to Saffron, the ones I was trying not to think about, would prove too serious for her to survive the flight.

She was still alive when the paramedic team loaded her on to the stretcher, and I kicked Lily Geldart out of the Wasp to answer all the questions that were about to rain down on us. As soon as they'd cleared the LZ, I put the power back up and lifted off. There was a policeman lurking in the background who looked like he might want to detain me. No chance.

There was no one I could contact by radio, and I ignored my phone when I got back to Blackwater Tower. The golf cart was exactly where we'd left it, and I zoomed up to the tower as fast as I could. This was partly to avoid thinking about what had happened, but driving a buggy doesn't take up nearly as much brain capacity as flying, so the image of Saffron lying on the basement floor came straight back to haunt me, just like images of Vicky dead on the Welsh hills, Vicky with a knife in her back, Dom Richmond's smashed pelvis, the arrow sticking out of Elaine's thigh…

For now, I had to shake my head and get rid of it. There was no trace of Douglas Geldart's light show in the tower's bricks, and my Third Eye told me that he'd ripped out some of the existing Glamours to create his Beacon. The more I considered what I'd seen and heard, the more I realised that we'd had a lucky escape. Very lucky in my case; less so in Saffron's.

The front door came into view, and there was a reception committee outside. Richard Geldart was sitting on the floor, his hands tied behind his back and his face a mess; Tom was standing over him, phone clamped to his ear. Lady Geldart was there, too, watching Richard with her arms folded in front of her chest.

Tom disconnected his call and waited for me to limp over. 'She's in the hands of the surgeons now,' I told him, then shrugged. 'I wish I could tell you more.'

He nodded grimly. 'Hannah is waiting for you to call, and she took it on herself to tell Saffron's mother. Mina is getting in touch with Faith, but she's not entirely sure why.'

'Because the Red Queen is either mixed up in this or hasn't told me something, that's why.'

I hadn't bothered with a Silence, and it was Eleanor who started to pull back the curtain. 'The Queen of Derwent was supposed to be maintaining Douglas's Bindings,' she said. 'Where's Lily?'

'In Leeds. She did a good job during the transfer and someone had to give the hospital Saffron's details. I think it's time to start telling the truth. Is there a fridge in there by any chance?'

'Lily keeps it well stocked with Diet Pepsi. Would you both like one?'

'Can you watch him?' said Tom. 'I need to find a bush to pee behind.'

'I can do more than watch him. It's about time I arrested him.'

'Oh. In that case I'll stay.'

The powers of magickal arrest go further and deeper than just telling someone they're nicked. The Badge of Office stamped into Great Fang is more than a symbol: it's a collection of Works which can severely dampen someone's magick and put them into a Silence. Along with the Enhanced Restraints which I was about to use, it would give Richard Geldart a taste of what his future held in the Undercroft.

I stared into his eyes, one of which was half closed. Tom had wiped most of the blood off his face but it was still trying to ooze out of his shattered nose.

'I didn't do it,' he said, and I saw that he'd lost two teeth as well. Blimey, no wonder the fight had gone out of him.

'Tell that to the Cloister Court. Richard Geldart, you are a piece of shit and you are also under arrest. You will be arraigned in due course. And if DCI Morton were not a gentleman, I'm sure he'd piss over you instead of behind the bush.'

I touched my Badge, and for the first time since it was struck, a Mage pushed back, resisting the Binding.

'You and whose army?' he said.

'Mother Earth,' I replied, touching the tip of Great Fang to the ground and drawing the power from the iron deep below the green grass. Geldart slumped back and tilted to the side, overwhelmed and for now out of the picture.

'I wouldn't do that to you,' said Tom.

'Sorry?'

'Urinate on a man you might have to transport in your helicopter,' he said mildly. 'Especially as I might be with him.'

I snorted with suppressed laughter, then coughed, then we corpsed together, and the only way Tom could stop laughing was to go and find his bush. He got back just as Lady Geldart emerged from the tower carrying a tray with three cans of Pepsi and Saffron's Badge of Office.

'I found this outside the tunnel leading to the old entrance. After all these years, Douglas could still remember the Work to unlock it.' She shook her head and put the tray down before passing us a drink.

I slaked my thirst, lit a cigarette and said, 'What do you know and when did you learn it?'

'My aunt told me when she was dying. We don't make a big fuss about it, but the Geldarts have our own title: Warden of Blackwater Tower. I succeeded my aunt as Warden, and she was Douglas's mother. She gave me the Stamp to unlock the Warden's safe and told me to bring the envelope on top.' She looked away and into the past. 'It was the first time I'd seen inside the safe, and there on the top was an envelope marked *To be opened urgently in the event of my death*. It was bent and marked from being lifted, but it had never been opened. She obviously thought it was so important that it should always be there. Always be the first thing she saw. I took it to her and she told me to open it and read it.'

'How long ago was this?'

'Coming up to ten years.'

'And what did it say?'

'It was short and to the point. The original is still there, but I can tell you pretty much what it said. *Douglas is still alive. He was Bound by the Red Queen and is confined to a nursing home in Beckthorpe. The money comes from the Black Sheep Trust, which you must always keep topped up. He must NEVER be released. NEVER.*'

She broke off to compose herself. 'The next part hurts the most. *His crimes must die with him. If he were not my son, I would have ensured that they did.*'

We waited. She shook her head. 'The first thing I asked my aunt was, *What did he do?* And she just shook her head and said, "Monstrous. I gave birth to a monster, and he married a worse one." Of course I looked in the archives and even spoke to the lawyer who'd handled his estate when his mother had him declared dead. No clues, but I knew he must have hidden most of his wealth.'

'And you didn't go to see him?' asked Tom, as if he were dotting an *i*.

'I thought about it. I was very tempted. And then a week turned into a month, and a month turned into a season, and I realised that I was afraid of what I'd find. He was out of sight and out of mind. Until I got the anonymous letter, I had no idea even that the Abbey had turned from a nursing home into an addiction centre. I presume you want to see the letter?'

Tom and I exchanged glances, and I let him ask the question. 'You're saying that you didn't know that his Bindings were loose, or whatever the technical terms are?'

She shook her head. 'No. No idea, until I got the letter. The original is at the Boathouse. Where I live. Let me Airdrop a copy to you both. It should be of special interest to Conrad.'

'It was addressed to you personally?' asked Tom as we got out our phones.

She didn't answer, but she did send two pictures, one of an envelope which was personally addressed to Eleanor Geldart, the Boathouse, Blackwater Tower Estate; the other was a picture of a letter, computer printed on A4 paper and as you'd expect, unsigned.

Douglas Geldart's bindings are loose. If you don't want the Fae or Conrad Bloody Clarke trampling all over your family, you'll get him out and lock him up at the bottom of Blackwater Tower.

'Apart from the effect this will have on Conrad's fragile ego, who do you think sent it?'

'I have no idea, and neither did Richard. He…'

Tom held up his hand to stop her and studied an incoming message on his phone. 'Excuse us a minute.'

He walked backwards, and I followed him. 'Can you put a Silence on us that will allow me to hear a phone call?'

'If you put it on speaker, I should be able to manage. What's up?'

'I've blocked all calls, but Elaine's just messaged me to say that I have to take it when she rings in a minute.'

I made the Work and we waited. And waited. Then his phone burst into life.

'Sir?'

Her voice had a weird quality, and I wondered if I'd made a mess of the Silence.

'I'm in the toilets,' she hissed. Oh. That explained it.

'Go on,' said Tom.

'There's a call come in just down the road from you, in Pickering. An old lady was carjacked at gunpoint by an old man answering Donald's, I mean *Douglas*'s description. She's at the local station, but they've put out a call for help.'

'Show me as responding, and quote the Angel of Death if you have to,' said Tom. 'Thanks.'

'You told her? About Douglas?' I said.

'Of course. I also told her that we had a suspect in custody for the murder. They weren't happy, but I said that MI7 would pay for the overtime on this case.'

'Fancy a swap, Tom? Mina for Lucy? I think you two are much better suited.'

'I'll tell her you said that. What are we going to do with Richard?'

'Leave him here and call for another Watch Captain to pick him up. I am not risking a desperate Mage in the Wasp.'

'You want to fly there?'

'Of course. There's bound to be a cricket pitch near the police station.'

We told Eleanor that we were leaving and that someone would collect Richard. She didn't look happy, but I suspect that happiness is a long way off in her calendar. 'You drive the buggy, Tom; I need to message Faith and the Boss.'

He seemed uneasy. 'You're going to ask Faith about this business with the Red Queen? Wouldn't it be safer to ask Matt Eldridge to look into it?'

'Faith has pretty much severed all ties to the Queen of Derwent. She might not be happy, but happiness is in short supply today.' I paused, my hand on the metal struts of the buggy. 'You've lost your grandfather, Tom. You were there when he was in hospital. Me? I got married yesterday and spent last night as a guest in Valhalla.'

He nodded. 'Send your messages before we go. And finish that drink. I don't want you getting indigestion or hiccups while we're in the air.'

Chapter 46 — Gone to Ground

'This is Conrad Clarke. He's with me on work experience. He's thinking of joining the police now that he has to leave the RAF.'

As an excuse for having a man in uniform sit in on an interview, it was appropriate for the witness, I suppose. Did nothing for my ego though. I smiled at Mrs Jeavons and added, 'Just ignore me.'

I wouldn't dream of describing our witness as a *little old lady*, even though she was most certainly little, definitely old and very much a lady. She looked at me through the top half of her glasses and said, 'Aren't you a bit old to be joining the police? And how will you chase people with that bad leg?'

Tom smiled. 'He makes a good cup of tea, so perhaps we'll find room for him in the office.'

'It'll need to be a big office to fit him in it.' She tasted the tea I'd made. 'Perhaps you're right.'

'Just to be sure,' said Tom, 'are you feeling up to going through it all again? It sounds horrific.'

Mrs Jeavons shifted in her seat. 'Could you show me the ladies room? This is my third cup of tea, you know.'

'Of course. As soon as I find out where it is.' He leapt up, shouted for help, and one of the Pickering officers led her away.

We were in their only interview room, and they'd had to squeeze in the table with recording equipment alongside something less intimidating. I had taken the chair normally reserved for suspects while Tom and Mrs Jeavons were going to have a civilised chat in two padded chairs over a coffee table.

Tom was about to say something when Faith finally messaged me back – I'd been checking my phone constantly since we landed twenty minutes ago. *This is bad news. I don't know all the details, but Her Grace is negligent not culpable. Do I have your permission to tell her before we speak? I will know more that way.*

I read the message to Tom. 'You know them, Conrad,' he replied. 'I don't. Not yet.'

'It could come back to bite me on the arse either way.' I drummed my fingers on the table and made a decision. 'The Red Queen is a lazy cow most of the time. If she can offload a problem, she will.' I picked up the phone and typed *Do it. I'll Whatsapp video you in an hour or so.*

Mrs Jeavons was shown back in, and she'd taken the chance to freshen her lipstick. Tom made sure she was comfortable and began by asking where she was heading when it happened.

'Into Pickering to change my library books. And those of some of the villagers who can't get out so easily. And some shopping. And maybe a visit to the café. Wednesdays are a big day, you know,' she added with a smile. 'I need to rest on Thursdays.'

She found it amusing, but I couldn't work out whether she was being ironic or making a joke out of declining health.

'And you were on the road which passes Blackwater Lodge?'

'I'll take your word for it, Inspector. I just know it as the Pickering Road. Mind you, I've often wondered who lived in the big house. They don't appear in our village.'

'I know you've gone over this twice already,' he said, lifting her signed statement off the table to show he'd read it. 'It's just that what happened to you may be connected to a more serious case I'm working on.'

She sipped her tea. 'More serious than being threatened at gun point?'

Tom hesitated, then said, 'Yes. I'm afraid so. A murder enquiry over in Beckthorpe.'

'Aah. I thought so. The man who took my statement was very cagey when I asked him if they were connected. Very well, so long as this is the last time, let's get it over with. It was like this. I don't go very fast down that road with the woods on either side because it's quite narrow. I came round the corner, and there he was, an old man standing in the middle of the road looking lost. I stopped and wound down the window and asked him if he needed any help.'

'Could you describe him, please?'

'Of course. He was about my age, I suppose, and didn't look very well cared for. You know: badly shaved and hair a mess. He was wearing a very old checked shirt, trousers cut for a much younger man and velcro training shoes. My first thought was *Is there a nursing home near here?*'

She had described Douglas Geldart to a tee. Tom didn't break eye contact with her to look at me while she spoke. He really is very good at this.

'I can understand that,' he said. 'What did he say?'

'He said, "You are most kind," in a very hoarse voice. Well educated by the sound of it. Then he said, "I seem to have got lost. I've got my niece's number written down. I'm staying with her for a bit and went for a walk. Do you have a mobile telephone with you?" It was the way he said *mobile telephone* that made me take pity, especially when I saw his hands. Terrible arthritis. He couldn't even use one of those phones from Age Concern, the ones with the big buttons. I felt ever so sorry for him. And for his niece.'

'You're a true Good Samaritan,' said Tom.

She blushed every so slightly. 'An apt comparison, Inspector. I must confess that thought did go through my mind: the outcast who helps the victim found by the road when others won't. Other cars must have passed him, you know, and that was my next thought: I was in the middle of the road. Not safe.'

'No.'

'So I said, "Get in and I'll pull off the road." He struggled with the door, but he managed, and he said, "I believe I saw a track round the corner," so I drove round the bend, and there was an open lane marked *Blackwater Tower*

Estate. Private Drive. I was quite proud of reversing in.'

She finished her tea. I'd read her statement, too, and I knew what was coming next. She was holding up well, but going over traumatic memories is never easy. She turned in her seat. 'This may be my third cup of tea, but it's by far the best. Shame they only had Jammy Dodgers left, though. They do stick to my palate.'

'Take your time,' said Tom.

'Well, I'm not entirely sure what happened next, but he touched my shoulder, and it was like a really bad charge of static electricity. Do you think it could have been a cattle prod, like they have on the telly?'

Tom and I had discussed how to account for this. 'Most likely a small hand-held TASER,' he replied. 'Nasty but not dangerous.'

'Quite. I may have screamed. I don't know. When I looked up, the road had gone fuzzy, and I thought for a second I might be having a stroke, and then I saw the gun.' She shuddered. 'It was an automatic, small but clean and very deadly looking. But that wasn't the worst thing.'

'It sounds bad enough.'

'It was. No, the worst thing was his voice. It was the voice of the dead. No more lost old man.' Tom said nothing, waiting for her to continue in her own time. 'He said, and I'll never forget this. He said, "You will do exactly as I say or I will shoot you and flag down someone else until I get what I want."'

She breathed out. 'I don't know what came over me, but I said, "How do I know you won't shoot me anyway?" and he laughed. "Because I need the company while we wait," he told me. "Get out your phone and dial this number, then hand it to me. And don't try pressing the emergency call button."'

'Was the number written down?'

She looked uncomfortable. 'No. He knew it off by heart, and I'm so sorry, but it went in one ear and out of the other. I feel so *guilty* for not remembering it. I used to be able to. Had to.'

'We're already looking it up,' said Tom. 'You have absolutely *nothing* to feel guilty about.'

'That's as maybe. I dialled the number and gave him the phone, and I wish I could tell you what he said, because I think he must have shocked me again.'

'Why do you say that?'

'Because his lips moved and no sound came out. What other explanation could there be?'

That she'd been placed under a Silence, but we weren't going to go there.

'What happened next?'

'He gripped the phone in both hands for a second, then dropped it in the cup holder. "Now we wait," he told me. "Put the radio on if you want. Your choice." I looked down at the gun in his lap and thought about being a strong independent woman who can look after herself. And then I thought about the electric shock, so I put on Radio Two and tried not to hyperventilate.'

'It sounds like you did superbly,' said Tom.

'Being a headmistress for thirty years prepares you for a lot of things, but this was new.'

'Did he say anything else?'

'Not while we waited, no. And I was too scared to start a conversation, so we sat through two songs and then the news. He perked up at that point and listened carefully. I think I know why now, if he's a murderer, but it was the national news so they didn't mention what had happened in Beckthorpe.'

'He's not a suspect in the murder enquiry,' said Tom diplomatically. 'So the car came just after the hourly news?'

'It did. I told you the road looked funny? Well, all of a sudden it changed, and a big Mercedes appeared. I couldn't tell who was driving it because of the sunlight on the windscreen. He said, "Aah. Here we go. Keys, please, and stay in the car until I've gone." And then he went. He got out, dropped a stick of wood on the seat and shuffled off to the car. Arthritis in his hip as well as his hands. As soon as the car reversed on to the road, I tried to use my phone, but the screen was black, as if it was burnt. Your colleague has it now.'

'I won't bore you with the car,' said Tom. 'I know you went through that, and well done for remembering the registration number.'

'The *index* you mean,' she said with an attempt at a smile. 'Yes. Did I get it right? Your colleague wouldn't tell me.'

The local officer had gone through Mercedes models with her on Google, and had obviously run the index. 'You did remember it correctly,' said Tom. 'Unfortunately, they were cloned plates. Unless you mistook a thirty-eight tonne Foden lorry for a Mercedes G Class.'

She sighed. 'Never mind. I forced myself to wait five minutes, then ran into the road. Do you know that *three* cars drove past before someone stopped to help me.'

'Thank you, Mrs Jeavons. We are very grateful, and your information could make a huge difference. I believe your daughter is coming up from York?'

She was having trouble holding it together now. 'She is. As soon as I call to tell her I've finished. When will I get my car back?'

'I'm sorry, but organising a car transporter is out of my hands.'

'I don't want it transported anywhere, I just want it released. I have spare keys. I imagine your forensic people have been analysing it.'

Tom shook his head. 'Budget cuts, I'm afraid. Your statement and witness evidence will be enough. I'm going to leave you in the hands of the local police now. Someone will take you to a phone so you can call your daughter. Thanks again.'

She didn't get up, and we shook hands and left her to stare at the Jammy Dodgers. Tom updated the sergeant in charge, and we left the station and headed to the cricket pitch. 'Why didn't you show her the video of Douglas?' I asked him.

'No point. Same with forensic evidence. He'll never face trial for this, will he?'

I sighed. 'No, he won't. I doubt there will even be a chance for a Watkins Trial.'

Tom shot me a sharp look. 'I've seen a couple of references to them. What are they?'

'Josiah Watkins murdered the vicar of his parish. Very publicly. In church, in fact, during holy communion. I think it was something to do with an image of the Virgin Mary. Or a woman called Mary who should have been a virgin but wasn't. One or the other. That was back in the 1690s, and there was a big fuss.'

'I'd imagine there would be. He was a Mage?'

'He was. A fully paid up member of the Invisible College. The congregation subdued him, and he didn't fight back, which left the Peculier Constable and the Cloister Court with a problem. Their solution was to sentence him to the Undercroft as usual and get a royal warrant for another Mage under Glamour to stand trial in the mundane court, plead guilty and go through a mock execution.'

'Is that what will happen to Richard?'

'Yes. Minus the public execution, of course. Assuming the Cloister Court convicts him.'

'Is there any doubt about that?'

'Even Augusta Faulkner would advise him to plead guilty. Unless he's going to blame Eleanor, of course. Not my problem.'

We had reached the clubhouse, and Tom stopped walking. 'Three years in the Undercroft instead of twenty-five in Full Sutton. Hardly seems fair.'

'Tom, much as I love to share my pain, I sincerely hope you never truly understand what it's like to be in a Limbo Chamber.'

'Another thing on which I'll have to take your word.' He stopped rubbing his scar and shook his head. 'Who did Douglas call, do you think?'

'Get Elaine to check all vehicles registered to the Blackwater Tower Estate. One of them will be a black G Class Mercedes. Douglas clearly knew there was someone in the family or on the staff who would help him.'

'One second.' He placed a quick call giving Elaine her mission, then said, 'Do you think he remembered that number all these years?'

'Who knows? Maybe there was a directory in the Tower and he looked at that. The big question is who he gets handed over to.'

'What do you mean?'

'I'm fairly sure he wants to go wherever his wife is. If she's still alive. Let's call Faith and see what she has to say.'

Faith took the call in the magickal version of a building site. Tamsin is working on creating the multiple levels which will soon make up a Royal Sídhe, but having access to the higher plane is only part of the construction: you need to dig out the chambers as well. And put in plumbing. And Wi-Fi.

'Are you alone?' I asked.

'Yes. I've cleared and sealed this level because it's the one with the router on it.'

Faith owns a High Unicorn, and tries to ride him every day she's at Staveley. She was still dressed for the saddle, and her hair was braided immaculately. That would be Alicia's handiwork.

'This is difficult,' she began. 'How is Saffron?'

She had a right to ask, I suppose, not that there was much I could tell her. 'As far as I know, she's in surgery. Lady Hawkins is on her way up from Oxfordshire, and there's no one else on site to give us updates.'

'Thank you, my lord. I take it that Geldart has escaped?'

'Yes. He called on someone local to extract him. Any clues you can give us about where his wife may be would be a great help.'

'The Queen of the Heather has her. And that Beacon he lit was to draw her attention.'

'Queen of the Heather?' asked Tom.

'What he said,' I added. This was a new one on me.

She looked almost affronted. 'Our great rival. Former great rival. The Queen of Galwyddel.'

Ah. That makes sense. 'Galloway,' I added for Tom's benefit. 'As in Dumfries and Galloway, just over the border into Scotland. And much of Ayrshire, too. And once she was Queen of the Firth, I believe?'

'Never!' said Faith with the enthusiasm of a fanatic. 'The only one of the People who gave her that name was herself.'

'Do I need to know the history?' asked Tom.

'You do. I'll fill you in when we have a plan. Faith, do you know if Douglas has any allies? Anyone who could help him assault the sídhe?'

'He once had a whole troupe of them, I believe. This all happened when I was confined to the kitchens as punishment, so I can't be sure, but that doesn't matter: the Beacon was a surrender. A *Come and get me*. And she will. She already has.'

I looked at Tom. 'I'm as clueless as you are, I'm afraid, so I'm trying to stick to what I can change. Do you know if she has People in Yorkshire? If not, she'll have to send transport.'

Faith twisted her lips and nose. She sometimes does that, an involuntary recreation of the open wound and scar which once disfigured her face. She looked down and read out an aircraft call-sign. 'Her helicopter. Our agents say that it has left her stables.'

Tom looked at me. 'How seriously are you going to take this?'

'Am I going to call in the cavalry, do you mean? I don't want to, that's for certain.'

'There is more,' said Faith, and now she looked really nervous. Not a good look on a powerful creature of magick. 'Her Grace the Queen of Derwent is about to declare that Douglas Geldart is her prisoner and that it would be a great offence for the Heather Queen to take him.'

'Shit.'

'Quite, my lord.' She took a very deep breath. 'Unless you declare him *your* prisoner, in which case she will bow to your will.'

Tom was starting to look tetchy. Any member of his team who knows him, and any suspect who doesn't yet know him, quickly learns that a tetchy Thomas is a thing to avoid. 'This isn't some courtly dance,' he said. 'How do we stop this escalating?'

'We can't,' said Faith. 'Mmm, you are well versed in the ways of the People, my lord, but you might not know that you could call on Nimue and make Geldart *her* prisoner. In that case, the Heather Queen would have to obey a summons, though that is not without risk.'

'The risk being?' snapped Tom.

'That Nimue would refuse and give Conrad to the Heather Queen.' She shrugged a liquid, non-human shrug that rippled up her blue equestrian top. 'There always has to be a balance, doesn't there?'

I hadn't realised that I'd taken my cigarettes out until Tom said, 'Not now, Conrad.'

'Sorry.' I was in a bind here. I doubted very much that the Heather Queen's helicopter would have filed a flight plan, and the Fae quite often fly without their automatic beacon in use. Calling the RAF would get me nothing but grief. Once Douglas Geldart was in the Queen of Galwyddel's clutches, he was effectively gone. The tetchiness in Tom's voice came partly from powerlessness and partly from being outside the circle of the courtly dance. *Courtly* dance? Maybe that wasn't such a bad thought after all. It was bonkers, but I couldn't see an alternative…

I took a deep breath and waggled my wedding ring. 'I'm going to take a risk. Princess Faith, I name you my deputy in this matter, as you are bound to me. Tell the Queen of Galwyddel of my decision and that she is summoned to … where would you suggest?'

Faith's smile told me that if we were IRL and not over the phone, I'd be seeing her extra teeth. 'There is only one place for such a meeting, my lord: at Gretna Green. On the battlefield.'

I snorted. Only the Fae. Only the Fae. 'Do it. I'll fly to Staveley and pick you up, and you can tell me all about Douglas Geldart when we get there.'

'As my lord wishes.'

This time I did light my cigarette. Tom moved to the side and said, 'You've been flying since first thing. Are you safe?'

'Yes. Safe and legal. Whether I'll be fit to leave Gretna Green is another matter. Do you want to know about the Solway War?'

He nodded.

'You remember the Wild Hunt of Trafalgar? When the Red Queen rebelled against her predecessor? Well, I told you she can be a lazy cow, and she can, but when she's in the field, there's no stopping her. The reason her rebellion succeeded is that she was the one who'd led their people in battle in the previous war. Gets you a lot of brownie points in the sídhe does that. Give her a sword and put her on the back of a High Unicorn and she's a proper Genghis Khan.'

'I can see that. I'd rather not see it for myself, but I can imagine it.'

'Quite. The Queen of Galwyddel – who is one of the oldest Queens in Albion – she had expanded her empire and declared herself Queen of the Firth. The Solway Firth, that is, between England and Scotland. Beautiful place, very wild. The current Red Queen led the Borrowdale People into battle and won. At Gretna Green. Have you ever been?'

'No. I've heard of it, of course.'

I stubbed out my cigarette. 'Funny place. It's part market town, part discount shopping mall and part wedding theme park. I went once, not long after Cranwell, when one of our intake got married at the Famous Blacksmiths Shop. Shall we go? I've got a special job for you when we get there.'

'So long as it doesn't involve bladed weapons, I can't wait.'

'Funny you should mention that…'

Chapter 47 — Skin in the Game

It was time to take a break. The flight from Pickering to Staveley in Cartmel isn't long when you can float majestically over the Pennines rather than queue behind the lorries, but it is quite stressful when you've been told to avoid half a dozen places and look out for a Tornado squadron. There was trouble ahead, potentially big trouble, and I needed a couple of hours to close my eyes and let my body metabolise some of the cortisol that was sloshing around my veins. Not only that, the Northern days are long in May, and the summons had been fixed for, you guessed it, sunset.

'I don't know how you can do it,' said Tom when he gave me a shake. I'd have preferred Alicia or Thistle to wake me with their soft breath and shining eyes, but you take what you can get. What? Did you think that because now I'm a married man I've suddenly lost my appetite for beauty?

'I couldn't possibly have dropped off to sleep after what we've been through today,' he added, placing a mug of tea on the ground.

'It's an important survival skill. Did you get it?'

'Yes. Liz sorted it out.'

'Thank you. That tea smells good.'

'And the bacon sandwiches smell even better.'

I did get to see Thistle, when she delivered the food. She looked grumpy for some reason, and kept casting accusing glances out of the Portakabin towards the meadow where Sophie was grooming Hipponax the Unicorn.

Yes, you read that right: we were dining in a Portakabin at the edge of the building site. At least I'd got to sleep in one of the completed underground chambers, even though it was on a camp bed, but I don't have time to investigate the politics of Faith's nascent Household, nor to explain the Skelwith Construction logo plastered on the Portakabin.

'What have I missed?' I asked Tom and Faith. 'And where did you get that tie from?'

Tom's earlier tie was no doubt languishing in the contaminated waste bin of Jimmy's Hospital after holding Saffron's dressings together, and he had a new silk number round his neck. He does look undressed without one.

Faith was still dressed for riding, but she'd changed from her hacking gear into something brand new, something more suitable for a cavalry regiment. As well as the gleaming white jodhpurs and high black boots, she was sporting a sky blue shirt and royal blue jacket. Maybe she'd chosen it as a tribute to Oxford *and* Cambridge. For all I know, she's got degrees from both places. And then I noticed that Tom's new tie was striped in the same shades.

'My colours,' said Faith. 'I hope that they become my Royal Colours in due course. The Sheriff's tie is in the same because I got some samples and there was one spare.'

Tom came close to an eye-roll as he shook his head and said, 'Saffron is out of her first surgery and doing well considering the amount of things they had to stitch together.' He looked at me suspiciously. 'Did you take a nap just to avoid talking to Lady Hawkins. It was not a pleasant experience. She went through every injury to make sure I'd got the full measure of it.' He managed half a smile. 'There is one thing you'll find amusing, but I'll let Saff tell you that herself.'

I tried to look as humble as I felt. If there wasn't a mission still in progress, I'd have reported to Leeds to get my tongue lashing in person. It says a lot for Celeste's priorities that she was still at her daughter's bedside. I know some Mages who would have tried to invade Blackwater Tower to get revenge on Richard Geldart rather than look to their child. And talking of Richard…

'Did Warren collect our prisoner safely?'

'He did. Eleanor Geldart sat guarding him until he was taken into custody; the family have locked themselves away, presumably awaiting developments. In other news, the Red Queen is washing her hair tonight and won't be going to Gretna Green. On the whole, I think that's a good thing.'

'It's a very good thing,' said Faith, with more of an edge than I'd have expected.

'On the other hand, her agents report that a large number of the Galloway People are mustering. The pubs of Gretna are doing a roaring trade.'

'So it's you, me and Faith against an entire People,' I said. 'Sounds about right.'

Tom hesitated. 'Not quite. As soon as word got around, Matt Eldridge insisted on going. Along with the entire team of Lakeland Assessors. And George Gibson. They're camped out at the service station.' He drummed his fingers. 'This was not my doing, but *someone* told your Pack. They will be there, too.'

I frowned outwardly, but inside my heart had swelled, just a fraction. I just hope I didn't make a stupid arse of myself. At least Evie Mason wouldn't be there taking notes.

'Lloyd?'

He shook his head. 'Down in London. He sounded distraught and said he was going to try and charter a helicopter, but he couldn't find one at such short notice, I'm afraid.'

I heard the crunch of gravel as light footsteps approached, but instead of Thistle with more sandwiches, it was Tamsin. She said hello and joined us, taking a chair to one side.

Tom glanced at her and said, 'I've also pulled together what I could on the history of Douglas Geldart and his wife, Margot Easterbrook.'

'Easterbrook! As in…'

'The Easterbrooks of Anglia,' said Tamsin. Her original family is the Pikes, old rivals of the Easterbrooks. 'This is before I was born, of course,' she continued, 'and being the last Pike Mage, I don't have access to any witnesses, but I've asked around a few people at Angel House who were willing to take my calls.'

She smiled meaningfully when she said that. Millie Easterbrook is a leading light in the Mages of East Anglia, and is Treasurer of the Mage stronghold in Cambridge, Angel House. Naturally, when you have a leading light, you also have plenty of shadows willing to dish the dirt.

'As far as I can gather,' said Tamsin, 'Douglas Geldart was something of an outcast from Yorkshire. He barely had any contact with his family after he left home to go to Salomon's House. He did his ChD in Cambridge, working in Angel House Library, and he married Margot, who was considered odd even by Easterbrook standards. Not that I'm biased or anything.'

'Of course not.'

'Shortly after, he resigned and more or less disappeared. My sources *think* that he had a base somewhere around there, but no idea where. I do know that Margot was never declared dead, though that's probably because there was no one around who cared.'

'Interesting,' I said. 'Did your sources say whether Douglas had any cronies down there?'

She shook her head. 'No one sprang to mind.'

Tom took over. 'And the next time they appeared was about ten years later, when something kicked off up here. Faith?'

'I have this from Her Grace's own lips, sworn and declared,' she began. If you've passed the Fae 101 module you'll know exactly what this means: everything would be the truth and nothing but the truth; the Fae *never* tell the Whole Truth.

'Prince Galleny wasn't always a complete shit,' she continued. 'A shit, yes, but not a complete one. He had good enough agents to be alerted when the Heather Queen put out hunting parties along the Eden Valley, and he was straight on it. A good job, too, because the Geldarts were on the hunt as well, and everyone was chasing The Intruder.'

I could hear the capital *I* in her voice, and raised my eyebrows.

'Lucas of Innerdale was not the first to breach the Wards around the Radiant Sídhe. Her Grace knew that some mortal had been digging around, and she knew their Mark, but she had no idea what they were doing. We called him The Intruder.'

I sat back, stunned. 'Douglas Geldart broke into the Radiant Sídhe? Her grace *must* know what he was up to. It's her property!'

Faith set her lips in a thin smile. 'If this were not such a crisis, Her Grace would not have admitted it, but the Radiant Sídhe is *not* hers. It belongs to the Morrigan: Her Grace is but the Custodian, and many Queens have put creatures in there over the centuries. In fact, it was Her Grace who stopped taking deposits. Since she was proclaimed, the Radiant Sídhe has been declared *full.*'

'Deposits,' I said. 'They are not cheques, they are living creatures.'

Faith didn't look happy. She knows full well what sort of creature has been filed away and forgotten under the green mats of the Repository. 'Tonight may provoke some sort of crisis, my lord. I think perhaps that there may be changes.'

'Too right there'll be changes,' I muttered. 'Why was the Heather Queen in the field?'

'It was her property in the Repository which Geldart had violated. According to her, anyway.'

'Go on.'

'There was never a song written for that night, so I can't be sure. It seems that Geldart was trying to rescue his wife, who was also fleeing, but the Heather Queen found her first. Shortly later, Galleny cornered Geldart, and he surrendered. When all the parties gathered together, there was something of a stand off.'

'Quite.'

I have been there. I know what it's like when interests collide in the brutal world of magick. I could even picture the scene, somewhere in the high meadows of the Eden Valley. An abandoned car, Sprites flitting from tree to tree, steam rising from the breath of horses, and everywhere in the night, blades glinting. The Queen of Galwyddel would be on her Unicorn, and in the shadows, the grey shapes of the Derwent Pack would be circling, yellow eyes like fireflies in the long grass.

And at the centre would be a Queen, a Prince, the late Lady Geldart and the hunted pair, Douglas and Margot. We were pretty much going to recreate that scene tonight, with fewer horses, yes, but with added helicopters instead.

'How on earth did Douglas end up in Beckthorpe and not on the end of a spear?' I asked.

'The Heather Queen had no Cause to detain Margot; she was deep, deep in our lands, and she was outnumbered, so she couldn't claim Douglas by force. Douglas would have been punished by Her Grace – the Red Queen –, but that punishment would not have been for life. He would have walked away. The thought of denying the Heather Queen her prize was too delicious to turn down.' She looked at Tom. 'The Sheriff has told me of the late Lady Geldart's letter: that she could not condemn her son to death. He agreed to be Bound for Galleny's lifetime, and his mother agreed to sustain him. In return, Margot agreed to serve and be cloistered in the Galwyddel Sídhe.'

'But no one expected Douglas to outlive Prince Galleny,' said Tom, 'and please stop calling me *Sheriff.* You'll encourage Conrad.'

'And when Galleny died, so did the Bindings?'

'Some of them. The Mortal Crown persists. Any Noble from the People could anoint him to death.'

What a phrase: *anoint him to death.* 'Is that the Ink around his head? The thorns?'

'It is. It causes no pain to wear, but it acts as a strong deterrent. As Detective Chief Inspector Morton has discovered, it was often used when we had more mortal servants.'

'I think the word you're looking for is *slaves,* but we'll leave it for now. Why don't you call me *Tom?*'

'Because you are wearing my colours but not in my household,' said Faith, as if it were the most obvious thing in the world. 'To use your personal name would be an insult. To you, that is. I am honoured that you wear them.'

He shook his head. 'Never mind. Stick to *Sheriff* if you must. So there we are: Douglas Geldart and Margot Easterbrook will be in the Field of Gretna Green at sunset.'

'So who's coming in the Wasp? Tom, you're up front, and Faith of course...'

'Can we fit three in the back?' said Faith.

'With a squeeze. If they're not my size.'

'Good. Tamsin has cause to be there, and I have a special request that Sophie be present. She knows about Raven, and she knows that – somehow – Douglas Geldart is responsible for her mother's conception and birth.' She put on a haughty expression. 'And we need a servant, don't we?'

Tom looked at me. 'I don't know how you put up with it.'

'Oh, you know, it's nice to see a naked hierarchy in operation. Everyone knows their place, then, don't they? Could you summon Thistle? I need a coffee and a fag before I fly off to possible annihilation.'

As soon as I was alone, I called my wife.

I promise I'll stop saying that soon, but I'm sure you'll indulge a newlywed for a little longer. Tom had got Lucy to bring Mina up to date, but it must be said that there were a few Chinese whispers going on. Once we'd sorted that out, she forcibly changed the subject as her way of trying to ignore the fact that I was, indeed, heading to potential annihilation.

'It is most inconvenient, Conrad. I'd much rather that you and your new toy were parked in the Elvenham paddock than up there, because then you would be able to airlift Myfanwy to hospital. Ben's mother is fairly sure that it will be soon. Possibly *very* soon.'

'And I'm equally sure that Myfanwy will be fine.' I reflected for a moment. 'Actually, I take that back. I think I've got the easier hand to play. Her labour will take a long time, but my troubles will soon be over, and if it all goes wrong, I won't feel a thing.'

'Okay, now I am glad that you are at the other end of the country. If you weren't, I'd have to snub you and ignore you for saying that.'

'And I love you too.'

'Good.' She dropped the act. 'Remember everything we've agreed, Conrad.'

'How can I forget? It was in our vows.'

'Then remember that I will always be by your side.'

I broke the call, and it was time to go.

Chapter 48 — Champions

'Can you see anything?' said Tom over the intercom.
'All good,' I told him. What I didn't have time to tell him was that a Fae Wood makes a perfect landing beacon when you have your Third Eye open.

The Queen of Derwent had planted the wood and made a small bower in the meadow near Gretna Green. It's what you do to rub your enemy's nose in their defeat and you have forever to gloat about your triumph.

The Queen of Galwyddel's helicopter had landed in a corner near the road, and I decided to show off by putting the Wasp down nearer the woods. It meant I wouldn't have so far to walk to the spring, because that's where we would gather: around a nice source of fresh water.

I took my time making sure that everything was shut down properly; after all, the Wasp would be spending the night here, even if I didn't. No night flying for me. Not yet. That was on the agenda for more peaceful times. So perhaps never. Shut up and get on with it, Clarke.

Shadows turned into people and creatures who look like people. The creatures who didn't look remotely human stayed in the shadows, but I could feel them all around us.

You know who is on Team Conrad here, and they were behind me, keeping a safe but close distance. I shook hands with Matt and George, and thanked the others, especially Karina, her bow strung and ready, her black combats already merging into the dusk.

'Don't I get a kiss?'

Erin stepped from behind Matt and puckered up. I obliged and said, 'What are you doing here?'

'Evie Mason asked me to come up and video it, and as I had nothing better to do, I said *why not?*'

'Evie. I might have known. No other reason for coming, was there…?'

She blushed a little and stepped back, and I stepped forwards to stand between Tom and Faith, with Tom to my right and Faith to my left. Tamsin and Sophie, both sporting some version of the Oxbridge stripes, stood together in the line of assessors.

The Fae Wood had been planted to the south of the battlefield, and I stood facing north. In the just-set twilight, I wasn't surprised to see a black dot descending from the sky. I turned west, and there was another. Odin's raven chose a proud oak tree, well away from the Fae Wood, because that's where the Morrigan's bird roosted. The Queen of the Heather saw them, too, and pointedly turned her back on Hugin or Munin, or maybe even the Allfather himself.

The Queen of Galwyddel was wearing traditional Fae green hunting garb.

Appropriate. Being a Queen, she stood alone. There were plenty of her People here, though. Around forty that I could see, clustered around a Princess and a Prince, also attired for the hunt, and that left two. Plus their guards.

Douglas Geldart was being held to my right, Margot to my left. Doug looked nothing like the helpless man in the video: his eyes were sharp and his jaw was set despite the heavy chains around his wrists and between his ankles.

His wife was staring at him over the divide. She had also been Bound for the night, though her chains were lighter and only her hands were restrained. She looked even older than Douglas. Perhaps the Heather Queen had worked her hard, or perhaps she simply was that: older. Her hair was completely white and put up in a bun, her face was lined and her cheeks almost hollow. Shadows hid her eyes, but they never wavered from Douglas.

The traditional way of greeting the Fae is *Well met*; it says that you are there in peace and hope for the same. I never got the chance to say it, because Douglas shouted out before I could open my mouth.

His jailors cut him off, but he still got out the first words, 'Tell Saffron I am sorry. Is she…'

An interesting way to begin. Of all the things weighing on his mind, why had he chosen that one? I didn't get the chance to respond, because the Heather Queen spoke up, and her voice was anything but soft and springy. More like *Thistle Queen*: all hard and spiky. Definitely Scottish, though.

'Let's get this charade over with, mortal.'

'Certainly. May I introduce Detective Chief Inspector Morton? He has something for you.'

Tom took out the piece of paper which Liz had expedited for us and showed it to the Queen. 'This is a warrant from the Cloister Court,' he began. 'It's for Douglas Geldart to appear before the bench and answer charges of attempted murder and grievous bodily harm with intent, and the Deputy Constable would like to serve it on your prisoner. Do you wish to read it?'

'You can use your fucking warrant to wipe your arse, you wee shite, 'cause that's all it's worth. You should know better than to pull tricks like that, Witchfinder. Your mortal court has nothing to do with me.'

As agreed, I just smiled politely. Tom folded the warrant carefully and said, 'The Deputy Constable is aware of that, thank you. The warrant is for Douglas, not you, and we intend to serve it. You cannot keep him prisoner with a warrant outstanding, no matter what your grievance with him.

'Or what, precisely? If that's all you've got, I'm going haem.'

'Lloyd! Take aim,' I shouted. A green light flickered in the trees. 'Excuse me, your grace, I had hoped to avoid threats, but my blood brother is keen to try his hand at being a sniper. He's been working on some new ammunition.'

The Queen stiffened for a second, as she had every right to. She also had an expectation on her shoulders: bowing to mortals, or even worse, bowing to a Gnome would be a humiliation she might never recover from.

She thought for a second, and the Princess she'd brought earned her keep for the night by shouting something in Fae. A broad smile spread across the Heather Queen's face.

'Shit,' said Faith under her breath.

The gist of the message soon became clear when the Queen said, 'If you're going to be all legal about this, how about we sort out the Summons first, eh? You used the Old One to bring me here, so let her decide on custody. After all, you keep telling the People that your Badge shows you work in her name. Call Nimue, as you said you would, and if you don't I'll tell her that you've been using her name without authority.'

I smiled to myself, wondering whether Evie would be so gauche as to quote Hamlet. It would very much be sport to see this engineer hoist by his own petard. 'Thanks, Tom. I'll take it from here.'

He shoved the warrant firmly in his coat. 'I've come this far, Conrad.' And then he stood his ground, as did Faith.

Nimue may have moments of wandering, but she is not psychotic. Tom was in no danger from her. Me, on the other hand…

I touched Great Fang and felt the Essence of the Nymph, the smell of spring flowers and the taste of sweet water. In but a few seconds, she was before us. Now that I can see more clearly, her face looks sharper, more defined. And more concerned than ever before.

'Guardian, the realm is troubled, I see. What matter have you raised in my name?'

I bowed low. 'My lady, if you would be so gracious, I would have you decide whose prisoner that man should be.' I pointed to Douglas Geldart. 'His crimes…'

'I forgive your ignorance, Guardian,' she said smoothly. 'When you dispute with the People, they must bring the body. After that, it is between you. Let it be today's lesson.'

She shrank back with a great splash, sending water flying everywhere. When I looked up, the Heather Queen had all her teeth on display. 'A challenge, mortal. Single combat to decide who gets to judge the thief in chains.'

'Fuck,' said Tom. 'Are they real?'

It was the first time there'd been enough Lux and power floating around for him to see what the Fae jaw can look like. It still makes me queasy, and I've seen it plenty of times.

'Only too real, I'm afraid.' I stood tall and raised my voice to its full parade ground volume. 'For those who were not there and did not know, yesterday I was groom to the fairest ever bride to walk on Albion's shore. In the vows we made, I foreswore single combat for any prize but my own life. If I would not fight for Mina, I will certainly not fight for Douglas Geldart.'

'Really?' said Tamsin from behind me. 'Wow.'

'Let me,' said Faith, shocking me with a touch to my arm. 'Let me be your Champion. It is permitted in the rules, I swear.'

'In Odin's name, why?'

'Not in *his* name. In *mine*. She was the one who cut me. It was because of her that I wore the scar for forty-five years. My lord. Please.'

'Why? What happened?'

'I will tell you if I live. If I die, it matters not. Or you can ask Her Grace.'

I looked around the gathering darkness. Somehow, despite the gloom, I could still see the two ravens, blacker dots against shadows. 'Very well,' I said, and withdrew my arm. 'I accept your challenge, your grace, and I appoint Princess Faith of Staveley in Cartmel as my Champion.'

The hisses, murmurs and squeaks were loud enough for me to hear and as deep as the frown on the Heather Queen. 'It is beneath me, but I have no choice.' She turned theatrically to her Princess. 'Prepare a body bag. I would not be accused of sullying the Rouge Queen's land with filth.'

Faith hissed at *Rouge Queen*, clearly an insult that went way over my head. There was movement as the Fae drew closer, to form a ring and to get a good view. My own team did the same, except Tamsin, who rushed forwards.

Faith turned and held up her hand to stop the onrush. 'Don't, Tammy. This is People's business. And my lord's. If you love me, please do me the honour of being my second. Someone needs to hold my coat.'

Tamsin blushed to her roots and looked as awkward as a teenager singled out in class. She nodded and helped Faith remove her coat. On the other side, a body bag was being theatrically laid on the grass while gestures and handshakes told me that bets were being laid by the Fae, presumably on how long Faith would last before being cut down.

The Heather Queen handed over her scabbard to her Princess and got ready to take position. Faith had just finished rolling up her sleeves, and was about to get her own blade when I said, 'You won't be needing that.'

'My lord?'

I took Great Fang off my back. 'As my Champion, you fight with my blade or not at all. Up to you.'

They knew. They all knew immediately what I'd done. If the Fae ever come across cold-forged iron, or *n'Haeval* as they call it, they won't even touch it to dispose of it. A dropped sword or arrowhead will be left where it lies, or swept away with a long-handled broom. For Faith to take my Gnome-forged sword, with it's cold-forged edge would be to take on a reputational burden which might crush her.

She considered the Badge in the hilt and the Old High Proto-Germanic runes chased into the scabbard. There were plenty more in the blade. 'I would not dream of going against my lord's wishes,' she said, with an inscrutable tone that was close to Fae in its inflection. Without saying more, she grasped the hilt, hissed in pain, and drew the sword.

Great Fang growled, and the surrounding Wolves answered with howls. Faith held the blade aloft, tested its weight and went *en garde*. I stepped back, pulling Tamsin away from the ring of light which had sprung up around the combatants.

The Heather Queen's blade was a gossamer shimmer of death, light and sharp and impossible for me to see in detail. It could shift from plane to plane, avoiding a parry and reappearing to cut down its opponent. But only if the opponent is there.

Faith dodged left and right, swinging Great Fang like a broom handle. It was gut-wrenching to watch, but I had to believe that she knew what she was doing. A thrust from the Queen hit Faith in the left arm: in, out, blood.

Faith staggered back, pain and fury mixing on her face. She lashed out again, and it was agony to see a genius with the blade reduced to behaving like a child with a wooden sword.

Twice more, the Heather Queen ducked under the n'Haeval edge and scored a hit, once again to the left arm as Faith was forced to protect her face, but it was the thigh wound that spelled the beginning of the end. With that in place, it wouldn't be long, and when the blade had gone in, it had almost seemed like Faith was offering her left leg as a target, bright red standing out against the white of her jodhpurs.

She limped back, was forced right to avoid the glowing line, and when she came face to face again, it was all over. And I was to blame.

Faith had spent hours teaching me to compensate for my titanium tibia by taking the weight unnaturally on my right leg. It was agony to do for more than a second, but a second was all you need to play a shot in cricket, or parry a blade, knock it down and use the cold-forged metal in a back-handed slash that cut off the Heather Queen's jaw and severed her windpipe. She was still trying to scream when Faith plunged Great Fang into her heart.

Time stopped. Gravity did not, but time did.

The Heather Queen's body slid off the blade of Great Fang, slowly at first, and then with a thump. Faith remained motionless, frozen in some localised timewarp which spread to everyone in the field except me. And the two Elderkind.

Odin was standing at the foot of the oak, his face hidden by the cowl of his cloak, his spear Gungnir in his left hand. The Morrigan was already striding towards me, a look of thunder on her face. I was bowing as low as my back would let me before she breached the circle.

'Macavity Clarke, eh?' she boomed. 'Two Queens dead at your instigation but neither at your hand. You're the Lord of Death in all but name, yet your hands are clean. She moved slightly, flexing the tree-trunk muscles in her legs and sending a ripple through the fabric covering them. The record is four, you know.'

I kept quiet, but I did stand a little straighter. She cupped her hands to the wound in the dead Queen's chest, then stood impossibly tall, her giant fingers making a ball to hold the fragile creature. When she opened her hands, the yellow and black insect buzzed loudly and flew drunkenly towards the wood.

She span on her heel, looking from the Allfather to me, shook her head and stood astride the Heather Queen's body. She bent her knees, squatted low and stretched out her arms, then launched herself into the sky, arms become wings and the royal corpse held in raven's talons.

'You're wrong,' I told her (once she was too far away to hear me, of course). 'My hands are not clean: you're just looking for the wrong coloured blood. Saffron's blood is red. Mortal red.'

In two more seconds, she was one with the night, heading for the Galwyddel Sídhe to drop off the body and turn the palace into a tomb.

And time moved again.

Faith dropped Great Fang and collapsed to the ground, clutching the wound in her leg. I had used the timewarp to shift closer, ready to pick up my blade and deal with the chaos which would follow. I never did find out whether anyone else noticed that I'd translocated by ten metres because I'm not allowed to ask.

In the stunned silence, of all the possibilities, the first thing I heard was the bizarre sound of Erin speaking into her phone. 'She's dead! The Scottish Queen's dead!'

'Seize the Geldarts!' I ordered, turning towards Douglas.

All around me, the field erupted with pushing, shoving and shouts. Tom ran for cover, and Karina shot like lightning to seize Margot Easterbrook; Tamsin and Sophie dashed to comfort Faith. On the other side of the circle, the Galloway People descended into chaos. I approached Douglas, and his guards took one look at Great Fang before high-tailing it away. Matt Eldridge arrived, and I left him to secure the prisoner.

My main concern was that one of the People would try to become a hero by taking revenge. I needn't have worried. There was a fierce struggle between themselves, blades flashing and magick dancing in the air. Several bodies dropped to the ground or staggered away clutching wounds. In seconds, the Princess who'd been the Heather Queen's second was a captive, half a dozen of her own People gripping her tightly and holding her struggling body upright.

The Prince strode towards her, drawing his dagger. He stopped two feet from her face and showed his teeth. He said something in Fae, and there was a ragged shout from around him, then he cut the Princess's throat and let the blood spray all over his body.

Wolves were already circling our prisoners and forming a protective ring around the rest of my party. I stepped away from where Faith was being treated and gestured for the Geldarts to be brought forwards.

Matt and Karina had read the reports. They stood behind their prisoners with weapons drawn and allowed others to lead them to me. Again, Douglas was the first to speak. 'Is Saffron badly injured?'

'Yes. She's serious but stable.'

'I am so sorry. Tell her. And Kathy? Is she in trouble.'

'The only thing that Kathy is guilty of is trusting you,' I told him. 'Douglas Geldart, you will be arraigned in the Cloister Court…'

'No I won't,' he said forcefully, his voice raw from lack of use. 'Margot! Is The Legacy secure?'

His wife raised her head. 'It is.'

Before I could regain the initiative, he lifted his hands, silver shackles glowing brightly. 'The Heather Queen made these bonds, and without her they wither.'

The manacle around his right wrist dissolved into sparks, and I was raising Great Fang in defence, but I was not his target. He sent a Blast of magick that was sharp, focused and deadly. It pierced his wife's heart, and she barely had time to register shock as she fell backwards to the grass.

And then Douglas became tonight's final victim. Three of us were closing on him, and he used the Ink in the Fae chain dangling from his left wrist to wake the mortal crown around his head. You can't Blast yourself to death with magick; it just won't work. But you can activate another Work, or Charm, or Ink. If you really want to.

As soon as the knots and spikes of silver burst into life and dug into his head, we all looked away. At least it was quick.

Chapter 49 — Tea and Sympathy

Matt Eldridge looked stricken. He takes his duties very seriously, and even though it was my responsibility, losing a life like that was going to hurt him more than it hurt me. His jaw worked hard, and he swallowed hard. 'I'll clean up, Chief. You have other things to worry about.'

'Thanks, Matt. Tom? Can you call Mina.'

'No need,' said Erin. 'She heard everything.' I frowned in confusion, and she gave me a silly grin. 'You didn't think I was really talking to Evie, did you? I just said that to wind you up, big man. Mina wanted someone who wouldn't be in danger and who wasn't needed to fight, so she chose me. Maybe I'll become a magickal war correspondent. Beats being up to your elbows in ink.'

'Shut up Erin. And thanks, but mostly *shut up*. Tom, could you call the Boss after you've spoken to Lucy.'

'Of course.'

I went to see Faith, and she looked weak: the Heather Queen must have nicked an artery somewhere. Tamsin was feeding her an energy bar from Karina's rucksack while Sophie finished First Aid. I squatted down next to her. 'You had me worried there.'

'All under control, my lord. Tonight is going to light a fire under some very interesting songs, I think.'

Karina offered me a hand, and Sapphire Gibson emerged from the trees with her harmless laser pointer, and after kissing her husband, she came to me. 'How did I do?'

'You did brilliantly. Thank you, Sapphire. And that was a genius idea, by the way. Wouldn't have worked without it.'

She grinned and went to join the women ministering to Faith. A discreet cough made me turn around, and there was the portly figure of Gustav, Chamberlain to the Red Queen. 'Excuse me, my lord, but Her Grace would like to send her supreme thanks for what you have done. In addition, she has made ready Solway Lodge for you and as many who want it tonight.'

'Thanks. I take it there is transport?'

'Of course, my lord.'

'Bring it as close as you can to Faith, and get ready to help them load her into it.'

He bowed, and I moved slightly away, so that the entire company was in front of me, and my back was to the oak tree. 'Thank you!' I shouted. Everyone turned to look, and Tom lowered the phone from his ear. 'We're done here, unless you've been given a job by Matt. Faith, Tammy, Tom and Sophie will be joining me at Solway Lodge. Be on your guard for a Fae war, and Matt, I'm going to ask you to liaise with Depute Constable McCabe in Edinburgh. Once again, thank you all.'

Erin being Erin couldn't resist. She started clapping, and a couple joined in, then just about everyone. I nodded and turned away. It doesn't do to keep the Allfather waiting *too* long.

The darkness around me grew deeper as I neared the tree, until there was nothing but the two of us. He lowered his hood, and the avuncular workman I'd left in Valhalla this morning was gone. The figure before me was every inch the god of the gallows.

'My lord. I am sorry that I could not bring Douglas to Justice.'

'He was a powerful Mage. You did well to stop him disappearing again. Did you learn anything?'

'I will be going to the Radiant Sídhe at noon tomorrow. I think the answer may lie there.'

He nodded. 'I will join you. It seems a long time since breakfast, Conrad. You must be hungry. Go well.'

When the darkness dissipated, I grinned all over my face. Bouncing over the grass was a bright red Rolls Royce. Now *that's* what I call a victory ride.

I left Faith alone when we got to Solway Lodge. Most of the night had been what you'd expect: reports, plans, news gathering and a very fine dinner cooked and served by the Red Queen's household. The lady herself dropped in to the red drawing room when I was having coffee and a smoke after dinner. I say *dropped in*, but I'm sure that she'd been lurking somewhere the whole time. Maybe she even tossed the salad. No, only joking.

I wouldn't have chosen a room painted deep red and edged in black to reflect on a day soaked in blood and tinged with tragedy, but it was the only inside smoking room. As ever, you've got to get your priorities right.

The Queen bowed to me, her red velvet dress at one with the upholstery, her hair turned a severe black since we'd last met. She dropped to one knee and her voice almost caught in her throat. 'I never thought that submitting to you would bring such opportunities, my lord. I will almost be disappointed when my submission ends next week.'

She had submitted until the first full moon after the wedding, and there was going to be a combined wedding celebration and liberation party in the Derwent Sídhe.

I was very much looking forward to that, but today's business was weighing very heavily: when you've seen three human corpses and watched your partner being sliced open, it's not something you can shrug off, no matter how succulent the beef. 'Tell me true, did you know anything of Douglas Geldart's unbinding?

Still on one knee, she lowered her head. 'I did not. Here, see for yourself.' She slid up her sleeve and showed me her left arm. Lux boiled and swirled over her skin, and she pointed to a series of squiggles. 'This is the closest I can get to proof, and if you summon Faith or one of her People, they will read it to you. It tells of Geldart's capture, and that I left his Binding to Galleny and knew not the details. I had no idea he had linked it so closely to his own life.'

'We'll leave Faith to recuperate. Rise and tell me of your plans.'

She rose elegantly and effortlessly as a sympathetic twinge in my leg reminded me that I would never do that again.

'Would you like a drink? I have some damson brandy you might like.'

'Is it better than damson gin?'

'Infinitely. And unique to the People.'

'Thank you. Take a seat when you're done.'

It was a very good brandy indeed, with sweetness to temper the fire after a long day. We drank a toast to the future before I asked her how much of the Heather Queen's land she was going to seize.

'We began last night while the confusion was at its height,' she said, a glimpse of teeth slipping out. 'I've been wondering for a while where to draw Faithful's boundary in the east, and I've decided to let her have the middle Lune Valley, including the current Pack Hall. Harprigg can move to Scotland.'

'Will the Madreb be keen on that?'

She looked puzzled at my question, then shrugged it off. The Madreb of her pack is Prince Harprigg's lover, and he's as devoted to her. For once, not my problem.

We chatted a little longer, until a knock on the door told me that the Boss wanted a three-way video call with McCabe. 'Until the full moon, my lord.'

'Until then, your grace.'

I really did get woken by Thistle the next morning, and although she was no less a cheery sight, she was still grumpy. Nothing wrong with her breakfast, though. I asked after Faith, and when told she'd had a good night's sleep, I took our heroine a mug of tea and some toast; Thistle had already delivered the full Fae breakfast at dawn.

Faith was propped up in bed, a silk dressing gown hiding the bandage on her left arm. 'What's up with Thistle?' I asked after checking her over and discovering that she could walk with crutches.

'You do not want to know, my lord. The first time you get your heart broken is always the worst.'

'But she's thirty-five years old!'

'She is, but there has been little love in her life up to now. She will recover: the heart is but a muscle, as we say.'

'Do you?'

She sipped her tea. 'We do. How else could we live this long? It can still be broken, though.' She ran her finger round the rim of the mug. 'The heart was what made the quarrel between the Heather Queen and myself, and it was not over a man. Or a woman. It was over a child.'

My mind leapt to *A Midsummer Night's Dream*, and the fairy war over the pageboy. I was wrong.

'I have borne only one human, my lord. A little girl, forty-eight years ago. The Red Queen lost a big bet with the Queen of Galwyddel, and my child was demanded as the price. The Heather Queen wanted her as a Changeling.'

That would be unbearable for a mortal mother. I said nothing and waited to see how it affected the Fae.

'I was summoned to the Galloway Sídhe and ordered to bring my child. The Heather Queen demanded her in settlement, and you may not believe this, but the Red Queen is indeed merciful. She asked me if I was happy, and I said no. I did not want my little girl's body sweated down to a pair of ovaries.'

'I can't imagine having to make that choice, Faith.'

'The Heather Queen rose up in fury. She held me in place and cut my face, and then she demanded that I wear the scar forever as a sign of my disobedience and that I be chained in the lowest chamber until I took my own life.'

'But you weren't?'

'The Red Queen said that I would have to give up my child for adoption. She said that I would serve in the kitchens for as long as the girl was of child-bearing age, and that I would wear the wound until my daughter died. Submitting to you broke that order.'

'I see. I think. Thank you for sharing that. It must have been hard.'

'No, my lord. Shame is dirt you can wash off in the morning. A lost child is something you can never erase from your skin.'

Having seen the Red Queen's arm last night, I caught a glimpse of what she might mean. 'I'll let you rest a little longer. You're sure you're ready to travel?'

'I am. Is it wise to take the Sheriff? I mean Tom?'

'He's not going. He's already left for Cairndale and a conversation with Commander Ross. I'll collect him and we'll fly to Yorkshire once you and I have investigated the Radiant Sídhe. Under the Allfather's supervision.'

Faith did not look happy at that prospect; it wasn't going to be my highlight, either. 'It is the Morrigan's land.'

'I'm aware of that, Faith.'

'As my lord wishes. Thank you for the tea.'

Mark Hayden

Tom was so preoccupied when he got in the Range Rover that he didn't think what might happen when they got to the end of their journey.

He looked around him as the driver worked her way from the Solway Lodge to the motorway. The Lodge was a pleasant, Victorian building near the mighty estuary that forms the firth, and it was surrounded by dairy farms, all belonging to the Red Queen, and all the farmers ignorant of their landlady's true nature. It started a train of thought that followed him back into England and all the way through the great valleys of the Lake District.

The first stop on his thought-train was waking up in the comfiest bed he could remember, the elfin Thistle by his side, putting tea on the bedside table.

'Your clothes are hanging, Lord Sheriff. I hope you slept well.'

'I did thanks. And you?' He had only had one previous conversation with Thistle, and his polite enquiry was a way of not thinking about it.

'Too busy putting the stick about,' she replied. 'Her Grace's Household could do with a few stripes on their back to gee them up a bit. Took ages to get your shirt sorted.'

He waited until she'd left, sipped his tea and went to see what she was on about. He hadn't been looking forward to putting yesterday's clothes back on, and discovered that he didn't have to.

His suit had been cleaned and pressed, his underwear washed and his shirt? It was gone, replaced by a new one. A shirt which hadn't existed when he'd gone to bed and which some creature had knocked up in the night, under threat of a beating, presumably.

And then he was taking the thought-train back to Elvenham, stopping on the night he had first seen Odin, and the night the happy couple had been whisked off somewhere, taking Thistle's trainers with them.

The little Fae had run over the Elvenham drive to fetch something and returned with blood flecking her bare feet. He'd expressed concern and she'd shrugged. 'You get used to it. So long as I don't mess the carpets, I'll be fine. I've suffered a *lot* worse, you believe me.'

His brain kept telling him that the petite, sexy bundle was older than him, but his eyes told him otherwise.

'Was that in Lord Tiree's sídhe?'

'Aye, but mostly in the studio. I could cope with the bondage, but those snuff movies really *hurt*, you ken?'

Tom froze to the spot. '*Snuff* movies?'

Films of young women being murdered for pleasure were an urban legend; it was well known in law enforcement that videoing a crime and trying to sell it for profit was about the fastest route to jail you could imagine.

'Aye. My lord got good money for letting them do it. Private parties, you ken? And even more from the blackmail afterwards. I only did a few, and I didnae scream enough, so he sent me back to the kitchens. And the black

372

bedroom. Can I get you another drink?'

He tried to focus on his present situation, heading to Cairndale. On things he could control. Things from his world.

Conrad had nearly come unstuck last night. Conrad *would* have come unstuck if Faith hadn't stepped in and settled the argument with blood. Fae blood. She was part of an entire species living in Albion, like parasites in a host body. One of several species, and the Nāgin who'd blessed the wedding (and no doubt planning to lay eggs) was just the latest immigrant. Even the shy, self-contained Mannwolves were part of a mix which also included the Elderkind and a water Nymph who got to play god even if she wasn't classed as one.

And Tom couldn't look away from all that. For goodness sake, he'd just referred to Britain as *Albion* in his head. He was in deeper than he thought, and he *really* didn't want to lurk on the fringes of Conrad Bloody Clarke's campaigns any longer. It was time for a change before Conrad became unstuck and Tom got covered in glue. His thought train came to the end of its runway, and he called Ross's PA. He apologised profusely and said, 'Could I move my appointment back half an hour? I really need to see Lucy.'

The Commander had a soft spot for Lucy, so Tom should get away with it. Then he messaged Lucy and said he would have time to see her before he spoke to Ross. She sent half a dozen kisses and heart emojis by way of reply.

A couple of hours later, he climbed the stairs to Ross's office and found several civilians clustered around the PA's computer monitor. They looked up at him and the women giggled. 'What?' he said.

'Might have to change your nickname, Tom,' said Ross's PA.

Tom made a point of taking a joke in good part. After all, if he didn't, how could he make them himself? 'Go on. Do tell.'

'Have a look for yourself,' she said.

The others stood back, and the PA rewound a video. It was the station's own CCTV and time-stamped barely a few minutes ago. He watched as a black Range Rover swept into the compound, bypassing the security barrier with magick and stopping right in the middle of the yard, blocking a patrol car which was trying to get out.

At the time, Tom had been so intent on his upcoming conversation that he hadn't noticed, and he certainly hadn't planned for a large man in a black suit to leap out and open the door for him, dark glasses obscuring the Fae Knight's identity.

'We'll have to change from calling you *Sheriff* to calling you *The Godfather*,' said a receptionist. 'Quite an entrance. Dancing with Tara Doyle one week and now this.'

'Neither are going to be repeated,' he said. 'Is the Commander free?'

The office staff scuttled off to share the news, and the PA checked that Ross was ready. As she showed Tom in, she stroked his chest (which was even more alarming than it sounds). 'What a beautiful shirt, Tom. That fabric feels absolutely gorgeous. In you go.'

Inside his oak-panelled lair, the Commander, stiff-backed as ever, was reading an extensive report.

'Is young Lucy okay?' he asked.

'Fine sir. I just had to run something past her before I came in.'

'Oh yes? We'll come to that in a moment, I presume. For now, take a seat and tell me all about this nonsense at Beckthorpe Abbey you've been involved in. I tried to prise details out of DC Fraser, but she was tighter than a clam at low tide.' He peered over his reading glasses. 'In the name of God, don't tell me you're going to do the same!'

'I have one thing to say, sir: *Special Constable Clarke.*'

Ross groaned and took off his glasses, then threw the report in a box marked *Secure Shredding* behind him. 'Was there a body? Is there actually a prisoner, and if so, where is he, because he's been remanded in custody but the system does not know where he is.'

'Yes to all of those, sir. Especially the prisoner part. He will be on the system soon, and he will go to trial eventually. We even found the missing old man, but that might not be on the system either. Donald Bell is being taken care of by his family.'

Ross pinched the bridge of his nose. 'The man makes a mess in Yorkshire and *still* drags you in? Conrad is like an octopus masquerading as a human being.'

Tom closed his eyes and tried not to let that thought become an image. 'About that, sir.'

'What? About Clarke being an octopus?'

'No, sir. I saw Liz Skelwith yesterday.'

'Not you too! Her name is *Swindlehurst,* for God's sake! Why is everyone suddenly calling her *Skelwith*? She's not getting divorced, is she? And Swindlehurst is her maiden name anyway, isn't it?'

'No sir, it's a joke, sir, but she does want to apply to take her Inspector's Board again.'

Ross couldn't sit up straight because he never sat any other way, but his whole body came to attention. 'Go on. Why do I think this isn't just about Liz?'

Tom's senior detective sergeant, Les Gartside, had reached as far up the greasy pole as he wanted (and as far as his second wife would permit). His other DS was different. In lots of ways. For one thing, Liz is a Daughter of the Earth. For another, her children are now in secondary school, and she wanted to try for Detective Inspector.

Commander Ross may or may not know about magick; this is a hotly debated topic. What he does know is that some people in the Lake District answer to another law, and that Liz is connected to them.

She had passed the exams, but couldn't take the Board without Ross's permission. So far, he had told her she wasn't ready as an excuse: Tom knew that in reality, Ross simply didn't trust her.

'Liz is ready, sir. She should be running CID here, not me. Not only am I too high a rank for this division, I think I could serve justice better elsewhere.'

'*Serve justice*? What do you mean, laddie?'

'I've been offered a part-time recorder's job. In the courts dealing with national security cases. I could go back to Professional Standards part-time. Once Liz has passed the Board, of course.'

Ross blinked several times. Some said that this was his cyborg computer brain at work; others said that he liked to think before he spoke, unlike Dozy Dave in Traffic.

'Good,' he finally announced. 'Unexpected, but good. Tell Liz that the same day she hands in her application, it will be on its way to the board with my full support and encouragement. And was this what you were talking to Lucy about?'

'In a way, sir. She would support me in anything, and vice versa, but I wanted to tell her I'd made my mind up and that I'd let her choose whether to live here or in Yorkshire. I inherited a house near York a while back, and I'd have to sell it to buy over here.'

'And what was her decision?'

'That we've got a while to think about it. Her business is all on this side of the Pennines.'

'Quite. Well, it's not up to me, but it sounds like a sensible thing all round. From what I've seen, Ms Gorrigan would be an excellent deputy if Lucy moves east. So long as Bridget doesn't stumble over any more bodies.'

'I don't think she plans to, sir.'

Lucy and her friend Bridget had been witnesses to a murder only a week ago, and Bridget had almost single-handedly solved it. Ross was pleased to make the arrest, but less than happy that Bridget had accused the murderer in public first.

'I'm sure she doesn't,' said Ross with a dark look. 'Are you staying here or heading back to your family? The funeral's next week, is it not?'

'It is. I'm going as soon as Clarke picks me up in the Wasp.'

'The what? No! Don't tell me. Instead, tell me who services your car.'

Tom was on his guard. 'Why's that, sir?'

'Because when I get a courtesy car, it's tiny. When you get one, it comes with chauffeur and bodyguard. I hear they're still lurking near the station.'

Tom stood up, the formal business now over. 'They're waiting to take me to the LZ, sir. The Wasp is a helicopter, and Conrad said he'd collect me on the ninth green. Or was it the eighth?'

'Get out!' roared Ross. Then he chuckled and picked up the next folder on his desk.

375

Chapter 50 — Burial Plots

Sheep are often terminally stupid. Just ask any farmer. Even the densest Texel knows it should avoid a helicopter, though. They scattered from the wash, and I found a nice clear spot to land thanks to Faith's clearing the Wards from the Radiant Sídhe from the air. Even better was the sight greeting me at the entrance to the higher planes: a nice green transparent slope.

Walk a little to the left and the slope disappeared to be replaced by a grove of trees on gentle mounds; walk a little to the right and it became a solid path to walk up. This was a big change in the field's topography.

Instead of having to navigate the tortuous path through the Midgard trees, someone very powerful had restored the original entrance, last walked up by the Radiant Queen herself, nearly a thousand years ago. I found the bad news standing at the top, wearing armour and carrying a spear. The Morrigan.

I hadn't realised what I was doing until I tripped over Faith's crutch and fell on my face, nearly rolling all the way back down the hill. Oh. I hadn't tripped: she'd deliberately tripped me.

'Don't look at her face,' said Faith. 'It stops you fleeing. No mortal can stand the sight of her War Face.'

'Keep your crutch there. Hang on. Up we get.' I struggled to my feet, keeping my eyes on the distant Black Coombe. 'Tell me that's not blood on her face.'

'What else would it be. Hurry up.'

I walked backwards until I felt the magick. 'Great Lady. Thank you for welcoming us.'

'Do not presume to question the ways of the Elderkind,' she pronounced in a voice that sounded exactly in proportion for a nine foot tall warrior queen. Scary isn't in it. And had I seen snakes for hair? Wasn't that what really happened to the snakes in Ireland? None of this nonsense with Saint Patrick – The Morrigan had taken them all to make a living wig. As you do.

'She's gone,' said Faith. 'You can turn around and stop shaking now. And she's left you a gift. You may not want it, though.'

She was right on both counts. Lying on the grass where the dread goddess had stood was a key. A big iron key. It wouldn't unlock any door, but the magick inside it was palpable and exactly the same toxic colours as the nightmare repository just over the ridge. I was now the proud custodian of the

Radiant Sídhe. Marvelous.

'I preferred her other wedding presents,' I said. 'Do we need that to get in?'

'No.'

'Then let's leave it there for now. I doubt anyone will steal it.'

We plunged into the sulphurous fumes of the pens, and I regretted not bringing breathing apparatus. Then again, as I've said, it doesn't do to keep the Allfather waiting.

He stood beneath one of the deformed trees, spear in hand. 'I cannot see in here,' he said, so softly that I had to strain my ears. 'My other eye would know.'

'Let me, dread lord,' said Faith. 'When she died, I saw her Name. I can find the Heather Queen's property.'

She limped to the middle of the roiling mass of sealed pits and looked around, then lifted her crutch and pointed to a dark corner. I followed the Allfather's giant stride as best I could.

Many of the chained creatures here are constantly struggling to escape. The green carpets covering their cells buck and writhe as they push for freedom. Not here. This plot was quiet.

'Help me, my lord. If you take that corner, we can peel it back easily.'

It was like artificial grass to look at, but nothing like it to touch. Think *lab-grown elephant hide* and you'd be closer. I should have brought gloves, too. Faith broke the seal and we lifted back the covering so that the Allfather could peer inside.

'Herja. My sweet, sweet child. What have they done to you?' said Odin, staring into the chamber.

A six-foot tall woman lay below. Her body was wasted, her golden hair fallen out and ringing her hollow face. Her eyes were dull and vacant, but I could feel that there was life inside. On her abdomen, just left of her navel, was a scar. Of course. Douglas Geldart had removed an ovary. And he'd left behind neat stitches forming the Infinite Circle which the Warden had shown me.

'She must have escaped from Ragnarök,' said the Allfather. 'And the Heather Queen must have captured her. You cannot keep a Valkyrie in ordinary chains, and these have stolen her mind. The essence of Herja is gone.'

Faith and I stood in silence, trying not to cough. I couldn't help myself, and after a minute, I had to clear my lungs. The noise stirred the Allfather from his reverie, and he took off his cloak.

He laid it on the ground, jumped nimbly into the chamber and picked up Herja in his arms, snapping the Binding Chain like cotton. He leaned over and laid her on the cloak, then jumped equally nimbly back out.

'I will take her to Valhalla to make one last sacrifice, to die and to rest in peace for eternity. I have a gift for you, Lord Guardian. You know what to do with it, I think.'

From underneath the cloak, he somehow produced a great axe. Not a battle axe, but a lumberjack's sturdy felling axe. He handed it to me, and my eye was drawn to the polished steel head. On the top, stamped into the metal was the Valknut, and all through the face of the axe were runes. When I looked up to ask a question, he was gone.

'Oh fuck, Faith. Are you thinking what I'm thinking?'

'That he wants us to cut down the trees? I'm afraid so.'

'Won't they escape?'

She shook her head. 'The trees give life. It's the Southern Road which keeps the Sídhe stable.'

'I was hoping you wouldn't say that. I really was.'

'I'll hold your uniform jacket, shall I?'

'You're a supernaturally strong magickal creature. I was hoping for a bit more help than that.'

'There's a flask of tea in the Wasp. I could text Thistle and ask her to bring it up here.'

'Ha ha.'

'I cannot wield an Axe forged by the Gallows Lord.'

'Oh. Right.'

It wasn't easy, but I didn't have to use muscle power alone. The magick in the axe helped bite through Wards and wood alike, and one by one the Fae trees fell to the earth. Faith was right: none of the creatures escaped, though they did struggle even harder as their supply of life and Lux drained away. I tried not to look.

I left the biggest tree till last, a solitary Yew at the far end which looked just a little like Yggdrasil. 'Go and wait at the bottom. And pour some tea.'

'My lord?'

'If it goes tits-up, there's no point in you dying as well. And that's an order.'

'My lord.'

I waited until she'd limped out of sight, down the slope, then I took one last look at the pens. They were almost completely still now, their occupants consciously or unconsciously rationing the Lux which kept them alive.

This repository was monstrous. The creation of the mutant, twisted abominations which lurked underneath was worse. That the Morrigan sponsored it was more of the same, but the most monstrous thing of all had been the scar on poor Herja's flesh. We are no better than them, and some of the time we are much worse. Whether our mortality makes us capable of being better *some* of the time is not enough. Human nature is like Fae blood: mercurial. I hefted the axe and swung it into the tree.

As the flowering yew crashed to the turf, I sensed lights going out all over the field. Maybe there was a Queen imprisoned under there. Maybe I'd become the Lord of Death by default. I waited a moment, to see if time would stand still again. It didn't. I put the axe over my shoulder and strode round the perimeter, eyes firmly fixed ahead.

At the top of the slope, I bent down and gingerly picked up the key, using my jacket to avoid physical contact. Many moons ago, I'd bonded myself to the First Mine of Clan Flint, allowing a little of its magick to enter my body and merge itself with my Imprint. I had no intention of becoming in any way Entangled with the Radiant Sídhe.

As I descended the slope, my attention was focused on the great Celtic Cross made of iron which ties together the Ley lines of south western Lakeland, and I didn't notice what my people were up to until I heard raised voices.

Sophie and Thistle were standing either side of Faith, mutiny written on both their faces. Sophie's arms were folded and her shoulders hunched protectively. Across the grass, Thistle was alternately pointing at Sophie and pleading with Faith. She said one more thing, then folded her arms to mirror Sophie, and I did not like what I heard: 'Either she goes or I do. There's plenty who'd have me!'

The Fae are incredibly, biologically loyal to the Queen. It goes way deeper than family loyalty in humans, but although Faith would soon be a Queen, she had not laid the egg from which Thistle had hatched. Those bonds *can* be broken.

'Enough!' I shouted. 'Faith, what is going on here, and why is this the first I've heard of it?'

Oh, that didn't come over well, did it? I hope to be a father one day, and I very much hope I never say anything like that to my children. Then again, two of these three are immortal; it's the human I'm worried about.

Sophie was close to crying and full of rage at the same time, I was going to go and comfort her, but as soon as I'd broken the argument, she unfolded her arms and ran away, stumbling over the tussocks and wiping her eyes as the tears started to fall.

'Thistle, go away for a bit. Over there,' I said, then found a pair of moss-covered boulders to sit on, after I'd dumped the key and put on my jacket. I was sweating buckets after my stint as a lumberjack, and my throat was parched. Faith handed me a mug of tea and took the other boulder.

'Yesterday was so sudden, my lord,' she began. 'I had not expected you to return so … abruptly. Nor for us to be at war in a day.'

'I didn't expect it, either. My body clock is telling me I got married two days ago, not two weeks.'

'There has been an issue in the household,' she said as if she was beginning a report to her CO.

'I can see that, Faith. Why is Sophie so upset?' I asked, trying to cut through the crap.

'Thistle has a right to be upset, too. As did Alicia.'

I didn't like the past tense there. And come to think of it, where *was* Alicia? And why was Faith's hair in a collapsing braid and not freshly groomed?

'Is Leesha okay?'

'She will be.' Faith sighed. 'My lord, no mortal I've ever met has come closer to understanding us than you.' She tilted her head. 'Maybe your sister. In a different way.'

I frowned. 'I didn't know Sofía had been with you at all.'

'I meant Rachael.'

That was even more alarming. 'Tell me you're joking. It is allowed.'

'Oh, no. I'm serious. The Red Queen showed you her Ink, I believe. Not even the mortal who gave her the First Seed has seen that. Rachael understands a different part, that's all, and you know I would rather die than see any Clarke get into trouble. Except you. I cannot avoid seeing you get into trouble.'

'You're changing the subject, Faith.'

'No I'm not! I'm trying to tell you something. We have a saying which translates literally as this: you can't tell the colour of the wing from the egg. It's about who we are and what we become.' She played with her braid, found it wanting, and started to unfasten it.

I lit a cigarette and waited patiently. When she'd unhooked a knot, she continued, 'Try to imagine all the eggs a Queen lays in her life, and try to see them as a huge pile of brightly coloured balloons.'

'I'll try…'

'That's us. We inflate slowly, and we can grow to a huge size, sometimes, but we can also burst. I am beginning to think that Thistle may have reached her limit. Maybe I'm wrong.'

'Humans are like that, too,' I offered.

Faith did not agree. 'You are not. I wish I'd seen my daughter grow up. It would help me understand you better. You are more like, I don't know…' She cast her eyes around for inspiration, then gestured at the Radiant Sídhe. 'You are more like a plot of land. Some are big and some are small, some have great views and others don't, but the size of the plot doesn't determine whether the building is beautiful or ugly, well-made or shoddy. You build your own lives in ways we cannot.'

I opened my mouth to object, then closed it. It was something I'd have to think about some other day.

'Interesting. Where's Alicia?'

'As I said, my lord: there was an incident. I also need her to see what it means to run a Royal Sídhe from a mature perspective and not just as a Sprite. We see things differently when we have wings. I have sent her away to gain experience, that's all. And yes, to let things calm down a little.'

'And Sophie? You know how much I take responsibility for her.'

'You are not the only one, my lord. Thistle will have to learn to like her bed. I will see to it. I give you my word.'

'Fine. Let's get this finished.'

'Did you not fell the tree? I swear I felt it, and I certainly felt the life going out around me.'

'The tree is down, the prisoners are at peace. It's time for some demolition.'

'My lord?'

I stood up and pointed to the key which pulsed gently on the grass. 'That's more than just a key, isn't it?'

'Yes.'

'Next time you see her, tell the Morrigan that she needs to update her metaphors. A remote control would be more appropriate than a key, wouldn't it?'

'I think a pair of virtual reality gloves comes closer to the mark, and you can tell her that yourself. My lord.'

'Stop arguing and pick it up. Use it to figure out exactly where the Ley line runs into the sídhe while I get in touch with Matt.'

I turned my back and went to the Wasp. I shut myself in and sent a message to Matt and Karina rather than calling. I didn't want them to talk me out of this.

Faith was standing a short way up the slope, shimmering in and out of sight because she was right on the liminal margin. 'Here, my lord. What are you going to do?'

I picked up the axe by way of an answer and opened my Third Eye to its fullest extent, and boy was I glad I'd got Faith to scope it out.

There was such a mess of Lux down there that I'd have mistaken the main Road for the supply line to the Radiant Sídhe and promptly blown myself across the Irish Sea as well as collapsing half the magick in the Particular. What I planned still wasn't without risks, though.

Cutting a working Ley line is like cutting through a live power cable: you *can* do it, but you'd have to be mad. And well protected, and I was neither mad nor insulated. Cutting the fastening at the end is still a huge risk, but a calculated one.

'You're staying close by this time,' I told Faith. 'For one thing, I might need you to pick me up and carry me away from the collapsing realms. For another, if I die, Mina will kill you because she can't get hold of the Morrigan.'

'I find that so comforting, my lord. How close to certain death do you want me to stand?'

'Don't be a wuss and stand two axe lengths away.'

She took up position and dropped her crutches. I really was going out on a limb here.

'Three, two, one…'

It was a good job she'd stood uphill, because the severed end of the Ley line whipped up and thrashed backwards, towards the iron cross.

'Run!' she shouted, haring past me and carrying her crutches.

Oh shit. I gripped the axe by the shoulder and tried to outrun the wave of collapsing reality that was pushing earth towards me in a tidal wave.

Something told me to leap forwards like I was trying for the crease in a cricket match. The violet shimmer in the ground might have played a part in that. In mid-air, a shock wave hit my back and propelled me and the axe into Thistle.

'Ooof. You are not a soft landing, but thank you,' I said once I'd rolled off her.

'And you're a geet lump of wood, so y'are.'

I crawled to my knees and looked for Faith. She was gripping her leggings, and darker black told me that she'd ruptured something in her thigh. 'Thistle…'

'Look to Her Grace!' she cried, dragging Sophie back from her sulk. I left them to it and turned to look behind me.

Where once there were gentle mounds, there was now a small hill with uprooted trees scattered on it, some clinging on to their place and some fully flat. I flopped back and let the magick in the ground seep into me.

Help was on its way. Leaving Faith here had always been the plan, and a car was due in ten minutes. Thistle and Sophie worked to stabilise the wound again, and Faith assured me that she was in no danger.

'Well done, you two,' I told the girl and pseudo-girl. 'I hope you two can patch things up in the same way.'

Faith actually rolled her eyes when I said that. I am *so* going to need a manual on how to talk to your children. As I went to fire up the Wasp, I wondered if it sort of grew with you: as they get older, your skills keep pace. I shall keep that thought to myself for now.

As the engine warmed up, I checked my phone. All good. I paused another few seconds to send Chris Kelly a message: *Can I change the subject of my dissertation to "Demolition of Enchanted Structures"????????????*

I got his answer as I landed next to, but not quite on, the Cairndale Golf Club, making sure they'd seen me first. Tom's car was waiting and I chuckled at Chris's reply: *Ha bleeding ha. No chance. Good to have you back.*

It was good to be back, but first I had the helicopter version of a road trip to undertake, beginning with Blackwater Tower. Or that's what I thought.

Chapter 51 — Echoes of War

'We need to talk,' said Tom when he'd put the headset on. 'What time are they expecting us at Blackwater Tower?'

Isn't that just the *worst* thing you can hear? *We need to talk* has never been the prelude to a pleasant conversation, especially when there's no qualification: *We need to talk about the bridesmaids* I can cope with, but this…

'Vaguely this morning. I was going to ask you to text them when we lifted off … it's going to be eleven thirty or thereabouts.'

Tom grunted. 'I'll tell them twelve, then we can have a few minutes. Come on, let's go before we're attacked by marauding golfers wielding Nine Irons.'

'Sorry, Tom, but they need to know more than that. Wards…'

'Shit. My bad. Eleven thirty it is.'

As I flew us over the Pennines, I gave him the latest on Saffron – that she'd had a comfortable night and was doing as well as could be expected. The buggy was waiting for us at the LZ, Lily and Eleanor Geldart standing in the sunshine and looking about as unhappy as you'd expect a pair of conspiratorial Mages who've been found out to look.

'Change of plan,' said Tom. 'We'll talk at Beckthorpe.'

'Fine.'

Eleanor's first question was about Saffron, and yes, she did look guilty when she asked. Her next question was about Richard, though. In her shoes, I'd have kept quiet on that front.

I frowned at her and said, 'He was delivered to the Undercroft in the early hours, so he's off my balance sheet, as Mina might say. You can contact Deputy Constable Drummond's office for further details. Shall we have another look at that basement?'

'Of course. Anything in particular?'

'Let's see.'

We drove up the hill and walked through the Tower and down the stairs. 'You must remember Douglas,' I said to Eleanor.

'I do and I don't. He's fifteen years older than me, and he cut himself off from the family when I was only a child. He was nice to me, as far as I can remember, and he didn't hold it against me when his mother chose my mother instead of him to be named as her successor.'

Tom and I looked at each other. 'When did your mother pass away?' I asked.

'She's still alive,' said Eleanor. 'She has the Mage's curse even worse than Douglas did, and she had it from childhood. She never became Warden.'

So the late Warden of Blackwater Tower chose her sister with crippling arthritis over her son, and we know that Douglas was a powerful Mage.

'I think I may need to talk to your mother,' I told her.

Eleanor pursed her lips. 'Of course, but you'll have to go to the South of France to do it face-to-face. She's lived there for twenty years and she doesn't come back any more. I spoke to her this morning, and she was shocked. She swears that she had no idea Douglas was alive. None.'

'Didn't you ask any questions when he was declared dead?'

We had reached the scene of yesterday's confrontation, and the stones still bore Richard's bloodstains from where Tom had smashed his face into the floor. Eleanor stood where she didn't have to look at them.

'His mother had put it about that he had wasted his talents and gone into *music hall.*'

'It's a term of abuse in magick,' I explained to Tom. 'Mages who prefer to entertain the mundane world rather than focus on their Art.'

'But not illegal,' said Eleanor. 'His mother also said that he'd developed a drug habit and this had led to his death. Made it seem as if we were being generous by burying him on the Estate.'

Tom grimaced and shook his head. I keep forgetting that he's related to this lot.

'Shall we?' said Eleanor, moving towards the iron door.

'What's with the antique medical equipment?' I asked when I'd taken a look round the room – it really could be the set from a First World War hospital drama.

'I was hoping you wouldn't ask,' said Eleanor, 'Or not with Thomas here.' She took a deep breath. 'It was put in by your great-grandfather, Thomas Alexander Morton, so that the family could look for a cure for his wife. No one wanted to take it out after we failed. We've never used it much, and if you look further you'll see that most of the workshops are deeper underground.'

There was nothing here except painful reminders of what had happened to Saffron, and staying would be as uncomfortable for me as for the Geldarts.

'I see. Warren will be coming to make a full inspection tomorrow, so let's go upstairs and back into the light.'

Two plastic bags were laid on the dining table containing the anonymous letter informing the Geldarts about Douglas. There was also coffee, which Lily poured.

'Where's the file?' asked Tom. 'The Abbey file on Douglas. Richard went to a lot of trouble to get it.'

Eleanor looked nonplussed. 'Haven't you got it?'

'How could we?'

'Then Douglas must have taken it.'

'How could *he* have taken it? He was a bit preoccupied trying to escape,' said Tom.

'And I saw him running down the hill,' I added. 'He waved at me, and he certainly didn't have a bulging file stuffed into his trousers.'

'Then I have no idea. It certainly arrived, because I saw Richard put it down in the treatment room.'

Tom shrugged. It was important, but not so important that we were going to tear the whole Estate apart looking for it. If Eleanor was lying, she'd had plenty of time to destroy it. I'd put it on Warren's list for the search.

'Eleanor Geldart, I am arresting you for assisting an offender and for deliberate deception. You will be interviewed in due course.'

'Very well,' she replied stiffly.

'I think we're done here,' I said to Tom.

He drained his coffee and put down the cup. 'Yes. Shall we walk down to the Wasp? Some fresh air might be nice.'

The goodbyes consisted of curt nods all round, and Eleanor didn't try to ingratiate herself with Tom with any further condolences about his grandfather. I lit a cigarette and said, 'Thanks, Tom. A breath of fresh air is exactly what I need.'

He shook his head. 'Not quite what I had in mind. Are you really going to play no further part in the investigation?'

'This one? No. I was CO when an officer was hurt. Now that we're not in an emergency, Iain Drummond takes over. Warren's young, but he's got a few years under his belt. He knows what to do.'

'Good,' said Tom decisively, and I got the impression that the King's Watch had just passed a test we didn't know we'd been entered for.

'Besides,' I continued, 'it will give me more time to dig deeper into Douglas's past. Creating Raven can't have been his only crime, and you heard him: "Is the Legacy secure?" It was all he wanted to know before he murdered his wife. And himself.'

'And he clearly expected an old associate to rescue him, not give him up to his family. I wonder why she or he chose not to.' We were nearly at the helicopter. 'I've organised lunch,' he said. 'Let's find out what Kathy Metcalfe's cooking is really like. But she won't be joining us until afterwards.'

'Sorry?'

'You'll see.'

Going to Asgard for my wedding night had given me a fairly weird sensation when we returned to Midgard and found that over two weeks had passed. I got the same feeling in reverse when I landed on the lawns of Beckthorpe Abbey, and it had nothing to do with magick.

Since I was last here, yesterday morning, I've seen a revolution in Galloway, demolished a sídhe and watched my officer hacked open by a geriatric Mage. In Beckthorpe, they're still reeling from Simon Swift's murder and still suffering the suffocating police presence which goes with a murder enquiry, even though there is a suspect in custody.

We were met at the doors by Dr Mora McNair, butt of several jibes from

Kathy. I don't know why, but I don't have to live or work with her.

'Half the guests left this morning,' she said when Tom asked her how things were going. 'We had no choice but let them go once your colleagues said they were finished interviewing them. I've told them they're on remission until Sunday. We'll see how many turn up then. This way.'

'What a lovely staircase,' I remarked as we ascended it. 'One of the few original features unless I'm mistaken.'

Mora shrugged as if this was news to her and she led us to a room which must be over the kitchens. 'There used to be a dumb waiter here. Kathy wants it put back for some reason. Your colleague's in there, as is lunch. You know where to find me.'

Colleague? Who? Aah. 'Elaine! Hello.'

'Afternoon, Conrad. Everything okay?'

Her question was addressed to both of us, but she was looking at Tom. 'Fine,' he said curtly. 'What have we got?'

'Early spring soup, apparently. And a cake, but Kathy said she couldn't guarantee it wouldn't break a filling.'

Elaine poured mugs of tea from a flask and we sat down to a delicately scented light soup and fresh bread. I was about to surrender to my hunger when Tom completely spoilt the mood.

'I've asked Elaine here partly to save repeating myself.'

My spoon was in mid-air, and I thought about putting it down to listen. Sod that. 'Mm?'

He turned to his partner. 'Liz says I can tell you this, by the way. She's putting in for Inspector, and I'm handing over the reins when she gets it.'

Elaine *did* put her spoon down. 'Bloody hell, Tom. What's going on? Not that she doesn't deserve it.'

He turned to me. 'I'm taking a part-time job as Recorder to the Cloister Court North.'

I was stunned. 'You? Working for Marcia? How come?'

'Because she offered it to me, and because I can't cope any more.' He didn't let me interrupt and pressed on. 'Not the violence. I can cope with that. I think. I've no idea how you manage to, but that's your problem. It's the make-it-up justice. It's the drumhead courts and the single combat. It's wrong.' His mouth twisted. 'She won't thank me for quoting her, but I agree with Hannah: I want to be part of the solution.'

I pushed my soup away. Where on earth had this come from? 'Are you sure it was Marcia who offered you the job, not Lois Reynolds?'

He looked hurt. 'That's not fair, Conrad. If anything, I agree with you rather than her. At least about bringing the Creatures of Light inside the fold. By the way, I can't see the Fae agreeing to submit to human justice any time soon.'

'What are you on about?' said Elaine, who had lost track of things completely.

'The Fae, the Gnomes, the Dwarves, all of them,' said Tom. 'They're just so … alien. It makes *Justice* such an abstract concept.'

Elaine glanced at me. 'And yet I've always found *Justice* to be so very *material*. Solid. But what do I know? I'm only a train driver's daughter from Rawtenstall.'

Tom looked stung, then sheepish. 'This isn't going how I planned it.'

I reached for my soup again. 'I've got three things to say, Tom. The first is that you should read de Breasey's history of the Inquisition of St Michael, or at least the chapters on the Pale Horsemen. Having corralled all human Mages into the Church, they decided to deal with the Creatures by exterminating them, and I know that's not you.'

He gave me a dark look. 'And the other two?'

'First, I'm going to offload the Dual Natured Commission on to your shoulders. I really do have too much of a conflict of interest, and it'll help you get your feet under the table.'

'Eeuw,' said Elaine. 'Imagine feeling paws and claws and stuff with your bare toes.'

'That was more literal than I expected,' said Tom. 'And you are a piece of work, Clarke. If only I could find a reason to argue with it.'

'Excellent! And that leads me to who you're going to nominate as your successor in police liaison. I had Liz down as favourite, but…'

'But she has CID to run,' he interrupted. 'And that was another reason for inviting Elaine.'

'Me!'

'Yes.' He turned to me rather than his partner. 'You know Elaine hasn't had a regular job since leaving Leicester?'

'Sort of.'

'It's because of him,' she said, pointing at Tom with her spoon. 'Him and my husband.'

'Erm, Rob, isn't it?'

'When I met Rob, I thought I'd be marrying a PE teacher, not a star international. Unless he's injured, he could have another five years as a top player, and that includes two world cups.'

'You do realise that you'll have to call him *Chief*,' said Tom, 'and they'd love you to stay at Cairndale.'

'Maybe they would, but I don't want to stay there. I'd rather stick with Professional Standards and help the King's Watch part-time, even if it means another encounter with werewolves. And as an absolute minimum, I want one of them magic amulets that stop you getting shot. Minimum.'

'An Ancile shouldn't be a problem,' I told her. Then I offered her my hand. And a badge. 'Welcome to the Merlyn's Tower Irregulars.'

She shook my hand and stared at the badge. 'Why do I get the impression

I've just agreed to more than liaison?'

Tom wiped his hands on a threadbare napkin. 'Because Conrad measures things by the Clarke Inch – he thinks it's the same length as the Imperial inch, but it feels more like a mile. And he'll no doubt be setting you on the search for Douglas Geldart's associates before you've tried that cake. Assuming you're brave enough.'

Elaine squinted. I've seen her do it before with Tom, and it's her way of coping with his sense of humour. I just take everything he says literally.

'Brave enough for the cake?' she said in the end.

'What else would I mean? Shall I carve?'

'Who baked the cake?' asked Conrad Clarke when he limped into the kitchen. 'It was delicious.'

'DJulie,' responded Kathy. 'I was gonna send her to the shop for it, but she's a lazy cow at heart so she offered to bake it herself.'

'Hey! Do you think I'm deaf!' said an outraged dJulie from the open fridge door.

'Thank you,' said Conrad rather loudly. 'Very moist.'

'Bet you've never tasted a soul cake.'

'Sorry? What?'

Before Conrad and dJulie could get their wires completely crossed, Kathy grabbed her coat. 'You did want to see me, right?'

'Please. Any chance of a coffee? One more flight to go, and extra caffeine never hurts.'

'I'll bring it to the bench. Where we were last time.' It hit her. 'I mean *yesterday*. Bloody hell, was it only yesterday?'

'Thanks.'

When he'd gone, she put the kettle on and told dJulie, 'He's hard of hearing.'

'And I'm supposed to feel sorry for him? What does he know about *hardship*.'

Kathy retrieved a cafetiere and grabbed a tray. As the kettle boiled, she muttered to herself, 'If you could deep fry that chip on your shoulder, girl, you could feed the Abbey for a month.'

He was on the phone when she approached the bench a short while later, and he waved for her to join him. Not that she would have stood holding a tray in the middle of the grass, no matter how tall and rugged he looked in his uniform.

'Have they told you anything?' he asked when she'd poured the coffee.

'The first one to treat me as anything other than a suspect is Scarywoman…'

He winced when she mentioned DC Fraser's nickname. 'Who told you that?' he asked, then realisation dawned. 'Aah. Mina.'

'Mina told me not to tell the Inspector. Didn't say anything about you. Was that Mina on the phone? Did she get home safe?'

'She did, and she's almost forgiven me. I think. Anyway, she'll soon forget it – looks like our housekeeper might be going into labour.'

Of course he had a housekeeper. Didn't they all? Kathy couldn't help herself. 'Why isn't she on maternity leave, then?'

'Aah. Yes. She lives in, so… Anyway, what did Elaine tell you?'

'She gave me my phone back for one thing. I know you said you'd put in a good word, but you did leave rather sharp like yesterday, and none of the local coppers believed me. Finally got a chance to look you up.'

'Don't believe everything you read online.'

'Doctor Simon used to say the same thing until I told him that I always believe everything online is true, because it's a lot easier that way: I don't have to think about it.'

He took out his cigarettes and offered her one. 'You're going to miss him, aren't you? Doctor Simon, I mean.'

She shook her head. She hadn't begun to process that yet. It was too soon to imagine a future without him in it. Best to focus on today. 'Elaine said you'd arrested someone. Is that right?'

'We have. It's what I ran off to do yesterday. He's in custody and hopefully he'll plead guilty and save you the stress of appearing in court.'

'Good. I hope the bastard rots in hell.' She took a deep breath and asked the question that really worried her. When she'd asked Scarywoman earlier, the detective had looked away and changed the subject. 'Did you find Don?'

Conrad didn't look away. 'We did. I'm afraid that he died last night, shortly after his wife. You deserve an honest answer, Kathy, and I'm sorry to say that he took his own life rather than answer questions about his past. He did ask about you, though. He wasn't a complete monster.'

The thought of Don being *any* kind of monster was more than she could bear. Then again, it didn't look like Conrad wanted to answer awkward questions. 'I hope he rests in peace. And what's going to happen to Michael?'

'Out of my hands. I really don't know.'

'Elaine said he was adamant she pass on a message to me: *Sorry and can we meet one day so that I can explain everything?* Can I see him?'

'Up to you, Kathy. So long as you keep the conversation to his past and your future, I don't see a problem.'

The way he said it left Kathy in no doubt what he meant: *Michael is a cat.*

389

Don't let his curiosity do for you what it did for him. There were stains on Conrad's uniform which hadn't been there yesterday. Someone had laundered his combats overnight, but blood is very hard to remove. 'Message received.'

He rubbed his face with his hand, as if he were trying to reset some switch inside himself. 'I had a word with your cousin this morning.'

Cousin? What cousin? Kathy was too wary to say anything but, 'Oh yes?'

'Not that he knew he had a cousin called Kathy, and it was a guess on my part, but yes, Xavier Metcalfe is your cousin.'

'I know he is!'

Kathy tracked back through the wilderness years, the drunk years, and tried to remember when she'd last heard of Xavier, and then it clicked. 'He's got the same condition as me, hasn't he! I always knew she was a lying bitch.'

'And now it's me who's no idea what you're talking about.'

She shuffled on the bench, bracing her hands and looking at the grass. 'His mother never said who Xavi's father was, until all of a sudden she sends him off to boarding school and says his father played for Leeds United and was paying for it, only his dad was never a professional footballer, was he, and your lot paid for it, didn't they?'

'Another department paid for his schooling, yes, and now he really does work for *my lot*. Would you mind if he got in touch?'

'No skin off my nose. Didn't he go to some university in London? I'm surprised he has time for the likes of me.'

'And how are you, Kathy? I'm going to fly off in a minute, and I doubt I'll ever come back. At least not until your girls grow up. Is there anything I can help with?'

'The picture. The John Gould. Inspector Morton never actually took it into evidence, so…?'

'I'd hang on to it until after Richard Geldart has pleaded guilty, then do what you want with it. And when the police release the crime scene, you'll notice that some of Don's effects are missing. What's left behind is for the Abbey to do with as they see fit.' He hesitated. 'My housekeeper's going to leave in two years. I might give you a call then. Clerkswell is a lovely part of the world.'

'Maybe it is, but it's not Yorkshire.'

'No. It isn't. Goodbye, Kathy. And thanks again.'

They shook hands, and she stayed on the bench until he'd limped out of her life and flown away. For now.

The Fragrant Faye was in bits. Totally. Mingey Mora had effectively put Kathy in charge of everything except treatment, and Dr Simon's daughter had turned up and been no use at all. It was good to be needed. To have something to do. After all, if coming to know Don and Michael had proved anything to Kathy, it had proved that the Devil really does make work for idle hands.

Chapter 52 — The Spoils of War

She was waiting outside when the taxi dropped me by the main entrance to Jimmy's hospital in Leeds, after a half hour ride from the airport where I'd stashed the Wasp for tonight.

'How is she?' I asked.

'There's a chapel just down the corridor inside. I can lock us in,' said Lady Celeste Hawkins, mother of Saffron and someone who could make my life very, very difficult. Or kill me.

'Of course.'

It was a multi-faith room, as you'd expect, and it looked like Leeds's Muslim population cared more for it than anyone else. She wasn't joking about locking the door, nor about putting a Glamour outside saying that it was closed for a private service.

I waited until she'd sat down so that I could choose a seat out of striking distance. I looked at her face, and I could see exhaustion, hurt and anger, but I couldn't see the void of tragedy.

She looked down at her skirt and brushed it before she spoke. 'I'm under strict instructions today: Essy says that I must under no circumstances shout at you.' She looked up. 'I told her that depends. I told her that I wanted you to look me in the eye and say that there was nothing you could have done to stop her getting hurt.'

'No. There was nothing. Eleanor Geldart could have stopped it, and Saffron could have stood back, but then there would have been two dead Mages, I think, and Saffron couldn't have allowed that to happen. It's not who she is.'

'I don't think I know who she is any more. Not after this.' Her mouth twitched. 'As you'll discover. Isn't there a nice safe desk job somewhere for her? Like Vicky's?'

'It's the second thing I want to talk to her about, right after I've seen how she is. And how is she?'

'Healing. The arm wound needs another operation tomorrow, something to do with a tendon, but they want to do an MRI on her chest first and I want to look into the neurosurgeon. The trauma surgeon did a good job, but I want the best there is to fix that arm.'

'Quite right, too.'

'I had quite a tussle this morning with her, you know. About whether I should give her phone back. More than anything, she wanted to know what had happened. I think she was a little disappointed when you wouldn't tell her.'

That sounded like Saffron: very quick to think people have a low opinion of her. 'That's not what I said. I said that I'd tell her in person, and if I could, because I had other things to do and because I wanted to see her.'

'You run a very tight ship, Conrad, I must say. I tried to get Jay to find out from Vicky, and he laughed at me. No one seems to know what's been going on. At least none of the ones who'll talk to me.'

'You need spies in the Fae, Lady Hawkins. They know everything.'

'I'm sure they do. She's in the surgical high dependency unit, which is only half a mile from here. Rupert's with her and she's coming back to Cherwell to recuperate.'

I was dismissed. 'Thank you.'

The surgical dependency unit was a lot closer than half a mile, but only if you took a short-cut through administration (which I did). Saffron's father was by her side and leaning over his daughter when I knocked at the door, and if the hulking Viking back of Rupert Thornhill hadn't been there, I'd have walked straight on, because it wasn't Saffron in the bed, it was Sammi…

'Wha… Erm?' I said from the doorway.

'Hello, Conrad,' said Rupert, rising and stepping aside. 'Five minutes only, and I'll be standing outside timing you.'

Rupert has no magick, as you may remember, which is why he was here with his daughter and not stalking her CO in the multi-faith room. I am not a parent yet, so I wouldn't venture an opinion on this. The door closed behind him, and I stared bug-eyed at the girl in the bed.

'Side-effect of the healing magick,' she said, brushing her newly ombre-d locks.

'But I didn't do any healing magick!'

'Nor did you remember to remove my Artefacts before dropping me off for chest surgery. You could have killed a theatre nurse.'

Shit. She was right. 'I'm sorry. Truly sorry. Did you wake up and remember?'

'No. Lily Geldart took them off, and it was her who did the healing magick: a special reinforcing Work, except that she didn't know I was wearing a wig, and so my hair healed to match it. Could have been worse: I could have permanent D cups.'

'Erm…'

She reached up a hand, desperate to hold mine. I closed the gap and took it.

'Thanks, Chief. Thanks for forgetting about Artefacts and just about everything else and for getting me here. And before you say anything else, it was all my fault.'

She had to pause to take a breath; cracked ribs do that to you.

'No, it was the Geldarts' fault, Saff.'

She shook her head. 'It was mine. GG and I have been experimenting with a Work that allows me to bypass the Badge of Office, and that was what allowed Douglas to steal my knife.'

I tried to keep poker face. Tried and failed.

She gripped my hand. 'Please, please don't tell Mum. She'd hit the roof and go into orbit, and I'm the one who's suffered.'

I squeezed her hand back. One day, when she's better, I'll tell her that if she hadn't been so stupid, Douglas Geldart's brain and its memories would be in custody and not spread over a field near Gretna Green. Not today, though. 'I'll leave that out of the report, Saff.'

'Good. Now sit down and tell me what happened.'

The door opened. 'Two minutes left.'

'Sod off, Dad. I want to know what happened.'

'One minute fifty,' said Rupert, closing the door.

'Douglas and his wife are dead, as is the Queen of Galwyddel in Scotland. Richard is in the Undercroft and Iain Drummond is investigating Eleanor. Now do you want the important news?'

'How the fuck did the Heather Queen get involved, and what could be more important that that?'

'I'm relieving you of the Cleveland Watch. You can't police a region where you've had a deadly encounter with the biggest family. I'm going to offer it to Xavier Metcalfe.'

'You can't send me back to Mercia! That's not fair!'

'How about Watch Captain of the Marches and Deputy's Adjutant, based in Middlebarrow and with the promise of London when I leave next year?'

'What in London?' she said, jumping right over everything else, including the fact that I wanted her to work with Elaine Fraser.

'Vicky may be moving on, but I can't say more.'

'What? What's she doing and where?'

'Time's up!' said Rupert.

'You can give me your answer when you're better,' I told Saffron. Then I bent down to kiss her forehead, and she let me.

'I hate you, Chief. I really do. And I haven't told you what the surgeon said yet.'

I looked at Rupert. 'Oh?'

'You can tell him now,' said her father.

'I think he's on the spectrum or something, because when he came this morning he talked to the monitor not me, especially when he said that I should *think carefully before lactating post-partum*. I had to get the nurse to translate.'

I didn't need a translation, and the concern must have shown on my face.

'Relax, Chief. I'm going to get a full reconstruction. I hear there's a good place near Byford.'

'Take care, Saff.'

I left the room and ran into Celeste, huffing slightly from having to climb two sets of stairs instead of taking the staff lift like I did.

'Are you off again?'

'Back to the airport hotel, via a computer hire place. My flying is done for today and I have the mother of all reports to write.'

She hesitated, and I could see that there was something she really wanted to say, so I waited patiently.

'We need to talk, Conrad. Your operational secrecy may be top grade, but I know that you're up to something big. Something political.'

'Not me, Lady Hawkins. I'm just a tradesman with some powerful clients. That's all.'

'And I'm just a member of the Women's Institute. Take care. Oh, and congratulations on your wedding, if it doesn't seem rather late.'

'You have no idea, Celeste. Thank you. Thank you very much.'

She nodded and slipped into her daughter's room. I limped off and headed for the main entrance to look for a taxi.

Tom had said goodbye to Conrad at Beckthorpe because that's where his car still was. It took ten minutes to get the Crime Scene vans out of the way, and then he was off, after sending his mother a quick message to expect him shortly.

When he pulled into the Cloister, she must have been hovering in the hall, because she was out on the steps before he'd locked his car.

'Are you alright, Tom? Lucy has been very busy *not* telling me what really happened.'

He gave her a hug, something he had yet to see Conrad do to Mary Clarke. He shook his head, trying to clear the giant shadow of Conrad Bloody Clarke from his peripheral vision.

'It was a bit hairy last night, Mum, but I was never in danger. And best of all, I get to hand over the paperwork on this one. As soon as I've finished the report this afternoon, the whole mess will be someone else's problem.'

'Always a good thing. Let's go inside and I'll put the kettle on.' She paused. 'Where did you get that shirt from? It looks brand new and fits you perfectly.'

'I bought it for Conrad's wedding and it was dark when I left yesterday. I forgot I was supposed to save it for best.'

She raised her eyebrows. 'Look, your father has been in a foul mood all morning and only cheered up when I said you were on your way here. He's desperate to talk to you for some reason and won't say why. At least that means it's professional. He's in the study, and I'll bring the tea through.'

Tom dropped his briefcase and headed for the north side of the house, where his father had a gloomy room covered in law books which made you think he came from a long line of barristers instead of having grown up on a farm. Tom knocked and went in. 'Hello, Dad.'

His father was trying to read something on his laptop, which he'd made difficult for himself by placing it at an odd angle to the side. In the centre of his desk, where the computer usually sat, was an ornate oak box slightly larger than a church bible. In fact it was about the right size to *contain* a church bible.

His father looked up and shut the lid of the computer before coming round to stand in front of Tom and work his mouth as if he didn't know what to say. In the end, he pointed to one of the club chairs in front of the gas fire and plonked himself in the other.

Tom hung his jacket on the oversized coat stand (full of judge's robes) and put his phone face down on the coffee table. 'What's up, Dad?'

He should have guessed what came next. Should have. All he could blame for his lack of foresight was that he was so used to keeping magickal and mundane apart that it simply never occurred to him.

'Eleanor Geldart's been on the phone,' said his father.

'Oh? What did she tell you?'

'Everything she wanted me to know, which I suspect will be less than the whole truth.' He steepled his fingers, then squirmed in his chair, then got up and took the box from the desk, fiddling with some sort of catch. With his back to his son, he said, 'I was never supposed to get this. If your great uncle hadn't accidentally lived over the broom, this would have stayed in North America instead of coming back here like a raven coming home to roost.'

He turned and showed Tom that the box did indeed contain a book. A leather bound book with the title stamped on the front cover in red. *Blackwater Tower* it said, and underneath, *A Tale of Magick by Thomas Alexander Morton, First Baron Throckton.*

'I got it two years ago,' said his father. 'Along with a phone call from Eleanor saying that it was true. It's yours now, as the heir to the title, but I wouldn't be in a hurry to read it.' He closed the box. 'How did it happen, Tom? How did you get mixed up in magick when the Geldarts have been trying to keep us out of it for generations?'

Tom was thunderstruck. His father *knew* about magick? Had known for *two years* and said nothing? Then again, Tom had said nothing either.

His father took his silence as an avoidance tactic, and pressed on. 'Just tell me it wasn't them. Just tell me it wasn't Eleanor or Richard who Entangled you. Is that the right word?'

Tom coughed. 'Yes. That's right. No, it was nothing to do with them. Do you remember when Elaine got shot by an arrow? Well, it was fired by a madwoman while we were being attacked by Mannwolves. That's how it started, and the man to really blame is Conrad Bloody Clarke. In fact, he's to blame for just about everything in my opinion.'

'The man from Operation Jigsaw? The man whose wedding you went to? How…?'

'It's a bloody long story, Dad. And it gets worse: I'm resigning from CID in Cairndale and taking a post as Recorder to the Cloister Court. And talking of all things Cloister, I need to ask you something about the house.'

His father looked like his blood pressure had just gone up rather too high, and Tom was relieved when his mother knocked at the door with tea. 'I think you'd better get another cup and join us,' said his father. 'I don't think I can cope with this on my own. And you'd better bring more biscuits.'

I think I must have been living in the country too long, because the sound of aircraft has never bothered me before. I did a quick search and discovered that the last flight to Leeds-Bradford arrived at eleven o'clock. Fair enough, and there was a gap between the last two arrivals which should allow me a decent chat to Mina, once I'd finished clearing up all the other crap. However, Tom Morton had other ideas. At least he had the grace to add *again* when he messaged me at tea time: *We need to talk. Again.*

The poor man looked even more harassed than I did when we connected later. 'What's up, Tom?'

'It's my father. He's been Entangled for two years and never thought to mention it to me.' He laughed. 'And neither did I to him, for some reason.'

'At least it didn't take a bomb for your family to discover what was going on.'

'Might have been easier. No. Sorry. I didn't mean that. Here. Have a look at this.'

He lifted a properly Gothic book to the webcam and let me read the title. 'According to Dad, it was our ancestor's way of making sure that we Mortons know what a shifty bunch the Geldarts are.' He put the book down. 'I think I gathered that for myself. Do you know what they did? Do you remember I said I went there once as a teenager?' I nodded. 'Guess what they were doing? They were assessing me for any Gift, as they did Fiona and Diana. And my cousins. Bloody good job we didn't have one is all I can say. Eleanor rang him this morning to get in her side of the story about Richard, because with a Watkins Trial coming up, Dad would know all about it.'

There was more of this for about ten minutes and then he got round to the real reason for the call. 'Just how rich are you, Conrad?'

'Why do you want to know? Has somebody said something, because believe me, Mina accounts for everything. You wouldn't find so much as a stray fiver if you audited us.'

He laughed. 'I know, which is why I wouldn't bother. No, this is for me.' He glanced away for a second. 'I asked Dad for a loan today. An advance on my inheritance or something. Unfortunately, the Bank of Mum and Dad became rather overdrawn when Di bought her Hackney loft.'

'This sounds serious,' I said, to show that I wasn't about to make a joke. Then I made one anyway. 'You'd think that a high court judge would have a few grand squirreled away offshore. Or has he sent it to that Prince in Nigeria?'

'It's more than a few grand. I need two hundred and fifty thousand, and I need it in cash. I want to buy Tara Doyle out of Lucy's business.'

That was unexpected. 'Ouch, Tom. I had no idea things had got so far. You wouldn't want that on your declaration of interests, would you?'

'Sod that, Conrad. I just don't want her in Lucy's life.'

It came from the heart, and I was the only person who could hear what he was really saying. I also knew that what he was asking was impossible: once the Fae are in your life, it's up to them whether they stay there. And up to Lucy, too, but I wasn't about to tell him either of those things. When it came to money, though…

'I can't help you, myself, Tom. I simply don't have that sort of liquidity.' I held up a hand. 'What I *can* do is to suggest that Rachael takes a stake. It's a perfectly sensible investment for her clients. If she knows you'll guarantee it, off the record of course, then there shouldn't be a problem.'

He burst out laughing. 'Which begs the question of whether the Clarkes are more trustworthy than the Fae.'

I tried to look hurt. 'You know we are.'

'I know no such thing. I think I'll have to sleep on that one.'

'Probably a good idea. For both of us.'

'Everything else okay?' he asked. 'How's Saffron?'

'Much changed, Tom. Much changed. No, seriously, she's on the mend.'

'Good. Thanks for listening, Conrad. Safe flight home.'

'Goodnight, Tom.'

I did get my Facetime with Mina, and all she wanted to talk about was whether or not Myfanwy was suffering from late Braxton Hicks contractions or whether they were the real thing, and where was the midwife when we were paying so much money to have her on retainer?

Mark Hayden

And then suddenly, in the distance, I heard a piercing scream. In Welsh. If you can scream wordlessly in a foreign language. And Mina was gone. At midnight, I turned my phone off and went to sleep.

Chapter 53 — Peace Dividend

Myfanwy's labour was in full swing when I touched down at the Grange on Friday morning, having left Leeds-Bradford as soon as ATC would let me, and I made myself useful by taking Scout for a walk.

Seriously, other than having the Wasp on standby for an emergency, there was nothing I could do that the midwife, Ben, his parents, Miss Parkes, Nell from the shop, Mina and the actual mother herself couldn't do perfectly well without me.

I was making tea (and Scout was exiled to his kennel) when I heard a roar of male pride from upstairs and stuck my head into the hall. 'It's a girl!' shouted Ben's father. 'And there's a boy on the way!'

And twenty minutes later, there they were, one in each of Myfanwy's arms and both of them suckling greedily.

'I think I might have got the date wrong,' said Myvvy when I'd finished adding my congratulations and telling her that they were beautiful. 'I thought they were early but the midwife thinks they were full term. Anyway, this is Seren on the right, and that's Welsh for *Star* 'cos she's my little star, and this here is Arthur. Ben's choice.' She checked to see that Ben wasn't listening. 'He was so set on Arthur, and then he tells me it's because he wanted an English name. Didn't have the heart to tell him that Arthur was British, not English, and that he should have gone for *Alfred*, and there can't be two Alfreds in Elvenham, not that there's anything wrong with *Alfred* of course. Or Mary or Conrad or Rachael or Sofia…'

Thankfully even Myfanwy gets tired giving birth, and I managed to escape shortly afterwards, and passed Ben on the stairs. I gave him a man-to-man congratulations, you know the one, where you congratulate him on becoming a father rather than on the birth.

'And now the fun starts for all of us,' he said. 'And for you, it starts tonight. You're captain for tomorrow's away game, the first one since your wedding that hasn't been rained off.'

'What about Stephen Bloxham?' I asked, not because I didn't want to be skipper but because Stephen has, in truth, put more hours into the team than I have.

Ben gave me a funny look. 'Since the wedding, Stephen has been taking a sabbatical from the team. Jules said it was something to do with you. I thought you'd blackmailed him or something.'

I frowned. If I had dirt on Stephen Bloxham, I'd definitely have used it, but I don't. 'Sorry, Ben, you've lost me. Are you sure about me being captain?'

'Positive.'

'Fine. I'll send a team WhatsApp to announce both happy events.'

Mina followed me downstairs, looking thoughtful, and helped me finish making mugs of tea. 'Shall we go for a walk when we've passed them round?'

I hesitated, mugs in hand. There was a tone in her voice which hinted that *We need to talk.* Actually, we did. 'Sounds good to me.'

'I'll take those two mugs and see you in ten minutes by the stables.'

I was slightly shocked when Mina emerged from the house wearing sturdy trainers and her workout leggings. Looked like she meant a *serious* walk rather than a stroll. Scout would be happy.

'In all my time here, husband, I have never been through the woods. Shall we?'

It had rained a lot while we were in Asgard, apparently, hence the lack of cricket. 'It'll be muddy through the woods. Are you sure your new combat uniform wouldn't be more appropriate?'

She gave me a venomous look. 'That is one of the things we need to talk about: Liz Skelwith tells me that Elaine Fraser claims to have pictures. I think you took one and passed it to her.'

As if I would do a thing like that. Elaine is perfectly capable of doing that herself. Or Tom.

We set off through the gardens, which looked immaculate. Apparently Ross Miller has been retained to keep on top of things until Myfanwy can do it herself (so quite a long time then).

'I understand something now,' she began, and I was expecting some profound feminine insight into motherhood. 'I now know why we are still in the second largest bedroom: it's because it's the furthest from Myvvy's room.'

'Maybe.'

We sat on the well for a moment, to give Scout a chance to finish sniffing. The air was alive with the smells of early summer, and I could hear the bees from the new hive, the mundane one at least, and if I could hear them, they must have been making an absolute racket.

'We have a lot to talk about, don't we?' she said. 'Starting with what the Allfather said to you in Asgard when you went off for your male bonding time.'

'It's a long story, and I'd rather not tell it sitting here, thanks. Too many associations. We also need to discuss what *really* happened at the Hen Party, why Lucy's car ended up in the Manchester Ship Canal, why Alicia has been sent packing to Ireland and what's going on between Thistle and Sophie, and that's before we get to the goings-on at the wedding. I'm sure you know all about it by now.'

Scout trotted back and looked up. 'Arff!' he said, which roughly translated means *I'm bored now. Why are you sitting down????*

'And him,' said Mina. 'You need to know the real reason he's in the dog house.'

I stood up and Mina took my hand. 'You can pull me up the slope if I get tired going up this mountain.'

It was soon going to be like the wedding all over again at the Grange: Erin has already left the Lakes to come and stay, and on Sunday morning, Vicky is bringing up the Boss. Vicky is coming to see her friend's new babies, the Boss not so much. On Sunday afternoon, we will gather in the library under the watchful gaze of Douglas Geldart's bust of Homer and figure out where to go next.

That, however, is a story for another day. Right now we have a different sort of mountain to climb. Okay, it's a hill, but you have to allow my wife a little hyperbole. Relative to her leg-length it might *seem* like the Himalayas. I couldn't possibly comment.

Bees. The wind in the trees. The skitter of doggy claws on fallen leaves. The startled rush of wings when a bird flew off. If I really focused, I could still hear the Sounds of Peace. Good enough for me. Hand-in-hand, we threaded our way through the trees, escorted by Scout and heading for the sunlit uplands. I'll let you know if we get there.

Conrad gets answers to his questions, and the full truth about the Hen Party is revealed in Three Ring Circus, the Twelfth Book of the King's Watch.

Author's Note

As Conrad said, it's been a while…

The first and biggest thanks are due to you, my readers, for waiting patiently (and not so patiently) over the last eighteen months while I struggled with this story. Thank you for your patience and for keeping the faith in the King's Watch.

A short while ago I did a "How to publish your book" workshop for aspiring writers. One of them asked me whether it was stressful to have readers asking about where the next book is. My response was this: "I'd much rather have that stress than the stress of having no readers."

You, the reader, are why I keep going with this madness.

I have written elsewhere about *why* this book took so long, and I have nothing to add here except that now that you've finished reading it, I hope that the wait was worthwhile.

And the good news is that (if the gods are willing), you won't have to wait anything like the same length of time for the next book. Work on *Three Ring Circus* is already well under way, but I'm not going to give myself a deadline.

One thing I will mention is that I took some time out last year to help my sister write her debut novel, and she is giving all the profits to charity. If you like a cosy mystery and you haven't already done so, please check out *Murder Within Tent* by Ruth Ward on Amazon. It features some of the non-magickal characters from the King's Watch tackling a mundane murder in an English village.

Shakespeare said that A good wine deserves a good bush. In other words, a good book deserves a good cover. I'll never be able to prove it, but I strongly believe that The King's Watch would not have been the same without the beautiful covers designed by the Awesome Rachel Lawston.

An additional note of thanks is due to those who read the first draft – Asen, Lore, Lucy, Nina, Paula and Sheila, and lastly to Ian Forsdike for casting his eye over the final draft. Any remaining typos/errors are all mine.

Finally, this book could not have been written without love, support, encouragement and sacrifices from my wife, Anne. While I was having a torrid time getting this book out of the mire, she kept faith and waited patiently for me to get my act together. It just goes to show how much she loves me that she let me write the first Conrad book even though she hates fantasy novels. She says she now likes them.

Until the next time,

Thanks,

Mark   Hayden.

Printed in Great Britain
by Amazon

39235851R00229